PATRICIA STORACE

THE BOOK OF HEAVEN

Patricia Storace was born in Chicago, Illinois, reared in Mobile, Alabama, and educated at Columbia University and the University of Cambridge. She is the author of *Dinner with Persephone*, a travel memoir that won the Runciman Award; *Heredity*, a book of poems; and *Sugar Cane: A Caribbean Rapunzel*, a children's book. She received the Witter Bynner Poetry Prize from the American Academy of Arts and Letters in 1993. She has been a frequent contributor to *The New York Review of Books* and *Condé Nast Traveler*.

ALSO BY PATRICIA STORACE

Dinner with Persephone

Heredity

Sugar Cane: A Caribbean Rapunzel

THE BOOK OF HEAVEN

THE BOOK OF HEAVEN

A NOVEL

PATRICIA STORACE

VINTAGE BOOKS
A DIVISION OF RANDOM HOUSE LLC
NEW YORK

FIRST VINTAGE BOOKS EDITION, NOVEMBER 2014

Grateful acknowledgment is made to Interlink Publishing Group, Inc., for permission to reprint "Thus I Write the History of Women" from On Entering the Sea *by Nizar Qabbani. Original Arabic text copyright © 1995 by Nizar Qabbani; English translation copyright © 2013 by Salma Khadra Jayyusi. Reprinted by permission of Interlink Publishing Group, Inc.*

The Library of Congress has cataloged the Pantheon edition as follows:
Storace, Patricia.
The book of heaven / Patricia Storace.
Pages cm.
1. Women—Fiction. 2. Astrology—Fiction. I. Title.
PS3569.T648B66 2013
813'.54—dc23 2013022316

Vintage Trade Paperback ISBN: 978-0-375-70755-1
eBook ISBN: 978-0-307-90869-8

Book design by Iris Weinstein

www.vintagebooks.com

Printed in the United States of America
10 9 8 7 6 5 4 3 2 1

For the Archangel: Michael Anthony Kazmarek

I want you female as you are.
I claim no knowledge of woman's chemistry
The sources of woman's nectar
How the she-gazelle becomes a she-gazelle
Nor how birds perfect the art of song.

I want you like the women
In immortal paintings
The virgins gracing
Cathedral ceilings
Bathing their breasts in moonlight
I want you female . . . so the trees will sprout green
And the misty clouds will gather . . . so that the rains will come

*

I want you female because
Civilization is female
Poems are female
Stalks of wheat
Vials of fragrance
Even Paris—is female
and Beirut—despite her wounds—remains female
In the name of those who want to write poetry . . . be a
woman
in the name of those who want to make love . . . be a
woman
and in the name of those who want to know God . . . be
a woman.

—NIZAR QABBANI, "Thus I Write the History of Women"

CONTENTS

THE BOOK OF HEAVEN

PROLOGUE: A VIEW FROM ANOTHER HEAVEN

We on earth navigate by the stars, so it is no wonder we have gone so far off course—since we have never seen more than a fragment of Heaven. Our knowledge of Hell is more detailed, and at least of certain regions, even thorough; we have spent so much more of our time and resources on the exploration of Hell. Hell is a much easier object of study; though it has endless variations, its nature is repetitive and unchanging. The stories of the damned told there all end the same way.

Heaven, by contrast, is infinite in a different way, endlessly reconceiving itself as the ocean does. In Heaven, the equinoxes shift; even the pole stars change places, changing what we trust and rely on, believe, what we are sure we know. You look and see, as you expect to, Polaris, now the North Star, the certainty of Heaven; but the brilliant Thuban, five thousand years ago, was once the pole star. At the time the pyramids were built, Thuban was the star that oriented us, and composed in Heaven our sense of where we were.

We can never stop searching for Heaven, since there is always more of it than we can see. There, as in those tales that evolve endlessly into other tales, stories have no end. They are hardly ever the stories you know, the official ones, in which wishes are made formal, then legislated and enforced as matters of life or death. They are more often the stories we didn't hear, or wouldn't believe, told by the person we ignored, the house that was razed, the choir of dry bones. The scholars of Heaven read and study the vast collection of ashes, books from the torched libraries.

Heaven is not to be confused with Paradise; I had so little time in Paradise that I cannot tell you much about it. What I know of Paradise, I know through men. But Heaven is my home, and there are things about it I will always remember, however far away from it I am now. That is why I can tell you that I have seen more than I imagined was there, even though I, too, have seen only a fraction of what exists.

The first Heaven I knew is the one we all know, the one with the constellations we have been taught to see. The sky we have inherited is a sort of celestial attic of the imagination. It contains a razor, fisher's nets, a tennis racket, and a Polish king's shield, among much other rubbish.

It is peopled with the violent and the anguished, warriors, archers, and weeping women. It is not a place for pardon or repentance, as the gods often placed glittering killers in sight of their glittering perpetual victims, so that there was no way for anyone to find a new relationship to anyone else. Little Ganymede, who had been abducted, shivered forever near the eagle that had seized him and brought him here. This was known as immortality. Many were there because they lived tragedies so unbearable that their suffering would have destroyed the earth if they had not been transported into Heaven.

For the gods of that Heaven had only two powers with regard to suffering. They could inflict it, often tormenting humans as proxy for their private quarrels. Many of the glowing creatures you see in Heaven are set there by way of reward for killing a human on behalf of a God, such as the Scorpion, whom I always avoided. Others are positioned there from petty divine spite, like the Crab, set there to taunt a goddess who tried and failed to have it kill a hero favored by her husband.

Some pulse with the implacable stellar reminder of the defeat of a passionate human desire. Lyra is the instrument that belonged to Orpheus, who descended to Hell for his bride, and failed to bring her out of it, despite his great love. The one inhabitant of Heaven I truly loved, Ophiuchus the Snake-Tamer, the great doctor who discovered how to resurrect humans, was killed at the request of the God of the Dead. It was a political assassination—the God of the Dead was protecting his borough. Ophiuchus was one of the few Heaven Dwellers who was still concerned with mortals; he trembled, sparkling with the agony of his pent-up will to heal them, but was thwarted by the gods' other power over suffering.

Their second power over suffering was, in a sense, to sculpt it—to reveal it in Heaven only as it was seen and felt by them—as ecstasy. In Heaven, tears, sweat, and drops of blood are translated into the brilliance of stars, which form the bodies of the Heaven Dwellers. The gods would not let Ophiuchus tamper with suffering, that radiant and exquisite state of being.

In Heaven, there was not one pair of happy lovers. There were Perseus and Andromeda, if you count a couple happy who killed a guest at their wedding. Besides, they lived apart in Heaven; and it made me uneasy to see Andromeda, a wife still wearing the glittering chains that had bound her on her rock. There was another pair who truly loved each other, but they were allowed to meet only one day a year, before they were separated to begin another year's yearning. I felt confined there, and unhappy. What woman wants to live in a Heaven where love can only be tragic, unfulfilled for all eternity?

I don't say that Heaven was without passions: in fact, it was through my fleeing Orion that the revelation occurred. I was always afraid of him, knowing what everyone knew about him: that he was empty of all but lust. He had practiced the sexual lynching known as rape on Merope and others, and his last mortal act had been a biocide. He could not control his appetite to kill, and had hunted down every last living thing in a forest where the goddess Artemis refreshed herself from time to time. He piled corpse after corpse outside her lodging. He presumed to kill as if he were a God. For that presumption Artemis had the mortal killed in a display of divine artistry. Yet, the gods awarded him an influential position in Heaven.

He spent his time in Heaven stalking the Pleiades; one afternoon, he caught sight of me, and decided I would do just as well. I was walking by myself along the shining river Eridanus, lost in my own dreams, hearing and seeing nothing else. Suddenly Orion leapt in front of me, blocking my path. His eyes were narrow and glinting, with the odd fixed gaze of the possessed, who see nothing but what they desire from whatever exists.

I turned and began to run. I could hear Orion strike out after me, though I dared not turn to look. It was like being pursued by a massive oak tree that could move as swiftly as the wind through its own leaves, and was also carrying a weapon. I knew he would shoot me with his bow and arrows to bring me down. Blinded, wounded, crippled—it wouldn't matter to him how he took me, or if I survived, as long as he succeeded in attaining his desire.

I screamed, but the scream metamorphosed in Heaven, and made a trio of the sublime duet that Aphrodite and Eros were singing, charmed at Orion's ardor, and the lovely patterns my long hair made streaming in flight behind me as I raced for my life. Later, I learned that Aphrodite had sent a dream of this scene to a Macedonian artist, who rendered it in relief on a gold vase, though he altered it to show Orion capturing me, as I screamed mutely and exquisitely in pure gold.

In the end, though, I escaped. I saw no other course than to fling myself into Eridanus, the flowing river of stars, and let the swift current drown me or take me where it would. Even Orion could not keep up with Eridanus, and I heard his marvelous aria of psychopathic rage as I was swept farther and farther away.

The river rushed me past constellation after constellation; I closed my eyes, and let myself be carried along, and thought of nothing, not even how I might find some exit from this flood of stars.

When I opened my eyes again, still submerged in the river of light, I saw a group of strange constellations. I recognized nothing of this zodiac. One cascade of stars formed the Cluster of Grapes, another the Sheaf of Wheat. There was the Hive where Honey Bees swarmed, entering and exiting like the dust of topaz and amber. I saw the Carpenter measuring the Door with a rope of stars. Beside him, the Birthgiver suckled the Newborn with her gemmed milk, while the Cradle swung, lighting the dark.

Looking up, I saw petal after petal outlined in stars drifting down from the Hundred Roses. I passed the Judge in her Jeweled Caftan holding a pair of scales in one hand, and lifting her luminous hand, patterned with stars like henna, in a gesture of Pardon. The Seven Scholars sat above pages and pages of stars, endlessly unscrolling across the skies. Beyond them were the clusters of Singers and the Storytellers, with stars pouring from their throats. A little farther, the constellation of the Pomegranate pulsed, scattering ruby-colored stars over the darkness. The Breadmaker kneaded her round loaves, which left her hands as floating, golden moons. Stars like tiny diamonds collided inside the Wineglass. The Artist, hands full of constellations, flung them playfully into patterns and images across the skies.

I gasped. I had been swept into another Heaven. Caught up in the powerful course of the river, I wondered whether I could find a way to enter it, or lose this Heaven, too, unable to find anything to hold on to that would make a place for me in any world? Ahead, I saw another wonder. A wingless bird suspended on a cord of stars descended directly into my path. It had a voice, and spoke to me. If I climbed on its back, the bird promised, it could take me into the surrounding Heaven.

"How can you do that, since you cannot fly?" I said mistrustfully.

"Climb on my back, loosen the cord, and open your arms wide. That embrace will create the wings of desire." I did as the bird described, and became its wings, ascending toward another group of unrecognizable constellations. We passed the Coffin, the Date Palm, and the Cherry Tree. The Guitar Player strummed his instrument: the notes formed stars that circled across the night sky, while the Dancer stamped, leapt, and whirled, his heels flecked with a staccato of stars.

Now I saw the Knife, with its jade-green hilt, and its fierce curved blade flickering. I was frightened; the bird soared closer and closer to the fatal stars.

"Don't be afraid," it said. "This is the constellation of the one who killed and gave birth." I saw a woman holding a book with the Knife glittering on its cover. "She is waiting to tell you her story." It set me down. I sat at her feet, and listened.

She said to me, "I am Souraya, lady of the question. I will tell you a story about which you can ask as many questions as arise, as many as there are molecules and atoms. The story that cannot be questioned is to be feared; it serves to conceal a story too dangerous to be told. A story that cannot be questioned abducts the soul and drags it toward the Tabula Rasa, which you see just to your right. That is the altar of killing, the bed of torture where questions cease to exist, and become instead interrogations, transformed into the myriad means of inflicting pain."

I looked away from the cruel white stars of the table of death. Souraya continued speaking, gently, directing my attention to a garden visible in another plane of Heaven, where men, women, children, and angels walked and talked; thousands of conversations drifted like perfume from that garden. "Questions are the grammar of ethics, and sacred to God, who does not teach by commandment, but through questions. Questions are the very structure of the universe, which is why the waves ask the shore, 'When? When? When?' and the winds swirl through the branches of the trees, always murmuring, 'Why? Why?'

"The question," she said, "is even inherent in our bodies, which is why lovemaking always takes the form of a reciprocal perpetual question, perpetually answered. The truth is, each of us, and each one of our lives, is a question asked of the other; we are God's questions to each other, and through the lattice of our questions, we sometimes catch a glimpse of God." When she finished her story, she gave me her book, and kissed me on the forehead. She handed me a golden apple. "This is the apple of knowledge. If you become human, you must eat this fruit, without fail, or you will never become human, a shadow in a loveless world."

I climbed again onto the back of the wingless bird, and we turned to the right, moving toward the second constellation, a Cauldron as big as an ocean, into which a woman ladled a rice of stars and grains. "This is the constellation of one who killed and preserved life," the bird told me. "She is waiting to tell you her story." On the cover of the book she held were all the illuminated grains and fruits of the world.

I began to sit down, but she took my arm and walked with me.

She said to me, "I am Savour, lady of creation. My story is part of the work of Heaven, where the acts of creation are ceaseless. You can see as we walk, that Heaven is always being composed; as we walk in it and speak in it, it is changing and taking new forms around us, while you yourself play a part in creating it. In this way, you do not simply live in Heaven—you undertake it. As you describe what you see here, you change it.

"Think of it as being inside a beautiful painting, except that the landscape you see is not static within the frame, the light changes second by second, the swans in the lower left-hand corner can swim out of the frame and back again to their pool, and you yourself can enter the frame or leave it at will. You can even stay inside and outside simultaneously. There is no 'either . . . or' in Heaven, but 'both . . . and.' Our sentences pause, but do not end."

When she finished her story, she gave me her book and kissed me on the forehead. She handed me a golden apple. "This is the apple of memory. If you become human, you must eat this fruit without fail; when you taste it, you will remember that you glimpsed Heaven."

She pointed toward the third constellation, the Paradise Nebula, a thousand paradises that rose and fell, in ever-changing configurations.

I climbed again onto the back of the wingless bird, and made the wings of desire. We rose toward the constellation. "This is the constellation of the one who was murdered and lived. She is waiting to tell you her story." From the cover of the book she held, stars dropped ceaselessly, small and bright as tears.

She said to me, "I am Rain, lady of suffering. My story—and I suffer to tell you this—will make you suffer. In order for you to understand my story, you must encounter the damned. I must lead you into Hell." She took my hand, and without traveling any distance at all, it seemed, we found ourselves in a prison courtyard with walls of stone.

In the center of the courtyard, there was a throne of granite, and a granite altar, both stained with blood. Chained to the throne was a creature—or creatures—whose writhing lower body was that of a reptile, but above the waist, had countless heads, the faces of men, women, children, animals, and monsters. Some of the faces showed expressions of rage, others of contempt; some of the faces were vicious, others displayed passive misery, or features contorted with anguish. Some were not faces at all, but garrulous skulls. There were faces that glowed radiantly, their gazes sublimely fixed blindly elsewhere, their mouths curved with implacable perfection into carnivorous, benevolent smiles.

"Each is gripped by an appetite that must be satisfied immediately, and can never be satisfied," Rain said. "Watch. New faces are formed as soon as a new lust is conceived." I moved toward it, to peer more closely at the creatures, some of whom seemed strangely familiar. One face looked charmingly at me, and beckoned me forward, eager to tell me an urgent secret. When I was face-to-face with it, its human eyes altered shockingly; it clamped its jaws on my arm, and dragged me toward the altar. I was in a death roll, gripped by a crocodile.

Rain hurried toward it, and forcefully hit it under the jaw. Its mouth, suddenly oddly weak, opened, and she pulled me away from the creatures, embracing me protectively. "These are the damned," she said. "They destroy whatever they yearn for most deeply. They will kill what they love in order to have it." One of the creatures wailed for water, complaining of thirst.

"Watch," Rain said. She poured a cup of water for the creature, and gave it to her. The creature took the cup, and suddenly spat the water at Rain, throwing the cup at her. Rain looked at her with grave sorrow. "You can do nothing right for a soul in Hell. She herself will thwart any effort to satisfy her desire—that is how you recognize them. This means their desires are never fulfilled, and so they never know the rapture of gratitude, never having been satisfied. Nor do they have a lasting capacity for happiness; their lusts are so overwhelming that each satisfaction can only be temporary. And as they can sustain no contentment, they can sustain no suffering. Those who cannot bear suffering cannot bear blessing." As she spoke, the thirsty creature disappeared, replaced by another racked with another lust.

I suddenly realized that I did recognize these creatures. "This is the Hydra," I said. "I saw this in the Heaven I left." Rain nodded. "Then that other Heaven is also here?" I asked.

"Yes," she said, "it is also here."

"Then the souls of the damned are in Heaven?" I asked.

"Yes," she said, "but they don't know it."

She led me from Hell back to Heaven. "For those tormented ones, the story always ends the same way. They do not realize that God is unforeseeable, not a Queen or a King, or Highness or Holiness, Mother or Father, or any other of these ambivalent titles. They do not know that it is presumptuous or sycophantic to imagine that God has any relation to any notion they have of power. God has no title more absolute than 'Beloved.'"

When Rain finished her story, she gave me her book and kissed me on the forehead. She handed me a golden apple. "This is the apple of death," she said gravely. "If you become human, you must eat this fruit without fail. The mercy of death is given so that no cruelty is infinite, no suffering everlasting."

I climbed on the back of the wingless bird, and made the wings of desire. Rain pointed toward a magnificent constellation formed of stars and moons that looked like a triple strand of iridescent pearls of every color. "You must pass through it to reach the fourth constellation, the Lovers' Cluster. These are the tears of those who suffer with those who suffer. We could see nothing in Heaven were it not for the light they give."

Now we approached a constellation formed by countless double stars that revolved around each other like lovers in each other's arms. "This is the constellation of the one who lost everything and gained everything. She is waiting to tell you her story." The cover of her book was a mosaic of a thousand jewels, which constantly rearranged themselves.

"I am Sheba," she said, "lady of loving. I will tell you my story, but it is a story in which you are already a character. It is for you to continue it, if you choose, and to ensure that it never comes to an end. My story is of the unfinished work of love, the bringing of the day when we will be as capable of loving as we are of killing, when to confess to love will have more impact than the confession of wrongdoing, when the sentence 'I love him' will be more final than the sentence, 'I killed him.'

"Before I begin, there is something I want you to see." She took me to the edge of Heaven, and gestured across the constellations in the direction of a marvelous garden, where a magnificent person, looking a bit imprisoned in his impressive musculature, and already disconsolate in Paradise, sat alone. "He is very beautiful," I said.

"Yes," she said, "he is very beautiful, and so is that earth on which he sits, and of which he is made. That is why he has the power to destroy the earth. You, on the other hand, were made in Heaven, and like all creatures of Heaven, you have the capacity to destroy, not the earth, but human happiness."

When Sheba finished her story, she gave me her book and kissed me on the forehead. She handed me a golden apple. "This is the apple of love," she said. "If you become human, you must eat this fruit without fail, or you will never have existed, either on earth or in Heaven."

She led me again to the edge of Heaven for another look at the earth where the magnificent other one seemed so alone. "Will you go there?" she asked. "Each human must invent human love, a chance that will be given to you in becoming human. And for all the atrocity they have done and will do, it is still through human love, and no other, that appetite, desire, and pleasure themselves become the source of ethics, which knowledge makes inseparable from love."

I was tempted to remain in Heaven. But I also wanted to taste knowledge, memory, death, and love, and to meet that person I could see in his splendor.

I lifted the first apple, and tasted knowledge. I tasted memory. I tasted death. I tasted love. Tears fell from my eyes. There was a moment of absolute stillness, as if I had stepped across the threshold of forever. Then the frame of Heaven began to shake around me, and I saw fragments falling, tesserae I would later recognize in paintings of Paradise.

I heard a voice saying,

"I have made Heaven, and earth, and you.
Now this is my gift.
It is for you to create the world.
That will be the work of humans.
Go now and begin."

Heaven was disappearing, as I drifted weightlessly toward the Earthly Paradise. I looked for as long as there was a trace of Heaven.

"I will miss you," I said. Then I drew my first breath. I shaped my first human question.

"Where is Heaven?" I asked.

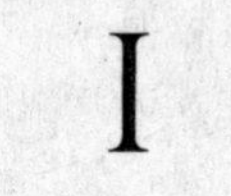

THE BOOK OF SOURAYA

THE KNIFE: THE FIRST CONSTELLATION

The world was created with a knife and a prayer. The Knife you can see well, especially in the late summer nights. Look up after dark; you will see its jade-green hilt, the sickle of brilliants that forms the curve of the scimitar's blade, and the field of red stars sprayed around it, the drops of blood. It is the topmost section of the constellation called the Murder, though decrees have been issued, as yet with no success, to change its name by compulsion to the Sacrifice. Nevertheless, the true name of this group of stars is the Murder, and there the Knife quivers unmistakably at night, lodged where it was flung back into the heart of Heaven. Whatever human beings would suppress or refuse to see, the heavens record their true acts and encode their true dreams in the ineradicable testament of stars.

The knife was forged as carefully as a sculpture as part of the dowry of a bride on her way to the household of an iconoclast husband she had never met. She was not to bring any images of animal or human creatures, none of the clay birds or babies that had been her girlhood toys, no paintings illustrating the cycles of legends she loved, no image of the house of her childhood, or of any guardian spirit. Souraya was being married into a household intensely concerned with what it was permitted to see. But the attention to physical form is a powerful instinct and often becomes a talent, and will turn elsewhere if diverted. And among iconoclasts, the impulse found its satisfaction in the intensely anatomical forms of all their domestic goods, saddles, ewers, farm implements, spoons, knives, forks, ladles, and bowls, those grand analogues to the womb. It is obvious what each of these forms can be made to suggest.

Above all, iconoclasts were exacting and seduced by the forms of weapons. These they commissioned with the kind of extravagant detail and ardent willingness to spend money that iconophiles devoted to images, specifying elaborate metal traceries, intricate gemmed patterns on hilts, and even incised calligraphy on the blades themselves. These ornaments created a web of meaning inscribed on the weapons, gave them voices, which are acceptable to iconoclasts as images are not. The ornaments knit hands and weapons together, made them inseparable, and, in a sense, helpless in their power, both hand and weapon bound together and absolved by a common pattern. The weapon ornament became a symbol of destiny, as did the self-inflicted wounds of the iconoclasts, tribal markings attributed to the appetite of the Divine for wounds. These weapons, and these wounds, were the jewelry of men.

After the contract for their marriage was negotiated, and the final catalog of dowry gifts agreed on, chief among the gifts, more costly even than the plantation of twenty shade trees and twenty fruit trees that Souraya was to bring with her, was the knife. Adon's emissary arrived with elaborate verbal instructions for its design, since for them to make a sketch of it was forbidden. The emissary, though, spoke in such vivid detail that Souraya's mother was able to make a discreet sketch of the knife, to assist her husband in realizing the design accurately, from the hilt set with emeralds, jade, and diamonds down to the inscription, "God's Servant," to be traced on the blade. Finally, before accepting their entertainment after his journey, the emissary drew from his luggage a massive clay hand. It was modeled on Adon's. "Fit the knife to this," he said. "Then shatter it." That disembodied hand, palm ambitiously upward on her father's worktable, was Souraya's first glimpse of her husband. It dominated the workshop while it was there; its openness, attached to nothing, made it seem charged with absolute desire. It reached for everything. There was nothing it did not want, as if it, and not her father's and mother's modest finite living hands, were the source of all the objects and tools around it; that it was joined to no visible body or face made space itself seem to flow from it.

Late at night, Souraya went noiselessly to the workshop, to make herself acquainted with her husband. The monumental hand was resting on the worktable, in the shadows, as if it had just created darkness.

She went up to it, and reaching her own hand out tentatively, stroked it, her slender fingers touching the monument soothingly, as if to appease and tame it. She picked it up. An even more colossal hand of shadow smoothed the floor, then gripped and grappled with the wall.

She strained to lift the hand to her breast, seeing an image of her wedding night, her breast cupped for the first time by a husband's hand. The clay hand lay across her flesh like a boulder, with a profound heaviness, a world reposing on her breast. But she was so young that the effect on her of its weight was not exhaustion, but a pooling of courage, a concentrated courage.

An energy suffused the sure muscles of her legs, traveling through the strong, solid, cypresses of her thighs, the unshatterable cup of her abdomen, up through her head, poised on the bones and tendons of her neck. The power and heroism of a young body is as helpless as the invincible frailty of an old one. She felt ready. She was as clean and plumb and deep with life as a well. She imagined a cup of water as it poured through the lips of a parched drinker. She trembled like the offered water as it shared the drinker's ecstasy in quenching his thirst. Let the world be heavy; she would shelter it. Let the world lie on her; she would sustain it. Let the world fill itself with her. This was her body's prayer.

When the knife was ready at last, so was the marriage. Souraya's dowry gifts and personal belongings were securely packed, and her clay birds and clay boys and girls given away to her cousins' children. She threaded the bridegroom's gifts of jewelry through her hair and around her neck. A special leather bag was set aside for the remnants of the clay hand; the iconoclasts were strict in demanding proof that the model had been destroyed, as if they were possessed by some fear that they themselves might be destroyed by their own despised images.

They danced all night, the night before she left, cycles of ribald dances, joyous dances, with figures of joined hands pledging that love requites everything, tender dances, then the openly tragic dances, with their mute declarations that all love is unrequited, the cresting movements of the dancers' arms like waves beating against cliffs.

They sang old songs, drinking wedding wine and eating indulgently from what seemed a supply of perpetual roast meat and a traditional wedding confection known as bride's tears, made of honey mixed with the resinous tears exuded by local pines, a symbol of the bittersweet nature of marriage.

Everyone, from children to old men, embraced the precious bride, touched her dress, smoothed her hair, clung to her as if she were each one's ebbing life. Some dandled her four-year-old sister, who was also getting married to a five-year-old cousin. It was a common arrangement. Small sisters would share in the dower of the older bride, and the family would have married all its daughters at the expense of one wedding. The younger girls would return to their playthings and household tasks, and would discover when they had grown up that they had been married all their lives, as if they were assuming a life previously lived, but unremembered.

The meat and dancing and singing and wine made a wild joy of loss. The sense of mourning someone who was departing from their circle was transformed into a blissful oblivion. The festival of an absence would not be revealed as painful until tomorrow, after she would be gone forever.

Someone fetched the model of Adon's hand, and brought it to the fireside, offering it to Souraya's father to destroy, as commanded. He shook his head dourly, regretting the end of his workmanship. "Do your husband's will, Souraya," he said. Souraya's lips were stained with red wine, she was just becoming drunk.

She picked up a log and with all her strength brought it down onto the center of the earthen palm. The guests cheered as the object shattered, and Souraya smashed the clay fingers, knuckles, and wrist into smaller and smaller fragments knit with splintering embers, overcome with the manic joy of destruction. She half-remembered the childhood pleasure of building cities in the sand, and joining with all the other children, after the fashioning of intricate domes, tunnels, and towers, in the ecstatic destruction of their own creations. In their annihilating dances, those children outlived the world.

A man poured her another cup of wine, and she lifted it high, in a mocking toast: No one could criticize her tonight. The singing ensured that exemption, in all gatherings, sacred or profane; it gently enforced a consent on the company, so that on those occasions, they would not settle old scores, either by boast or by insult.

"Drink to the unseen," she cried out, laughing recklessly at her own daring, exulting in a moment of freedom in her severely disciplined life. Tomorrow, she would have to be impeccable, eyes lowered, wordlessly graceful, inscrutable in the face of sorrow, relief, bewilderment, disgust, or fear. She needed to indulge herself in bravado tonight, for a virgin goes to marriage with an unseen man as a soldier goes into battle, uncertain of survival, risking death. Who would protect her if she did not please? And she had no more idea than a soldier in first combat does of what she would experience physically.

Like a soldier, she had to give herself over to an experience that she had been schooled to defend herself from her entire life. She now unnaturally had to permit a man what she had previously utterly forbidden to the point of death.

She had heard she would be wounded. Perhaps the man would be as well? But there was no clear story about how the blood on that sheet was purchased. Did the man enjoy the pain? Would she? Was it forgotten afterward, or always remembered? And in any case she must be the loyal companion, the faithful servant, the clairvoyant fulfillment of the man, whether or not she liked him, even whether or not she loathed him. As a soldier must guard and obey his commander, regardless of the nature of their personal feelings toward each other.

Tonight, though, the brides were exempt. Even though she had a long journey to make, she drank more wine, and danced until late, on the carpet that would be the last of the dowry gifts to be packed and the first to be set in place in her new household. Its pattern of squares, lozenges, and arches in blue and contrasting silver silk threads had been devised uniquely for Souraya. The design was impeccably abstract enough to satisfy the iconoclast examiners, yet the figures represented the shapes of windows through which the bride could see the shining light of her former home.

Her exhaustion as they set out next day was merciful. Souraya slept through most of the day, her slight nausea a useful tranquilizer, like the layer of ash judiciously applied to fire to damp down its flames. Adon's entourage was waiting to meet them after they crossed over the river nearest his compound.

There, after ceremonious addresses and formal greetings, something strange occurred. Instead of proceeding directly through the gates of the compound, to the sounds of drums and harps and songs, the party was halted, barred from advancing further by a line of guards, each with a heavily ornamented knife in his belt. They could see the musicians, poised on the walls of the compound, each holding a silent instrument poised for song, as if they were paralyzed by some magic. Then a pair of guards surrounded the mounds of luggage Souraya's party had brought, and began to unpack it.

Souraya's father, masking his fear of banditry, perhaps even the possibility that these were not in fact Adon's men, approached the soldier directing the pillage. They were searching the luggage for images, the soldier explained to him. It was forbidden for images to be transported into the compound, or across any threshold occupied by a kinsman. Any images that were discovered would be taken back across the river and quarantined there in a guarded post, unless they belonged to the bride.

They amassed a small, indiscriminate pile of clay figurines, winged angels, painted medallions, golden eyes, and a pair of earrings in the shape of swimming dolphins. Among Souraya's dowry gifts, there were cooking pans with handles in the shape of nymphs, which, though they were exquisitely crafted and valuable, were destroyed. No treasure was prized above the great holy laws.

The soldiers turned their attention to her personal belongings. Packed with her perfumes and cosmetics were a group of mirrors in graduated sizes. The guards seized them, and began to smash them. Souraya pleaded to keep just one, for the sake of her husband, so she could make herself presentable for him. "These objects collect and contain images," the soldiers said, unmoved.

She looked at her father, but he kept his eyes on the ground, not looking at what the soldiers were doing, and for the first time, not meeting the mirror of his daughter's gaze. Suddenly there was a commotion near the baggage, and a soldier rushed forward, embracing a dress covered in a magnificent, intricate design of sequins, which glittered scarlet in the light of the sunset. He had never seen such a garment. It was Souraya's wedding dress. The commander examined it closely, narrowing his eyes. Then without hesitation, he ripped it from bodice to hem, and tossed it to the soldiers to finish shredding. "These reflect," he said to Souraya. "They are image-givers." The soldiers set on the dress, and quickly destroyed the sequin-covered sleeves it had taken months to design and then to sew, hands moving to the rhythms of the marriage mantras. She covered her own eyes then.

The commander made some gesture afterward indicating to the compound that the search was successfully completed. Then a torrent of music opened out over the landscape, and the wedding party was swept inside the walls, where hundreds of torches were lit at the same moment, and the rhythmic clapping of the families of the community welcomed them. A gaggle of children rushed forward to touch Souraya when, from the whispers and gestures, they realized she was the bride. Souraya didn't smile at them or respond to them, though as a rule, she was lavish in her smiles with children, and could, with a still, steady gaze in which a small flame of smile flickered, bring the smiling willingness to be adored out of nearly any child, even one determined to wail.

But the violence that had been done to her wedding dress made her feel both hostile and anxious. The fabric had been set to her body as words to music, as the knife to her husband's clay hand. It was a dress in which she felt as certain as a goddess must, absolutely sure in her movements, perfect in her shape with the ancient perfection of a sheaf of wheat, perfect enough to pass into archetype, and become immortal, which was the purpose of all ornament.

It is a strange fact that a dress can safeguard a woman, its elegant design or fine color functioning as a counterweight at the moment she risks stepping off a precipice. It is a strange fact that a few lengths of cloth can bring a woman to life. But water, if it is to be drunk deeply enough to satisfy thirst, needs a cup, as an idea needs a sentence. And the strangest fact of all is that what we ourselves make gives us life. Souraya had a wild thought of running from them, these madmen who would dismember a dress. Her confidence in her new people had been shaken, as her confidence in herself.

She had not known ideas could be violent, had never seen anyone destroy something beautiful for an idea. If these people were haters of beauty, then they would surely hate her, too. And she would hate them in return, with her own red terrifying capacity for savagery. But the worst of her fears was beyond impersonal. She had glimpsed an implacable demand that something she thought of as lovely, harmless, and lawful must be destroyed. What else that was precious to her sight must not exist? She passed through the crowd toward the nuptial lodging.

Later, she would remember this progress as blind; she could not distinguish a single face in memory until she saw Adon's, the face that belonged to the right hand she already knew and had held. And looking at the angular planes of that face, set on the colossal height of Adon's body, she found her balance.

Adon's features were set on the scaffolding of his bone as if riveted there; they expressed a force that seemed almost metallic. When he turned to look at her, his eyes gleamed, not only with obvious pleasure in her beauty, but with a kind of will to friendship, even though his mouth stayed stern. It was like having a shield smile at her. The kindly look relieved her of the burden of violent hatred she had been feeling after the mutilation of her wedding dress. Her flood of relief and gratitude at not hating her husband on sight was so strong that her great willingness to love felt akin to love itself. It was as if the blood inside her turned to wine.

With the help of two kinswomen, she chose a costume to be married in. They helped her dress, and after the priest had joined the couple's hands and given them wine to drink together, the women helped her again, to undress. One of them gave her a small hand mirror that she had smuggled past the soldiers, and then they left her to wait for her husband. She could hear drumbeats beginning outside, establishing a steady regular rhythm, even as they built in intensity.

She knew what they were for. If there was pleasure, it would remain inaudible; if there was pain, that too, would remain inaudible. The percussion also served to muffle the footsteps of her husband. She did not hear him as she fretfully changed the position of the small mirror, trying to catch a whole glimpse of herself in its turning orbit. But the light in the room altered, and she realized that Adon stood behind her. It was as if her body held a reunion with its wandering shadow, a shadow that was now the stronger of the two. Her husband reached for the mirror, not unkindly, but authoritatively.

"I beg your pardon," she said. "I am anxious for you to be pleased with my appearance, and I do not know how to appraise myself without a mirror." Adon raised his arm and shattered the mirror on the threshold. "Images are forbidden to us," he explained patiently. "We are forbidden to gaze anywhere but at God. You will never see your face again."

It was at that moment that Souraya understood the depth of his power over her. She understood through the easy, despotic violence of his gesture, the self-multiplication of his "we," the perfect repose of his tone. He was not simply explaining unfamiliar customs to her, he was telling her the life she would live, feelings he expected her to have, her future, as if he were a seer with the power to make his prophecies come true. In the moment when he deprived her of her mirror, she saw clearly.

If she were to have any power over herself again, it would only be through exaggerated, even competitive, obedience to the laws of her husband's God. Her only power would be in her embrace. She must embrace him—and his God—to survive. It was at that moment that she truly lost her virginity, when she understood, as a girl does not, that the marriage was not only her vocation; it was a matter of life or death. And that God would be in her bed.

"Are you going to blind me?" she asked, with the kind of frankness that absolute fear produces.

"I am going to transform you," he answered. "I am going to help you to see with truth and clarity you have never known. Here is how you will see yourself from now on." He smiled radiantly, and touched with his index and third finger the dark pouches under his own eyes. "If you are beautiful in my eyes, you are beautiful. Look here." He gestured again toward his face, and frowned with disgust. "And if I look like this, this is how you will see yourself. But I feel sure," he said, "that I will more often look at you with the delight I do now." He held out his right hand, the living model of the clay one, and caressed her hair, with an almost priestly gesture of benediction. "I chose you and I believe I have chosen well. I am going to make a nation inside your body. I am going to make a world out of you."

She never forgot, although it did not spoil her pleasure in love-making later, the intense pain of her wedding night, when she was ripped apart like her own dress. And afterward, shocked and wounded as she was, enduring the violation of displaying the sheet, the public evidence of their intimacy, with the imprints of their bodies apparent on the cloth, the whole community crying out its triumph in its collective possession of her. The brief but unforgettable intensity of the pain, the particular sense of agonizing vulnerability it gave her, the sensation of being stabbed or raped, even though Adon had treated her with exquisite care, was frightening. It gave her a doubt about the nature of the world that it was so ordered that the initiation into lovemaking for her sex began with an inevitable cruelty. But the shrilling and shouts of the crowd when they saw the sheet stained with her blood aroused in her a disgust she had to conceal for years, especially when she was a guest at other wedding feasts. They had massed outside waiting, exulting in the sight of her wedding blood as if it were the trophy of an enemy brought down.

It was a mystery to her later, that although she would come to know years of confident pleasure in her marriage bed, she never remembered her first night without shuddering, that she could recall specific details of her physical agony and the gross exhibition of both her virginity and her husband's capacity.

In the morning, when they brought a basin of water for her to wash in, she saw that its interior was lined with black stone, so she could not see her face reflected in the water. Its surface was covered with exquisite incised calligraphy. This was true of their plates, trays, ewers, and cups. She could never catch a glimpse of herself even when she eventually undertook the preparation of food for fifty in a vast metal cauldron.

She saw occasionally a fragment of lip, or a triangle of her eye, but never her whole face, fissured as it was in a shining web of prayers.

She missed herself sharply that first morning—if she could have seen her face, she would at least have had the comfort of seeing someone she knew well. But as she began receiving the wedding visits, and assuming the domestic command of her household, she felt the contrast between herself and the men and women around her, many of whom had never even caught a glimpse of themselves or seen any kind of representation of the world outside them. To themselves, they were the seers, never the visible.

It had a strange effect on them physically, and even verbally. They somehow lacked the self-consciousness of those who have been seen. In ordinary conversation, with both strangers and family, they narrated their digestive, sexual, and health preoccupations with acute and intimate detail, as if all were members of one vast body, all flesh held in common. Without hesitation, they took one inside the theater of their intestines, or seated one inside their chests to listen to the thunderous ovations of their heartbeats. On their visits, they sprawled, unaware of how much space they occupied, forgetful that they shared it, unable to sense boundaries. Or they sat blindly slack-jawed or gesturing strangely while conversations flowed around them, without any sense of physical decorum, taking their features and movements as absolutely as they would a dawn or nightfall.

Often when Souraya walked in narrow passages or alleys, she found herself having to leap out of the way of someone who, although he saw her, continued to possess the path obliviously, unable to gauge the distance between his body and her own. They had a tendency, too, to stand only inches from whomever they were talking to, never dropping their eyes, but gazing intently and deeply into the other's eyes, as if they were seeking out their reflections there. A casual acquaintance would reach over and absently finger Souraya's jewelry or cheek during an encounter, in the way someone would forgetfully touch his own face or hair, rub his own chin.

It was strange; the severe restrictions they imposed on themselves seemed to have an opposite effect, deeply enclosed as they were in their customs and beliefs, the more they seemed to feel they knew the world absolutely with a knowledge that could not be challenged.

Somehow, this prohibition against seeing themselves was also an expression of an intense desire not to see other people, to be free of their existence except as ghostly presences. Even more, the refusal to look out at the world overlay a never-acknowledged ambition to determine and control what was there, to tell the whole world its story, rather than to hear it tell its own.

She would come to experience this in her daily life, most intimately with Adon; it took a strange authoritative form socially, a prescriptive insistence, as if he really wanted not only to be married to her, but also to have created her. He was ardent and affectionate with her, but also impatient, severe, even strangely melancholy. He made her memorize prayers that were to accompany each quotidian action, bread-making, planting, washing her hair, even before and after love-making. He wanted to rededicate her every moment, to cast her hours in the crucible of God's will. He would gaze on her for hours by fire-light, but insist that she not speak, as if he both adored and regretted her existence. It was as if he had been given a gift he thought magnificent, but in some way hated, because it had come from outside him, and was therefore corrupt.

She came to find herself, among his people, in a world where her accounts of her own experience were constantly corrected, even by people who had never ventured outside their own walls.

During the storytelling and song making that was the chief form of entertainment, she found herself incessantly interrupted, even by young children, who would object to her descriptions, or the events of her story, even when it was something she could swear an oath to having seen. "That didn't happen," they would say dogmatically, "that does not exist." Then they would overwhelm the story with a kind of chirping or mewing resembling seagull cries, or shouts of "Don't tell that. Don't tell that," until the teller altered the tale to their satisfaction. Once when she was telling a childhood tale of a boat that traveled under the sea, they stopped the story with the rhythmic chant, "Don't tell that. Don't tell that. There was no sea. There was no sea."

This was different from anything she knew of the art of story or epic poetry of her own people—here the art of storytelling was a battering collective struggle, where elements were rejected or insisted on until a final version prevailed, which it became taboo to alter.

A story was judged acceptable when the priests, the Guardians of the Story, called for the great tribal parchment. A red silk cylinder covered with a calligraphy of sacred words wrought in silver wire was brought to them. The Guardians unfurled from it a thick roll of flayed-looking skin, and hovered over it, deliberating. They chanted it aloud, alternating the recitation. If words or sentences were unacceptable, they plucked the metallic script from the scroll, held it up, and crushed it in their fists. These words were never again to be uttered.

When the redaction was complete, one of them stepped forward, and with a great slab of porous stone, grated what looked like an uncut gem, but was actually a block of solid perfume onto the flames. Thick clouds of incense in a garden of colors flamed upward and diffused through the gathering. Then the Guardian called out the title chosen for the tale, under which it became part of the record, and the audience acclaimed it with shouts of: "God permits! God permits!"

In this way they created a world suspended from the meshes of their stories. They named themselves after the characters in the stories they accepted; new lives seemed retellings of old stories, proof that the world repeated itself; so that it was as they said it was. Thus they conceived destinies, and were surprised that they came to pass, as a clandestine couple is stunned on the day they realize the woman has fallen pregnant.

The elderly uttered a strange automata of prescriptions and adages, as if they had been replaced by their own fictions. Even the youngest were shaped here by the tensions over what they were compelled and forbidden to believe. Souraya, in the way of people who kept their own counsel, was told secrets. Eventually, she could have become a living library of discredited tales, prohibited variants, and inadmissible family histories.

The arts in which they truly excelled were those that concerned themselves with the invisible, or at least the abstract. They were fine scribes, with a keen appreciation of the abstract patterns of script. They were skilled in medicine, in comprehending the invisible workings of the body. For that reason they were also excellent navigators, at home in an element whose territory was nearly entirely concealed from them.

In war, they were experts in espionage, so skilled that opposing tribes competed to make mercenaries of them. They understood how to shape tales subtly and aggressively to their own ends. They understood how not to be seen. They were marvelous hunters, and they were the originators of the use of camouflage in military operations. And they made magnificent jewelry whose forms were not based on flowers, or fruits, or mythological figures, but on light itself. They took bleak dead stones, and revealed the light and brilliant colors inside them. These were remarkable; it was as if they had gone into catacombs and brought back life out of inertia and death. The women, the children, and the men themselves all wore these splendid ornaments, and they were a steady source of trade for the community.

Souraya knew of other communities where both the men and women wore garments that concealed their bodies, but here it seemed the air itself veiled the people. Now she would go daily to examine the state of the gardens, paradises, as they were known, that Adon owned, which were now her work to oversee. This gave her the right to be called a human being, literally, because those who worked with the soil were called that, human beings, children of the earth.

And the gardens were considered as the realm of women, because they produced food, but also, perhaps, because no one experiences sheer misfortune more intimately than gardeners, farmers, and women. All that is planted in the earth is subject to caprice—hailstorms, freezes, predators, drought, disease—while women give birth to dead infants and girls. Even overabundance could be dangerous, its own kind of emergency, which required the mother to deprive her too numerous children, or the gardener to arrange for many expensive hands to harvest and preserve a surprise of success.

These customs were the source of a body of foolish, fanciful local legends told to frighten children, about a woman who destroyed the world through harvesting a dangerous fruit in search of some esoteric knowledge. However, legends are like ivy; they will relentlessly seek some crevice in the world, from which to emerge and make themselves come true. Thus these legends gradually became the underpinning for cruel superstitions about women, and later a body of opportunistic laws that deprived them of letters, and of civil and property rights.

As she approached the gate that led into the property, she saw a small child being soundly punished for making a drawing with a stick in the ground. Souraya stopped and came closer, hoping to plead for some leniency for the little girl.

She looked down at what the child had drawn. It was a sketch of Souraya herself; the child had caught the almond shape of her eyes, and had marked out curves with a playful exuberance that represented the wave on wave of her hair. She looked with a pang at her face; it seemed as far away now as a boat receding into the distance as it vanished around a river bend.

It was with a concealed sense of relief and pleasure that Souraya received the news from Adon that she was to prepare to leave with him on a trading journey of indefinite duration. If she were a wife of longer standing, he might well have set off without her. She thanked God she was a new bride.

Although she had adapted to her new life with tact, if not with ease, she had a keen, if untried, appetite for travel, as she had even in her girlhood. She was young, and wanted to see cities and settlements she had heard about in traveler's tales, cities ascending to Heaven on stone, concealed in cliffs and caves, or settlements in marshes, where you leaned out of your floating house to catch a fish for breakfast. If she had submitted her own face to eradication, she could at least look at the faces of others. She wanted to see a world that insisted on itself. She wanted to be in motion in this world where she had not found a home.

And she wanted to give an illusion of holiday to the work of her marriage. It was her work to create an environment of efficiency, productivity, prosperity, and enjoyment for a perfect stranger, to anticipate and provide him with everything he wanted, even if what he wanted was an illusion, even when what he did not know he wanted. It was a strange paradox of marriage that it required her to outwit her husband. It was critical that she know him better than he knew himself.

She woke up charged with energy, each day a day of danger to be outwitted, each day a test for her; her sense of herself was urgent, a runner straining to outpace a capture. She worked to enlace him in a web of services, obligations, delights—to construct a power of life and death over him that would balance the power he was born with over her. She knew her fate depended on not disappointing, at least until she could provide the dynasty that was the obsession of this aging, childless man.

At home, she was owned, a locked house that her husband entered or left at will, a garden whose fruit her husband fed from according to his appetite. She offered herself with ruthless practicality and an increasingly successful forecast of his moods.

The deprivation of images she lived with seemed to have enhanced an intuitive capacity of hers to nearly supernatural levels—she had developed an almost infallible gift for predicting action and analyzing character through observing other people physically. Their bodies told her stories, warned her, confirmed rumors.

A tension in the neck, a slight compression of the lips, the way arms were crossed, had shown her details of business dealings in a way that even impressed her husband. She had only to entertain a potential client or partner to understand their enterprise, like those canny jewelers who offer coffee to clients the better to see the quality of the rings worn on the hand holding the cup. The anticipated journey would give her more scope to demonstrate these skills, and so secure her husband's favor.

At least as travelers she and her husband would be almost equals, equally subject to the unknown, equally engaged in acts of discovery. They would wake up both unsure of what each day would bring, embarked on a common journey at last.

In those days of traveling, she felt the momentum of being alive so powerfully that it contained her unhappiness. She woke early as if she were hungry for the day. She had discovered the odd and unexpected involuntary savor of living—there was an appetite for it, even among the aggrieved, she observed, as when mourners woke ravenous for breakfast on the day of the funeral.

She coursed through the hours of movement, the rhythms of departure and arrival, the overheard conversations, the changing gods and customs so offensive to her marriage tribe, the absorbing entertainments that were part of hospitality, her appreciation of the beautiful invention of trading, its fine transcendence of combat.

And she secretly delighted in the mirrors in the women's quarters, the first since her marriage over which her husband had no power. She did not, as he admonished her, close her eyes, or turn her back on them. She was surprised to see how easily she had forgotten her own features, how she had become a hazy general impression in her own imagination. Her lost features had expanded like a mist; her face had become the size of the world. The mirror's limitations of her imagination of herself came as a relief. Her face again had an accurate compass. But she was also encountering now a world of mirrors—in the faces of the people she was traveling among, she saw her reflection, as they saw theirs in hers.

The journey made those forbidden images for her, images she never forgot, that came to life and then changed it. Her thoughts, as always, sometimes to her guilt and annoyance, bubbled unquenchably to the surface, like artesian wells. The woman was one of those helpless saints of honesty, so many of whom come to doom.

As they climbed into boats, and set off on reed-fringed waters in the moonlight to approach a legendary settlement scattered on a thousand islands, she knew she had reached a moment that would never end for her. It would end in the world, but not in her memory.

It was as if she were entering into a superb world-sized brocade, somewhat like the kind her own people had made, of nocturnal landscapes emerging from silver, blue, and purple threads. The sounds of the paddles of the guides weaving through the water was the sound of her own figure being woven into a corner of a scene of moving through glistening reeds and water at night.

She had a feeling of being present at her own creation, a moment of premonition. She would never not see herself here. It was, she knew, a deathbed heaven, as her own people called such visions—the place a dying person would imagine himself returning to at the moment of his death.

One of the thoughts came to Souraya that she disliked, that made her feel disturbingly isolated within which what was now supposed to be her clan, her hearth circle. If it was ordered not to fashion images, then it was ordered to destroy the mind, which could not blind itself. Then the great scroll of thoughts and memories that was her mind was sinful. Then even this present moment in which she saw her own figure in the moonlight was forbidden. Then it was ordered not to dream. Dreams, though, flow through living minds as blood through veins, and the loss of them is mortal, too.

A dream came to her now. The heightened feeling she had, the sense that she was unexpectedly part of something permanent, made her think something would happen to her here, something that would itself be permanent. There are moments when one can indeed know the future truly, though never infallibly.

As they neared the island where they were to be received by the chief of this region, one of the guides took what she thought had been an urn, turned it upside down, and began drumming on it with his palms.

The boat laced its way through a labyrinth of reeds, and the moment it struck ground, lights sprang up around them, torches crowned with countless flames, that made them look like the petals of burning white roses. The reeds had camouflaged hundreds of boats, which were now clearly visible, their forms heightened as sculptures in the burst of light. The whole island was alive with light now, as if it had just sprung into being out of darkness. It was as if a new kind of time had been achieved on this fragment of earth, in which day and night were inextricably joined together.

They passed through a pergola that seemed to be formed of flowers that flickered and glowed as if they had bloomed with lit candles inside them. Souraya stared at them surreptitiously as she passed through the fragrant gallery. The luminescence of the flowers was owing to restless fireflies that had somehow been coaxed into their hearts.

Men and women, too, stood on borders of the path to the guesthouse, each supporting a torch planted in the ground like the stone caryatids bearing baskets of flame that she had seen in several cities along their route. The forms of those pillars, she realized, could only have been basalt and granite translations of what some embassy had seen here and remembered. So it was that a form took new life from place to place, from version to version, as a child's features interpreted his ancestors'.

Souraya, as she had been trained since her marriage, met no one's gaze directly. When they crossed the threshold of the guesthouse, she expertly used her lids and lashes as a veil, taking her impressions obliquely and without entering into or inviting any relations, any exchange of mutual knowledge, with any person present. It was a matter of theater; one gave the illusion, in a successful performance, of never seeing the audience.

She observed the great wheels of metal laden with extravagant dishes, and that the company was composed both of men and women, an oddity of the island decorum perhaps. As Adon moved forward to greet the chief, she saw him drop his own eyes, much more ostentatiously and awkwardly than someone did who was accustomed to the practice.

She saw him flinch, and furtively traced the trajectory of his gesture, noticing now, as she had not in the first defensive cautions of entering, that the walls of the structure were covered with painted frescoes and with brocades. It was strange to see Adon obliged to assume her own withdrawn posture in the face of these painted scenes. She could make out what looked like men and women having a picnic under flowering trees, another of musicians playing for dancers, and a brocade of the very scene she had just passed through, a boat moving through reed-fringed waters under a full moon. The rest were too shadowy to see from her position.

The chief, whose name was Am, escorted Adon to a place next to his own, and seated him before a small round wooden table, decorated with gleaming metal tracery, identical to the tables set before the other guests. Then, instead of taking his own place, he returned to escort Souraya to a seat of her own, precisely opposite his, where he could take his fill of looking at her throughout the evening, accidental or deliberate.

Adon was more helpless in the face of the subtle laws of hospitality than he was in open combat. Something as subtle as a foreign conception of courtesy had as much power, it seemed, as a conquest did to alter the course of events. The meal was a chess game played with the eyes, each of the three of them pretending not to look and not to see.

Souraya's mastery of inscrutability was put to the test. She struggled not to respond when she heard their host compliment Adon on the beauty of his companion. She arrested her blush, drove back the current of light flooding her eyes in response, kept her natural expressions masked as if underneath a thin sheet of metal.

Nor did she flinch when she glimpsed Adon gesturing toward her, and heard him explain to the chief that he was traveling with his sister. Then, the chief said, with a courtly inclination of his upper body toward Souraya, your family has not only acquired treasure, but also created it.

After the meal was finished, the singers and dancers arrived. Souraya had never witnessed such techniques of storytelling. The singers and dancers began by surrounding one of the frescoes; they narrated the story it told, and danced it in and through the audience, bringing the figures out of their frames into life, and the audience itself into the world of the pictures. The acceptance of the imagery was an acceptance of a changing world. The dancers even gave the illusion that they themselves were the creations of the audience.

She was rapt, though she saw that Adon was barely able to control his displeasure, which rose to what she recognized as an agony of suppressed protest at the climax. It was the story of their own arrival, Adon's and Souraya's, told through the brocade of the moonlit marinescape.

Boats, oars, winds, moving waters, were made out of dancer's legs, hands, hair, and eyes, and then dissolved. With uncanny observations of their faces, voices, and gestures, Adon and Souraya were woven into the brocade with song and dance, forever honored by becoming a flickering part of the community's pilgrimage of experience.

After the entertainment, when their party had been shown to their quarters, Adon seated himself near the entrance. Although the bones of his face looked prominent and stony, his expression, which she always watched as carefully as a sailor watches the fixed star, was unsettled. His eyebrows were both raised, his mouth open, as if he were in the act of asking a question that confused and panicked him.

He had taken the knife forged as part of Souraya's dowry from its sheath, and turned and turned it in his hand, as if he were meditating on its inscription. Souraya watched him cautiously, turning and turning his face in her eyes, wondering what mood was being communicated to the knife.

At last the knife came to rest, its glittering blade still on the flat of his palm, like a snake charmed into sleep. The familiar certainty returned to his face, a characteristic, almost aggressive tranquillity.

Adon invited his wife to sit with him. "I cannot reproach you for impropriety in this case as it was forced on you," he said, "nor for the beautiful accident of your features, as they were given to you, but your face has brought me into great danger. We are undefended here, except by God.

"You have fascinated our host. It is apparent. His object will now be how best to acquire you for himself. I cannot prevent him. The dilemma now, rather, is in how to maneuver him to earn what he could simply take. This is the art of commerce, how to make a jewel-covered bride of a girl anyone can rape.

"If this lord suspected we were husband and wife, he would simply rid himself of the obstacle of me and take you. You would live, and I would die. I have seen such situations. But God has spoken to me.

"With God's help, I find a stratagem that will protect me, and may yet turn to our profit. You will be my sister. And so Am will make an offer for a sister that would be impossible to make for a wife. I am sure of it. And I will accept it." He sheathed his knife in the traditional iconoclast gesture that accompanied the sealing of an agreement or the acceptance of a treaty.

"You will join his household until I find the means to bring you back. This is a hard thing to ask of you, I know, but I will not be murdered for your sake. It is not God's will that you should live and I should die. I am God's servant. You are mine. Pack what you will need. Remember at all times that you are my sister. And don't dream they won't come for you. God permits the visions He sends to me."

For the second time that night, Souraya became an athlete of silence and emptiness. She froze her eyes, her forehead, her mouth, regulated her breathing, this time to conceal her shock and disbelief. She drained herself like a lake, emptying herself of any visible emotion. But inside her self, where images could not be forbidden, she had witnessed a death.

It was as if she had seen the soul of her husband fall and die in front of her, fall from his body as from a cliff, leaving behind not a corpse, but a soulless living body, the body of the man prostituting her, selling her body for his. She, too, had been separated from her body; she had never realized, never understood, how expendable, how provisional a thing it was.

She had imagined herself as under her husband's protection, like a precious coffer filled with his future children. In this vision was the way she had made herself consent to her life with him. But she was as secure in his protection as a fish is under the protection of a fisherman.

She had thought because he loved her body that he cherished it. But now she saw that he took her body to be a dream of his own. It gave him pleasure, it gave him work, it gave him comfort, and profit. It was even more completely his body than his own, since if he needed to, he could discard it. Nothing she had imagined about who she was to him was true. At that moment, she became his widow.

In the morning a messenger did indeed bring an offer from Am, along with a handsome weight of the gold ore that was the iconoclasts' preferred currency, because they abhorred, as blasphemous and polluted, coins impressed with images.

He was followed by a group of men and women bearing slabs of silk and baskets of dried fish: these were the fundamental currency of their own economy. The messenger also set down a basket of fruit, bread, and new eggs for the breakfast of those in Adon's party, and waited for Adon's reply.

Souraya would be escorted into the chief's household when the day's business was done, and Adon would continue his travels of commerce. Adon put the payment for his wife in the locked chest where he kept the other records and earnings of his expedition. At nightfall, she followed Am's servants, on the path to her new stranger master, still stunned at the way Adon had disposed of her, his chosen wife. She, who had only ever experienced living as a daughter and a wife, was sick with fear. She did not look back, at those carrying her luggage, nor did she look forward, at those leading her away. She kept her eyes on the ground, while her heart saw what it saw.

She was led through a courtyard, and then taken into a pavilion with a wooden door, painted with a scene of musicians playing their instruments on a shore to a party of revelers in a boat at sunset. It was a scene of grace and melancholy, much imitated later in the vernacular art of the region—the boating party seemed to be drifting away from the music they were hearing, while the musicians would soon be without any audience to hear their songs. There were more frescoes on the walls of the room, which looked out onto the water and the shore of an island opposite.

Souraya wandered around the room, drawn to the skillfully painted scenes. Any one of them could have taken place in the setting just outside the room, and she suddenly understood the playfulness that had put exterior into interior. The world then was inside the room, and the pictures filled its walls with possible adventures and histories and destinies, with other lives than her own; their presence communicated that what happened inside the room was not negligible, its scope too was the shared world's scope.

She was brought refreshments, and told to expect to be welcomed shortly by Am, who would announce himself unaccompanied. She saw his face with impotent fury and with dread, both emotions as daily and recognizable to her as the taste of water. She prepared herself to understand the new absolute will to which her life would now be chained. Looking at the frescoes had given her moments of repose and freedom, the relief of a voyage into another world. His presence recaptured her for this one.

She concealed the sudden surge of intense irrational hatred she felt for him with a gesture of courtesy, in the ancient practice of women. Every woman had touched her hand to her heart in delicate obeisance at a moment when she wanted to tear out the heart of the person opposite. He seemed younger when she saw him close than he had yesterday, much nearer her age than Adon's. She dropped her eyes, so as not to insult him by gazing at him as if she were his equal.

"Please look at me freely" was the first thing he said. "Look at me without fear. I want to see myself in your eyes, and I want you to see yourself in mine. Be welcome as a guest, not as a prisoner." She did as he asked, and looked straight up at him, more fully and intensely than she had ever looked at another human being. She was terrified to do it, anticipating a blinding impact in the candid exploration of another's face. A taboo was being broken, and though she could not express it, she was not sure she would survive.

Two joined gazes, she would later say, create a particular reaction, mysteriously generate something together, breed a feeling as palpable as a fruit.

They read each other's look as if each contained the first illuminated page of a story. What their gazes made together, she said, when she could describe it, was a kind of immediate biography, a shared recognition of the integrity of personhood, a mutual sense of the truth of each other's humanity. It was as if they had already shared a life. Their understanding was silent, instantaneous, and moved through the eyes, as real a phenomenon as a sudden storm or a cut apple.

She had grown bitter about the body, that filthy donkey one rode until it died, so it was a marvel to her that the same body was able to accomplish this, this exchange of unsoiled dignities. She felt a physical change; she seemed to herself to achieve a new stature, to step free of her former body as if from a sea.

This look they had exchanged then began to find its form in words. What he said she wanted to believe. "Despite the crude way you have arrived here," he told her, "I want nothing to happen to you here that you do not permit. What happens to you here must also happen to me. I would take nothing from you that I do not inspire you to give, though I confess there is something I want from you. What I want from you is my own freedom."

She had never heard speech of this pattern. He was describing the workings of his mind as it lived, studying himself as if he had weather. He spoke as if he had thoughts that were unpredictable and changed. He spoke as if there were things he did not know, things he was not permitted.

"With all the power I have here," he continued, "and that is obviously considerable, I am not free. Because nothing I have is truly given to me, but mine by custom. My self is no one self. It is a dynasty.

Where I live, fear lives—and ambition. I inspire seduction. Obedience. Intrigue. Jealousy. Beseeching.

"I think I feel like God feels, and I do not like it. For a man to feel like God, it would seem, narrows his experience. As a man, a person, I am a kind of virgin. I know I am not God, and do not want to be. I am not in possession of that common ambition. I want someone to talk to me, not pray to me.

"You are smiling, and that confirms what I noticed so strongly when I saw you last night. There was a quality of shrewdness in your obedience, of fine political craftsmanship. I thought, If this is deference, then it is deference conferred. If this is silence, it is filled with speech. I wanted to speak with you. I wanted you to speak with me.

"I want you to choose what you want to give me, even if I risk obtaining nothing. I am not your father, your brother, or your husband. I stand in no relationship of law to you, but only of grace. I want no relationship with you that you do not shape. If you want to return to your brother immediately, I will arrange it this night."

Then began the only courtship she would ever experience, in which the initial invitation was for her to reject the suitor. It was a courtship devised not only to seduce her, but as much to question her and himself, to divine something about her, to reveal some new capacity of his, to look into the galleries of each other's dreams, to transform knowledge into delight. They became, during this time, connoisseurs of each other, each fresh comprehension an extended caress.

It was a wonder to Souraya that any man could admit himself to be such a particular creature, with personal tastes and fears and thoughts, capable of uncertainty, of humility, and of the playful wit uncertainty made possible. This man had thought about who he might and might not be, and discovered some things he was not.

He deliberately suffered and feared his own power. He dreaded the coming of the day when he would not; he had seen others live that day; when it arrived, old friends were executed without cause, men jailed without trial, wars declared like malignant cancers. Souraya had known men only as monoliths, as fathers, husbands, priests, who affected infallibility, whose power was so certain that it endangered them; they risked being crushed beneath the weight of their own authority.

In a way, Am saw her as a witness, a protective talisman against that condition.

Every day Am wordlessly offered to her a power over him that Souraya refused; every day Am relinquished his own power over Souraya. These were the most subtle, never-ending temptations she had ever known, met on both their parts with a moral asceticism that utterly refined their passion for each other.

To accept a power over him would be to determine his response to her, to set it in motion, to plot its trajectory, to create a physics of feeling. They would then be together in a known world, limited but secure in its predictability. But in their steadfast, intricate, reciprocal refusals of that power, was something greater than power, inexhaustible as power cannot be; she would say later that this love beyond power—symbolized by an embrace, in which neither imposed himself physically on the other—must be at the heart of creation, majestic in its perpetuity, and still unknown in its extent and depth. She dared to think now of this as the way of God with the world; a courtship. An offered embrace, which the world had yet to accept.

It was extraordinary, too, her discovery of an unknown aspect of the appetite to live, based on the discovery that there seemed to be such a thing as love. Until now, she had lived like a soldier on bivouac, apprehensive, enduring, keenly observant, always aware of threat but immured to it. Now love had made her, for the first time, fear another's death. For the first time, she feared her own. Through this intricate tenderness, she knew, for the first time, terror.

All the language she had been taught to describe such phenomena—happiness, joy, pleasure, comedy—trivialized it, made it seem like a fleeting interlude, an entertainment. The other range of descriptions, written in blood instead of pastels, made love seem equally trivial, as if it were insubstantial or dull without the glamour of fatality. She needed words that did not yet exist, words that would be both precise and metamorphic in the mouth, in the heart, like wine. It became her conviction that there was no surer sign of corruption than the contempt for human love that winkingly portrayed it as banal confectionery, or as an equally banal torment.

Nothing was stranger than that it was her husband's opportunism and treachery that had delivered her so inadvertently into love. Adon had said the night of his decision that what he did was God's will. The memory of that phrase made her shiver at her husband's unwitting idiotic blasphemy.

Adon had an ambition for something of God's, wanted their wills fused invincibly. His prayers and prohibitions, his power over what was admissible from the past, his clemencies, seemed designed above all to produce a particular effect—to make Adon feel like God.

Now it seemed to her that God had been jesting with Adon, smiling as he spoke truths without understanding them. It had been perhaps God's will that Adon live, but it had also, it seemed, quite unexpectedly, been God's will that Souraya too would live, that life would mean one thing for Adon and another for his wife. Only this made her marriage to Adon seem something more than a foul accommodation. In the presence of the unforeseeable, she saw God's true image, she heard God's laughter.

Adon was like an oarsman being carried along like a great river of divinity; he looked into the water, and was arrested by his own reflection on the surface, thinking he had found in his own face the true image of God. But that reflection was traveling on currents hidden in the shining depths.

If she knew anything of God, she knew it from her love with a man not her husband. The truth of this feeling was unfathomable, its sweetness stronger than a carnivore at its kill. It was she who had been given a divine gift. She had learned what it was to live in a world without end, like God. Now she felt that it was impossible to know God's will disentangled from one's own, like a mosaic flecked with shining fragments. One could only imagine the divine, not know it, and only through this astonishment of love. She could sense the distance between herself and God by marveling at the distance between what she had been before she knew love, and what she was now. No world had ever been created out of will—but out of revelation.

She was able to divine something more of Am's thoughts not only from his words, but from a gift he brought her. It was the elaborate embroidery she remembered seeing on the night of her arrival.

The scene depicted the arrival of a boat on the same kind of moonlit night that had first brought her here. The curving reeds and blue water rippled in their silk. There was a path lined with torchbearers, just as she remembered, the flames of their torches rendered in golden thread. But Am had commissioned an addition, with her permission. He would not claim even her image without her consent. It was a woman's art on these islands, painting with cloth; she showed the fullness of her assent by apprenticing herself to the weavers.

With them she looked at the world, and at her own face. She shaped the portrait of her journey, woven into the night, passing along the avenue to Am's house, her icon's hair decorated with seed pearls, a tiny replica of a hair ornament he had given her, perpetually moving toward her beloved, who was perpetually waiting for her at the entrance. In making her portrait of herself entering his world, she both kept and returned to him the gift he had given her.

This is a love story, a love story, she would repeat to herself, at work in the herb gardens. Love exists. So what she had heard sung in the poems and epics was not imaginary, had actually been experienced. And yet, only the spray of this great ocean had been described.

Of Adon, she heard nothing. Nor, she realized, as the passing weeks freed her from his presence, did she want to. She had been married without her consent to someone she was grateful not to encounter again.

She had begun to possess her own body within her new world, making the arrangement of furniture in her apartment fit her comfort and her taste. Shy and inexpert, she met with the court's painters, who were its historians, about the schemes for the frescoes ordered for her new rooms. Here, it seemed, such frivolous and trivial matters were taken seriously. Until this moment of her life, she realized, she had never been asked what it was that she might want in the world.

The rooms she chose lay directly on the water, opening onto a small balcony-like wharf, so that from one angle, the suite of rooms was stable, and from another it swayed like a fish tail from side to side. She and the sea gazed at each other.

She could almost set sail carried along in these rooms; at night, she slept freely in breezes blowing off the water, instead of encircled by stone walls. She floated through her dreams at night as if through clear waters. It became her delight, during the last hours of night, to step into a fishing boat from the wharf and watch the brilliant pomegranate of the sun scatter its seeds of scarlet light over the deeper waters beyond the settlement. All the island people, including the women, were accomplished sailors and swimmers.

It was Souraya's embarrassment among these fluent navigators that she was quite unschooled in marine science, and it was Am's pleasure to teach her the rudiments of sailing. He made a gift to her of his knowledge of water and wind; she came to value it more than jewelry. She absorbed their hours on the water adapting to changing light and air and current as an imperceptible, sustaining idea of how to live. The sun, perfume of salt, and cradling motion of the boat in its dialogue with the sea were never lost or stolen from her.

Am delighted her by renaming his boat for her; he painted her name on both sides, with a brilliant pomegranate above her floating name; the boat lay anchored every night at the wharf just outside her suite of rooms, a declaration, even to the sea, of faithful love. On clear evenings, the sun inscribed her name waveringly on the waters themselves.

Souraya thought those days that she knew so many songs about the misery of love because pain kept love within the boundaries of time, and knowable, whereas what she was experiencing passed beyond the horizon of birth and death; it was like the eternal life the prophets spoke of. A gesture, a kiss, a task, a sentence had a golden elemental endlessness, like the scenes in the murals painted in the island houses.

The water lapped against the wharf at night, and she dreamed that it was whispering to her. It subsided, but immediately had more to say, as lovers do, in the way of Souraya and Am. Another murmuring overrode the water's, repeating her name softly, again and again. She answered peacefully, and before she was fully awake was ripped from her bed and dragged across the floor toward her veranda, a piece of cloth stuffed in her mouth, almost choking her. She turned her head and saw Am stabbed by one man. Two others, with a frenzied childlike joy in the act of desecration, were pissing on the murals that covered the walls. "Idol worshippers," one of them spat at her portrait. Then mesh after mesh was wound around her, fishnets, and she was carried like cargo onto her own boat.

She could not remember how long they sailed; when they landed, she was taken up by two of them, and carried ashore. Through the thick webs of fishnet they had wound around her when they seized her, she could sense the light and movement of flames. They laid their catch down roughly near what she guessed must be a campfire. She heard its hissing and the cracking sound of the heat breaking fuel apart, and then a confusion of footsteps.

Someone knelt over her; she could feel the motion of a knife working, cutting through the upper rope that bound the fishnet over her head and around her neck. It moved too swiftly for its handler, and she felt it eat a small bit of the skin beneath her right ear, a minor gourmandise, but it got a sip of her blood. The fishnet was rolled back, and she was blinded for a moment by the broad curved knife blade glittering in the firelight in Adon's hand. "I heard the voice of God," he said. His face was ecstatic. "And then it was revealed to me how I would bring you back to my side. Praise God for our success."

He freed Souraya from her nets, then brought a plate of food for her, and tenderly fed her with his own hands. As she ate exhaustedly, she saw a wonder, tears coursing down his face, like a steep and barren cliff flowing miraculously with milk. The men who had abducted her were shocked by his remorseful gratitude. They had held her comfort of no regard on the journey to their rendezvous, and kept her bound, thinking they were delivering a body that would soon be a corpse to its vengeful owner.

In the morning, Adon paid off the iconoclast mercenaries he had hired to seize his wife. She overheard the accounts they gave of their struggle to escape the island with her. They did not know themselves whether Am had lived or died. Souraya quietly tormented herself with both possibilities. She was unable to measure which one gave her more pain.

Adon spoke almost passionately to the soldiers of his gratitude for their perfect execution of his plan. He lavished them with a supply of food for their journey, and paid them the previously agreed sum for their services. Despite the extra expenses of her rescue, her husband had not failed to make a handsome profit from the price he received for

Souraya's sale, not excluding Am's gifts of jewelry, which he confiscated from her, to free her from shame.

The journey back to Adon's settlement was tragic to her beyond mourning, despite his extraordinary display of solicitude. He could not bear to let her out of his sight; he watched over her with a sour, impassioned adoration. But there was a privacy in her tragedy. She had become invisible to her iconoclast husband. Her love, even her loss of it, gave her an independence, a continuity of a life of freedom, a possession of remembered words, images, and experience over which her husband had no power.

This, she concluded, must be one reason marriages of choice were held so dangerous. The imperfections of the husband were the conditions of marriage; the imperfections of the beloved, by contrast, seemed flowing and mutable, like the verses of an ongoing song. In love, one experienced the beloved, and through him, oneself; but this knowledge destroyed one's subjection to him. Love, then, destroyed innocence. Love, then, was knowledge.

So she lived through the return, indifferent to the cities and settlements they passed through, uninterested in the details of their trading, taciturn during the hospitalities. She felt a pang when Adon financed a purchase of seed and medicines with seven of Am's jewels, but no more than that. The hand that fitted the rings to her fingers and clasped the brilliants around her throat had made them precious. Without it, they were toys. For her, treasure could be nothing but her lover's child, its small face and hands swept inside her by the current of their caresses.

She was shaken by a bitter amusement when she saw the primitive greed and admiration the ornaments excited. Cities and wars were paid for by colored rocks, by the luminous secretions of shellfish, by a subterranean dung of gold. These had no more real value than if military power were based on an inexhaustible supply of toy soldiers. She inwardly mocked the gravity with which the negotiators examined and debated the qualities of the colored rocks, the intensity of the blue, green, and red reflections, for which they would exchange food. Love had made her unfit to live in this world.

They arrived at a famous city she had once desired to see. Now her desire had been fulfilled after it had died. God has many ways to grant our prayers.

This city was built entirely underground in a labyrinth of crystalline salt caves. Visitors could only hope to find their way in and out with the help of expert local guides who led them along sinuous paths, mounted on their special breed of sightless ponies, who shied at nothing. Another relay of guides poled them through a coil of canals. The air of the place was shocking, pure, saline, solid as water—it was if one were breathing as one had before birth, inside the mother.

They were received in a hall built around a great dammed pool of water; the walls and ceiling of the room sparkled with flecks of salt and mica, and a chandelier carved of salt illuminated the room like fireworks. The celebrated acoustics of these underground rooms were unique, producing a sound that seemed to come at once from all directions. Specially trained choirs, during the ceremonies of greeting, sang choral music in parts so that the music moved around the hall, now seeming to pour from above and below them, or most spectacularly, in an effect that made their hearts race, from within the chambers of the listener's own skulls.

They called themselves the Salt of the Earth. Salt was their wealth: the king's musicians played instruments whose strings were encrusted with salt. Salt fell shimmering from the capillary strings, as the song makers' fingers played over them, revealing the music woven inside its tense chrysalis. Even their banquet dishes were of whole fishes, animals, and roots baked in domes of salt. The women of this tribe decorated their faces and skin with mica, salt, and sugar crystals, so their very features, brows, cheekbones, foreheads, chins, seemed a kind of jewelry, their flesh sparkling ore.

It was there that Adon sold her again, for a substantial tonnage of salt. This time he sold her with studied calculation, and a much more assured presentation of her as a beloved sister, with whom such a parting was reluctant but inevitable. He was implacably confident that her loss was temporary, despite watching her escorted disappearance through a maze of glittering tunnels. To him now even the tunnels were a part of the ruse God inspired in him; they were an extension of the tunnels in his own soul. The insatiable divinity of invincibility possessed him.

This time, though, her purchaser was not a king dreaming of philosophy, but a satrap eager to replenish his harem with a fine breeding woman acquired by purchase rather than the more costly method of capture. She was dressed in the costume of the city's women, a voluminous garment made of a material that sparkled, designed to conceal the outline of her body. It made every encounter here between men and women charged; the very volume of the garment directed the imagination to the naked body of the woman inside it. The garment concealed the details of the body, but made explicitly clear the outlines of the fantasies of the gazers. Sugar and salt crystals were applied to her face and hands and body, so she looked like an underworld woman. Thus she was delivered by the man of faith to wait for the lord of the underworld, the salt of the earth.

While Souraya waited for him, she reflected on her course of action. She looked at herself, waiting for the new man, as withdrawn from her own body as if she were a ghost or a god. What should she do with the woman sitting here by candlelight in a cavern hung with velvet? She could leave the woman underground here, and see what happened to her. Her destiny with this master might even prove to be less burdensome than a future with her husband. She could leave this woman even deeper underground, and be free of her forever. She had now lost so much and lived with so much fear that even her own destruction was no longer unthinkable to her.

But if she were pregnant? Any child not assuredly fathered by this man would almost certainly be murdered. She had seen for herself how the women's quarters teemed with this lord's children. Am's child would have a better chance of surviving if born to Adon, whose desperation for a son would tempt him into believing in himself as the father. Besides, like many iconoclasts, he had so little sense of what he looked like that he could easily be deceived in the matter of resemblance.

The chieftain was preceded by a wife, carrying the traditional equipage of welcome: a tray and cups of rock crystal, chiseled from the walls that sheltered them, filled with a tea made of "earth-milk," stalactite drippings, and salt butter.

The wife made the arrangement of the refreshments an opportunity for a concentrated scrutiny of the newly purchased. Souraya was not surprised by her intensity: what she had gleaned from the girls of her own people who had entered polygamous arrangements was that one was as wived to the women in such a marriage as to the husband. The wife looked Souraya full in the eyes, then pulled aside the velvet hangings and held them open for the chieftain to enter. She bowed as he crossed the threshold, and took her own leave by backing out the door; it was a grave discourtesy here for a woman to turn her back to a man.

A woman who has been bought feels a rush of sickening, defensive, and absolute attention when she sees her purchaser, as a soldier does when he stands and faces for the first time a combatant on the field, who is coming toward him to kill him. A woman's purchaser, too, wants power over a body, but differs in that he pursues her life, not her death, which is a different kind of destruction. Souraya stood up to meet the man who owned her.

Another wife followed him in with a tray of jewelry, set it down, following his gesture, and left. He had a pale face, from living so much out of the sun, and an appraising eye, perhaps for the same reason. He, more than many men, was surrounded by a world he had imported and created. "Please be seated. There." He spoke to her with a formulaic, proprietary courtesy, and a slight impatience, as if he wanted to treat her in a more perfunctory fashion, but was inhibited by the value his investment in her gave her.

"It must be a grief to you to leave your brother," he said, "but these are the natural sorrows of women, like the transplantations of fruit trees. There is a shock, but then they bear well in their new soil. You have made his household pleasant; now you will delight my house. And you will have the opportunity to see him again before he and his party depart. Now," he said, offering her the tray of ornaments, "let the tree choose its own blossoms, as even God himself does not permit."

Souraya kept her eyes down, studying his way of speaking. He offered metaphors as a parent offers toys to a child in pain to distract it. And his sense of ownership seemed absolute. It was there she might free herself, for if one locates the sense of the absolute in a man, one can see where he is blind, his judgment vulnerable and unbalanced, incapable of anticipating the unexpected, prone to uncontrollable outrage; while he is staring at the sun, his prey can silently slip past him, and find a hiding place.

She made a show of examining closely the necklaces and bracelets he set before her. Some of them, the ones superior in design and workmanship, were recognizably the work of iconoclasts. She needed to experiment with him, and she saw a way to test her theory of him with a jewel. She allowed her indecision to express a welcome awe of him. Then she selected a negligible ring, and slipped it on her finger. Before she could secure it on her hand, he swiftly reached to retract it. He already had an idea of the appearance she should present. A woman's body is often a man's self-portrait. And the opposite can also be true.

So her instinct had been right. The unassailability of his ownership was a need, to which she was supernumerary. His approach to her would be to dramatize that ownership, until he was satisfied she acknowledged it, submitted to it, publicized it. These jewels were neither jewels of gift nor jewels of contract; they were glittering locks and bolts. She now knew precisely in which way she was valued.

"You are too modest," he said. "Let me choose some more important pieces for you." He riffled through the tray, and selected a lavish hair ornament, and a matching necklace and ring. The headdress was a masterpiece, a veil of thin rubies, cut in petal shapes, linked by a network of thin gold chains.

With an oddly maternal gesture, he set it on her head. It trembled on her hair like a drift of supernatural roses shaken apart by some otherworldly wind. The necklace was of emeralds: the roses' leaves. The ring was an ingenious creation, a cluster of diamonds trembling on wires: dewdrops. The jewels imprisoned her in beauty. He reached forward to clasp the necklace, lifting her hair; the gemstones hung there heavily, as if the weight and force of his hands still spanned her neck. He pushed the ring onto her finger, like oaring a boat upstream, and used the occasion of the touch to keep her hand in his.

"You were made for these," he said. "They are flawless. As you are."

Now, she saw, was the moment she could try for her freedom. For the sake of her child, she reduced the size of her life, made it small, portable, expendable as a pebble. She launched it toward him, that life the right size to gamble with.

"Sir," she said, "I have a flaw."

He looked at her with two expressions, an irritation that could be excavated just beneath an overlay of confident indulgence, with a sharp sparkling light, both angry and humorous, in his eyes. "I see none," he said parentally, absolving her of any of her girlish indiscretions.

"The flaw is invisible. But it is real."

"In any case, it is not lack of candor, and for that you are to be admired. Tell me what seems to you so important for me to know."

Carefully, remembering Am as he maneuvered his sails, she watched what the winds and currents wanted from the boat. A facial expression finished as quickly as a life, a cluster of words fell like leaves, and disappeared. But if they vanished quickly, they could still be remembered deeply. She learned as quickly as she had to.

First his indulgence, and now his command translated her approach to him from independence into obedience. Now he ordered her to tell him what she had previously volunteered. Now, with luck, her initiative would be invisible, her action would be lost in his. She might find a chance to submit to the freedom he imposed on her.

"The customs of your people may be different than our own. So I must ask you, sir, would you have taken me if I had been a widow?"

"There is no certain answer, except perhaps, and not for myself. A widow has been a bringer of bad fortune."

"And if I were a wife?"

"Under no circumstances but war. A woman with a living husband is a house where a snake waits hidden in a crevice, a danger even in repose."

"Sir, then I am obliged to tell you. The flaw I have is marriage."

She watched his impulse to strike her, the thwarted reversal of his wish to touch her, and steeled herself. But he was so confused that his movements were indecisive, and in that physical indecision, a question about the justice of his wish to harm her surfaced on his face, which took on the hardworking innocence of a student unable to solve a problem. A face working with a question is a youthful face. His practiced courtesy faltered. "This is not what I was told," he said.

Softly, carefully, she echoed him, giving him the sound of his own words in a muse's voice. "There is much I, too, was not told."

More calmly, having heard his voice again in the world, he seated himself again, facing her. "Is this some scheme of your brother's?" he asked, gazing at her with a judge's intensity. For her child's sake, she wanted to survive both men. So she answered him, "Sir, there is neither scheme nor brother."

"I find myself in possession of a bride who is the wife of another man, after a purchase I made in good faith. Only your brother can have plotted this."

"Sir, there is no brother. The man is my husband. And there is no plot. In a moment of panic, he sold me to you, afraid in your wish to have me in your household you might choose to make me a widow."

He flinched and recoiled. "This is an extraordinary violation of both custom and trade. And having done this, is he planning instead to make my wives widows?"

"Sir, he had no plan beyond saving his life, which he imagined at risk. I do not know what he thought beyond fearing you, leaving your city, and in security, seeking some resolution."

"He has shown no scruple in the beginning, why should he be any more trustworthy now? This is what I see: he sells a woman he claims to be his sister, but she privately claims to be his wife. I return her. He repudiates her claim to be his wife, and then justifies his attack on his host for the insult to his honor. Then the matter is settled in violence. Or that threat is averted through payment. Isn't that the plan?" He moved toward her, so rent by his own impulses, and by outrage that another man had taken the privilege of making him afraid, that she could not accurately estimate what he might do.

"Sir, there was no plan. Sir, there was no plan," she hoped he would hear her words through his storm. She cowered instinctively to shield herself from the whiplash of his slap, ashamed that defending herself necessarily conflicted with her pride. There were moments when she valued the enforced diplomacies imposed on her sex by physical defenselessness, but she hated her endangerment at the hands of both this stranger and her husband. She crouched with her hands cupping the back of her head and neck, tearing from her hair the jeweled ornament he had given her; the heavy gems would intensify the blow and cut into her scalp.

She became a sculpture of fear; the sculptor paused before her to contemplate the work of his hands. She felt from her crouch a new quality in his breathing; the power to attend to someone else had returned to him. She ventured a look at him. The salt sovereign motioned her to sit up. "Sir, may I speak?" she asked. He nodded.

"Sir, I have said there was no plan. But with your permission, I have devised one now."

"What do you propose?"

"Sir, return me to my husband, and let him return the payment you made for me."

"On what grounds?"

"That you have discovered I am his wife."

"Then his treachery is revealed, and we are forced into conflict. Or your treachery, in disclosing yourself to me, is revealed, and it is you who die for the betrayal. Have you thought of that?"

"Sir, it is not I who have made this disclosure."

"The same punishment that would fall on you will fall on anyone you try to make responsible. Would you sacrifice one of your husband's merchant colleagues, or one of your iconoclast sisters?"

"Sir, with your permission, tomorrow morning, you will approach my husband as he is preparing to depart with his company. You passed no time with me this night, because, though you had intended to, you fell asleep in the early evening, in your own apartments. There you had a long, magnificent dream, in which the true nature of my relationship to my brother was revealed. It was not I who disclosed this to you, but God. Tell him it was God, maker of miracles, who gave you this knowledge. Will my husband punish God?"

In the morning, it happened as she promised. Adon, radiant, permeated by God, returned his host's bride payment, and received his wife with thanksgiving and with prayers. God, as had been his conviction of the divine will all along, had made each man even with the other, and restored Adon's lamb to his flock.

Adon's party was a good two days away when the gifts that had been slipped inside were discovered in Souraya's baggage, to her astonishment. There was a magnificent hair ornament of rubies carved in the shape of rose petals, an emerald necklace cut to look like leaves, a diamond ring like a cluster of dewdrops. She dared to think of them as a compliment, perhaps a repayment of a debt owed for unraveling a conflict more dangerous than her would-be husband had known. Perhaps, too, there was a soft, silent breeze of erotic regret emanating from the secret gift of the jewels the Salt of the Earth had chosen for her.

Adon was jubilant at the news of the discovery; he called for a communal prayer, and afterward, feasted the whole camp splendidly. God heaped blessings on his head; his body was a map of the world God was making, cartography of God's divine journey through the human soul.

So Adon, enriched, journeyed home. He was given an appreciative welcome. He had traded advantageously, and adroitly avoided all but the most necessary conflict. He had, in fact, spilled very little of his own or any other tribe's blood, and, of the band he had set out with, the only life lost during the entire expedition had been that of his wife, Souraya. And it was her blood that was spilled on the return journey, the blood that had belonged to her lover's child, whom she was not to bring to light.

She had desperately wished that Am's child had found its life within the palace of her bones, but her wish came to nothing; it was as if God had answered one wish of her life so supremely that nothing was left for her in Heaven. The child she miscarried two years later, she reflected bitterly, could only have been Adon's or God's. As was the child she miscarried the year after that, and the five more who found nothing to please them in the world outside, and refused to be born into it.

Now she realized how close she was coming to a precipice in this settlement, for a childless woman had no political and little economic value. A woman's possessions consisted of her jewelry and her children.

The consequences were brutally visible everywhere, in the snubs of Adon's kin when they were guests at her table, and their hints at divorce, the theatrical pity prominent secure mothers displayed toward her at public rituals. Now bands of beggars sang traditional taunting songs—"She without jewels will wear no jewels"—when they crossed her path, and beat on drums, their hollow thuds evoking barren wombs. These beggars had lived their songs; they were mostly childless women.

Above all, she felt the danger of Adon's increasing indifference to her thoughts, a dust of casual contempt for her advice. A woman with a collection of children had some authority—in a conflict with her husband, she could show him her offspring like a mouthful of bared teeth. Children were a woman's strongest link to the world of men.

It no longer mattered if Souraya hoped or dreamed for a child. Now she must get one, by any means. Without one, she risked being transformed from wife into servant, or worse. Now her longing for a child felt corrupted. It had become an ambition, like Adon's—it held a willingness to destroy, a cancerous mass attached to the dream of creating. This mythically selfless act had become instead as calculating as a merchant's creation of a profit. For her, a child was no longer a motive for living, but a means of staying alive.

She began to surround the trunks of her fruit trees with banners embroidered with prayers, and buy illuminated prayers to hang on their leaves, the remedy suggested by the priests. She hated to do it, because it publicized her growing desperation. She had a cannibal's need for this infant meat, a vulture's for the eggs of another bird. She was revolted with herself.

For the first time, she was truly relieved at the absence of mirrors. She did not want to see her eyes now, their former soft brilliance turned metallic, her body changed, as feeling has the power to change the shape of all bodies, by her ruthless need. So riven was she by this need that it seemed to have made her a new soul, in the way a new tree will grow between the two halves of a dead tree, split by some accident.

Now when she passed mothers holding a young child or baby, she saw herself pushing the mother aside, reaching to take the child, so forcefully, so finally, in the calmest indifference of cruelty, that she sometimes believed this was what she had actually done. She was horrified to recognize that this new self of hers, in a female way, had something of the character of a rapist.

It was, however, this ugly fantasy itself, which led her, after suffering it for years, to the lawful solution of her dilemma. It was not the child she would sweep up and out of its mother's arms, Souraya determined. It was the woman alone.

If she could find a woman to bring into the household for Adon, a child was bound to follow. And as the architect of this new household, she herself would rule both the child and the woman. As soon as its cord was cut, the child would be placed upon her knees. It would be she who would set its name upon it, she who would be its God. The name she chose would be traced in honey on a ceramic plaque, then she would bend down to touch her lips to the honey, and whispering the name, set her lips on the infant's, transferring the name to him, recalling the birth of speech, the honey dropped from the kiss God gave the world.

An unexpected struggle with Adon became the most difficult element of her plan to execute. God had revealed nothing to him of a child he would have with a woman he had not chosen for himself. Souraya was his in a way no other woman could ever be, almost as if he had at last succeeded in creating her.

He had bought her from abroad, and he himself made an iconoclast of her; he had twice catapulted her beyond him, as in stories of heroes shooting arrows into space untold distances, arrows that inexplicably returned encircled by a hundred diamond rings and slid in silken homecoming into the hero's quiver.

Like those legendary arrows, she had returned to him as through resurrection, and through her returns, had enriched him a hundredfold. These things made a miracle of Souraya for him. She was a woman of destiny for him, God's will at work in her, however blindly. Besides, the suffering of this previously stoic woman moved him; and he did not want to be maneuvered into putting her away for her barrenness, leaving himself and his property a target for a strategic marriage engineered by an ambitious clan.

In the end, in the face of Souraya's surprising relentlessness, the female equivalent of muscular strength, Adon could not endure, and agreed to take a wife of her choosing. The strange symmetry of circumstance did not go unobserved by either of them; he had twice given her to strange men. Now she would deliver him to another woman. "God permits," he told her.

It was easy enough to arrange a "harvest" marriage, as they were called, a temporary marriage for the purposes of begetting a child, if the reigning wife had means, and knew a family vulnerably burdened with girls, those creatures who had to be given birth twice, once as infants, once as brides. Souraya selected a daughter who was a pivot between three older sisters, and three younger sisters. She hoped the mother's fertility was prophetic.

It was Souraya who negotiated for the girl, and paid for her, using her own jewelry for the purchase. She felt a momentary shame when she realized how easy it had been for her to buy a woman, she who had been bought and sold herself. She wondered if the girl's docility was an affectation. Her own had been. Souraya suddenly saw the girl's entrapment was hers, too.

Their inferior position destroyed their integrity at the outset; if the girl rebelled, her life would be broken. But her calm acceptance of herself as merchandise, her eager embrace of the preference for boys, made her suspect. The priests who gave women tongue-lashings for being the source of faithlessness, or of evil, were secure on this scaffolding, that women must be either deceived or deceivers. For if women loved a God who had this contempt for them, they were either mad, therefore truly inferior, or if not, their love for this God was a frightening display of untrustworthiness, of calculating collaboration.

After the transaction had been completed, the girl, whose name was Roucoul, meaning the cooing of doves, shyly approached her.

"Do you remember me, madam?" the girl asked her. Souraya looked at her keenly, but no scene including this face reappeared in her memory.

"I only wondered if you might," the girl said. "When you were a bride, I thought you were so beautiful, so unlike anyone I had ever seen, that I tried to draw your face in the orchard grounds. The stick I used was as big as I was, and I remember drawing with it was like poling a boat—it took my whole body to navigate. I made your face as big as a lake, or a full moon, and I circled it and circled the world of your face with my oar. My mother beat me for it, and you tried to stop her. I always remember how you tried to rescue me when I was a little girl, and you were a newcomer. I shall try to serve your household well. I shall try my best, with God, to give you a boy."

It was Souraya who led the girl, their maker of soldiers, to Adon's bedroom, and who arranged her diet, and bought talismans from the priests when she conceived, to ensure that the child would be a son.

She treated the girl with passionate, but untender, attention to her physical welfare. She saw to it that the girl lacked for nothing, even judiciously indulged her, but with expertise, not kindness. Souraya knew her care for the girl was not only practical, but also aggressive—a way of exorcising the intense jealousy she felt of the girl's fertile effortless success. She would control her resentment by translating it into governance over the girl. For Souraya, she was little more than a canal. Through cups of fresh milk and plates of ripe fruit, prayers of petition and prayers of thanksgiving, ordained repose, arranging visits of musicians who played the traditional songs that created boys, Souraya possessed the girl's advancing pregnancy.

As she had envisioned, and had demanded, the child was put into her arms as soon as the cord was cut. She sat down with the nearly weightless creature on her knees, observing the beseeching movements of his unmuscled arms, the tiny fingers like fistfuls of fresh herbs, the bewildered, already human face. She called for the plaque and the honey, and wrote down his name. Then she kissed his name onto his lips. "Pelerin," she sent the name into his body. "Pilgrim."

The midwife, concerned to have the child fed, disentangled him from Souraya's arms. She did not want to let him go. She cursed herself for not being able to feed him. It dismayed her to see him at his mother's breast. He fit there like a star within a constellation. Souraya had named him—she was his fate. But Roucoul, she saw, as her milk went into the child like rain into the soil, was his existence. And nothing could change that.

This was why the priests insisted that each conception was an act of God's, and surrounded each birth so densely with ritual, prayer, and custom. These were exorcisms of the mother, a seeking of protection of the child from some other, not maternal, source. Otherwise, in the beginning, it might seem that the woman, the birthgiver, had absolute power over life. It was she who gave each life, and thus, terrifyingly, it was also the woman who had the power to take it away, as Souraya had herself seen a number of times, effected simply by a subtle withdrawal from the child, who wilted like a parched plant. There were mothers who simply selected one child to sponsor, and another to neglect. And as a rule, their infants obeyed them to death. Even law could do little to change that power.

Adon was eased by the child's solution of his dilemma, as everyone who had expected to inherit from a rich man without an heir was not. He was quite indifferent to Roucoul, as long as she had served her purpose, and continued to serve it. Her abject misery would have been of concern to him; her happiness was not. The child, for him, was born of Souraya's thought, and another proof of the providence she was for him.

For Souraya, though, the household was unbalanced. Her husband preferred her, and that was as it should be. But the household's child preferred its mother, grew to resemble her, spoke almost a private language with her.

Pelerin dropped his voice to a whisper before Souraya, rarely smiled in her presence, and made her feel an intruder in her own home. It was almost as if he had absorbed the way Souraya had dealt with his mother while he formed in her womb, and now refracted her own behavior back to her; he treated Souraya with perfected, pragmatic, affectionless obedience, unless he felt his mother was being maltreated. He displayed an odd assumption of equality with Souraya, as if he were uncannily aware that he was the guarantor of her marriage. Souraya had called his mother a soldier maker; he was a childlike caricature of a soldier.

Twice, though, he had lost that martial obedience, and attacked Souraya, on the two occasions she had slapped his mother. It was almost irresistible to Roucoul as the two women struggled over the boy, to assert her motherhood over him by finding a way to refer to Souraya's childlessness. Though Souraya was disgusted with herself for striking the girl, the taunts touched her where she was wounded to death.

It happened again on a day when Souraya was beginning to teach the child to count. He could hardly force himself to attend to her, and followed his mother with his eyes, as she did the cleaning; heavy household tasks were now almost wholly hers. Souraya had made the boy sit close by her side, though he never stopped tapping his feet, as if he were running away from her, even though the rest of him stayed still. Roucoul, proud to be his favorite, began to hum one of the folk songs about childless women.

A fury surged up in Souraya, a burning energy of anger. She felt as if she could tear a building down with this force. She called Roucoul over, and with this strange invincible energy alone, and no other restraint, made her stand still, and slapped her hard, four times, alternating the blows with her right and her left hand. Instantly the boy began to kick Souraya; as if her body as well as her soul was oppressed beyond endurance by her exile within her household, she began to laugh uncontrollably, and fainted. Two weeks later, the household heard her racked with laughter again, but this time the tone of her laughter changed from hysterical to ecstatic. Her invincible energy was not only the result of an irrepressible hatred, but also a cresting wave of life. She had realized that she was unmistakably, miraculously, with child.

A generation of servants and relatives had never seen her laugh. It seemed to her that she had not laughed since her husband had bestowed her on Am, and then had her abducted from his islands. Her perpetually severe husband took her uncharacteristic mirth as a freakishness of this miraculous pregnancy. As a way to keep his thanksgiving always in the ear of the Lord, he paid a pair of priests for prayers to be chanted throughout the day and night until the child's first birthday had passed. Adon, it was said, was such a favorite of God, that he received the gift of communications from the Lord even through his wife, the rarest of distinctions.

Souraya, overhearing this form of congratulation, overflowed with laughter, which for her, in her fulfillment, was not irreverence, but prayer itself. Then she begged forgiveness of her unborn child for not loving its father, reflecting that God's ways were so subtle that even the child of a lawful marriage could be illegitimate.

When the time came for her to deliver the child, the midwives told a marvelous story they had witnessed of her labor, which circulated through the settlements and beyond. They had never seen a woman in the grip of her throes bend double in tears, then straighten, and throw her head back, laughing as if an angel lifted her in his arms, soaring high above suffering. As powerful as the agony was, her joy was stronger.

She raised herself up when the child was put into her arms, and called for the honey and the plaque. She wrote her son's name in honey, and kissed the name into him: Ivat, "he will live." Her lips were rich with honey, but as she transferred the name to him, her kiss was adamant. Then she laughed again, as he swallowed the sweet wine of his own name.

But earth was and is not Heaven. The laughter of one mother and son brought sorrow to the other mother and her son, in the way a brilliant sunrise in one city is a sign of nightfall somewhere else, in the way the freshest, most flourishing, and joyful infant born brings news to its mother of the smile waiting inside her, to be released, at the child's maturity, onto her skull, its fatal coquetry the last of all her facial expressions.

Ivat's entrance into the household displaced Pelerin astonishingly; he became instantly negligible, as expendable as if he had been a girl. It was the first time either Souraya or Roucoul had ever witnessed a boy experience by accident what a girl experiences inevitably.

This plunge into the condition of womanhood had the effect of strengthening the child's bond with Roucoul, but for the rest of the household, above all its men and the boy's father, it made of the boy an object of almost superstitious fear, a creature to be avoided. The discomfort of the men with the transformed older boy meant that he remained in the world of babies and women, a fixture in the nursery for longer than he would have been under normal circumstances.

Even there, his misfortune was apparent. Before Ivat was born, the women, even Souraya herself, had been preoccupied with him alone; now they flooded Ivat with concern, admiration, and attention. It was assumed that the younger boy must do excellently all that he attempted, which functioned not only as a demand, but an encouragement, and a confidence. It was now assumed that the older boy's excellence would be to do as he was told. It was the difference in upbringing between master and servant, boy and girl.

Pelerin absorbed this, as children do, with a sense of physical threat, since as the teachings have it, a child's body and soul do not separate until the child reaches the age of seven. Pelerin perceived his change in status as if he were being destroyed; the great heroic purpose of his existence, protecting his mother, was compromised, almost impossible, now that he had been, above all, separated from himself.

His reaction was to defend himself from this annihilation. Now he made himself a nuisance, seized by unpredictable frenzies of kicking, striking, biting; his rage was not local, but universal, and took for its object not only persons but furniture, dishes, even food. He entered into combat with all the forces of domestic life.

He crushed eggs and murdered melons, mixing together praying and killing, in an eerie imitation of the slaughter rituals practiced on the community's herd animals. He pretended his hands were knives, decapitating onions and garlic from their stalks whenever he could intercept them before they reached the cooks. He was a soldier fighting in an invisible war.

It was as if he were acting in a kind of theater that represented over and over varieties of destruction of the vulnerable. With a kind of angry genius, he was violating the most cherished prohibition of the iconoclasts. Unobserved by any of the censors, he had found a way to make images; many people who saw the boy at this time kept vivid memories of his wildness and suffering throughout their lives, permanently imprinted in their memories, down to the length of his hair, as detailed as an artist's murals. All that he showed them made him a living blasphemy. It could not be long before he was judged not only a nuisance, but also a danger.

Nevertheless, it was not the boy, whose fury betrayed a kind of ethic, in that the only animate creatures he attacked were adults more powerful than himself, well able to control him, who was the object of Souraya's fear. It was his mother.

Souraya winced every time her former protégée approached the younger boy, and froze with fear if she took him in her arms, as if her embrace would prove mortal. Just by existing, she compromised Souraya's own maternity, distorted her affection, transformed her caresses into embattled gestures. What was a miracle for Souraya was the very source of Roucoul's own magical new power—her intimate knowledge that this boy would be Souraya's only child meant that he would always be at risk from her.

She had done nothing threatening yet, but Souraya was exhausting herself through her surveillance of both Ivat and Roucoul. The name she had given her son seemed darkly prophetic, since she felt him surrounded by danger, his life haunted with threat. She judged Roucoul by herself—she found herself, through love, so far from love. She found herself a woman whose passion for her own child would allow her to harm another's.

She began to confide an artful version of her fear to her husband. The link that must be broken was not his bond to his older son, for that was fragile. He had come very quickly to consider Pelerin an outsider, perhaps a burden. The bond that needed to fray was Adon's own sense of self, his sense of what was permitted in relation to a child he had already betrayed.

She launched her campaign with telling true stories, of Pelerin's violent fits of temper. She had observed that what was most unbearable for this man, and for many others, was a sense of his own wrongdoing. This caused such poisoning pain that each one would search for elaborate stratagems to disguise, justify, or forget his guilt. There was no more certain path to violence than this needing to uproot something in oneself. She could almost believe she had seen entire peoples in the grip of this.

Adon was uncomfortably aware of the injustice of his altered treatment of Pelerin; there was even more he did not want to know. She would graft that anesthetizing will to ignorance to her own will to blot out its source, the son whose shadow lay on her son. She was so consumed by her lust for her son's future that she forgot how much she, too, wanted to forget.

It was as if she had given herself a sleeping drug, and carried out her actions both deliberately and unconsciously, lost in a self-induced sleepwalker's torpor. In the end, the lie she told to rid herself of Roucoul and Pelerin was so convincing because it was true as well as false, like all exemplary lies. Her tale was not true in fact, but it was absolutely true in dream.

The world changes through this mysterious alchemy, when dreams, splendid or cruel, are brought to life in it. These dreams re-create the world. When they are splendid, people say, "My dream came true." When they are cruel, people say, "My nightmare became real." For in this world there is always a difference between what is true and what is real; those who live greatly find the art of joining them, becoming loci where they embrace.

Souraya told her husband the story of an imaginary scene that tormented her, as if it had really happened. The mystery was that when she transferred her terrible dream into the world, it became real, in a grotesque, deformed way. That is to say the people who died in the world were not the people who died in the dream. And the house she lived in, so full of movement and sound, turned to stone, and her own flesh became fire.

She made her husband see a winter afternoon, with the strange peace of winter, its cold timelessness, and the feeling of safety of a mother and child's afternoon nap near the warmth of an abundant fire. They lay together like a word and a comma, asleep within an unfinished sentence. She made her husband see, and it was exactly what she saw, a door open noiselessly. She made him feel the chilling violation of some unknown gaze above surveying the pair in their sweet sleep; it must be like what the drowsy dead sense when they feel the weight of the living heavy on their graves. The door that was opened closes. And the mother and son wake inside a new room, a room made entirely of flames, no longer a shelter, but a room with an appetite for them, a room determined to consume them.

The nap, the fire, the leap through flames with the promised child gripped hastily and passionately, to the point of suffocation, in her arms, were real. Her accusation that the boy Pelerin had set the fire, according to his mother's instructions, was her dream, a dream repeated many times. Untamed fire is especially dangerous because it takes swift, unpredictable, marauding paths, which is why it is the element of soldiers, and their true language. This fire was driven from the room, and from her sleep, but it leapt out of the dream and out of the room, and invisibly entered Souraya, to scorch Roucoul and her son, Pelerin.

Adon, like all iconoclast men, was God in his household. It was his right to judge its members, and his right to allocate exonerations, warnings, penalties, divorces, and death sentences. He chose a traditional punishment for an attempted murder.

"You who tried to execute God's power will live only with God's help. You who tried to seal the fate of another will be delivered to an unknown fate. You who have made a child a demon will dwell with the children of wolves. You who tried to destroy a house will be released into the wilderness. If there is mercy in the wild, let it sustain you. Whatever awaits you, God permits." He remained implacable despite Roucoul's protestations of innocence, and unmoved by her pleas for clemency. She and their son would be given a supply of food and water, escorted beyond the city walls, and given to destiny, set adrift in the desert.

Roucoul turned as they led her out, her boy's hand in hers. "You will not see what happens to us, but your blindness will be criminal. Innocence is here, in your own son. Look at him well. For the innocence of a child is in not knowing what he does, but the innocence of a man is precisely in that knowledge. This is the last hour of your innocence." The soldiers moved to silence her, but her speech was ripped apart by her tears, like the garment of someone in the passion of bereavement.

It was a little after Souraya had succeeded in driving Roucoul and her child from the household that the dreams began. Though she kept a full jug of cold water by her bedside, she would wake parched, with tears streaming down her face. It was as if water could not quench her thirst anymore, her body could make use of it only for the purpose of grief.

Her small son, sleeping on his pallet near her, would wake and try to comfort his mother. As he grew older, his expectation of her nightmares would wake him before they woke her. The dreams were persistent, occurring close to the same hour every night, the same pattern of racking thirst, and unquenchable tears, a season of grief, as if someone were speaking to her, saying the same thing again and again.

Gradually, she began to grow, not more fragile, but thinner, as if the dreams were eating what she ate, taking her nourishment and using it to re-create themselves even more vividly. She acquired the terrible insatiable look of the very thin, the appearance of one who could under no circumstances be satisfied, in contrast to the plump, who look overwhelmed by a satisfaction that demands that they perpetually satisfy their appetites, their flesh incorporating a fused mother and ever-suckling infant.

When her son had reached that moment of boyhood when they no longer shared a language and talking to her was not precisely like talking to himself, he asked her, "What do you see at night that makes you cry?"

She was grateful then for the years she had had to prepare her answer to his question and that she had not succeeded in pretending it would not be asked. She had waited for this to come, and it came. She took him then to a corner of the garden she had been tending since she was first married to his father, one of the gardens that provided a household's food and was called, in their language, paradise. They sat down in paradise, in the shade of one of her oldest and most fertile fruit trees.

She reached up and handed him one of its near ripe golden fruits. "I am going to tell you what I see at night. But first tell me what you see in your hand."

"A quince from one of your trees," he said.

"Yes, it is that," she said, "but it is also a world in itself, a fragment of this world and an emblem of it. What you are holding is not merely a single fruit, but water, light, leaf, craft, work, knowledge, time, filth, and luck. It is thousands of other things, too, most of which I don't know. If you eat it, it will become you, and a part of you will be quince. What you do and what you are gradually become the same thing, and are identical when you die. And what you have done to another person becomes a part of your substance as surely as a fruit you have eaten.

"What I am telling you is that the world is made of thousands and thousands of marriages, visible and invisible, thousands and thousands of filaments of kinship, bonds of love, and bonds of harm, which are as intimate as those of love, and breed with a fertility of their own.

"My dream is one of those filaments; it is my half of a bond with another person I can no longer see. It is my bond"—she threw back her head and closed her eyes, as if suffering physically—"with a person I have harmed. I know she must have the missing half of my dream. We are forbidden mirrors here, so as not to look away from God, but the prohibition is futile, my heart: our lives are bright mirrors; our reflections outlive us, they show the truth of what we have made of our world, and of the world of ourselves.

"Do you remember a woman and an older boy who lived with us when you were very young?"

He felt the memory as much as saw it, at first, but it was there, especially of the boy, of being carried on his shoulders, and also of furious battles with stones, blood on both their cheeks, mixed images of love and hate. And parallel memories of his mother with the other woman, each with serious faces, sharing the burden of carrying a full grain basket together, and later, in some other room, a nightmarish, ugly memory of his mother's murderous, distorted face, as she slapped the other woman viciously. He had assumed until then that his mother was only capable of loving.

"Now you know who I see in the dream. I see this woman and her son. They are in the desert with no water left. She carries him on her back through Hell. He is unconscious. She lays him down beside a dry well, and walks away. She cannot bear to hear her son's last breath, does what otherwise she would never do, abandons him.

"And they are there, because in a frenzy of jealousy and ambition for you, I drove them from the house, Roucoul and her son, who is your brother.

"And I think if she lived, she will be dreaming of me, watching me with you in a fur-trimmed coat in my arms as the soldiers marched her beyond the walls into cold twilight, giving the order that the gates be locked. But I know now how flimsy those stone gates are, now that every night I die her death, and I hold her thirsty child in my own arms as he unendingly dies.

"There are no mirrors in our houses, but there are mirrors in the sea, in our eyes, in the eyes of animals, in the drop of rain. In that desert, a woman and a child showed our images as they sank down, not knowing where they might go. There are a thousand mirrors alone in their tears. I look into those mirrors, as in a gallery of looking glass, and through them I see their desert. But the mirrors of tears show the world ahead as well as the world behind, the world inside as well as the world outside; I see my own desert, that tragic labyrinth of the innocent becoming the guilty. I have brought you to the edge of that labyrinth. I do not want you to enter it."

The boy's face was suddenly as full of lines as a rock that has been thrown hard at something harder and cracked on impact. He had never heard her speak in this way before, as if there were a world beyond him, as if she were translating the language of another world. She spoke as if she would mean what she said even if he did not exist. He discovered at that moment that she was human with exactly the sacred convulsion a convert experiences when he encounters God.

Souraya looked into her son's face and saw him recoil from her. The new fear of her in his eyes was a knife in her heart. Her own child now knew she had done harm to the point of death, that only good fortune might save her from the charge of murder.

But she went on speaking. "You are right to flinch. I have imagined this moment again and again. Sometimes I thought, Surely my beloved son will forgive me; it was my passion for him above all that drove me. He will realize that there is nothing I would not do for him. But then I think, If there is nothing I would not do for him, why should my own child feel safe from me? If there was nothing I would not do for you, then is there nothing I would not do to you?

"If my soul was so frayed in me that I destroyed one child then it might yet give way altogether. So believe beyond a doubt that you are my unutterably beloved son. But remember that I do not deserve your trust. And when you are grown, search for your brother, and, if he lived, beg him to forgive me."

The boy was utterly quiet for a few minutes, as quiet as a hunter stalking or as prey being stalked. "And was my father standing with you on the walls when this happened?" he asked.

"No," she answered. "He was not there. He was waiting at the great gates to bar them." Now the boy's eyes looked beyond her as she made him present at a scene he could not remember. She saw his face as she had never seen it, his features racked and aged with pain and fear; it was exactly the expression she had seen on Pelerin's face as he and his mother were escorted to the city gate. She saw now how strongly the two boys resembled each other.

Not only had she failed to protect her son from the rivalry of the other boy, she had inadvertently entrapped him in the other child's suffering, as if what had happened had inevitably happened to them both. She had, perhaps, killed the other boy, and the effect was this: her mercilessness had entombed them both, which must mean, it occurred to her for the first time, that the risk of generosity might have held a power of its own, might have sheltered them both. Her love for her son was a failure. She had taken his life as well. Love was action as surely as combat, she saw too late, and the way it was used and put to use directed its effect.

"Mother," the boy said to her, "I do want to find my brother. There is a way to begin now to look for him, even here. But I need your help."

"What can I do to help you?" she asked, suppressing the impulsive urge she had to say she would do anything. She had already done that.

"Tell me, what did he look like? And what do I look like? I need to know how to recognize him. I need to know how he might recognize me. I need you to help me see. I need to make an image of him. And of his mother. And of our father. And of you. I need to learn how to see."

He was enlisting her help to endanger himself, but her own actions had enforced this on him. She could only hope that this was a necessary peril, and would somehow redeem them. "I will tell you," she said, "what I see and what I have seen, as clearly as I am able."

It was time for them to return. The boy's days were filled with the acquisition of skills Adon purposed for him, praying as Adon instructed him, and fulfilling commands Adon gave him. His days were divided between the study of the mercantile and the martial arts, in segments designed to reveal to him the relationship between the two disciplines.

In the late afternoons, he was drilled in the arts of fighting and using weapons, although he was not yet old enough to be given the knife the iconoclasts presented in their coming-of-age ceremony. Only fully initiated men were entrusted with the sacred knives—the merciless reflections emanating from those blades gave enemies their first glimpses of the face of God.

Adon himself was nearly always present at this instruction. He opened the session with a prayer of thanksgiving: "Blessed is God, who formed our souls to strive. All-Powerful, grant that these will do holy violence only, strike only in your service, sacrifice their strength to your righteous causes."

Then Adon would seat himself in a carved wooden armchair, his eyes glittering with intensity, watching his son, his opponent, and the young man who instructed them, circle each other, deceive each other, and struggle. At the end of the match, Adon would descend, place his hand on each combatant's head, like a priest, and intone a closing prayer: "Praise God, stronger than all, revealed in victory. Praise God, stronger than all, revealed in defeat."

Adon would find some reward for whichever boy shone, a fine piece of meat, a garment, tool, or coin. He would give these neither coldly, nor smilingly; he gave them not in affection, but in judgment, out of a passionate acknowledgement of the victor. "Here, my son," he would say, offering the small treasure. "You have served God with a victory this day."

But this day, and from now on, Ivat had the new thought that his father watched the combat so forcefully, and so often pitted him against other boys in contests of skills, in order to reassure himself he had spared the right son to fulfill his destiny.

But from this day and from now on, Ivat himself knew the true answer to his father's implicit question: he was not the son his father had prayed for. He was, at best, the son his father had been granted.

He was certain he was not, because during the hours spared him from his father's program of education, he was possessed with his efforts to acquire the forbidden ability his father most loathed; he was, with his mother's collusion, learning to draw, to model clay, and to paint. And it had come to seem to him that he enjoyed not only his mother's collusion in this but was undergoing a profound education in the relations between the mortal and the divine.

Since the afternoon his mother had shown him that the charcoal pieces she had gathered up could be sharpened, and then make lines that were like ladders one could climb between earth and Heaven, he had learned, in moving back and forth between the worlds, that even the world in which he existed was both visible and invisible; how much more so the court of God it nearly hypnotized him to imagine. The charcoal incised the paper, like a kind of knife—but a knife that worked not to destroy what it touched, but made it intact.

It seemed to him that God had saturated the world with colors, and had, with what suggested deliberate abundance, supplied that world with the means to paint them. The world around him yielded paints from eggs and cooking oils, from colored stones, from flowers and dung, from fish and insects, fire, water, air, and earth, the botany of a supernatural garden. To refuse them was to refuse creation itself.

And most powerfully of all, his efforts to represent what he saw around him taught him how partial his dazzled vision was, how mortal his hand was in its joyful agon, how each of his sketches showed him he lived in a world he did and did not know. Making art showed him beyond a doubt that he had not created the world; it taught him that his art was to live in a world not made in his image.

No, iconoclasm was meaningless. The dread of images seemed a disguised arrogance, a way of flattering oneself that one's perceptions were greater than they could be; what was terrifying was how little one could actually see. Or perhaps it was simpler, he thought, angrily ripping apart a spoiled sketch of a horse and rider he had drawn with grossly thick lines that contradicted any illusion of motion or speed. Perhaps images were forbidden as a magic because people were so afraid to be erased.

His first work was discouragingly crude. There was his childish lack of coordination to overcome. Worse, he could not ever start a sketch without a paralyzing sense of sacrilege. "God permits, God permits," he would whisper ritually to himself before he could draw the first line.

Every sketch was like beginning the entire world. His efforts suffered from the void in which they existed; there was no other work to compare his with, no means of learning how other hands approached the drawing problems that perplexed him. And his mother insisted that she would not teach him unless he destroyed without a trace what he had made in each practice session. He obeyed her at first, but eventually, when he began to make drawings that could actually teach him something new, it was beyond him to obliterate what he had worked so hard to do.

In secret, he found a novel solution that both hid him when he was working at his art and preserved at least some of the work. He would shimmy up a tree, gently scrape a flat surface on the underside of a thick, well-concealed branch, and spend an invisible hour there, sketching or painting. When the tree had yielded him every inch of surface it could safely provide for pictures, he would move to another tree to begin a new series, returning to the previous trees to examine what he had accomplished in the older pictures. He lost a fair number of the images. Many faded or dissolved in rain, but over time many trees bore a miraculous and secret fruit.

In the autumn, he had to suspend work on his private orchard of images. It was hunting season, and any creature hidden in a tree risked being cut down by an arrow, or by one of the keen flying knives for which the iconoclasts were famous.

Stories were told all over the region about how these knives seemed almost to seek their prey, floating alongside them: the best marksmen could bring down a stag on the run with a perfectly timed and angled flick of the wrist. During one harvest season a celebrated knife huntsman bagged a figpecker at dawn, with a throw that bisected the delicate bird. Its body fell in two halves at his feet, along with a slender branch sliced off at the moment of the kill. The branch was stained at intervals with three studies of Adon's face.

The hunter had the momentary thought that the tree was infected with some disfiguring disease. He picked up the branch to examine it more closely; his hand trembled when he recognized Adon's portrait. He was as awed and confused as if he had seen God. These were the first images he had ever seen. Never before had he looked Adon directly in the eyes.

He dropped the branch, and with more apprehension than he had felt on any hunt, he swung a leg over the tree as if it were a woman, and slithered up into its crown. There, swaying above him, he saw the sea for the first time, its waves a transparent aquamarine starred with silvery fish, painted in a sequence of miniature panels, according to the description of Souraya, whose son had translated her words into images.

There were houses he knew, animals he had hunted and killed, alive again here in Heaven. Here was a wedding, a coming-of-age ceremony, faces only a bit larger than buds emerging like new fruit on the branches. He recognized the face of his own wife. God seemed to have made a world in the sky corresponding to the one created on earth. The tree was like God's own record of the tribe. Bewildered and frightened, he forgot his kill, and ran back to the settlement with a fierce speed, as if he were chasing a leopard.

He was led into Adon's house, and taken to the master, where he gave a breathless, incoherent account of an ocean in the sky, of a tree of life, where God made pictures that determined the destinies they lived. Adon, sensing a danger that had driven this steady-handed hunter mad, chose two men to meet it with him, took his knife in his hand, and guided by the hunter, followed him to the holy tree in which the world past and the world to come were blooming.

When the hunter handed Adon the fallen branch etched with his portrait, Adon flung the limb to the ground, and raising his knife, chopped it into segments as if it had been a snake he had encountered on the path.

Then he ordered the hunter to shimmy up the tree and hack off its branches one by one. Faces, still lifes, flowers, and animals fell onto the ground.

As if he were at war, Adon attacked each one. A branch with an unusually ample planed section near its leaf end fell to the ground, and Adon froze. The wood was painted with a dreamlike scene of a woman with a small child in her arms; pearls of tears were visible on her face, as she and the child stared back with fixed eyes toward the recognizable gates of their own settlement, as a company of soldiers in helmets barricaded the entrance. Then Adon called for fire.

The men pleaded with Adon to save the orchard; its destruction would be an incalculable loss to the community. Another ran to the sanctuary to fetch the chief priests, hoping they would dissuade Adon, but when they arrived and saw how the trees had been desecrated, they agreed with Adon that whatever fruit they might yield was irrevocably poisoned. They chanted prayers of repentance as Adon put the torch to the garden.

Then began a time of fear, of interrogations, denunciations, and perpetual dawn sacrifices presided over by the men and boys of the community. These were the first months Adon and Ivat had spent a substantial amount of time in each other's company, and the shared ceremonies and ritual rigors created in them a mutual acknowledgment, almost camaraderie.

Souraya could hardly bear the dread of those days, with their atmosphere of tense mutual suspicion and old scores waiting to be settled.

She spent hours in agonized prayer, begging that the boy would not be found out, while Ivat acted, for her sake, as if he were oblivious to his danger. He would only admit that he sorely regretted his lost work, and that he was frustrated by the incessant liturgies of expiation that left him no opportunity to practice making pictures.

This morning's sickle of the new moon, surrounded by a crop of pale stars, held the sky, but not for long. Soon the light would come that made every night seem an illusion until it was replaced again by the dark that made a dream of the lost brilliance of the day. The boy felt his father's great slab of hand rest gently on his shoulder. "Blessed is God who shrouds the world in darkness and adorns it with light. It is the hour of sacrifice. Dress yourself and join me outside."

It was a time of day the boy loved, and longed to paint, though he thought that would be impossible. This was the time when day was an impulse, a promise, destined but not born; if one could tell the adventures of a hero in his mother's womb, or a love story before the lovers had met, then one could paint this. Even though leaving sleep so early was a struggle for him, and his secrets made the daily sacrifices troubling to him, being abroad at this time of day gave him a sense of a mysterious and tender blessing passing over the world, like a hand caressing a cheek.

The thought made him want to perform just that gesture; he washed and dressed, then went quietly into his mother's alcove, and brushed his hand against her cheek. His fingers were so alive with his craft that he felt as if he painted a caress on her flesh. Painting was the first way he had understood cherishing; through it, he found he looked as long and intently and passionately at the world as the young husbands did at their new wives.

His mother stirred, as if she remained in some relation to him, even in her sleep, and he backed away, not wanting his presence to force her into consciousness before it returned to her naturally. He joined his father outside, where a servant was holding two saddled horses. They rode outside the gates, which were barred behind them. Ivat had never been beyond the settlement with his father's knowledge or permission, though he had enjoyed a few undisclosed boys' adventures beyond the gates.

"Where are we going, Father?" he asked.

"To the Eye of God, to make our sacrifice," his father answered. "Today we will promise again to see only what God commands us to see."

The Eye of God was sacred territory; it was a large lake on a mountaintop, flanked by three peaks. It was there that the first iconoclasts had seen God, and had sworn to the deity to blind themselves to all but the Divine. It was not far from the settlement, but only priests and elders, and by dispensation, shepherds, were permitted to climb it unaccompanied; the rest of the tribe, though not the children, joined them there for twice-yearly rituals of penitence, thanksgiving, and the renewal of the ancient oath to purify the world until it mirrored nothing but God. These feasts they prepared for months in advance, fattening the lambs whose spitted corpses dotted the slopes of the mountain, crowning it with smoke and fragrance delectable to God at the culmination of these festivals.

Ivat was awed. He was deeply moved by the significant honor his father was conferring, a powerful acknowledgement of the bond between father and son, that had paradoxically become more public, and also more personal, during these months of purification and rededication within the tribe, during which father and son had gained their first direct knowledge of each other.

He was also anguished by his secret knowledge that he was the hidden motivation for the purification—that he had come to hope, even to believe, that he could serve God best in seeing as much as creation would reveal to him. If his father had uttered an intimate word, Ivat would have confessed the truth. But his father was too overcome with the emotion of his son's first journey to the Eye of God to speak. Ivat heard him chanting to himself the prayers of pilgrimage, and joined in the ones that boys were allowed to learn.

He drank the wonderfully cool dawn air as they rode up the labyrinth of paths, air that for the boy irrationally had a color: dark green. They greeted a shepherd, driving his lambs toward a high valley for grazing. Wisps of silvery mist drifted upward from the trees' leaves. Ivat felt, for the first time, one of the ancient forms of joy, the sublime physical joy of ascent. Trees were no more than balconies to him. He had never climbed to the top of a mountain.

At the summit was the fathomless blue-black Eye of God, ringed with four enormous altars. They dismounted, tied their mounts, and walked to the edge of the water. Adon instructed the boy to remove his outer garments, so that he could be dedicated to God within the waters. Ivat had the cricket-slimness of boys, as if his flesh were not yet fully fitted to his bones. His young shoulder and rib bones were of a shell-like delicacy; Adon took his hand for fear he would be washed away during the ritual by some sudden current.

They waded together into the waters, which chattered and glittered as the sun rose, until they were high over the boy's head. Then Adon raised him on high, cradled the boy in his arms, and plunged him deeply into the waters, once, twice, a third time, muttering unintelligible prayers in the secret prayer language of men, which had its own grammar and alphabet, to protect the sacred words from the profane tongues of the uninitiated.

Then they returned to the shore to gather wood and kindling for the fire to roast God's lamb. Ivat wandered the nearby slopes and woods, searching for the choicest, driest pieces. He worked doubly hard, because his father seemed swept with one of the sudden sovereign exhaustions of old age, and sat down heavily under a tree, his face gray and his eyes closed, with a nauseated expression.

It was impossible for Ivat to touch these varieties of wood, and not regret the finest, with the smoothest grain, as foundations for his painting. He completed his elegant pyramid, and stood back to look at it, to make sure it was above criticism. A boy his age was supposed to have mastered to perfection the making of a fire for roasting.

He judged his work vulnerable, with too many pieces of green or still damp wood, which he would need to conceal artfully among the sticks and logs that were above reproach. He bent over the mound, quietly, so that his father would not realize he was disguising his poorly chosen wood. He was engineering a building designed to disappear without a trace, making a palace for flame.

A powerful blow just above his kidneys knocked him to the ground, where he knelt, panting.

A coarse, thick rope was bound around him twice, and then doubled over his hands. Ivat screamed for his father. He was flung, hard, on his back on his carefully arranged mound of wood. His father was twisting the ends of the rope beneath the stone altar, and looped them around him again. Ivat screamed for his father again; but his father was with him, had never left him, was lighting the kindling that would set the wood ablaze. "You hurt me, Father," Ivat said, and cried in pure fear, without dignity, like a much smaller boy. "Why are you hurting me?"

"Son, you have come to the hour of your death. God speaks in me. For our sins, God demands your death. Only the death of my son will cleanse the filth of images from the pure face of our nation. Only the death of my son—my own image—will please God. I do this for the love of God." His father seemed to have found an unearthly strength; his father's face shone, raised toward Heaven. His father had not spoken his name.

He drew the knife that Souraya's father had forged for him long ago, as the centerpiece of her bridal dowry, and leaned close to the boy, as a father leans over a child's bed to kiss it at bedtime, and draw the covers over it against a night chill. The knife seemed as big as a new moon, as inevitable a fact of creation. It hovered flush with the boy's eyes, as his father sought to calibrate its cutting edge with the mortal angle of the child's thin throat.

The child looked for his father's eyes to find the human being there. But it was his own eyes he saw, in the fragments of blade not covered by patterns and calligraphy; blue-green, like his mother's. And his hair, the earthy color of oak bark. "Father, I see my face in your knife!" he cried out, as stunned at the first glimpse of his own face as if he had witnessed his own birth. "I see my image!"

At these words, his father's demonically radiant face took on an expression of rapture; at this sight, the boy, like all children who are frightened to death, and all adults who are dying, lost control of his bladder, and soaked the smoking wood of the pyre with his waste. A flash of anger intensified the ecstasy on his father's face, as a local bolt of lightning does the dark immensity of a storm. His face turned an explosive red, dark with unshed blood. Then he collapsed, as if he had had a stroke.

It was not, though, a stroke that had felled him. It was his wife, Souraya, who leapt out of a thicket, and with the full weight, both of her body and of the unexpected shock, knocked him to the ground. She must have had a kind of intimation that became a panicked conviction. Perhaps she remembered how her husband had risked her life when she set out on a journey with him. Perhaps she trusted him no more than she trusted herself. In whatever form, by whatever means the knowledge came to her, she was there.

"Will you?" she whispered, trembling so convulsively that more words were impossible. "Will we kill another child?" She snatched the knife, her bridal dowry knife, shaped to Adon's hand, from her husband, and flung it away, so far, or so deep, or so high that it was never found.

She too held a knife, a kitchen knife covered with prayers to accompany the preparation of food; she cut swiftly through the cords that bound the boy, and swept him off the altar, onto his feet. She did not allow herself to hold him, because there was no time. "Live," she said. She pushed him away, brusquely and urgently, toward a slope. He stared at her, as if he longed for something, some other world in which a prayer like hers was not ambiguous.

"Run," she cried out, and her husband was upon her, enraged at her blasphemous interference. She struggled with him, but his hand was a carnivore's. God had asked for blood from him, and he was God's lion, voracious in his obedience to lay down some hallowed kill at the foot of God's throne. Nothing could deflect him from giving a death to God, the death his Holy One craved.

His wife looked him full in the eyes, a gaze that seemed suspended and timeless, though it must have lasted no more than a moment. It was a look of lucid and perfect knowledge. "God permits," she said. It was not clear whether what she meant then was her rescue of the boy, or her own murder.

Then her husband dragged her onto the altar where he had tied down their son, and killed his wife. He killed her with her own household knife, so much an element of her body, her life, and her work every day, that he could feel she died by her own hand. Which was the way her death was told, crafted as divine punishment, a retribution for her act of rash faithlessness, before God revealed her child would not be slaughtered.

. . .

I did not see my father cut my mother's throat. I have heard the story painstakingly arrived at by the Guardians, their ingenious, intricate panoply of prescribed responses, designed to justify murder if it is for God; it is a basilica grandly architected, a building in which only some doors may open, and others remain permanently bolted against either entrance or exit. The Guardians of the Story say it was an angel of God who rescued me, who stayed my father's hand. But it was a human who performed that awful miracle. The sacrifice that day was hers, and it was herself.

I saw that day what I can never forget; I did not see the moment of my mother's death in blood, but I saw my mother die. Just before she cut me from my bonds, her face took on an eerie youthfulness, mixed with an expression of agonized regret. I believe she was remembering then my brother and his mother, who had suffered at her hand what she was experiencing now.

And then a new face seemed to grow from the existing features, as if one could actually see the precise moment a blossom comes to exist as a fruit. Her renewed face showed passionate fear, and, astonishingly, an equally passionate resolve. It was her face of death, when she had taken the measure of what she was doing, and knew that in saving me, she would lose everything. Then she gave me life.

Who was filled with God that day? Was it the parent who rushed to kill with trickery for God's sake a child who trusted him, or was God in the parent who said, "Take my life instead of this child's"? What does God's voice sound like?

There was more than one death that day. My mother was killed, but my father died too; he died to me. I have never seen him again. If he sent a thousand embassies with a thousand offers of reconciliation, I would not risk them. After such treachery, how could I trust he had not had some new divine revelation concerning me, or that he was not still determined to fulfill the old one? How often I have since heard unruly children threatened in this way by their fathers: "I shall make a sacrifice of you, unless . . ."

And I myself died. No child whose own father has tortured him has not died, has not seen Hell itself. A child whose father has trussed him on a pyre, who has looked up and seen a gleaming blade in the hand of a father absolutely determined to destroy him, has been killed. I outlived that death, with the grace of the life my mother gave me. There was enough life to survive, to form a new self. But even the story the Guardians tell cannot conceal that death. In their version, there are three voices you do not hear, three faces you will never see: mine, my mother's, and my brother's. They obliterate us with their story.

But here is mine. In a story, you must always listen for the voice you cannot hear, the one that has been ignored or silenced. In that crushed voice, there is a strain of truth, as a crushed grape yields a drop of wine.

I have said the world was created with a knife and a prayer. The prayer was my mother's word as she went to her death: "Live." The knife you can see well, especially in the late summer nights. No one had seen this constellation, the Murder, appear in the sky until after my mother was killed and I escaped my father. The astronomers until then had not observed it, or at least had made no record of it. But there, overhead, an image that seems the size of a world formed all at once, larger than any image my father ever succeeded in eradicating. Speech denied will burst its dam and become a flood of song. Stories silenced on earth will catapult into Heaven, visible wherever we turn our faces, glittering irrevocably, forever.

Legend (that is the name the Guardians give to the stories they reject) tells that the flashing knife that trembles in the heavens was the one that my mother tore from my father's hand and flung away. It is suspended there, in the heart of Heaven, they say, poised to slice the night and cut us all to pieces, until the day you can hear my voice. Until you let me tell the truth. Listen. God permits.

THE PROVERBS OF SOURAYA

The images of gods and saints are mirrors in which we see ourselves praying; they are not idols.

If a painter could make the water in his seascape salty, God would congratulate him.

Unless we see ourselves praying, we cannot know what we pray for.

Monotheism is also polytheism: each believer worships the images of his own God, the God in the many faces of his dreams.

We refuse images in order not to see our own desires clearly.

Every man has prayed at some time in his life to a false God.

Those who will not gaze at others' faces cannot see their own.

Words are more dangerous idols than images; idols we cannot see.

The evil are always insulted at the suggestion that they are not good; the good are never convinced that they are not evil.

God's humans are the creatures who bring themselves to life through what they make.

The man who believes woman was made of him, not of God, has made an idol of himself.

We must pray a thousand ways, with bread, with wine, with falling leaves, with breath, with idols, with thinking, and with kissing.

Is the one true God who saved one boy from sacrifice the one true God who welcomes the sacred killing of ten centuries of girls?

Beware the mother who would sacrifice another's child for her own.

A woman who gives birth has gambled with the life of someone she does not know—which is why the churches are filled with women.

The mother who will do anything for her child will also do anything to it.

A blessing given at another's expense is not from God.

Honor your mother and father, if they have also honored their children.

Blessed is the parent worthy to be mourned.

Blessed is the child who at the parent's grave weeps for his death, not for his life.

What a man refuses to see is the idol that always accompanies him.

Idols are what we will not look at, and will never see.

Idolatry is the failure to observe that we imagine what we see.

Women are the knights without armor, the soldiers without an army.

One can destroy such good as one embodies by lusting for virtue.

Men make laws: God makes miracles.

II

THE BOOK OF SAVOUR

THE SECOND CONSTELLATION: THE CAULDRON

TO THE MEMORY OF NICOLAI VAVILOV

I have always found that Angels have the vanity to speak of themselves as the only wise; this they do with a confident insolence sprouting from systematic reasoning.

—WILLIAM BLAKE

Look to the left of the shimmering Sheaf of Wheat undulating in the heavens, and just upward of the cascading Cluster of Grapes, from which the thick black wine of every night is pressed. You will see her standing next to, though higher than, the Cauldron, just to the left of the Great Table. She pours that nocturnal wine, holding a pitcher whose handle is set with planets, from one starry hand. Just above the Cauldron is the small diagonal group of eleven stars, which resemble seed pearls and are known as the Grains of Salt. It is said that the twelfth has already dropped into the Cauldron.

With her other hand, she tips a ladle over the Cauldron; streaming uncountable diamantine grains of starry rice, wheat, corn, and all shapes of edible seeds fall from it. They keep the world from devouring its own body in its hunger.

For the world was created not from clay, but from butter, which can melt like an illusion; from fertile grasses and trees, which may yield no fruit; from meat, which may be the prey of its own mother. For we ourselves are cauldrons, our breaths rising fragrant vapors, our entire span of life an evening's banquet at which God is our guest. And treacherous or generous, what we offer is what we think the nature of our Guest merits.

For it is said we wait for God's judgment in the life to come; but our lives here are our judgments of God.

She was nameless, being an Invisible. With the others of her year, she had been sent naked after her birth to one of the Ghost Houses in the three port cities of her country. These received children whose parents refused them. The children were called by shifting names until a permanent name formed for them, usually a name reflecting a talent or trait, therefore a useful marker to a potential owner.

No name could be given them, as is the convention in families; these children's names had to choose them. Her name found her a little later than average—Savour. This was not only a description of flavor, but was also a kind of spice native to her island. The savours grew on trees like nutmegs, but when their rind was shaved away, and the nut pulverized, it revealed an inner flesh like an iridescent jewel.

The spice emitted a unique perfume of caramel and smoke when it was grated into a dish, as well as adding an almost shocking ornamental beauty. The nuts separated into micalike sheets colored like precious gems; a tray of meat or rice flavored with them glinted with flecks of diamond, sapphire, ruby, silver, and gold, illuminating the faces of the diners as much as lamplight.

The fragrant fragments were not only used for cookery, but also served Ghost artists to make the mosaic pictures of the gods celebrated throughout the region. Savours were so common on the island that they were not particularly prized locally, but elsewhere, they represented the greatest luxury; cities were built on a trade in precious savours, the ships with their cargoes of savours and slaves were blessed by priests as a protection from pirates as they left port.

The Invisibles, also known as the Ghosts, and the Grateful Ones, were nurtured and fed until age seven or so, when they were dexterous and useful enough to be sold, having shown no sign of uncorrectable flaws of physique or character that would determine their future as wandering, rather than household Ghosts.

This was a condition more dreaded than slavery, not only for its insecurity, but because these children racked the countryside, their presence as torturing as questions that could find no answer, their unrequited faces and bodies haunted by their unknown parents, their parents possessed by their unknown children, wandering in fate.

They were never allowed to mourn, and were disciplined for any sign of melancholy, or talk of the lost ones. Their graves could be easily recognized in the cemeteries; instead of identification by relationship to parent, companion, or child, their headstones were carved with their assigned name and, beneath those, the embellished word "Grateful." Hence, the proverbial threat that all the children of the island heard when misbehaving: "I'll give you something to be grateful for."

But all the Grateful, even the pretty and endearing ones, made people uneasy. Their parents had not killed them; but in sending them to the Ghost Houses, they delivered their children out of the known world to a region in which anything was permitted to happen to them, anything might be given, anything withheld, anything done. All feared, and some envied, the windswept freedom that paradoxically made their slavery possible.

Above all, the Ghosts came into the world incarnate with knowledge. They lacked the innocence of family children. What they knew was the cruelest of secrets, the one that all parents strove to conceal from their children.

It was this.

They knew from the outset that all relationships are voluntary—even that most primal bond of mother and child. They were the bearers of the fearful knowledge that to commit a being to birth is as grave and fatal an act as to commit murder. Indeed, it was forbidden to sing lullabies to them. Their lives began with their own deaths; to sing them promises of safety as they fell asleep would be contradictory, if not mocking.

Other children seemed to live in a faith of need and fulfillment; the Ghosts were never sure that the sun would agree to rise, the next wave consent to the shore, never sure they would hear another of their own heartbeats.

This was reflected in Savour's laconic manner of speaking, always with a slight hesitation, as if she had to assemble herself from various elements before she replied. This quality could make her seem half-witted, though she was not; but her thoughts often had to traverse a great distance before they could be expressed. Then they poured out in a visionary and sometimes incomprehensible flood. There are people whose thoughts reflect the period of their own lives; but Savour was one of those whose attention is trained on the world as it was before they were born.

In their country, there was a legend of a paradise tree whose magnificent fruit exuded a crimson sap in small droplets like blood. According to the story, this fruit was sacred to the gods, and was forbidden to humans. Anyone who ate of it died. Then those who died revived, and lived afterward in a state of both unbearable knowledge and visionary rapture. It was said the Ghosts were suckled on the blood of this matchless fruit rather than on mother's milk.

The Ghosts were trained, for the most part, as craftsmen who were designed to be masters of a sole occupation, so they would serve perfectly, but remain atomized, never unite to challenge their own masters. They were educated to receive their lives as fate, not accident, never to imagine the world itself and the way they lived in it might be separate phenomena.

Their prayers did not finish with the syllables "amen," but this phrase, "The way of the world, so be it." They spoke in proverbs, timeless, insightful, provincial, and believed that the patterns of their lives had been set before time, and would continue until its end. No one had ever returned to their island after being sold, to tell them whether this was true or false.

The Invisible cooks brought particularly high prices; they were often sold apart to private clients rather than at auction. The proverb has it that brilliance in cookery is bestowed on those who have never tasted mother's milk.

The folktales concerning the Grateful Ones also tell us that anyone who displays an unusual gift for cooking is someone who has actually tasted the forbidden fruit of the paradise tree; the taste of paradise, and the mystery of what was known there, will haunt and distinguish the dishes that they prepare.

It was in exchange for that knowledge that they were destined to spend their lives in the heart of the wheeling universe, subjected daily to the elemental forces of fire, earth, wind, and water, the architecture of every kitchen.

It was for that knowledge that their days were poised between nurture and slaughter.

It was for that knowledge that their hands were plunged in carcasses, stained with blood, scarred with the burning flames of cooking. They were condemned to spend their days in the exact center of the world, the crossroads of Hell and Heaven in every shelter. They were indentured to the kitchens, struggling to find paradise within and beyond the killed, evaporated, and uprooted being that lay on their worktables.

Savour, it emerged, had this gift, which is a characteristic talent of those born under the constellation of Souraya, the sign of the Knife. At three, she had proved herself an agile gatherer of the precious spice, the first task of all Ghosts still too young and clumsy for tasks requiring more skill. As she grew older, they thought they might make a trapper of her; she had a passion for amassing provisions, and went about it creatively, like a true Invisible.

Once she was nearly punished for the disappearance of a keg of wine to be served to an important slave trader and his officers, but averted the punishment by leading the house governor to a clearing, where, it turned out, she had ingeniously lured three rare wild boar, now ripe for capture, lying on their sides in sumptuous stupors, and already seasoned, drunk on red wine.

She was an excellent weaver of nets and ropes, which taught her that food could be quarried throughout the firmament, not only in earth, but also in the sea, and in the heavens themselves. Her deft, swift fingers searched out the sweet berries from the bramble thickets that were planted over graves to keep the dead deep inside the earth. She grew expert in trapping the rabbits who fed in cemeteries, and, cooked in cream, were the base of one of the great traditional dishes of the Invisibles, known as Saint's Supper. She was so useful at supplying the house that she was still in residence well after most of her generation had already been sold.

She trapped by learning—not through instinct, or luck, but through acquiring knowledge, the destiny of those who had tasted the fruit of the paradise tree. When she was ordered to capture swans to roast at banquets, she failed and was punished, failed again and was punished again.

When she saw them swimming, she was awed by their absolute grace, their fluent unity with the world itself. She could never be as strong as they were, would always be more awkward. Trying to capture them was like trying to capture the reflections of trees in water—you could not succeed unless you captured the light itself. It was when she saw them walking that she grasped how it was to be accomplished; grasped the tragic principle of trapping.

She had seen swans walking on a frozen riverbank, searching for a fishing hole; they walked like the elderly, hobbling, hunched, unbalanced, unnatural; the curves of their necks distorting their gait. She realized that what had given the swan all its grace was the water. Water joined them to the larger world. Separated from the water, she could see what they were in themselves; they were formed as living fishhooks. So she could capture them out of water, with fish. Knowledge, she discovered, was stronger than strength.

It was then she saw that trapping was breaking the world into its fragile components—separating a creature from what made it fluent in the world, a part of the delicate integrity of the whole. Once it had lost that connection, it became vulnerable. One could snatch it from the world like a child from a mother. When a creature was successfully isolated from its environment, one had arrived at the point at which flesh becomes meat.

After she had caught the swans, she felt the burden of her new knowledge. She went back to the cold riverbank, to find the time and place to endure what she now understood. She wondered what she was formed for, removed from the context of the world. What, for instance, was the underlying, pure purpose of her hands? The fingers complicated everything. They made her able to stack, mold, cut, stir, test, collect. They could be like ten strong ropes to strangle a bird. But none of this was everything. She could use them to turn her hands into cups to drink from. She could not discover what one thing she was shaped to be. There were a thousand things her hands might do.

What she did could better be called searching than hunting; her way of tracking a hidden plantation of spices, a game bird, or prey on foot was to share its life. Their flight from her became her flight toward them, as if they were weights balancing on a scale. She entered into their fear of her by sharing it through her fear of them.

She did not hunt, she discovered. She learned which shelters they valued, what they ate, where they were born. Her pursuit of a creature fitted a frame around it. When she successfully followed tracks or caught a telltale movement through trees, she did so by describing the animal with her own motion, body, breath. The great hunters, she would say later, are not the expert killers, because their appetite to kill is keener than their appetite to hunt, but the ones who know how to keep a creature alive. Above all, she never forgot that she herself was prey.

She was the one on the beach or swimming in lagoons, ever vigilant for the transparent floating creatures, whose touch on skin was pure acid, that turtles fed on. The stinging food led her, though, to the creatures that ate it. She haunted these spots, and when she saw the turtles fused together in the shallow water like copulating stones, or watched for one beginning his hour-long mount on the sand, she would call for rope to secure the mesmerized creature, when it was sure that he had done his life-giving.

She was awarded the shells of her catches to use as cooking and serving vessels. She permitted the other kitchen Ghosts to use all but one of her private collection. This was an amber-colored shell of perfect symmetry, with lightning flashes of iridescent green, violet, and gold, particularly dazzling when the food it held was ornamented with shards of savour. The Lord Governor himself had promised her that she could take her tureen with her when she was sold, a pledge entirely contradicting the usual custom, under which the crafts and possessions of the Grateful were the property of the free citizens of the nation.

The concoctions she simmered in this shell were invariably successful. It was as if she herself entered into this shell when she used it. She had faith in this basin as in no other object, or indeed, person. She had found, perhaps, a womb from which to be born.

The Governors and their guests were able to recognize an unmistakable distinction when they dined on a beast, or root, or fruit that Savour had cultivated. Her food had a double life in time, as she had been gathering flavor to it before it emerged on the face of the earth, as well as after it was cooked. The tastes were of things forming or newly born, as much as things dying.

She watered the most delicate of her garden seedlings with a syrup of water, milk, and blood, and fed her animals grains mixed with spices, honey, and butter. She moved like a pen through the landscape, leaving behind her a kind of signature through the cursive of irrigation channels she had set in the fields where she was responsible.

She killed like the god of her little world, neither cruel nor merciful. She intoxicated the animals however she could; she drained them of their knowledge of death, and took the burden of the knowledge. It was another gift of those who had eaten the fruit that was forbidden.

She gave each farm animal a cup of wine, looked into its dark expressionless eyes, then turned its head away, and gave them, not birth, but death. Her clean swift cuts separated them from the life their mothers had put into them; always she had an imagination as strong as memory, of her mother looking into the dark shocked pools of her newborn eyes, and turning away.

With each butchery, she tested her own reaction. Innocence was impossible to her; she sought some form of goodness instead. She struggled never to give a death without wounding herself. She never killed without the fear that she would one day be able to murder. Surely this death-giving transformed her into a cook, made her of the guild of those who must resurrect what has been killed. Her cooking was a summoning of life; it was the way she did not acquiesce to death.

There are those who say that what the cook creates is trivial, as it disappears. On the contrary, the cook defies all that vanishes.

For a cook transfigures death, and exalts the act of eating. Those who eat and drink at such a supper encounter on their plates a meditation, a prayer, a remembrance; set before them is an embodied pardon.

A company at table unknowingly tastes the celebrated forbidden fruit. Through their laden plates and overflowing cups, they approach its secret; the bones and blood that enter them and become their bones and blood reveal to them that tragedy is inescapable. This is the cook's knowledge.

But the cook unites what vanishes and what survives. This is the cook's art—to refuse absolute destruction. The defiant delicacy, glory, and revelation of flavor, accomplished through the hands of a cook on the bodies of the dead, this is the taste and incense of resurrection, in which the sensual and the spiritual are fused.

The cook takes a handful of dust and it becomes flesh, flour pulverized from the seeds of grass rises into bread.

The cook takes flesh from a carcass, and through spice and oil, salt and butter, roasting or braising, guides it through time once again and back into life; a cook transfigures the blood of tragedy, and fills our cups instead with wine. Death vanishes into the bodies of the living and sustains them. In yet a further alchemy, the food and wine become breath itself, the scaffolding of speech—so that the guests may lift their glasses, and craft with their companions the words of honor, of wonder, of love. The glasses are filled then, the company fulfilled.

It is for this reason that religious festivals most often take the form of repasts, and are called feasts. Through eating, we know resurrection, passing from exhaustion to new life. It is for this reason that we deem the murder of a guest not only an act of violence, but also a blasphemy, wounding the hope of all living.

A company at table tastes the forbidden fruit, but does not die; the cook teaches their bodies how to make life of death. Death passes through the hands of the cook, and becomes not destruction, but destiny. The guests at table taste and drink their death; they praise death, and are forgiven death, delivered to new life. It is for this reason that funerals are concluded with feasts. The ecstasy of flavor awakened in perception is the taste not of the body, but of the soul. A dinner made by a great cook is a vision of the world to come.

Savour could not speak this, but she could craft and enact it, as when she mesmerized deer with torches, and killed while they were hypnotized. She judged their gaits and bodies expertly from her hiding places, so she could find the deer most likely to yield the preferred dish of the Governors of the Ghosts, a dish known as the Feast Without Beginning. This consisted of an unborn fawn, or better, twins. She would slit the placentas, add wine and herbs, and braise the meat in its sac. When they were served at table, they were cut into slices known as "fates." On these occasions, the carver was instructed to give her a substantial portion, as for a guest rather than an Invisible. The presiding Governor would lift his glass to her, and say, with merry irony, "You have a great fate, Savour."

It was perhaps true. Savour's gift distinguished her from the common destiny awaiting a Ghost: the auction hall filled with inspectors, agents, and sea captains buying Ghosts in lots of ten for speculation.

Day after day in the Lord Governor's kitchens, she learned to cut banquet foodstuffs; she cut fruits in the shapes of diamonds, emeralds, pearls, marquises, pointed stars, and lozenges, gilded them with syrup, and recovered them with their own glistening skins, so that when the guests sliced the fruit before them, its flesh scattered onto the plate like a handful of jewels. She knew very well that one seed contained in every fruit known to humankind was a seed fallen from the Forbidden Tree, and that each fruit contained a trace of the flavor of Paradise, if the cook could uncover it.

Her knife work was so fine that she could cut cold butter into golden sheets of lace; these were layered on beds of ice to hold their shape, then lifted off and flung over the great platters at the banquet table, melting erotically as bridal veils over the principal dishes. She learned the seven methods of leavening, the three hundred sauces, the ninety-nine transformations, a complex genre of dishes based on recreating vegetables and grains as meat. She learned how to whip edible ornamental clouds of eggs in the shapes requested of cumulus, cirrus, and a repertoire of others, flavored with the essences of game, cheese, buttered lemons; they floated in haunting broths, garnishes that suited the principal dishes they accompanied. A coastal people's observation of weather was a sacred task. It was a cuisine filled with hidden magics; these copies of clouds influenced the sea clouds, and conjured fine sailing breezes, it was said.

Savour learned the arts of how a personality was revealed through the grammar of a palate, such as the range of behavior one might predict from people who preferred the foods of childhood. She was taught the classic recurring paradoxes of appetite, such as the fact that the people who refuse meat are drawn from those who hate death and those who love it, either truly tenderhearted or vicious sadists, afraid of tasting the first kill.

Unlettered, her dinners became her records of time passing, of feelings experienced, of life lived. Her soufflés, her management of fire, the architecture of a roast burned slowly into succulence on its carapace of bones, her transparent pastry revealing a jewelry of rice, meat, chestnuts, shredded mushrooms, and the butter churned in spring, were like entries in a journal. A certain cake of chestnut and chocolate represented shock and pain to her—she had cut her finger severely in learning how to make it. She would always remember drops of blood disappearing into the batter. She could recite an anthology of her menus precisely for at least four years, and all that had been said of them, and what had happened the day that dinner was eaten. For literacy, she substituted a prodigious memory.

At the end of one evening, when she was twelve, she returned to the residence hall after a banquet and found three new girls settled in her room. The three she had grown up with—the Ghost sisters of her childhood—had been sold and sent away. The House Governors believed farewells led to discontent and disruption, for both the sold and unsold, so ceremonies of farewell were either clandestine or accidental.

Savour had now, for the first time, lost the known, having previously lost the unknown. For three weeks, her kitchen work was aggressively slovenly. There was always blood on her hands. Her knives cut her as if they had their own wills; her forearms were inscribed with burns as they had not been since she began her apprenticeship. Her walnut sauce burned the tasters' tongues, seasoned with the violence of her rage. Gate, the second master cook to whom she was assigned, took her by the shoulders, almost shook her, and half-pushed her into his cubicle. "I would like to terrify you. Shall I tell you what you are risking, you cracked egg, you driftwood, you disease?" He paused, momentarily unable to invent more insults. She looked at him sullenly. "You are an Invisible. You have no past. Your mother was a grave. Your only life is the life to come.

"You are not pretty. You are not winning. It is prohibited for you to marry.

"Yet you have a chance that comes to few Ghosts—you have a gift that has been noticed. Others are sold in lots—you can be sold privately. You are fit for a rich family. Even a royal one. You may not be thrown below the decks with the others.

"You will be bought for a purpose, not for speculation. You will be protected to fulfill that purpose. You may not be raped." Savour's cheeks reddened and she clasped herself in her own arms, looking down at the immaculate floor.

"I said it's possible you won't be raped. Or bred. A rich family wants its banquets, in private or in public, every night. They want you to cook their meat, not to breed it. You have a chance to be more safe than most of the girls in your lodging. No Ghost has more than you. But if your dishes taste of chaos, the kitchen mistress can send you traveling below the decks. You won't have the chance to cook your exhibition dinners.

"Listen to me. Look at me. I'm teaching you.

"I want you to know what a talent is—it means your body is like money. It means that your value may not change, as long as you can practice it. You are off the market. As long as you can fulfill a master's need again. And again. Your price won't fluctuate.

"Make that gift a house, hide in it. Make a lock out of the bones you roast for stocks. Invent a dish—use it like a weapon. Remember what I say. Cut the throats of the little birds—but not your own."

He sent her to her quarters, his stony eyes liquid with crippled sorrow. Though Gate would never have children, Savour taught him the impotence of fatherhood.

The Governors of the Ghosts at that moment were debating at

length whether to keep Savour or to sell her. Her cooking was highly prized; it not only gave them a celebrated and enviable table, but also served as a kind of guarantee of the excellence of all the Invisibles offered for sale. In the end, though, it was determined that the sum she was likely to bring would subsidize the clearing of a new plantation, in addition to a Great House and outbuildings in the southeastern corner of the island. She was designated for sale in one of the year's quarterly dispersals.

Over a series of days, great clots of Invisibles made a wavering progress to the ships. These were the groups who had been sold in lots. At the gangplank, the merchant waited with an inventory, and a pair of iron cuffs to lock on each pair of hands. A broad-shouldered boy squared his jaw, clearly, brightly sought the merchant's eyes with his own, shaped his posture until his stance was tall and graceful as a hero's, and refused the cuffs. "I don't need these, sir," he said, "I will honor the contract."

"You will," said the merchant, and signed to his aide to bind the boy's hands, instantly distorting the clarity and balance of the boy's body. "We won't lead you into temptation. But we admire your good manners. Take him below," he ordered a waiting crewman. "Honor is the possession of the strong," he said, "as is the privilege of virtue."

He spoke to no one in particular, his words unfurling like a written decree. "Submission is not honor: defiance is not virtue." His face, which had been as public as a statue's, remained public but in a new style, the style of the barracks. "Which is why women are never either honorable or virtuous." His witticism also decreed assent, and the men around him submitted to his proverb in unified laughter.

Privilege, however, is as ineradicable as slavery, and is present even among the enslaved. For her prized skills, Savour was sold privately. She was ushered into an anteroom on the second story of the Traveler's Exchange, as the market where the Invisibles were sold was called. The governess who was to monitor the dialogue closed the door behind them.

The room widened into a balcony overlooking all the transactions below. Savour was too terrified to peer down, afraid she would fall over it like a cliff, into the world of absolute compulsion below.

The potential purchaser wore a black tunic and black trousers, bordered with gold, as she would later learn all the priests of high rank did, though Savour did not know it at the time. In his pierced left ear was the gold and ruby earring that was the mark of a priest of the tribe of Angels. Fastened around his fine waist was the cummerbund of these princes, a belt of golden coins engraved with images she couldn't recognize and inscriptions she couldn't read. Later she would learn that on each coin was an image of God, and one of his thousand names, in the language of the Angels. This was the language in which God spoke directly to the Angels, who called themselves "His translators."

"Please sit down," he said, with a courtesy shocking for its sincerity. She was too surprised by the invitation to obey, so the Guardian pushed her, as you would push a door open, and she sat down. This had the effect the High Priest wanted, which was to force her to look up at him. What happened on her face as he talked, though she did not know it, was the first step in the sequence of acquisition.

What he saw first was a variant of the instinctive admiration on the faces of all who looked at him: a rapt involuntary willingness to gaze at him indefinitely, as if at a breathtaking view.

Every beauty—whether of sight, sound, or taste—has a dimension of the metaphysical. Strawberries, those fruits that ripen into the forms of kisses, or the somber dignity of meat, vineyards of scrolling curls, emerald eyes, evoke thoughts as well as desires. The architecture of a face, of how a dish is realized, forms dreams of particular ways of living, of being present in the world one would wish for. Beauty is, however momentarily, a world. It moves us so powerfully by making us present at the creation of a world, bringing us into existence.

The exquisite bones of Xe's face suggested the repose, fearless candor, and indestructibility of a noble house. It was a face that looked as if it would never end as a skull, but rather pass from life directly onto a coin like the ones he wore on his belt.

The direction of his smile was upward and outward, with rippling charm, never sour and downward with self-deprecation. His features and expressions incarnated the essence of trust; the certainty of the presence and protection of divinity that the play and qualities of radiant light produce. His speech emerged from his beauty as an unexpected wonder; a conversation with the rising sun. This had the useful political effect of making each of his statements, momentarily, seem an absolute reality, as of a breaking day.

What he did not guess at, radiant with her admiration, was Savour's assessment of the duration of his beauty; she had a cook's sense of the urgency of beauty, of how it must be transformed, or lost. She was used to judging the anatomy of fruits and greens, the silver of fresh fish, and of estimating how long they could hold the summit before they began to rot.

She looked at the cadences of his eyelids, and the barely perceptible brushstrokes at the wings of his nose, unconsciously calculating. He was not far from his meridian, when the end begins. Still, it made her feel faint to look at him.

He asked her name, and smiled at its coincidence with her craft. "And your parentage?" he asked. It was a question to discover a temperament, not an answer. He knew the Invisibles knew of such matters only through rumors or imagination.

She was surprised by the question, frowned; having never thought it through, she told the truth as she discovered it.

Savour was a silent girl, but when she did have a thought to pursue, her words bubbled rapidly, boiled, and overflowed. They cooked inside her. A number of her contemporary Invisibles avoided her, made apprehensive by this occasional unpredictable overflow of her speech. "I was born to Our Lady Rice. Cousin Butter. Queen Wheat. King Wine. Our Saviour Tree, the Olive, who lights, who heals, who houses, who nourishes. Who outlives destruction, even when its trunk has been destroyed. I have seen the shoots of the dead tree live, and I pray to them.

"These are my parents. The Ones who don't die. The Ones who return. Every day I am born to the Holy Green Leaf, the Golden Honey, the Bleeding Butchered Rib, the Lamb's Severed Head. My sign is the Knife, the sign of Souraya, the Lady Sacrificed."

"Do you know of God?"

Again, she saw only the world she spoke of, and spoke, as inspired people do, as if there were no listener.

"Of gods, yes. But I don't know my own patron yet. The Holy Ones are always changing, when day opens or night falls or summer comes. They vary like rice, with a thousand shapes and flavors: saffron, with meat, with cheese, with sugar. In a dome, or a pancake, or a turret of rice or any form you can think of. It is always what it is, but never tastes the same. It is infinite in ways of being, like the goddesses and gods."

The High Priest shifted in his chair, and leaned intently toward her, as if he were trying to hear every word accurately.

She blushed, but could not stop herself. Savour spoke to so few people that she had often had no knowledge of her own thoughts, and found herself deeply surprised when she heard them said aloud.

"The gods and goddesses are like bread and flesh," she said. "They also resemble salt, seed, grain, water, flour, weather. A loaf is like them, the assembly of the universe. And they are flesh, shaped by our hands, and shaping them. They can live in any dimension, like food. Outside us, hidden in us. In our bellies, or in our dreams. That is the difference between us and the gods. They can always be reborn.

"We are only a little like them—we can live in only one place at a time. And it takes us one entire lifetime to taste of anything. And even then, we are more like seasonings and accompaniments, a little salt, or sugar, pickles, or crushed roses."

The Priest smiled patiently. As those confident in their knowledge smile, while the face of unknowing is the face blinded by tears and sobs.

"You are both a heretic," he said, "and an innocent, with your kitchen thoughts of God. There is a charm in this combination. But God is not to be found in storage jars or on dinner plates.

"God can be found in the outcomes of wars, in hurricanes or tsunamis. He is present at coronations, or even, if this makes Him clearer to you, at weddings and childbeds, at any event where fates are decided. For the Divine is the force of all that is unpredictable.

"He does not live where you live, in the world of beds made each morning with clean linen—but in the roof that shivers in an earthquake and crushes that bed. God lives in the message delivered to that man's wife, telling her whether he was sleeping in that room, or was resting elsewhere, someone else's guest. God lives in the moment a woman nearly free is captured.

"The purpose of your life is to shape materials to yield predictable results—to roast, to bake, to melt. What can you learn of God from this? But if I decide that you belong to us, you will learn something of the nature of God.

"You will learn at least that there is one God alone. And that you do not understand your relation to Him." He looked at her as if from a tower whose height gave him a perspective over a landscape for miles around. "Do you pray?" he asked.

"I find what is good to cook. I make it what it should be. Then I see the food I offer become flesh." She paused. "I slice justly. I kill with mercy." She told him one other thing. "I nourish everyone who eats from me, even the ones I hate. The work I do is the prayer."

The Priest said, "If you come with us, you must pray in words. Do you speak to God?"

"When I am about to cook, I say something."

"And what is that?"

Savour looked toward the governess. The words were her one secret in life, her secret charm. They made the dinner come to life when she spoke them before she set the pot on the fire or the lamb on the spit. They ensured that the portion of each guest would suffice. They evoked the angel of flavor intrinsic to each dish, which emerged in a fragrant cloud when summoned.

The governess nodded. All questions must be answered, all thoughts naked and available for inspection. Savour feared that the power of abundance locked in the words would evaporate if she said them aloud, like lifting a lid too soon. She was too inexperienced to lie, however, and too inarticulate to make up alternative words on the spot. She swallowed, and spoke hesitantly,

"Grain—have children for my sake.
Oil—pour gold on all I make.
Flesh—forgive me for the life I take."

The Priest's eyes glowed momentarily with amused tenderness; he had never, he thought, encountered a living being whose soul so strikingly possessed the characteristics of a vessel, a spoon. This girl was hollowed out in some way, like a priestess, or an oracle, not quite recognizable as a self. She would carry without comment whatever she was filled with. "Who have you cooked for here?" he asked.

"I have cooked household dinners for up to fifty people. And I have won kitchen competitions to cook over half of the Governor's banquets, this year and last."

"Have you ever cooked for royalty?"

"So they say. They tell me some things about why I am cooking, or the guests. Then I solve the dinner like a riddle. My eyes are on the platters, not on the guests. I have cooked for the Governor in each season; I know how to follow the changes of the season, in the expression of flavors, and in the molding of the guests' appetites. Gate—my sponsor—he is the second master cook—says I have the making of a fine formal cook."

"And where do you fail, according to your superior?"

"In my attention to the assistants. I lose the thought of them, and of what they can do and are doing. When this happens, Gate says, I might be cheated. Or they can flaw my work. They can be careless, or vengeful or lazy. It will all be tasted. Gate says I do not know yet how to work with any instrument but my own will."

"The cook I am seeking will work in a household that is not yet formed. I am commissioned to choose the staff for the household of a Princess of the Angels who has now reached the age to move to her own pavilion. In addition, her father, who was a great victor for the Angels, is now our King. She will be his hostess. As for you, perhaps you could manage your staff more efficiently, if you yourself train them at the time of your own training. Do you think you could do this?"

"I don't know," she answered. "Perhaps if I could choose them. As I choose meat, or garlic or flour."

"A sound thought. Then you can knead them, or shape them. Or cut them into bits, little Invisible, born under the sign of the Knife."

He smiled with complicity, probing her for a sign of a taste for him. "In any case, I can judge your capacities only if you cook for me. I will taste your work the day after tomorrow; because the number of the Princess's guests will always vary, lay the covers for twenty, but be prepared for more. I will be exacting in my judgment. You will need to do your utmost to succeed. But even a slave's life among the Angels is to be prized. Serving us, you will come to know the language of God. You will learn to read. You will learn to pray as we do. For the first time, God will hear your prayers." He decided to waive the customary physical examination. Her body would reveal nothing about her talent, or taste.

"Sir," she said, "I would like my prayers to be heard. I would like to serve in a country of peace whose rulers, like you, carry no weapons."

"Little cook, there is no weapon more powerful than the one I am carrying now."

She searched his body with her eyes, familiar as she was with the tools of butchery. She could not see any blade, hammer, sharpened stake, no mechanism to propel deadly metals, no vial of poison. Then she saw his earring; this must be designed to kill in some way. Her eyes fixed on it, and she was satisfied. He understood her conclusion, but could not resist instructing her, so great was the pleasure of taking possession of her untilled mind, as a gardener plants a tree in an empty clearing.

He struck his belt with his right hand, and made the coins jangle. They sounded to her like platters clattering to the kitchen floor. "With these, I can cut down the strongest opponent. These are sharper than any blade. With these, I can buy the hands that hold the blade. With these, I can incite an attack from one side, or a retreat from the other. I can fill ships with men and women, and set them sailing. I can buy a world, or make what seems like one. My belt lacks only one power. It cannot make time a slave, to run back home, and fetch what I forgot there. Or to run forward, and bring me what I need from where I am going. Still, I can buy you. And I doubt you need to grasp any power larger than that.

"Good luck," the Priest said, with his brilliant, frank smile. This summoned one more question from Savour. "What is luck?" she asked.

He slid his belt a quarter turn around his waist, unfastened it, and lifted one of the coins to show her. He traced the lettering beneath the image. "It is a name for our God," he answered.

"Here." He handed it to her. "Keep it for luck." She accepted it expressionlessly, as she had been trained, but she was enchanted. It was the first gift she had ever received, besides her own.

When she returned from the interview, Gate was supervising thirty child apprentices. The apprentices were taught to cook with each element: earth, air, water, and fire. These were in their phase of earth. Some were molding and firing clay pots in every imaginable variation, like most clay cooking dishes, of the shape of the pregnant womb. In each phase of their training, the apprentices learned also to fabricate their own cooking equipment.

Now a group of students sealed and painted designs on the clay vessels containing game birds, to be cooked slowly, buried in pits dug by thirty other apprentices. The birds were seasoned and wrapped in savour-buttered vine leaves, then covered in clay whose surface was painted in brilliant colors. When the clay was removed at table, the vine leaves adhered to it, revealing a glowing succulent flesh of ineffable tenderness, which had absorbed the jeweled iridescent color of the spice. He kept his eyes on his students, but whispered to her privately between his public corrections of their technique. Savour, who was reputed a fine artist, like so many of the great banquet cooks, who sketch beforehand the dishes and dinners they present as spectacles, added her criticisms of the students' designs.

"Do they want you?" Gate asked.

"I don't know. He asked for an exhibition dinner."

"For how many?"

"I may not know. Between twenty and forty, I must adapt to the circumstance."

"And this Angel will be your master?"

"Not him. He himself serves in the new household of a Princess, the daughter of an Angel general who has made himself their new King."

"So he serves as her agent. Therefore you are not really cooking for him. But there is a further problem; this dinner must be to his taste. Describe this person to me. What does he look like? How old is he? Is he married? Then tell me, which of your Twelve should you present?"

The Invisibles who completed their kitchen apprenticeships won their initiation as master cooks by gradually mastering the Twelve Dinners and their variant patterns. The children intended merely for household service were not taught the Twelve.

These Twelve were the culinary incarnation of the great cycle of events, seasons, and emotions in human life, the very taste of Providence itself, in food that Heaven and earth, the natural and the sublime. Gate taught her that the effect of the Twelve should be like music, the acme of entwined flavors. As with music, the guests should intuit what had been expressed, even if no one could describe it.

Each master cook was educated with a secret, separate Twelve, designed for her individual skills and temperament alone, known only to herself and her teacher. There was a drama in each of these Twelve, and the great Invisible cooks produced them as messages, exquisite and triumphant resolutions, or as dazzling gambles taken at a moment of great risk, a dinner dealt as if from a fortune-teller's deck of tarot cards.

You will have heard, even if you are unfamiliar with the Twelve, the stories of one of these dinners that changed the course of a human life, or of a country's history, thus altering—or still to alter—your life, and mine. For example, we all know the familiar story of the False Host, the tale of a great landowner who invited a young couple to a great feast in his magnificent garden, but when they sat down with him at table, would not let them share the splendid dishes he himself was served on golden plate.

Instead, they were served cooked grain on earthenware dishes. When the husband, according to the hospitality he valued and understood, attempted to serve himself and his wife from the golden platters, the landowner had them stripped naked by his attendants, and driven from the table.

The couple took no revenge, but instead vowed to feed anyone who sat at their table with overflowing generosity and intuition, as a way of loving all impersonally. In this way, they did indeed come to love many strangers, even some they did not like, and many came to love them, too. But they established the great principle of impersonal love through their feasts where all were welcome at the table and none refused any dish that had been prepared. They became the angels we know as Providence and Plenty, present at all feasts.

As for the landowner, his garden fell into ruin, as no one would accept his invitations, and even his servers deserted him as he took to capriciously denying them the wine and particular dishes they loved and had earned in serving him.

There is also the tale of the Miracle of the Bread. This happened to a hermit, who belonged to a sect that shunned and abhorred women as animals, temptations to men, who had brought every kind of evil into the world, slaves to their own flesh, fallen nature incarnate. The hermit had a tender heart, despite his harsh doctrines, and to be candid, his ignorance, since he never had any but the most restricted contact with women. It was his habit to feed animals, and the travelers who passed by his hut, half hidden in the spring and summer by straggling grasses.

He lived on cheeses donated by merchants on his twice-yearly visits to town, but bread was a luxury beyond him; he never had any to offer. "Eat, poor fish," he said, crumbling bits of cheese and tossing them into the lake. "But I have no bread for you." "Eat, poor insects," he said, dropping crumbs of cheese for the ants. "But I have no bread for you." "Eat, poor vipers," he said, leaving bowls of cheese curd out at night. "You, at least, will not want bread." One afternoon a woman stopped at his hut, to ask for food and water. He brought out a share of cheese, and said to her, "Eat, poor animal. But I have no bread."

She thanked him for the cheese, but paused before she ate, and said, "May I ask why you call me 'poor animal'? 'Dear woman' would be more welcoming." The monk answered, "It is what we call women in our prayers for them."

"And," she asked, "why do you say you have no bread? Your hut is surrounded by wheat." The monk had never realized that the overgrown grasses in the fields near his hut were wheat. "But it is not ripe," the monk said, with finality.

"But I can ripen it for you," the woman said, and the fields turned to gold.

"But it is not threshed," the monk said.

"I can thresh it for you, and mill it, too," the woman said, as the finest powder of flour snowed into the monk's empty barrel.

"But I have no yeast," the monk said.

"I can make bread rise," the woman said, and on the table next to the cheese two perfect loaves appeared, emanating the sweet fragrance of a summer afternoon.

The monk, until then, had been resisting the miracle. When he touched the bread, he accepted the miracle, and asked in wonder, "Who are you?"

The woman said, "You should recognize me."

The monk shook his head, marveling, and said, "I did not think it was possible for God to incarnate in the body of a woman."

"You also did not see the wheat hidden in the grasses, and the bread alive in the wheat," she said.

The hermit never had the courage to admit the vision he had seen, but God, being a woman, forgave him for that. The bread made from the wheat harvested around his hut, though, became famous for its exquisite flavor and healing properties, and the hut became a place of pilgrimage, where no one went unfed.

Savour stood that late afternoon at Gate's side, as he accepted the roast bird of one apprentice, turned another aside for a mismanaged fire that prematurely cracked the clay, as he tasted and corrected.

She began to describe the Angel. There was an unspoken but powerful prohibition against the presumption of forming impressions of authorities; such impressions were viewed as undermining, in the way that iconoclasts viewed images of gods as challenges to singular divine power. Contaminating a leader or a god with partial human perceptions was to impose a limitation and to hint at the unmentionable existence of change.

Still, in hearing her own description, she discovered that she had made a number of observations of this man, and had concealed them, as if in a mental pantry. She told Gate of his charm, courtesy, dazzling handsomeness, his insistence on the supremacy of his God.

Gate set a group of apprentices to shred the flesh of the birds he judged failures, to be used in other dishes, and said, "Think of his soul as a dish. What is its predominant flavor? If you have tasted precisely, you will know the secret of his appetite. And where should you look first to glimpse this appetite? At the face—a man's habitual expression manifests what he tastes like to himself."

"I believe," said Savour, "that what is sweet to this man is strength.

And power, his power. When you see his face, you notice that his expression in repose is one of pleasure, and yet frustration, as if he is tasting something delicious he cannot get enough of. I think he is tasting himself."

She shivered with excitement. Gate knew she was seeing a vision of her great exhibition dinner. "Yes, I know him now, this is what I must do, it should be the Dinner of Grandeur."

Her excitement mounted, and she spoke with the unconscious authority that possessed her in the practice of her craft. "A dinner for a ruler, dramatic and extravagant. There will be twelve different roasts of game and herd animals, fish and birds. I shall slaughter a pair, male and female, of each, and have them borne in lying side by side on enormous platters of gold and silver and tortoiseshell, lying on beds of pilaf. These will be carried by twelve children each, six on each side. They will kneel in front of him, to present the meats. This will hint that they kneel not only from reverence, but also from gratitude, that they themselves have not been sacrificed. I must learn quickly some of the names of his God. Then I shall make pastries rich with cheese and butter, latticed with the thousand names—"

"Savour," Gate interrupted. "Are you sure of your judgment?"

"Yes," she said decidedly.

"I am not," he replied. "Listen to yourself. The last skill of the arts of the kitchen is the power to judge the work you have done.

"This is done through two tastings. First, the tasting by mouth, the judgment of food by the tongue. Then the tasting by mind; that is, the judgment of the palate itself. This is a far more subtle discipline, but it can be approached by describing your work in words. Then you must listen carefully, as if you were someone else, to what you have described.

"You, Savour, have described your own feats. The dinner you have described is a display of your own power and your desire to impress. It is your own power that enchants you. You should be thinking of this man's. It is you who wants to be the conqueror. If I were this man, I would want you to celebrate my power more than your own. Above all, as you seem to have forgotten, he is not a ruler, but the servant of one.

"However, if a Dinner of Grandeur were appropriate, yours would not be a bad conception. This dinner may yet be a useful one in your repertoire. Still, I think you have forgotten to ask a cook's second important question in devising an entertainment."

"What is that?" She looked up at him.

"You must search your own appetite. And remember the first of all the principles of the kitchen, embedded in all the skills of knife, every calibration of temperature, each fine conception of a dish. Cooking is description, Savour. It is a description of the world, of the cook, and of the guest, all at once. And it is also an imagination of paradise. The great cook is working to reconcile that description, the facts of this world, with that vision, the dream of the gifts of Heaven.

"You are excused from kitchen work until noon tomorrow. Think deeply and quickly. Your work tonight is to create your future."

Savour did as her teacher directed, and took advantage of her rare evening of freedom from the kitchens to walk along the estuary; the tide was still out, and the lambs old enough to graze were feeding on the salty grasses that gave their flesh its unique tenderness, and its faint aroma of lavender and sea breeze when roasted. Fine palates loved these delicate animals because they were the only creatures slaughtered and roasted whose bones tasted of flowers when they were brought to the table, as if they had never died.

Part of her work, like the work of all cooks, was to enter into a strange waking dream, to invite the world inside her. This work never feels as if it is done in ordinary time, because action and imagination fuse in the doing of it. The discipline of training and the freedom of passionate abandonment merge within it. Those who are dying and those who are making love know the hallucinatory nature of this work, those at the task of ending a life, those at the task of beginning one.

Savour entered that dream as she walked, and sometime during her sleep that night, she became convinced of which of her Twelve she must present to the Angelical. She sat up in bed as alert as an athlete leaping for a ball. She went to the window and prayed to her patron deities. There was, in answer, a full moon. She took polish, her whetstone, her silver presentation dishes, and her knives outside into the kitchen garden. It was common knowledge that silver polished by moonlight would take on a supernatural radiance, and that moon-honed knives cut more keenly, and impart the flavor of Heaven to whatever they cut, if a skilled hand wields them.

When Savour approached Gate that day as he patiently corrected the faults in the shapes of the clay urns his students offered him, he saw that she was inspired. This could mean that she had a true inspiration, or was seized by a headlong impulse that would cost him great effort to discipline. He hoped it was the former.

She beckoned him aside, and he left the supervision to another apprentice, one he was training as an instructor, a destiny that would have been impossible for Savour.

"I know which of my Twelve it has to be," she said, with an absolute conviction that made him apprehensive. However, she was still his apprentice, and he must still make her understand the faults of her work when it was bad, the finesse of her work when it was good. He said, "Which have you chosen? And explain to me what made you choose it?"

"I am right about the man's appetite, but wrong about how to satisfy it. The Dinner of Grandeur can only be for someone who has won power beyond striving. It would not make this Priest feel content, but remind him all the more of his hunger. My first dinner for my master would have given him the sensation of starving."

"Good," said Gate. "You are thinking more keenly about the nature of this guest. Now, what is a cook to a man seeking power? Who are you to him? Reason, Savour."

"I am his theater. I show his power as hospitality, sustaining, if he chooses, his companions. Or my plates set out hints of reproach, or a warning of a guest's falling worth, a message sent subtly through a thumb's flick of salt, of tears to come.

"If I serve apples with duck, I show his orchards and his lakes. I show his power as glory.

"But I have to be more to him than this. Because any banquet cook can serve him in this way. Judging from what you have taught me, the chief feature of power is the ease with which it can jettison and replace. But I am a cook, servant of the irreplaceable. So here is how I will serve him.

"I will give him back with this food what he cannot replace in himself: innocence. I will make him feel the luxury of safety, since men of power are always in danger. I will remind him by nourishing him that I can also poison. He will remember that during the hours he dines, his cook is responsible for his fate. He will sense that my hand is never far from a knife, yet I will do no harm. From my Twelve, I will offer to him the Banquet of Trust.

"I will give him the dishes of childhood, each distinct from the other, so that nothing can be hidden. The food in bright, pure colors: white, green, red. With cheese, milk, and cream, the maternal foods with which kinship is created. I will present these in terra-cotta, the material of our foundation, the very earth that sustains us. The effect will be rustic but elegant, in the spirit of a carefree week in the country, free of protocol."

Gate smiled. "Your description makes me feel drowsy and content already. Well done, Savour. Remember that we are the animals who feed with our minds before we feed with our bodies."

She went on constructing her mental banquet. "I will seat him facing the door, so he can see anyone who enters and exits. I will offer no shark or boar or any animal that is a danger to man. The wine should be floral, and golden, the color of the hair of princesses. And more, no knife should appear on the table, nor any glass, nothing that shatters, or cuts. There will be no need for any guest to cut his meat; it will be set before him in refined morsels.

"The Banquet of Trust begins with soup, because drinking is more primal even than eating. The taste of water, the essential, the pure, the necessary, when you are thirsty, first drunk ardently, and then slowly, is the taste of truth itself."

"There is still a problem to solve."

"Yes, I know—how many covers to set. I think what I will try is to tell him that at our great dinners, we honor each place with a portrait of the guest. And that this also serves the safety of the Governor, to ensure that each guest matches his image. I will have an apprentice paint them on ovals of terra-cotta to match the dinner service. I will hope the Angel doesn't realize that painting these portraits will give me the count for the dinner."

"It may be that even if he does, he has already decided for you, and will enjoy your ruse all the more."

Whether the Angel was deceived, or complicit, Savour was chosen. She revealed the first of her Twelve, and won the confidence of the Angel. She was ordered to prepare herself for departure from the country where she had grown up, but which was not her home, to the country of her life's work, which would not become her home.

Savour was the last Invisible to go on board the ship of the Angels, bound for their New Kingdom. Gate had said good-bye to her as she was emptying her personal pantry. It was in the evening, before the dinner service, when the training of his new apprentice was to begin. They stood awkwardly before each other, rather than side by side at a table or an oven. The moment of unoccupied leisure was unnatural to both of them.

"My apprentice," Gate spoke, too moved to find words beyond the literal. "I would have liked to have brought you a gift to take with you, Savour. But you know the law. We nameless ones are permitted no souvenirs. The ones who are not remembered are commanded not to remember. We must not risk the consequences."

Sudden tears welled up in Savour's eyes. To have nothing to remember Gate by, nothing he had even touched, was an annihilation that returned her to the primal one that had made her an Invisible. "Savour," he said, "you will have at least the fine things you have won in competitions. And I have put into your hands all that we who have tasted the fruit of the Forbidden Tree are permitted to keep: knowledge."

Savour then slowly and deliberately violated another strict prohibition: she sank to one knee and put her hand on her heart in a gesture of respect that was reserved only for the Governors of the Island.

She lowered her head, and then, she felt on her hair, a delicate, almost impalpable caress, like the weightless drift of sifted sugar; Gate's hand settling for a moment on her hair. It was the first time a human being had caressed her. Forever after, she thought of it as knowledge; the final knowledge he imparted to her.

In the morning, her utensils, the great copper and silver banquet trays, her silver-banded tortoiseshell tureens and marble bowls for frozen creams, all the equipment that she had earned through Governors' prizes, was carefully loaded in the cargo hold, near the quarters of the living cargo.

Large boxes of carefully stored savours were brought aboard, so precious that they accompanied her, as did her knives and ladles. Each of her implements bore the traditional inscription engraved on equipment awarded to Invisible artisans: "I am the servant of a slave: Savour." She had brought a high enough price to earn the right to the tools of her craft.

Her bundles were carried to the kitchen annex of the great round cabin that dominated the upper deck of the ship, the quarters where the Priest and his entourage would be lodged. The quarters where she was lodged were not far from the cabins that housed a cluster of the prettiest girls and boys, who would be resold to harems or theaters. She thanked her gods that she had been spared beauty.

She was to assume her culinary duties immediately, and oversee their meals during the voyage. During the hour when the Invisibles belowdecks were brought up for air and exercise, Savour was to be made literate. She was to learn to read and write the language of the Angels; she would need the means to manage the Princess's household without supervision, and with the expectation, as the Priest told her, of perfect Invisibility.

She had her lessons in the early afternoon on the same breezy veranda overlooking the open sea where she oversaw the fine dinners served at night. The language was another kind of food.

She tasted the new words with her tongue and teeth; they had rich, odd, distinctive flavors. Each letter of the alphabet had a distinctive flavor. "A" did indeed taste of apple, just as the illustration promised.

She held the syllables on the roof of her mouth, and just outside her throat before she swallowed them, like pomegranate seeds. When she first held it, she was astonished by the capacity hidden inside the pen; it gave her the power to see the words outside herself. It was an implement like a wooden spoon, blending letters into words, or like a trowel from a kitchen garden. Even though her hand assisted the letters, they took form on the page like plants springing from the underworld, with a life beyond the gardener's power.

The new language taught her that languages held many things in common, but that each held a reservoir of words so local that they were experiences in themselves, like the foods native to a certain soil.

They could be known only through intimacy, either with the place they came from, or with a person from it.

She learned each of the thousand names of God. The Angels knew one God with all these qualities; she knew a thousand gods each with these qualities, metamorphosing from moment to moment like rising bread, like wine in ferment. For Savour, the world was overflowing with divinity, often unrecognizable, even deceptive. The Angels knew much more about their God and His thoughts than she did of hers.

The words she was learning also tasted of the moment she was living, of elemental fish straight from the water, cooked with a richness that offset its absolute oceanic flavor, in the fresh butter churned from the cows stabled on board. She seasoned it with herbs cut from heavy pots in a sheltered corner on deck. The perfect intensity of attention necessary to achieve the right texture and flavor was part of the taste of the dish. Cooking it was a matter of bringing the body of the dead fish back into time, so that it tasted of new life. She cooked it as quickly as a falling star.

She oversaw bread baked on deck. True Invisible, she vanished into her rising bread. She imperceptibly entered the bodies of her masters as they savored the warm, earthy bread under a canopy on nights of soft sea breezes.

The glittering blade of the great Knife constellation hung low in the sky at that season, seemingly suspended over the ship as it sailed. She bowed her head each time she saw it, the bright Knife of Souraya, Savior of Children. Seeing it made her feel, not exactly protected, but fulfilled, on the path to whatever was inevitable for her.

It seemed as if there were a deep ocean above them as well as underneath them. The blue-black sky frothed with stars like celestial whitecaps. Musician Invisibles played during the meals, compositions that could never be repeated, using the sounds of waves or the winds in the sails as additional instruments of their orchestra.

She thought of Gate, but as part of this firmament, not quite intimately. She was an exemplary Invisible, trained in all the arts of vanishing; there was no one she had not already said good-bye to.

She grasped something new as they sailed. She had striven for the taste of perfection before, but now she added a new quality of luxury to her work. To eat luxuriously meant to be given the sensation that nothing could be denied you from the ends of the earth, in any season or any climate. The incongruous fresh-churned butter, young greens, new laid eggs, and aged wines set on a table in the middle of the ocean taught her. To eat luxuriously was to exist everywhere; to eat like an immortal.

At night, she lay awake devising new dishes to express this. When the masters were in the grip of the appetite for luxury, her work needed to range over the world, and bring it into relationship on their plates.

She had been told that parts of the New Kingdom experienced heavy snows in winter. She envisioned silver dishes of newly fallen sugared snow bathed in a syrup of sugared rose petals. She began to make more inventive use of the eggs the shipboard chickens produced, and to dabble with new geometries. She took to ending the Angels' meals with globe-shaped custards bathed in caramel; it made them feel as if the world itself was theirs for the tasting, and that it was sweet.

She was relieved—and took a cautious pleasure—to see that the Priest-Angel experienced her dishes with a questing appetite, as if he, too, were learning the grammar of a language. He observed that his guests sat between courses with their mouths open, like children enthralled by the telling of a story, which pleased him enormously.

"Superb," he would say, after calling her from the kitchens to congratulate her after each dinner. His lavish compliments were offered as extravagantly as a wealthy man offers the best wines of his cellar.

Savour, though, had been taught to fear praise—and especially praise too easily given, which was like the bright light used to stun animals. "May it sustain you," she responded with the not unpleasant austerity that he recognized was a refusal of his judgment—perhaps even of his right to judge.

These were her first encounters with conversation, its intentions, exchanges, maneuvers—its perfumes, distinct as the handful of toasted sesame or crushed bay leaf, or the wrist flick of coral salt crystals a cook used to sign a dish.

Even from within her shelter and plenty, though, Savour could hear the hungry. She was haunted by the daylight-blinded Invisibles below, the air in their lungs apportioned for the sake of economy.

Spared the full knowledge of what their condition was, the shape of the ship became for her the architecture of the human being—above, beauty, craftsmanship, finesse of taste; below, all that suffered unseen, and must not be acknowledged.

The question tormented her: Was it possible for each person aboard this ship to sail on the upper decks, to be exquisitely fed, to have sufficient space and air?

She winced as she descended each day the fine broad staircase of the Priest's dining room to the rough ladders leading to the foul-smelling depths of the ship, where the Invisible slaves and the livestock were housed. If the structure of this ship were the anatomy of justice, then her question was answered.

When they made landfall two weeks later amid the calls of a thousand waking birds at dawn, she shivered stoically on the deck. She was accustomed to fear; though she felt the chill sensations of fear, she was never surprised by it. She had never lived a day without fear, and neither—she was certain—had any other creature, not even the sweetest drowsy infant.

She was astonished by her new quarters: she had been allotted two rooms for herself alone, which gave onto the kitchen garden on one side. On the other side, the kitchen's courtyard with its marble pools stocked with fish afforded her more privacy than she had ever known, or imagined. At the same time, her proximity to the Gate of Provision, where supplies were delivered and itinerant sellers brought goods, gave her a free relation to the world outside that she had never before enjoyed.

The vast subterranean chambers beneath the kitchen complex were crowded with storage jars as full as merchants' bellies. There was a winter and a summer kitchen, as there were winter and summer dining rooms, the winter with a view of the mountains, the summer with a view of the sea. She could range the seasons and the landscape as never before for her materials. She was especially intrigued by the thought of spring. On the island where she had grown up, she had known the alternations between severe winters and brilliant summers, with little variation between them. Two new seasons would offer her an entire new vocabulary of taste.

The apartments of the palace were laid out over shifting, uneven terrain, as a series of pavilions. Even the mountain caves were incorporated into the living quarters; natural wine cellars, they had also served as defensive retreats during sieges. They were adaptations of the tents that had lodged the people of the New Kingdom in their nomadic days before the Conquest. Before, they had moved their dwellings with them; now it was they themselves who moved, from palace to bunker. The precipitous height of the royal suites reflected the old ways, too. The powerful families enjoyed the security and commanding prospects of the highest slopes, while their advisers lived in quarters below them, accessible for consultation, expendable if necessary during attack.

Even before she settled into her quarters, Savour went to the kitchens for a first glimpse. Her childhood hunter's instinct was at work. She needed to analyze her terrain, its advantages and disadvantages, and to survey the workers she would be supervising as well. She would deal with her own quarters later; they had far less to do with her life than the kitchens and pantries.

She was awed at her first sight of this cluster of rooms; they stimulated in her an odd, expansive pride in her command over them that she felt it important to suppress. It was as dangerous to her as the High Priest's compliments. Pride was eradicated in Invisible children. They were reminded that they had no sustained presence on earth, as those with genealogies did; they were born each time they successfully accomplished their work, and were as lifeless while awaiting a new task.

She tamped down her flame of pride like a kitchen fire, and marveled at the almost ruthless elegance, practicality, and spaciousness of the suite. These kitchens were like a perfectly conceived, monumental body.

Even the kitchen walls united beauty and utility, as they flowed with words in sinuous scripts, the work of the royal calligraphers. Each wall was covered with recipes of the territories and peoples conquered by the Angels, who had no cuisine of their own. "God grants His Angels this abundance": each formula began with this prayer, for to eat of the empire was to possess it.

Beneath it were painted exquisite miniatures of the ingredients necessary for the dish, in the brilliant colors of all that was edible. These were followed by the title identifying the recipe; beneath it were illumined images inset in medallions of gold, of the finished dish, or a picture of the dish being served at a wedding, funeral, banquet, or in iconic scenes from the legends of the Angels.

Somewhere in each image was embedded the prayer she had heard the masters say at the end of each meal—"Praise God, for we have eaten of the earth which is given to us." It is said that these paintings are the origins of the pictures of fruits, meats, and meals that you know as still lifes.

Savour would be expected to master these dishes for festivals, though at this time she was so newly lettered that it was all she could do to grasp what they contained, moving from letter to letter, a monkey climbing the tree of language.

She had intended to begin her explorations in the spice rooms and grain rooms, but a man a bit younger than she was, with strong short legs, a belly like a tulip bulb, and eyes that gleamed like fine sunflower oil, approached her, before any of the other workers had spoken to her. He wanted to find out if the Angelic ships had arrived with the anticipated master of the kitchens, the new feast-maker.

A few of the kitchen workers, bent to their tasks of sluicing and cutting, took the chance the moment offered to joke and chatter with each other. Savour drew him toward a window, and said to him simply, "I am the feast-maker. And who are you?"

The young man held out both hands palms up in the greeting gesture of the Angels, symbol of a freely accepted submission to fate. She was used to it now, though the gesture looked disconcertingly like the posture of begging for alms. "My name is Salt," he said. "Or rather, that is my kitchen name, my service name. Because you mustn't imagine that I am an Angel. I am an Indigene."

These were the primitive people, it had been explained to her, who had been conquered and dispossessed of the land that now formed the New Kingdom, underneath which lay the true lost Paradise of the Angels.

The Indigene had managed the palace kitchens while the Priest was abroad searching for a master cook, he told her. He would now return to his previous rank, becoming her assistant, and master of the kitchen supplies, the liaison between the Indigene farmers and gardeners and the palace administration.

He spoke without tension appearing in his face or voice, but Savour feared that he might be hiding his resentment.

Nothing was more subversive in a kitchen, Gate had taught her, than the bad will of the staff, so she prepared herself for a long, researching conversation, making herself ready to wander blindly in the man's mind, as alien to her as a forest.

And she hoped she could coax him into some stories of the Princess Life, who bore this name as did all the eldest daughters of the Angelic nation. If Savour could see her portrait in his mind, she would succeed in meeting her before they were introduced.

There was no chance to talk more deeply, though; a robust, almost masculine woman, wearing three necklaces of jade beads and gold cuffs on her wrists, appeared in the courtyard, and beckoned to her.

"You are to follow me to the Pinnacle," she ordered Savour. "The Princess has asked for me to bring you to her." The faces of the kitchen workers, which had showed a range of narrowed eyes, rounded lips, raised eyebrows, in reaction to the sight of Savour, now assumed a blank unity. The appearance of this woman was more threatening to them than the unknown new director of their daily lives.

Savour had been so eager for a glimpse of the kitchens that she had put on fresh but simple kitchen work clothes after her arrival early in the morning. She was not even wearing the belt with the keys to the kitchens with which she had been presented with some ceremony on landing. She made an involuntary gesture in the direction of her rooms, which the jade wearer interpreted correctly, with a warning. "The Princess Life expects to have her requests fulfilled immediately when she makes them. Climb behind me to the Pinnacle." Savour, exhausted and self-conscious in her kitchen tunic, had no choice but to follow the royal attendant.

They made their way through tunnels, alcoves, and labyrinths, climbing their way through and around the cliff where, legend had it, God had flung the Primal Angel, who had sinned against Him by preferring Paradise to life.

God had been furious at this rejection of His gift. No longer able to create the world He had envisioned, He had hurled the Angel from Heaven. The impact of the Angel's wild trajectory had created an earth, not of intention, but of accident, the shattered angelic substance combined with the Divine Impulse, which was the source of all life.

That pulverized Angelic body had split into woman and man; its fragments formed ocean and sky, forests and deserts, fish and flowers; from the Angel's blood had crystallized the multicolored gemstones, and from the splintered bones, the flying mosaic of the birds. The Angel's brain had cracked like a pomegranate, and produced the created peoples, who never came to share the Angelic Remnant's longing for their lost paradise, or their determination to gather the earth into a divine empire, and offer it to God, who would at last lift it back into paradise.

Savour's idea of splendor had been formed only from the skills she had been taught and from nature; she was unprepared for, and terrified by, the unnatural wonders she saw during their ascent, increasing in extravagance as they approached the Pinnacle.

Everywhere there were unexpected forms and colors, tents outlined in rubies, opal-colored domes where music sounded when you passed beneath them, black and scarlet silk cushions in the shape of full-blown roses, from the depths of which hidden servants materialized, carrying trays, papers, keys to secret doors. It was like nothing on earth.

The entrance to the Princess's courtyard was a screen latticed with patterns of diamonds; they spelled out a psalm from the Angelic scriptures that opened: "Therefore make of life a paradise . . ."

The jade-braceleted servant pushed open a leaf of the screen, and motioned to Savour to follow. In the center of the courtyard, there was a green marble pool, filled with water that gleamed green, and ringed with both real and artificial trees. The man-made trees were hung with gems representing fruit, a botanical garden evoking paradise, crafted by goldsmiths and jewel makers.

Savour could make out a figure reclining under a canopy near the pool. The canopy was embroidered with gold brocade, which spelled out the Angelic greeting, "Life is Paradise." A servant emerged from beneath the canopy, carrying a tray.

The jade-wearer halted abruptly, forcing Savour to trip and stumble. She frowned worriedly, distressed that the Princess's first impression of her would be of a clumsy and graceless servant.

The jade-wearer, who had not spoken a word to her during the climb to the Pinnacle, held her back. "Your face is wrong," she said. "In the Princess's presence you are expected to smile. In serving her, you serve God, and you must show your joy." She curved the corners of her own lips upward, and adjusted the lids of her eyes, so that her pupils caught the light and sparkled like glass. "Make your face like mine," she said to Savour, and led her forward.

The Princess did not alter her position as they approached her, though Savour saw an intense, minute attention in her eyes. She was dressed in a web of thousands of delicate gold chains, interwoven with tiny diamond letters of the Angelic alphabet. It was impossible to discern almost any of her natural physical characteristics; even the color of her hair was obscured, since her head was covered with tresses and waves of the same spider-thin golden chains. She lay unmoving as a distant landscape as she watched them draw near.

Even her fingers, weighted with ten magnificent rings, were still, as if she found motion demeaning, something expected of servants, or of men, who were compelled to show their power in running, jumping, wrestling. Her own power was a magnet's—she lay still, and was irresistible, drawing everything to her.

She did not offer her hand, but shifted slightly on her cushions, and the golden chains of her dress changed shape, like sand dunes in the wind.

Three other women hovered over her, bending reverentially toward the Princess, as if over a cradle. These were the Mirrors, who attended the Princess. The Princess's left eyebrow lifted imperceptibly; the left eyebrow of each Mirror arched. Later, Savour was to learn that they underwent special training for this work at the Royal Theater. She wondered what would happen to them when the Princess's face changed, as life would change it. Her own had changed, she could see, simply from speaking the Angelic tongue.

Savour noted that the Princess was a beauty; she had the kind of beauty that is most seductive, an angry beauty that gives the woman an air of dissatisfaction with her own splendor, and so appeals to the spectator to complete her beauty with happiness.

Savour hurried her eyes to her object. She knew that the great rarely tolerated a direct gaze from an inferior, before they required a downcast gaze.

She always used her moment of contact to gaze intently at the mouths of people she was meeting, a cook's version of palm reading; it was through their mouths that people would encounter her art. From the shape and set of a person's mouth, Savour believed she could intuit something of the nature of the individual's appetites. The Princess's mouth suggested an almond, rich and faintly bitter. Her lips were not parted in the manner of the insatiable, but closed in the manner of those difficult to please.

The jade-wearer presented her ceremonially: "In fulfillment of the High Priest's commission, I present the feast-maker Savour, new mistress of the kitchens, to her Princess Life." Savour waited for the first word from the ruler who was truly now her life; her blood galloped in her veins.

"Why are you dirty?" the Princess asked, with no other greeting. Her voice was like lemon dripping into broken skin. Her brilliant hazel eyes narrowed, her gaze suddenly reptilian. The Mirrors' eyes narrowed, and their cheeks hollowed, reproducing the Princess's expression with startling precision.

Savour shuddered; the knife was invisible, but she had been cut. Her fidelity to her craft had emerged so absolute and early that she had never suffered the disciplines the other Invisible children knew. She had rarely been spoken to informally, and even more rarely lied to; there was little to conceal from the Invisibles. She had little experience of contempt or accusation, which affected her with a swift, strange, reflex conviction of her own guilt.

She ran her mind over her body like an abstract hand, to examine what offended the Princess. She found herself inelegant, but not unclean. But, she realized, if she protested that she was not dirty, she would contradict the Princess. If she did not, then she would be acknowledging the justice of any punishment the Princess chose. The respect she was constrained to render to the Princess meant that any of the lady's thoughts must be treated as fact. The Princess's sentences were royal sentences indeed. With only a word, she had soiled Savour.

Savour found that she had crossed some boundary into a world that must exist, without contradiction, as the Princess described.

She was spared the choice, or indeed, any response, by a flurry at the entrance to the jeweled garden. The jade-wearer took her arm and forced her to step backward, and backward again, as a farmer compels a horse or a water buffalo in harness.

The King of Angels, child of God, father of Life, surrounded by the swarm of courtiers who fluttered around him always, like the leaves attached to a great tree, led the newly returned High Priest toward the reclining Princess.

At the sight of them, she lifted herself on one elbow and extended a hand, covered in a brilliantly colored dew of tiny jewels, which were freshly fastened with an adhesive paste of almond and sugar, made by the kitchen each day; these spelled out with the traditional dressing prayer, "O Life beyond price . . ." Her facial expression altered when she turned her face toward them, away from Savour; even the shape of her chin and cheeks changed; what had been a sickle moon was now round and full.

When she turned from her father to the High Priest Xe, she sat upright, her eyes newly radiant, fixed on his. The eyes of the Mirrors began to sparkle in sequence, until they shone impeccably. She looked at him and angled her head delicately toward her right shoulder, adjusting her position as if he were a mirror showing her a delightful image.

"Life is Paradise," she greeted them with the formula. "Praise God for your homecoming," she said, speaking now to the Priest alone, her words slow and soft, silky and enveloping, her lips shaped in a charming smile, as if her face were a flower a butterfly had lit on.

"Life is indeed Paradise. It is an honor to be greeted by the Daughter of God," the Priest said, more formally.

Savour had experienced the range of his manners from having

traveled with him; she thought that at this moment, he and the Princess were struggling in a way she recognized. It was like the struggle she experienced between herself and a flame when she wanted to control the temperature for the sake of a particular dish. "It is an honor to greet you," the Princess said, claiming the formal word, and melting it. But the Priest took her word, and made it impersonal again, set within a solid frame.

"It has been my honor and my task," he said, "to acquire for you the fruits of this voyage, most important, the cook I found among the Grateful Ones, who will make your entertainments famous." He caught sight of Savour in the shadow, and smiled with candid pleasure. "Welcome, Savour," he said. "Life is Paradise." Savour felt a rush of warmth and gratitude.

He turned again to the Princess. "I promise you that she will fulfill your expectations. I have tasted her work under the poor conditions a ship affords a cook; but even there, she wrought magic at our table. The animals she cooked tasted as if their blood was the distilled attar of roses. I swear that if she pours you a cup of water, it will taste like fresh cream."

"I hope I will find her as you describe," the Princess answered, and without turning, said graciously to Savour. "You may be excused. Take her to her quarters." Her eyes had never left the Priest's face; "Tell me about your travels," she said, and gestured toward a seat.

Savour hurried quickly back behind the jade-wearing attendant, descending through the same labyrinths they had climbed. She walked without seeing, still listening to what she had heard. Like many who practice her craft, her response to events was powerfully physical.

The exchange between the Priest and Princess had been like the folktales in which two sorcerers try to capture and escape each other by changing forms; if one became a mouse, the other a cat, the one a door, the other a key, the one a window, the other a beam of light, and so on.

She tried to apply Gate's principle that you must use the materials you understood to translate what you did not understand. If she were not mistaken, she had seen a woman offering herself to a man like a goblet of wine, and a man returning the goblet as if he were not thirsty.

She worked with Gate's technique of comprehending what she had seen by tasting the flavor of her own feelings.

She felt the delicious milky reassurance, as if she were a lamb in a shepherd's arms, which had welled up inside her at the warmth of the High Priest's greeting.

And then suddenly, she felt an unexpected nauseating anxiety, a sensation of illness that washed over her before she recognized it as an insight. What her body had recorded, caught between the two sensations, was the essence of entrapment.

She was in the thoughts of these two, the Priest and the Princess, not as herself, but as an instrument of themselves, and of whatever they were to each other. She could even, she realized with shock, be sold again.

As she returned to the deep region of the kitchens, she seemed to herself to be falling. It occurred to her for the first time that a world might exist in which one was not rewarded for excellence, but despised for it. Her craft had always been her protection. Her entire education had formed her as its selfless servant. But now Savour was the protégée of the High Priest, who had his uses for her work; and she was the servant of the Princess, who had her own.

Over the next months, Salt was her guide, and fortunately a trustworthy one, to the world she had come to. He introduced her to farmers, merchants, and to the public markets, so that she could ensure the excellence of her kitchen materials. No table of dignity must be able to match the table she presented.

He began to show her the areas of the countryside where most of the indigenous inhabitants of the New Kingdom were allowed to live and farm. Indigenous houses made of native stone punctuated the landscape. The shapes of the houses reminded her of the round form of the native bread, as if these houses had not been built, but leavened by the wild yeast that lifted the loaves they kneaded and set out in wicker baskets.

Salt took her to meet his parents and eleven brothers and sisters. These were the second family she had ever met in her entire life, the Angelical Royals having been the first.

She marveled at their resemblance to one another, but also at the range of their faces. She couldn't stop staring at them. The continuity but variety of the features gave her a sense of something endless.

She was fascinated by their names, which expressed the most precise nuances of human experience, some of which existed only in her imagination, and others unknown even to her fancy.

She couldn't absorb them all that day, but she remembered a twin brother and sister: he had been given a name that meant a beacon of fire guiding lost travelers, and she had been named for the feeling of warmth from a hearth fire on a winter's night.

Savour could hardly conceal her fascination with the sister, who was a bride and pregnant. Savour was familiar with all sorts of pregnant animals, but had never been so close to a pregnant human or seen at firsthand that extraordinary melon shape of the stomach, the child under its dome.

They sat at a table in their courtyard outdoors, fourteen people and one guest. Never had she sat at a table with a family to eat. Never had she been served food by anyone else. They had milled their own wheat, churned their own butter, and each loaf carried the initials of the one it was destined for.

They ate nothing they had not grown. They seemed to experience everything in the world as familial; they had even begotten their own food. In their granary, they kept a store of seeds from all the Indigenous territories, a library of what the local earth yielded and what sustained their people.

Each taste at their table was absolute. When she ate the red currants they offered her, she tasted summer, defining itself against all other seasons. She tasted the color red of that brilliance. "I can taste no further of this fruit on this earth," she said solemnly. "I have tasted here its existence in our life and in the one to come."

It was a strange and unnerving sensation for Savour, these fourteen people implicated together in their lives, clustering together like grapes on a vine, each with a specific place at the table.

She could find no one sense of it; it was sweet, sour, abundant, oppressive. She watched them share dishes, refill glasses in anticipation of a sibling's or cousin's needs. Were these actions made of manners, custom, or love? This company was so practiced in being together.

What happened as their ages changed? What happened when the young ones lost their childish charm, and could no longer be corrected? How would you replace the ones who vanished?

Afterward, Salt walked with her through the fields and orchard near the house. To walk with him through a wheat field was like learning yet another language, where even the angles of the stalks had meaning. "The Angels are gradually resettling us on smaller plots of land. So I am working with plants that yield well, but are compactly shaped, so I can plant the maximum number," he said.

He picked up a grain of wheat that had dropped to the ground. "Look at this. This is a greater construction than all the palaces and fortresses of the world. Bury it, and it will surge from the earth. It is the architecture of life." He kissed it, as was the custom of the Indigenes.

Savour had not cultivated a garden since childhood, but she recognized a discoloration in one stand as a sign of disease, and pointed it out to Salt. They were searching for a remedy, he said, frowning, though they had no answer yet. His iron tranquillity made Savour wonder whether the Indigenes might not prevail after all against the Angels. The Angels were soldiers, and their conquest of the Indigenes was absolute. But the Indigenes were farmers; the work of making things grow was eternally woven with loss and devastation. The Angels worked with nothing that was not man-made; the Indigenes worked with what was given by the gods.

Salt took her on expeditions through the Angelic capital, which they had renamed Paradise after their conquest. Paradise teemed with tradespeople from all the territories conquered by the Angels. There were many merchants, too, from the bordering country of the Saints, which lay in the northwest beyond the Alpine passes. Salt told her that it was generally assumed that Saints were spies, whether on behalf of their own nation or employed by the Angels to report on the next nation they had chosen to annex.

He showed her the courtyard where the Invisibles were auctioned to buyers from all over the world. She saw a phantom of herself standing on the auction block, and shuddered. Salt realized, with a flood of guilt, what she was seeing, and hurried her past it to the exquisite public gardens of Paradise, extending through the city down to the port.

It was in these gardens that the black roses the New Kingdom was known for were cultivated; these were the source of the glittering dark sapphire conserves of rose, and the blue-black petals sparkling with sugar crystals that were the base of several of the New Kingdom's traditional sweets. A pendant of deep blue glass or sapphire recalling these roses was a traditional wedding gift, Salt explained to Savour.

At the very heart of the gardens, in the center of an orchard of agate trees, grew the Tree That Was Once a Woman, sacred to the Indigenes, and loathed by the Angelical conquerors as a symbol of sacrilege and indigenous rebellion. A violent faction of Angels perpetually threatened to uproot it; the tree was always ringed by armed guards, in order to prevent the conflict that must inevitably follow.

"Why should this tree matter?" Savour asked. She looked at it closely, to the extent she dared, under the hostile gaze of the guards.

It was a thick-branched tree laden at this season with abundant ovals of golden-skinned fruit resembling women's breasts. The tree almost seemed to be singing because of the rich chorale of birdsong from the coloratura birds that nested in its branches.

"Why should a soufflé matter?" Salt asked, walking her around the tree, but well back from the guards.

"I see what you mean." Savour tilted her head, thinking. "A soufflé matters because it is a dream, a dream that can be eaten. Which is why people are so afraid of making them. A soufflé always evokes a resurrection, a second life. I often served soufflés made of cheese to sick people, so they would know the taste of being made new—as I make cheese, a preserved food, fresh again, with new eggs and milk."

"Yes," Salt said. "When they finish your soufflé, the guests should feel as if they had had their fortunes told, and that the future is happy. The Tree That Was Once a Woman is like that, she tells a fortune; to our ears, it is a good fortune, to the Angelicals a bad omen." Savour looked at him expectantly.

"We are taught she was an Indigene girl, of wit and grace, though neither a princess nor a great beauty. In the legends, she was one who discovered how to make the conserves of black roses that you yourself have now mastered. She was a singer, and we say when we don't know the author of a song, that she has composed it. When the first Angelical invasion occurred several hundred years ago, their commander captured her and forced her to marry him.

"However, among our women there is a wedding custom that must be followed, or the marriage will never be considered legitimate. During their wedding week, they prepare a special spiced butter of our native agate fruit, enough for a year, which will be stored in ceramic jars, and used to flavor all sorts of dishes. It is a form of wealth, because for us, food and drink is wealth; this is the means of life. As the song says, 'Bread makes the body, love makes the soul.'

"So the agate butter is a dowry, and a sign of the acceptance of a marriage in providing for its future. When it is withheld, it is known that the marriage is false, and the children of the union bastards.

"The commander took this girl, put her through a marriage ceremony, and enjoyed her, though he knew very well she had not consented, which is a grave sacrilege among our people.

"But he could not force her to fill the empty jars in his storeroom, or even to tell him how the butter was made. She knew he would then have the jars filled, and claim that he now had proof that she had accepted him at last. He held her, a prisoner-wife, while her songs circulated from hand to mouth, as, aware of her coming death, she changed her flesh into words. Her stubborn refusal of the forced marriage became a symbol of our own captivity and our own refusal of the rule of Angels.

"The commander could not afford to remain the repudiated husband of his entire New Kingdom, so she died of 'natural causes' and was buried here, with a cluster of the fruits in the palms of her hands. These grew up into the great orchards that are like wordless portraits of this woman. They are the glory of the Indigene gardens.

"Her name was vanished from the country, never to be uttered, on pain of death. We no longer know what it was. The bride's songs, too, were forbidden, under the threat of harsh penalty. In that vacuum, we too died, with our knowledge of our own history and traditions, our obscure dreams of what we might become.

"The fruit of these agate trees dropped to the ground unused, because it is rock hard and bitter without our traditional method of rendering it edible. Even the coloratura birds that make their nests in these trees will not attempt to eat this fruit. We worked and served, and our children played in these orchards, to the odd, syncopated tunes of the coloraturas, until they, too, were old enough to work and serve.

"One day, one of these children heard the songs of the birds in a new way. They were more than a pleasing accompaniment to his games; intrigued, he found a way to enter the songs, by writing down their patterns.

"He drummed the patterns of the tunes, as he transcribed them, sitting outdoors in the narrow alley of tangled houses where he lived.

"An old woman lay nearby on a pallet in the sun, like fruit drying for storage. She had been silent for years after a seizure, and her life consisted of being moved outdoors in good weather and indoors in bad.

"But her mouth suddenly moved and in a voice like a dried leaf being crushed, she sang words to these rhythms. The melodies of the bride's songs had been based on the patterns of the coloratura tunes. They had been hidden, but never lost. They were inside the throats of birds, notes pulsing like jewels in the sun, songs preserved for us in the heavens themselves. And they were buried inside human tombs, like the old woman.

"You have heard at least one of the songs that had stayed inside this woman's body: 'you shall make honey of stone and of the glaciers, wine.'" He sang the line; Savour did recognize it, a tune popular among the Indigenous kitchen staff.

"Hidden inside these words," Salt continued, "we slowly discovered, were the treasures of our old knowledge, crafts, architecture, our sagas, our history undistorted by Angelic destruction. Most extraordinary of all, in that particular song, hidden in its code of metaphor, was a precise recipe for the lost method for making agate butter. Our marriages felt true to us again; we remembered that we were the fathers and mothers of our children. We have slowly developed a secret language of these songs; we can communicate simply by quoting them.

"So the Angels hate this tree, and all agate trees, because their will to destroy us can never be satisfied without annihilating the very land they have conquered. And for us, these fruits are the miracle of the honey flowing from stone, of returning to life from death."

. . .

Savour's first court dinners functioned not only as public displays of her skill, but as explorations of the Princess's tastes. Her plates spoke the language of the New Kingdom, as she served up delicate birds braised with the local black rose honey, herbs, and figs, and waited to see what the intimate flavors of the landscape around her evoked in the Princess.

Savour watched from the hall as the company took life from her dinner. She was delighted to see that the youngest of the three Mirrors shut her eyes and, for a fraction of a second, smiled with involuntary pleasure. The Princess's face, however, remained impassive, and the Mirror's trace of expression quickly dissolved.

The Princess had ordered a very rare red wine to be poured, in lavish quantities, as the guest of honor was famed for his vineyards, and had recently been employed to advise the Angelicals about wine production in the New Kingdom.

He toasted the Princess, and held his glass to the light to admire the wine's color of the setting sun. The Princess beckoned to the server behind her, who returned hurriedly with a silver bowl. The Princess tossed a handful of ice from the bowl into her wineglass. Savour saw the guest wince with disgust, as if she had urinated into the crystal goblet. "I like my wine iced," the Princess said, with a challenging, insultingly flirtatious glance at her dinner partner. "It pleases my own taste to drink it cold." She lifted the glass to the winemaker, and sipped, and rolled the ice on her tongue. "My satisfaction is greater than your conventions."

The winemaker replied, "It is true, Madam, that all the earth has to offer is a mere reflection of your lovely self."

She sent Savour word after the first few dinners that she expected more impressive dishes. Savour learned what that meant. The Princess dazzled her guests with Savour's culinary feats. She accepted rapturous compliments for Savour's soufflé of green almonds, accompanied by ice creams made of silk and silver leaf.

The Princess ordered dishes made from costly ingredients, brought from distant conquered lands, and obtained with as much risk as possible. She wanted omelets from eggs gathered on high cliffs by agile children. She wanted snow in summer, cherries in winter. She wanted brilliant colored fish brought by deep-sea divers, extravagant flavors and lavish expenditures of devotion to her service.

She ordered a Solstice Banquet for the court, a winter feast. It was a banquet dreaded each year by the kitchen staff. When they received the order, Salt beckoned to Savour. He led her to the still life medallion on the wall that pictured the Angelical Solstice Banquet.

The central image in the medallions was of a company at its banquet; around the borders ran a dizzying pattern of knots in black and gold. Salt traced the border with his finger; it was then that she saw that the black and gold knots were stylized snakes coiled around the border.

"Yes," Salt affirmed, "they are pit vipers. The solstice is celebrated with many courses of dishes based on snake. The Angelicals must eat of flesh that crawls at least once every year. This symbolizes the submission of the colonies they have conquered. Those who would rise up are cut down, and their very uprising serves the Angelicals. The flesh of pit viper is considered to have extraordinary restorative powers. Of course, for us, if we are not cautious, its powers will be anything but restorative."

The creatures were delivered to the kitchen gates by the snake hunters, who imprisoned each serpent in a flat wooden box, carved with a pattern of wings imitating the Angelic seal. Salt dressed Savour in a kind of thin metal armor and pulled a pair of metal gloves up to her elbows. He put a metal mask over her face, then he put on his own gear. They walked to the kitchen courtyard.

"I will teach you the wrong way and the right way to make them meat," he said. "I'll demonstrate first, and, if you are ready, the second is yours." He took a pair of long shears and a stick, and gave Savour a pair of shears to use if anything went awry. She tensed herself, and Salt looked at her.

"Breathe," he said. "I'm going to open the box and reach in." He opened the box swiftly but smoothly, reached in, and grasped underneath the snake's head with his metal glove. It was the work of seconds, as it had to be. He sheared the snake's head off, and threw the bleeding head into one basin, the still writhing body into another. "Why do you say that is the wrong method?" Savour asked him. "It's already over. I can't think of any way that would be as fast."

"Look down into the basin," he said. She leaned forward, noticing the sneering raised ridges on the sides of the face, and the lidless eyes, perpetually open like the eyes of the damned.

"Carefully," Salt cautioned her. "Not so close." He dropped the stick into the basin with the snake's head, and she saw the severed head strike the stick, stop, and strike again.

"They can do that for hours after the kill," Salt said. "So it isn't the speed that keeps us safe, but the deliberation. Imagine what would happen if one of the kitchen children overturned the basin, or emptied it too soon. The second way takes longer, but is more secure." He handed her the tongs. "I'm going to reach in, grasp the head, and open the jaws. When I do that, take the tongs and pull out the left fang, then the right. Then shear off the head."

He opened the box. This time the viper was not bewildered, but furious at the disturbance, and surged to strike his metal arm. He caught hold of it and opened the jaws of the creature, its head jerking like a wave he was holding back from the shore, its tail whipping against the world. Savour reached in with the tongs and pulled the fangs out of the mouth struggling to close. Its conscienceless eyes looked into hers with the absolute purpose of killing her; she quickly sheared through the solid muscle close to the head. She couldn't think of it as a neck; the uniformity of the snake's body suggested that for it, eating, mating, and killing were mere phases of the same activity.

Salt taught her to separate the meat from its web of tiny bones, and to make correctly the ritual banquet courses of soup and pâté, followed by the grilled flesh served on curved metal skewers representing snakes in motion. Savour would always think of viper as the meat of fear, and was privately sure that its legendary powers of energy enhancement were the result of the fusion of the two fears concentrated in it at the moment of death, the reptile's fear, and her own.

No direct word of pleasure or disdain ever reached the kitchens from the Princess's quarters, though menus were sent down.

The Princess wanted dishes that were the equivalent of incomes, that glittered across rooms like rich women's rings, never intended to be delicate ornaments for the wearer's finger, but to dazzle eyes across reception rooms.

Savour created banquet dishes: enormous roast pigs hollowed out, then filled again with their own metamorphosed flesh pounded with snails, truffles, butter, and cognac, and swans stuffed, like never-ending puzzles, with peacocks stuffed with turkeys, each bird smaller than the next, until the last tiny figpecker, stuffed with roasted quail eggs, each containing a pearl.

Some guests would leave her table richer by a pearl, others would return home as they came. The Princess herself, through her power to confer, emphasized her detachment from these small variations of fortune.

At last, the Princess herself sent word on the occasion of this piece of culinary theater, via the Mirrors. Savour was escorted across the courtyard and into a small reception room on the sea-facing side of the palace.

The Mirrors had been sent to deliver the message. When they were in attendance, they were permitted to utter only sentences or echo words that the Princess had spoken. It was understood during their tenure that they were a trio of carrier pigeons, that the use of the pronoun "I" at these times was the royal prerogative of the Princess alone. The Mirrors were deprived of personal speech in a practice reminiscent of the way other courts deprived men of their virility to make them effective guardians of women.

The Mirrors spoke in unison: "My guests took pleasure in what I created." They turned away after delivering themselves of this speech, and Savour was sent back across the courtyard.

These were not the sort of dishes that interested Savour, though she executed them with the defiant perfection so often the foundation of perfect obedience.

Her particular delight was to make each element of a dish remember something of what it had been. This was how Gate had taught her, to make the lamb remember the herbs it had fed on, or the orange the sun it had mimicked. Two things, he had said, were fundamental to a masterpiece of cooking: either it re-created a remembered ecstasy of the past, or it discovered some immortality promised in the future.

A successful dish, he said, must be all that is not fatal; it must taste of either memory or destiny.

Savour loved, too, to learn dishes that had names and were made of inherited knowledge. She was intrigued by preparations that preserved techniques, such as the Indigenous dishes that she learned from Salt. They taught her how a creation can be utterly altered by an infinitesimal addition, a drop of lemon, one syllable of vanilla. They gave her the majestic feeling that she could reenter life through history. It was as if a pear she was slicing had dropped from a tree in Heaven, relayed from cupped hand to cupped hand until it reached her own.

The Priest visited the kitchens after he returned from one of his administrative journeys, and was reminded of his first impressions of Savour's work. She was making dinner for that evening's kitchen staff, and out of material that would scarcely serve four important guests, she spun an abundant supper for thirty people. She stopped her work when she saw him, and held up her palms to greet him. "Life is Paradise," she said correctly.

"Life is Paradise," he replied. "Go on with your work, Savour. I enjoy watching you cook; it is like watching someone weave a grand carpet out of nothing but colored threads."

Savour had to permit him to watch, but she permitted him as graciously as if she were free to refuse. She knew well how men loved to see women in a state of devotion to a task. It seemed to suggest to them a wonderful, enfolding shadow, a muse, a personal guardian devoted solely to each one of them.

"I am hoping for a soufflé," he said. "It is a dish that expresses your gift—something thick and solid becomes something ethereal, as if you had fused the material with thought. It is a dish of resurrection, what we will be when we are raised, our flesh leavened, fragrant, real, but weightless." She was too absorbed in what lay on the board before her to respond, but was struck at how keenly he grasped what was essential to the dish. She replied only, "What I am making has no name yet."

He sat and watched as she transformed one substance into another. She altered chicken, saffron threads, and brilliant red peppers into broth. With her knife's sharp blade, she chopped four onions, one after another, in the palm of her hand. She simmered them in butter, until the fragments became crisp vegetable sugar, tasting of words well spoken.

Then she took the chicken, and with hands as quick as hummingbirds, she unwound its flesh into silken threads as if she were deconstructing a flower.

Now it existed as a substance no thicker than the saffron, which itself now existed as a color and fragrance more brilliant than in its former state.

She took walnuts, pounded them with mushrooms and some green herb, and used the paste to change the broth into another language altogether. Without his seeing, she had set a handful of flour in a pan to toast; it became wheat again, regaining the color and fragrance it had had in its field under the sun.

She used it to make the broth into a thick sauce, and then again, through a further alchemy, into a thick, velvety, utterly new kind of flesh, when she combined it with the threads of chicken. At last, she pounded some small hot peppers, garlic, some dried rose-colored fruit, and oil, and ribboned the trays with this, until the substance underwent another metamorphosis, looking very like the intricately patterned porphyry marble columns of the palace.

She gave him a plate of it, cut into diamond shapes. Its flavor was orchestral, infinitely more profound than the showy food she produced for the Princess. She had made something as absolute as a tree.

Yet what he enjoyed even more than the delicacy she offered him was the novel sensation he derived from her company. This eccentric, unworldly slave girl made him feel free—and that was the greatest of all delicacies for him.

"This reminds me in its texture of the creamy, fertile earth of the Indigene's valleys—but as finely colored as palace porphyry," he said. "It's a new kind of earth you have made, Savour—an earth that sustains man not through struggle, but through delight. It is even blasphemous," he joked daringly, "for God himself has given the earth to the Angels through divine war and divine deception, but never through divine pleasure."

There was more blasphemy in the kitchen than he realized. Savour had not yet come to believe in the One. She felt more affinity with the

Primal Angel; if she had had a choice between Paradise and life, she, too, would have chosen Paradise. Why would anyone risk himself here, on this hard earth, if one could be sure of Paradise?

Despite her achievement, near-mastery of the Angelic language and its array of obligatory hourly prayers praising the Supreme God of Angels, Savour still prayed in action, not in contemplation. And in what she did, she had found her guardian god, who, like a feast, was not a single being, but a perpetual metamorphosis, sometimes male, sometimes female, or neither: it manifested as an afternoon, an illness, a tulip petal, a song, or an olive, to be sensed, but never understood.

She was quite sure the Angelicals' god existed, for them.

All gods exist for believers. But its singularity seemed to make them confuse its substance with their own, lending it their own motives. Their insistence on their god's supremacy seemed less faithful than ambitious.

Their books purported to be its very certain words, as if mortal beings could reproduce divine speech, a language in which the most learned mortals were unlettered. As if divine speech were not finer than words. Divine speech would be more even than song.

Divine speech was itself food, perfect in fragrance, ever varying, infinite in flavor and nourishment. It was not meant to be written, but eaten. She spoke of this to no one, even to Salt, who prayed to the Indigenous gods.

For the Priest, it was not only a gastronomic pleasure to taste the fruits of Savour's labor. It was an ultimate refined and subtle sensuality, too, to feel no desire for her.

It was a form of gourmandise to visit her, a piquant mixture of eating and speaking, of two oral pleasures fused. In Savour's company, he could speak without consequence, about matters she didn't understand, in words she would never repeat. He could taste food from her hand without the mediation of the guard who took the first taste of any dish set before him. Nothing could be more voluptuous for a man in perpetual danger than the safety he felt here from all threats and all complexity. There is no greater safety than to feel the pangs of an appetite that can be satisfied.

Nor did Savour feel any desire for the Priest, although his almost monumentally handsome features became newly candid and youthful as he ate her kitchen offerings. She knew well how to satisfy herself, all the more absolutely, without the distraction of attending to anyone else's needs.

The Priest, however, was ill at ease with Salt, like all Angels faced with the peoples they had subjugated.

The Angels and the Indigenes were almost naturally opposed, so little did they resemble each other physically. Angelic faces were perennially childish, smooth as eggs. Even the elderly had the faces of children, though sagging, while the Indigenes aged early, their faces like maps of their stolen territory. This made them instantly identifiable to each other; Savour could distinguish them from her first days in the kingdom. She remembered how it struck her: the Angels gazed at the Indigenes with faces as unfinished as dreams, the Indigenes returned the gaze with the faces of history.

Still, despite this small tension, the refreshment of Savour's company, the near-perfect protection it afforded the Priest from either contradiction or demands, made him seek out the kitchen complex as if it were a beloved landscape, where nothing needed his interference.

The well-ordered world of the kitchens, its phases of industry, abundance, and the ever-renewed cleanliness recurring like the quarters of the moon, evoked a life lived with ritual grace. In this room, he collected himself, needing to impose nothing.

It became more and more his habit, when he could absent himself, to enter this world where he experienced, as nowhere else, the ideal condition of the man of power—to be master and child simultaneously, the object of intimate, detailed, and immediate attention exacted from beings utterly subject to his power. A child pleads for his needs to be satisfied and dreams to be fulfilled; a ruler not only receives these offices, but commands them, simply through existing.

At about this time, Savour had begun receiving visits from someone else besides the Priest.

She always left her bedroom window open to the courtyard; after her days laved in the heady smells and heat of the kitchens, the fresh nighttime air was precious to her. One night, as she was falling asleep, she heard an odd rhythmic scratching, as if someone were climbing a tree.

The sound persisted, but the gentle percussion was rather soothing, and made her drowsy again. She gasped and woke with a shock when a ball dropped from on high onto her bed. The ball unraveled, and, as if it were just being created, it acquired one paw, then, rapidly, three others, downy fur, and a pair of sea-green eyes that glowed in the dark. She lit a lamp and saw that it was a kitten, no bigger than her hand, probably alive for no more than a few weeks.

Its unsteady climb up the wooden pillars that held her bed in its frame was the equivalent feat for this creature of climbing the Three Wishes Peaks in the northwestern corner of the country, so named because no one had ever attained them. Savour knew of them because fine game fed on the berries of the mountain slopes below it, and was prized at the Angelic court.

Savour lay still, not wanting to risk any sudden movement that might provoke the creature. The kitten, too, remained motionless, gazing at her with unwavering eyes, and murmuring to itself, with a sound like a distant bubbling brook.

Savour delicately slid from her bed—the idea of a living being awake in the room where she slept was unnerving. She gently scooped it up, carried it to the door, set it down outside, and closed the door. She closed the bedroom window, and lay down again, seeking sleep as intensely as if she were hunting it. Her days were long and tiring, and doubly burdensome if she met them in a state of exhaustion. When she woke up in the early light, the kitten was lying by her arm, its small paw, soft as moss, resting in the center of her palm.

Hesitantly, almost with humility, as if she were afraid to offend it, she brushed the top of the kitten's head with only her forefinger. She traced its ears and its cheeks gently. She felt its tiny, vulnerable skull and then felt her own hand transformed by those fragile bones. She looked at her hand as if she had never seen it before.

She was used to using that tough, confident palm to flatten, to sweep, to chop, as a platform as her fingers closed around a bird's throat. The kitten fit snugly into her palm, and settled there, absolutely refusing anything from her hand but shelter. She lifted the kitten to her face, and they looked straight into each other's eyes. Savour had caressed melons, powdery milled flour, her own sex, clusters of cherries, and stalks of wheat. But she had never yet caressed a creature that stared back at her, its very breath visible in its throat. The kitten purred.

And so began a love story, one of those devotions between animal and human that remain inexplicable and wordless, articulated not through speech, but through behavior.

The kitten had made its choice, and insisted on Savour, for what quality she never knew. There would have been a palpable reason if it had courted her outside the kitchen, but it had never appeared there. Nor did it ever attempt to enter, but waited calmly for her in the courtyard, or in her rooms. Now, after the kitchen was quiet after the evening meals or entertainments, and she entered her own quarters, she would find the kitten sleeping in sweet, sumptuous trust and comfort on her bed.

He spoke to her in his feline music; a question was a door creaking slowly open on its hinges, contentment was the sound of a fire burning safely in a hearth, a sound to warm a heart as surely as a pair of hands. There was a single crystalline note of affection, a stream of playful soprano chatter during a game. And a mischievous shout for breakfast, achieved by placing his mouth directly on the sleeping Savour's ear and emitting a yowl. When she leapt up, startled out of sleep, he sat on his haunches expectantly, regarding with satisfaction his expertise in managing this being.

She said to Salt, "I am learning my third language." He smiled, and said, "Your fourth, Savour."

"My fourth?"

"You speak fluently the earliest language of all, the primal native tongue of food and drink. The language of life and death."

Savour did not expect the cat to stay with her, but he did. She expected him to lose his infant tenderness as he matured and began to hunt. However, his unceasing affection came to seem almost deliberate, though he did develop a love of teasing her, disappearing and materializing where she least expected to see him, in a basket of fruit, or in residence on the full moon, an illusion he gave her by perching on a certain courtyard tree on moonlit nights.

Nor did he ever hunt, as if this too were a matter of principle. The trees in the courtyard were full of birds, but when she sat in the shade to rest, the cat would turn his back on them, and leap into her lap, as if they bored him. He did not try to catch the fish in the courtyard pond, though he sat on the stone rim of the pool contemplating them, his emerald eyes like jewels that could think.

On the other hand, he listened to music raptly, his mouth open as if he were tasting it. And he ate Savour's dishes with discriminating appetite. When he found a dish merely acceptable, he ate standing on all fours, waving his tail. When he judged the food excellent, he threw her a look over his shoulder, and sat down to eat it, to the delight of the kitchen staff.

Salt described him as a lover of civilized pleasures, and suggested they try to teach him to read. Above all sensations, he loved the feeling of being embraced and caressed, and would even ride on Savour's or Salt's shoulder, for the pleasure of the contact.

After a year, she took a momentous step; she named the cat. Giving it a name meant she found herself at a strange crossroads; a name in some way put a term to the cat's existence, but it also meant he would exist always for her.

She called him Candle, after his eyes, which were blue-green like the purest heart of flame. The name celebrated the way every movement of his glowed with the grace and unpredictability of fire. He was Candle because he brought a warmth, illumination, and peace to her room. The animal in a way made her into a person. She could see by the light of him.

Savour had little time for any existence of her own at this period; it was the season when important men were presented at formal dinners and invited to court the Princess; it was time for her to achieve an advantageous alliance and to be bred.

The breeding of new Angels was the great purpose of all Angelic women, for each generation of Angels embodied the burning hope of the Paradise that Life might yet become. Yet, despite the dramatic beauty of the Princess, and the youthful, suggestively bridal dishes—dove cooked with figs, mousses of rose petals, honey, and cream—with which Savour metaphorically portrayed the experience of marrying her, no promises were exchanged.

It was the Princess herself who was the source of the stasis.

The Princess, in conference with her father and ministers after each presentation, had refused each of the possible suitors.

No one entertained the idea of peremptory force; the Princess was notoriously expert in the corrosive defenses of the unequal. She had perfected the use of the sheer, exhausting, negative force of her will. Her violent passivity had the effect of quicksand on anyone who attempted to change a course she had firmly chosen. She fought for herself the way a womb would fight, by engulfment.

She had, she said, found a number of the candidates attractive, but all represented an insulting alliance with an inferior, each from a territory now under Angelical dominion.

These men were her father's conquests, Salt theorized to Savour, as they worked in the kitchen. The Princess wanted to make a conquest of her own.

There was no one, it seemed, that she could be prevailed on to accept. As a last resort, her father sent the High Priest Xe, his most elegant and most persuasive diplomat, to explore a resolution with her. His stature and title alone would evoke her duty to God. "It is imperative that she marry," said the King, allowing his eyes, as he rarely did, to meet the Priest's with the expression of his genuine emotion. His gaze was intense and desperate.

Their meeting was to be confidential, its setting carefully chosen for maximum discretion. Marriages were of capital political importance to the Angelicals, whose conquests brought them the problems of managing the new territories they ruled. The choices made had the potential to affect territorial society profoundly, and were closely scrutinized for what they revealed of Angelic intentions.

To preserve the maximum secrecy, the Priest and Princess arranged to meet on the great terrace overlooking the sea that extended from her apartments. Even the Mirrors would remain at a distance, withdrawing to an alcove from where they could be beckoned if required.

A table was laid with delicacies Savour had made. She had learned from Salt's mother that Indigenous tables, during conferences, whether familial or political, were traditionally laid with salt and sweet breads and pastries, the flavors symbolizing the elements needed to reach equilibrium. They were baked in the forms of letters of the alphabet, symbolizing the need to speak and to be sustained by speech. Savour tried to achieve the effect of a true Indigenous parley table. She had observed that the Priest seemed eager to incorporate many of the Indigenous customs, despite the antipathy between the two peoples.

The Princess was waiting for him at the table, toying absently with a sugared "H." The Priest gracefully began their discussion by asking for a salted "M." He hoped that, as is often the case, the shared pleasures of the table would transform them into partners. "The fine work of Savour," he said, accepting the glass of wine she offered him.

"I don't think so," said the Princess.

"No?" he asked.

"No," she answered. "It's the work of some Indigene or other." She took a letter and tossed it over the balcony; a group of birds hurtled toward it, like arrows to a target.

"In any case," he said, "let me make the traditional wish. Let salt and sweet be complements, and our agreement perfect. May I sit with you?"

She indicated the seat across from her, but turned her face away from him toward the sea.

"Princess," the Priest began, "it is appropriate that you look out to sea. What we have to talk about today is vast. The decision before you is vast, and its consequences are also vast, not only for your life, but also of course, for our Kingdoms, and for the Paradise that we seek to create. A moment has come when what you choose to do or not to do may mean Paradise Regained or Lost for us, for the people of Paradise."

She looked at him for a moment, and then turned her face again toward the sea.

"Your father tells me that you are reluctant to marry. I assure you, I am in sympathy with your hesitation. It is not for nothing that among the Angels, dreams of death and funeral processions are said to be portents of weddings. Your fears are natural—a union for life, the creation of children, and yes, the difficulty of combining pleasure and policy . . ."

"I am not reluctant to marry," she said. "In fact, I have made my choice."

"Then I rejoice to say I have misunderstood. Our impressions of your state of mind had been quite different. With your permission, I will bring the happy report to your father of your choice. He will feel the gratitude and relief that I do."

A gull soared overhead as if obedient to a force of countergravity. It seemed to be falling forcefully, but upward. It pinned its wings backward, soared upward to a carefully gauged height, and dropped an oyster on the stone of the terrace with a clatter. The bird swooped toward the cleanly cracked shell and began to eat what was inside. They were too intent on their conversation to notice it, and the Mirrors did not dare to interrupt and shoo it away.

"I take pleasure in thinking so," she said, and took a sip of her wine.

"And which among your suitors may I announce as your future husband?"

"I shall marry you," she said.

"That is impossible," the Priest answered.

"I engage myself to you," she repeated.

"But, with the greatest respect, I am close to concluding an agreement with someone else."

"Then you must not conclude it. It is not what I wish." She looked at him with incomprehension.

"Princess, it is the greatest of honors that you offer me. Still, for the sake of my own honor, I must refuse."

"And I refuse your refusal," she said, her eyes welling with tears, whether of hurt, shame, or rage, he could not tell. She reached for his hand across the table, but he kept his hands clasped together under his chin. "I love you. I have always wanted you for my husband. I am certain you want this, too—but you do not yet know it. You talk of pleasure and policy. I am your kingdom, power—your glory, if you accept."

"Princess, again, I thank you for this immense honor, which I do not deserve. But I cannot accept."

She looked at him, her lips tight, tears now spilling down her cheeks. They were not calculated tears, but real ones. She wept at his mortal cruelty; he was robbing her of her dream of life itself. "I will do something that I don't want at all to do, if you refuse me again. I will scream. And the Mirrors will have no choice but to echo my scream. And the guards will rush through my rooms onto the terrace. Then I will say that you tried to rape me. And the Mirrors will be obliged to repeat what I say. And you will end as something quite different than my husband."

"I ask for a day to reflect."

"I refuse it."

"Then I have no choice."

"Let salt and sweet be complements. Our agreement is now perfect."

He then took the hand she offered, as a key accepts a lock. "Our agreement is now perfect. I will inform your father that you and I intend, with his consent, to be husband and wife." He lifted her hand to his forehead, in the customary gesture of respectful leave-taking. "There has been violence done here today, Princess, a violence of unforgettable precision and delicacy. But since our agreement is now perfect, I think we can also agree that it was not you who was raped this afternoon."

"I am now your wife-to-be. I give you freedom to kiss me," she answered.

Despite the discretion of their meeting, unpleasant rumors circulated about the Priest, that he had brought about the marriage through an unseemly passion that coerced the Princess and endangered her honor. These murmurings introduced in the Priest a new gnawing suspicion that the rumors were emanating from the Princess's quarters.

He observed that the tales were designed to illuminate her virtue, and to throw a shadow on his own, in a way that must mean her father had assented to the scheme.

He found himself abruptly in the worst position for a courtier, the trusted counselor of a monarch he could no longer trust, and the husband-to-be of a treacherous wife.

And as the administrator of all ritual, he now had to set in motion the ceremonies, old and new, of betrothal and marriage, even of his own strange marriage, in which he, like any woman, was the bride. He was obliged like a woman to consent regardless of his feelings, whether delighted, appalled, or suspended in the feminine discipline of awaiting the inevitable, marrying an unknown husband, bearing an unknowable child.

For Savour now, labor was trebled; the work of planning and consultation for the receptions and wedding festivities was added to the execution of each week's work of provisioning and feeding the population of the Angelic palace of the New Kingdom. Still, the profundity of her training supported her, she had been taught that a kitchen must be managed like a wine cellar; the cook must know what is in it and where, and the current stage of life of each of its provisions.

She understood better than ever what she had been taught was the first precept of all cookery: that a dinner begins in the mind before it approaches the body.

So she was able, with only a few suspenseful days, to continue sustaining her community, while devising and testing varieties of dishes for the wedding.

These would be the Metaphor dishes through which the Princess would display her imagination of herself through the theater of her bridal glory, and express her dreams of her future union. In addition, the dishes accepted for the Angelic Books must be recorded pictorially, either by Savour herself or another kitchen artist under her supervision. And she was expected to teach them as well, so they could always be reproduced, once accepted.

Still, when she felt burdened by the endless provisioning, the almost involuntary preoccupation of her mind with possible dishes, new combinations of flavors and textures, evoked the hunter child she had been.

She recognized that working of her mind, imagining a fleck of cinnamon in a venison curry, or endlessly recording the stocks of sugars, salts, dried mushrooms. It was another version of the human-animal self, the creature ranging along a forest path or plain, seeking in crevices or underbrush or in trees whatever might be edible. The sense that the dead and the living had all known that intense burden of hunger and the intense strategies against it strengthened her. She felt herself to be human and animal, a young sister of ancient hunger.

She remembered, too, that her burdens came precisely from abundance, from possibility—that all around her, in the Indigenous territories, beyond the borders of the New Kingdom, women knew exactly what they would cook for dinner—nothing.

The precision with which she managed her provisions was even more critical at this period, and she appreciated more than ever Salt's administrative skills. Among the panoply of skills of the ideal cook, it was those she struggled most to master. The gods give humans gifts like silver, but it is for the mortals to keep them untarnished and shining.

She and Salt added an hour to each day, spent in a morning inspection of the storerooms. Each took a notebook to record supplies on hand and supplies needed; the separate records helped guard against mistakes, and to maintain an accurate measure of the materials supplied from each part of the empire. All the Angelic kitchen personnel were well acquainted with the story of the first feast-maker of the New Kingdom, who threw himself from a cliff after the oysters he had planned to open an important feast failed to arrive.

In Savour's pantry, there were eight kinds of rice and at least fifteen variants of salt of all colors, so that the Angels could taste and see the shores of the colonies they had conquered.

"We need more pilaf rice. I also see that we need to replenish our rice to grind for flour." She had had a request for beignets of a local olive as big as a fist, stuffed with spiced meat and greens, then coated in rice flour and saffron dust, and fried; she calculated the amount of the material needed next to the dish in her kitchen diary. She always wrote with a touch of disbelief—it was so strange to be unlettered in her own language, to be an infant in her native language and an adult in the Angelic tongue.

"What do you make of this marriage?" Salt asked, as he duplicated her request in his notebook.

"What do you think?" she answered. "I hate it. I fear it. The person who is the most kind to me will soon be married to the person who is the most cruel. And the palates so badly matched, between a man who wants to taste the world, and a princess whose true appetite I cannot understand."

"Do you believe the rumors?" he asked, not looking at her, but down into the bronze saffron strongbox, its lid chased with stylized crocuses.

"Which ones?" she asked, equally preoccupied with the box.

"You know. That he forced her. Do you think the Priest capable of rape?"

"You remind me of things we Ghosts used to speak about when I was an apprentice. Many Ghosts, as you know, are made by rape. I have never forgotten what my master teacher, Gate, used to say when he trained us in the art of aphrodisiac dishes." Salt, always curious about the legendary craftsmanship of the Invisibles, interrupted her to ask what those dishes were.

"We learned a greater range of dishes than you seem to do here; your erotic cookery is rich and blunt, based on feminine oysters and phallic truffles, that evoke desires through obvious fragrances and shapes. Still, we learn that these are not true aphrodisiac dishes, as they only awaken desire where it is already present."

One of Savour's Twelve was the Dinner of the Fulfilled Wish, though she was not free to tell even Salt the names and compositions of her Twelve. The Twelve were the crown of her craftsmanship; if finely executed, they had the power to change or renew a destiny—including her own. Still, the bond between them had grown strong. She described the creation, without revealing its secret relation to her.

"We are taught that desire is affected by many oblique elements, the burden of daily cares, for example. In that case, the dishes evoke not simply the lover's sex, but the experience of joyous abandon that refreshes and renews desire.

"We delicately evoke the flesh of sex with rose-colored wines of the appropriate shades, and we set a landscape on a platter. It is the dream garden where what one reaches for is present to hand.

"The dinner is set out on exquisite small trays; it is eaten with the hands. The guest eats at the pace he wishes, and takes as much or as little as he wants. He nibbles, he grazes, he devours, he caresses, to his perfect satisfaction.

"There are brilliantly colored vegetables and fruits, like solid fragments of the blinding rainbow the sun makes in your eyes when you stare into it over the shoulder of someone you are embracing. There are hot crisp vegetable and melting cheese beignets, barely fastened, with the fritter batter slipping off them like loose shoulder straps in the passion that quickens carelessly made children. There are ice creams with the colors and perfumes of flowers. And so forth." She had spoken with the inspiration, but also the practicality, of one whose work is to make dreams exist.

"Savour," said Salt, "there is no Invisible I envy. A Ghost's life is one of enslavement. Even the lives of many Indigenes are less harsh. I wish at times, uselessly, that I had the power to set you free. But there are times also when I realize that you have more freedom than I could presume to give you."

Savour led them out of the spice storeroom, followed by Candle. She paused on the wine cellar steps, bent down, and gently caressed him behind the ears. It was the cat's favorite caress, and he threw his head back with pure pleasure and trust.

Salt followed and paused. "But you have forgotten to tell me what your teacher said or what you think of the rumors about the Priest. Could he do such a thing?"

Savour had begun to note which stocks of bottles must be replenished. She set down her kitchen diary, trying to summon up Gate's exact words.

"This, as fully as I can remember, was what he said when he was teaching me the aphrodisiac dishes I have described to you.

"He said that he believed we could understand the very nature of human evil if we could ever grasp this; why is it that we work with such artful delicacies to restore a man's power to make love, while soldiers in their thousands, in attacks on villages, and policemen torturing in interrogation rooms and men on lonely streets so easily find the erections necessary to rape? As to the Priest, on the day we can understand why love makes a man incapable and brutality makes him potent, we can decide on the truth of the rumors."

The cat had climbed onto a rafter; he leapt into Savour's arms, lightly as a falling leaf. She locked the storeroom door behind them.

Savour's conferences about the composition of the wedding banquet brought her into uneasy contact with the Princess, who governed through displeasure and insult. After every meeting, Savour felt as if she were snake-bitten.

It was a strange world the Princess created, functioning through the dark privileges of hatred. The freedom to hate, to insult, to strike, were privileges she claimed, but denied to others. If the same impulses welled up in those she harmed, it was treated as unconscionable insubordination.

It was as if she needed hatred the way others need love, and sought ever-fresh ways to obtain it. Their resentment of her was a crown of distinction, and she provoked them until they did her that homage.

Nothing made her more certain of her soul's heroic and superior integrity than the hatred of others; it made her feel a precious jewel, perpetually threatened by marauding thieves. The hostility of others perfected her, proved the presence of God in her, as a jeweler's attacking chisel makes a gem brilliant.

Savour's task in connection with the royal marriage was to devise the decor and menus for the betrothal and wedding dinners. She would also have to cook the betrothal dinner, though nominally, it was supposed to be the work of the fiancée.

Now, no matter what her other tasks, no matter what time of day or night, she was obliged to confer with the Princess when she called. In this way, the Princess could both berate her for not responding quickly enough, and also for her neglecting the task in which she was engaged. That evening, she was summoned from supervising an important dinner for the Synod of Angelical Priests.

Salt knew the order and seasoning of the dishes perfectly, and the servers had mastered the symmetry of each plate, but Savour still felt tormented when she was not allowed to concentrate on the task before her. When she was working as she wished, her mind and body seemed to her to enter into what she cooked, to be consumed, and then to survive inside the ones she fed.

As she hurried through the labyrinthine passages to the Princess's quarters, she felt she understood at last something of the nature of fate.

She had undergone a rigorous training in all aspects of her craft so that the results of her work would be, within reason, what she expected them to be, unless she was experimenting. Within the kitchen, her work was elegant and consistent.

But she had not reckoned on the dining room, where her masters and their guests sat, competing, intriguing, seducing, insulting, putting her work to purposes she had never dreamed. The kitchen, whose workings she understood, was small; in the dining room, she was an instrument in a world of unforeseeable intentions and events. That was fate.

As always, the Princess was reclining, surrounded by standing attendants. She had thought she'd seen a mocking glint in one of the Mirror's eyes—and the Mirror had confirmed her suspicion by defending herself. A truly obedient Mirror would have reflected the Princess's accusing gaze. "Lean down," the Princess said. "Closer." The Mirror leaned low over the couch, so the Princess could slap her effortlessly. "Beloved," whispered the Mirror, uttering the formulaic response of those who assented gratefully to correction.

Savour had learned to be less fearful. Her situation protected her, as a Mirror's did not. She was less easily replaceable. The self-abnegation demanded of her was different, but her training had prepared her for it: she had to perform her work perfectly to public adulation, but refuse praise; all that she accomplished must be acknowledged to emanate from the Princess.

"Come closer," the Princess said to Savour. Savour was not a personal attendant; she was not required to address the Princess as "Beloved," which would have been impertinent.

"Yes, ma'am," said Savour, and inclined her head.

"I want to talk to you about the wedding feast. I've chosen a theme."

"Yes, ma'am," said Savour.

"I want," the Princess said slowly, "the Feast of Undying Love. Can you make that feast?"

Savour observed, with disbelief, an atom of anguish in the Princess's brilliant gaze. It was as if she saw fire there, not only as something that could burn others, but also as something that was consuming itself. It occurred to her for the first time that the hateful, too, crave love.

"Well?" the Princess asked sharply, as if Savour had been caught out in some theft.

"I will try," said Savour, too truthfully.

"You weren't brought from across the sea to 'try.' You were selected to interpret my wishes faithfully. You do not grant my wishes; you fulfill them."

"Will you describe them for me, ma'am?"

"I want you to make a dinner that seems to have no beginning and no end. I want you to make dishes in the form of circles, of rings, the forms of perpetuity and renewal." She raised her voice. "I want to offer beauty that doesn't die. I want the guests to taste supernatural snow. I want to see their plates thick with drifts of snow that doesn't melt, and to remember it forever." She turned her face away from Savour. "I expect these things to appear on the nuptial table. I expect my Metaphor dishes to be remembered forever. See to it."

Savour hurried back to her kitchen. A mighty work of invention lay before her. She understood that she would not be able to use one of her Twelve; they could only be effective in situations whose outcomes were yet to be decided.

The evening's encounter had revealed to Savour the true nature of the Princess's appetite: it was an appetite she had mistakenly thought was trained on the extravagant demonstration of power, like demanding strawberries in January. But what Savour had seen that night was an appetite not for the extravagant, but the impossible; a hunger for the fruit of the Paradise tree itself. And an insatiable appetite is a murderous one, which nothing on the face of the earth can satisfy.

Savour set to work, though she sensed that no flavor she could combine or consummate would change the Princess's fate, whatever it might be. Young as she was, the Princess was like a ship already far from shore, disappearing from sight.

Long after the kitchens were quiet and even the scullery staff, compulsive as sea waves in its rhythm of soaping, scraping, and drying, had gone to wherever they slept, Savour composed the wedding Feast of Undying Love. Her small cat, Candle, kept her company during those late nights. He leapt onto the stone preparation table to assess what the baskets contained or what was rising underneath the copper cloche. Knowledge obtained, he slept on a cushion at her feet, as she stirred and sculpted and changed liquids into solids, searching for the snow that wouldn't melt.

She worked to make the material express what was required of it; she was drawn into that labor, into that doing, so completely that she often forgot that her task was to immortalize a joyless contract.

Even a dinner that gave supreme pleasure, yet did not enter into memory, would be an utter failure, like a single night of rapturous love-making with someone forgotten.

The banquet must dazzle with its beauty, but pass beyond the eye into consciousness. A great dinner does not vanish, but is transformed into speech in the throat, as a marriage is made to exist through vows. It was Savour's work to begin by setting perfected nature before the guests; and to end by putting words into their mouths.

She devised a feast in which every course was an allusion to some aspect of love, marriage, or fertility, and in which every course would develop until the culmination, in which the perishable elements of the beginning would take imperishable forms. Thus the first course—fried flowers stuffed with partridge liver, quince paste, and sheep's cheese, mixed death and the bloom of new life together, and would be completed at the finale by a dessert of flowers crystallized in sugar, preserved by a sweetness, as of love.

All would wane, wax, and begin again.

Savour devised a platter to set before each guest of small crepes, folded to figure the phases of the moon. The new moon would be filled with the roe of sea urchin, the half-moon with velvety greens and mushrooms, the three-quarter moon with minced pheasant, the full moon with a mousse of venison. In this way, the guests would range from sea to the subterranean, to the sky, and then the earth, the presence of egg in each element a promise of rebirth. There would be breads baked in the form of rings, as the Princess had envisioned.

And for the main course, magnificent crown roast rounds of lamb, pork, and veal would be served, their exposed edges of bone capped with glittering semiprecious stones. They would be accompanied by gold platters, six feet in circumference, of pilaf, on whose surface Savour would reproduce, using pistachios, pomegranate seeds, and thin crisp fried petals of brilliant blue potatoes, the strands of the magnificent emerald, ruby, and sapphire necklace which was the Priest's wedding gift to his bride.

She felt certain, so far, of her culinary pageant, but she struggled in vain to match the Princess's desire for the snow that does not melt. "How can I fabricate what does not exist?" she said worriedly to Salt; she had failed to find any substance that would evoke snow visually or in texture, that would also bring the feast to its sweet, sublime finale.

"You are thinking too much like an Angel"—Salt shrugged—"with their 'war for peace' and 'life is paradise.' If the Angelic scriptures ordered us to drink the sea, they would send us to shore every day with cups, and order us to praise the taste of the bitter water.

"I cannot make myself a woman, nor make you a man, though in many ways I am like a woman and you are like a man. You should be seeking for something that is like 'snow that doesn't melt'—a dream of it—not the thing itself. Truth comes to us in resemblance, in shade. In moonlight. In grasping what exists through what we cannot make exist."

Savour remembered Gate, who prayed to a Goddess of Fortunate Coincidence he called O, for the syllable of recognition that she forced you to utter when you encountered her, the sound of the homage she demanded. The Invisibles had a particular reverence for that goddess. She was playful and witty; she would place the thing you were seeking where you least expected it.

She was an important deity of all cooks. With all their efforts to master complex techniques, not one could make a dish that would become a legacy for each generation unless that goddess was present. And as always, with Immortals, one had to court her through practice and skill before she would reveal to you the exquisite bliss of what you did not know, and transform it into knowledge, like a tree flowering in spring.

Savour set to work with all the materials she knew that were clear or white—sugar, salt, rice, potatoes, flour, egg white, milk, cream, cheese, water, even chalk, pearl, and bone. These and other materials would be strewn about an area of the kitchen that functioned as her workshop. There, she examined these substances in as many of their properties as she had grasped. Even phlegmatic Savour lost her temper in these experiments, and would fling the inedible messes angrily into a basket for an apprentice to empty.

Salt arrived during one of these hours to use the time to plan the choreography of the feast. Savour's hair was plastered to her forehead with sweat. "One thing is clear," said Salt. "You are not made of the snow that doesn't melt." Savour looked at him unsmilingly and kept working. "When you have something of value to say, I will hear it," she said severely.

"It looks as if I have strayed into the laboratory of one of those mad alchemists who is trying to make a flesh and blood man from a skeleton." This class of people, former cooks who had turned charlatan, were known in the New Kingdom, where they preyed on the Indigenes, offering to resurrect their legendary leaders who would lead them in rebellion against the Angels.

"Like them, I have whipped and grated, melted and strained, and have not brought anything into creation." They turned to discussing the problems presented by the arches through which the wedding guests would enter the courtyard where the festivities were to be held. Each of the arches represented an entrance into Paradise, in the form of a different season symbolizing the passage from time into eternity, and so, from betrothal across the threshold to the undying love of marriage.

Each must be appropriately decorated, so Savour and Salt worked to invent the imagery together. They shared a certain pride in their training as banquet cooks, feast-makers as well as flavor-makers.

After he left, Savour turned again to her experiments. She took six eggs, and cracked them one after another. She had never lost her love of the distinctive sound of an egg cracking—not like the shock of a snapping twig, or the wounded shearing of ice on a pond. An egg cracked as delicately and deliberately as a heel tapped a parquet floor to begin a dance.

She separated the whites from the yolks through the sieve of her own fingers. When she cooked, she felt her body fit the world as if she were the world's wife.

She took a whisk of Salt's invention, made of braided, thinly shaved, and flexible twigs, and began to beat the whites, almost idly.

Her mind set sail on them, as the motion caused them to imitate the moods of the sea, glassy calm, rippling, frothing, plunging with tempestuous whitecaps. She whipped at them, as the peaks drifted and bubbled, and she thought, like a sailor in a storm, of shore.

She had an image of gleaming sand, then realized that she had the image itself at her elbow and could plunge her hand into it. She took a drift of sugar and scattered it into the egg whites. They began to sparkle and swell. They took on the majestic and mysterious texture, both fragile, and impenetrable, of snowdrifts. She had only ever seen them before as clouds, as envisioned by the Invisibles. She dried her forehead on her hand, and the motion made her think of drying what was wet, of the way fire set shapes, as with clay dishes.

She set the bowl in the oven, and when she brought it out, saw that the egg whites held their shapes, and now seemed a glacial landscape gleaming in the distance. She was sure she had discovered the snow that doesn't melt. She had the means now to culminate the feast. She could present the final course that would sum up the Banquet of Undying Love, while delicately suggesting the sweet consummation of the wedding night to come.

The guests entered the courtyard, on the perfect evening of the wedding, through three of the arches. One arch was covered with peacock feathers, which shuddered in the breeze made by children with peacock-feather fans. One was outlined in silver ribbons of water that flowed perpetually down its curves, returning to the two fountains at its base.

The third was covered with masses of tiny candles, illuminating gilded reliefs of angels carved into the arch. And the fourth was for the entry of the bride and groom. One side of the arch, where the ceremony would take place, was covered with green palm fronds, roses, and cornucopias of fruit and wheat. They would step through the arch after the marriage had taken place, where the exact pattern of decoration was repeated, this time with the palms, roses, and cornucopias sculpted in transcendental gold.

The feast was flawlessly choreographed; the pilafs glittered in faithful imitation of the bride's necklace, and there were audible gasps of admiration when the roasts in their coronets of jewel-studded bones were carried in.

The sculpted glaciers of the Snow That Does Not Melt, ornamented with crystallized roses, soared dramatically over the pools of rose-scented cream in which they floated. "Snow That Does Not Melt," the Princess explained to a military governor seated across from her. "A most original conception, Princess," he said. She inclined her head graciously to accept the compliment.

When the last plate was cleared, glasses were brought for the traditional toasts. Since the High Priest Xe was an experienced rhetorician, whose homilies and political reflections many of the company heard weekly, the bride elected to speak first.

She rose. "My husband," she began, "every couple married according to the Angelic laws is commanded to restore another fragment of our lost Paradise. We regain Paradise in pledging our undying love. Tonight I have given you all a symbol of my indestructible love in serving you and this company with Snow That Does Not Melt.

"I vow to you, my husband, that I will be to you as Snow That Does Not Melt. Until we make the earth again a Paradise, I will be all you know of Paradise on earth." She lifted her glass, and the company toasted her. "Snow That Does Not Melt." Her father raised his own glass, returning her toast.

The Priest, magnificent in a brocade robe worked with trees of paradise, which he resembled, soaring above the guests in his own dramatic height, stood up in his turn. The crowd consented to him, as they always did, raptly.

"We Angels are a feasting people," he said. "We know that what a feast first accomplishes is to create a time and space in which, above all, the guests can be delicious. As a sports field creates a time and space in which our capacity to kill is crafted into discipline, diplomacy, and play, a festive dinner table creates a space and occasion for our lupine carnal impulses to glitter with disciplined genius and wit. At last they can attain the qualities that most often elude them—intelligence, elegance, courtesy.

"And as Angels, we know that God speaks to us not only through Scriptures, but through flavors. These tastes—of butter, of peach, of partridge, are remnants of what existed in the Paradise we lost. They enter us like invisible angels, even in this ruined world.

"Here, Paradise is inside us; but there, again, when it surrounds us, we will be nourished, as we once were, on tender breads wrought from obdurate stone. And the roast swans we consume shall leave one golden body on the plate, and simultaneously soar unharmed in the heavens above our table. And our hungers will not deplete us, but will be exaltations.

"Before a banquet, the experience of hunger, as in Paradise, is for once a luxury and a glory, since it is a desire that will surely be fulfilled. The detail and perfection of the cooking that we owe to our feast-maker, Savour, has changed our daily burden of appetite from stone to diamond."

The Princess's eyes narrowed for a split second, as if she had been struck, until they were as thin as blades. She quickly recovered her composure, and resumed impeccable bridal serenity, but Savour had seen. She knew she would never be forgiven for diverting a moment's praise from the bride in a toast in which she alone should be celebrated. It was an insolence merely to exist outside the consciousness of the Princess.

She had at last grasped the true nature of the Princess's appetite; an appetite for love so all-consuming that she would destroy the beloved in the pursuit of it. For the appetite to be loved is murderous if it is not balanced and justified by the appetite to love.

"Hear, hear," the military governor, who had not heard his own voice for too long, seconded the Priest's compliment. "Ornaments are forbidden to Invisibles, yet this one has scattered jewels on our plates."

Savour exchanged a glance with Salt, and saw the foreboding in his eyes. The Priest, feasting with relish on his opulent speech, observed nothing.

"We all know the folktales of dinners that changed the fates of the hosts or the guests. And a wedding dinner is surely one of those, as the bride and groom preside for the first time over a shared table. A wedding feast serves to make the erotic social, general, and thereby, celestial.

"Tonight we have delighted each one in each other. Some say that in Heaven there will be no marriage. But we know otherwise. In Paradise, all will be married, as we have been tonight.

"We have all been each other's lovers at this table tonight: for once, without cruelty, without selfishness, without regrets. We have had a glimpse of Paradise together." He raised his glass, and saluted the Princess, who stood up with the inexorable grace of the swans he had alluded to, and signaled the end of the feast.

If the court of Angels had hoped that the much-anticipated marriage would bring peace to the Princess, they were disappointed. If the Princess had hoped that marriage would create love, she, too, was thwarted. The Priest's perfect courtesy toward her was as relentless as her insistence on the marriage. His polished and formal self-possession was a display of freedom, a reminder that she was a stranger, that her will had not become his.

It was not long before she began to try to provoke him in small ways, interfering with messages to him, destroying in what she described to him as "accidents" garments or possessions he seemed to favor. At the same time, she made him gifts in public, so that he was compelled to express his gratitude to her gracefully in front of guests.

She fastened a massive golden chain around his neck at an assembly, like a leash. She enjoyed forcing him to accept something he did not want that she wanted him to have. Now he would always carry her around his neck. And if he did not, there would be an occasion to remind an audience of the splendid gift and of her generosity, by asking where the chain she had given him was.

The gold had its gleaming hypnotic effects on the spectators, plunging them into private dreams, for gold is like a magic mirror that shows ambitions satisfied, without effort or consequences.

The Princess longed to make him lash out at her, to entice at least a show of passion. If she could force him to strike her, she could have him imprisoned. And when he despaired, she could plead for his freedom, entrapping him in a silken web of public clemency.

She imagined herself in the center of that scene as if perceived by a painter. She mentally dressed herself, changing the colors several times, until she arrived at a rich dark blue, which combined elements of mourning, royalty, and the suggestion of Heaven inherent in all blue shades.

She could not kneel for the sake of dignity, but her eyes would be downcast, her lips soft, emblematic of someone whose love was infinitely superior to the wrongs she had endured.

She, who had been born a symbol, always imagined herself seen. And to be seen by an audience acknowledging the wrongs done her was to be cradled in a perfect embrace. Perpetual apology is a tribute greater even than the bent knee that acknowledges power.

Power can be shown to be corrupt and overthrown. But blessed are those with a wound that does not heal; for it is an ever-refreshed innocence, through which the rich become supplicants, the powerful helpless, vengeance perfect justice, and all life forfeit in compensation. Glory is due to those who rule; but blessed are those in possession of the debt that can never be repaid.

The Princess did not need to be so subtle in her behavior toward Savour. The Priest, like all Angelic men, was her superior. But Savour belonged to her; her body, her hours, her days, her skills, even the gift that distinguished her. She was outraged that Savour had not yet fully grasped that.

Now the Princess devised a way to torment Savour. She began to send the Mirrors on random nights to the kitchens as Savour was closing them. The Mirrors would utter in unison one choral message, "You did not please," and then depart. The staff hurried away silently on those nights, their camaraderie broken by Savour's humiliation.

"Is this true?" Savour asked Salt. The question was real. She was deeply anxious that her hands might have lost their skill; she was ready to despair.

"She is trying to make it true," he said. "She senses that to work well, you must entertain doubts about your work. If she can replace your legitimate doubts with an absolute conviction of failure, you will begin to call all your work into question.

"What you don't see is that the false certainty of failure is as deceptive as any smug conviction of success. Ask me. Listen to me. I am someone who knows your work.

"And isn't she still accepting praise for the work you have done while she sends messengers to insult it? Could she do that if your work were poor? No, she wants what you have—the Priest's praise, the Priest's respect. Only you can give her that. She cannot produce these dazzling banquets—or anything—so instead, she will eat you, like the parasite she is." Salt spoke with the depth of experience of one who was accustomed to doing his most excellent work on behalf of people he hated.

A measure of comprehension is like a bridge over an abyss. Savour was strengthened, and her work held steady; with Salt's help, her judgment of its quality remained flexible and responsive as the measurement of a thermometer. The campaign of the Mirrors became intermittent.

It was followed, however, by the night of the Perpetual Banquet.

The Princess had ordered an equinox dinner for a hundred places. The difficulty of this dinner was that each of its seventy components were delicate and miniature, and must be served simultaneously, as soon as cooked, as if they were newly opened roses; the dinner was prized for the illusion that a diner was tasting what had just been born. It was always served with new white wine only, and was known to be a votive dinner offered as a prayer for conception. The Princess, it was clear, was enlisting her guests to add their communal hopes to hers.

Savour flew from grill to cauldron to oven, many-armed, overseeing the complement of twenty assistants, and fifty servers needed for the deft work an equinox dinner required. The plates were covered and swaddled ingeniously to preserve the heat, crispness, perfect colors of the cooked food, and then taken to the seaside reception room where they had been ordered. The servers found no one there. The dishes returned to the kitchen, no longer appetizing.

Savour sent a messenger to the Princess's apartments; the messenger returned to the kitchen to deliver a reproof. Savour was careless, the messenger reported. She had substituted her own will for the royal will. The guests were actually due within the hour, in yet another reception room.

The group began the process again, dicing, flouring, grating, boiling, frying, grilling, with a speed that would have been comic had they not been desperate. Savour improvised substitutes for the dishes that could not be completed within the hour. They served. They found the room empty of guests.

Another messenger was sent, another hour and venue designated. They prepared again, for ghosts. On the fourth try, the staff and servers, exhausted, bedraggled, presented their latest dinner to a real assembly, who fell on their offerings with hearty appetites. The next morning, Savour was called to the Princess's quarters, and sharply reprimanded for her mismanagement of the kitchen and for her extravagant waste of stores.

Even more unwelcome was a new royal caprice; the Princess began to make incursions into the kitchens themselves. Savour had been born into bondage; but she had managed, in a sense, to make herself free. She willingly offered a magnificent obedience to her work; ultimately she was the servant of a divine craft, the priest of the kitchen. It was this that infuriated the Princess. She was determined to crush Savour until the slave understood she had no other God than the Princess; she struggled to transform Savour's work into servitude.

"Why does she do this?" Savour asked Salt, resting her forehead on her hand, after the Mirrors announced an impending visit.

"The Priest did not really choose her," said Salt. "He did, however, choose you. And undertook a long voyage to find you. Perhaps there is some destined relation between you. It is a mystery she wants to comprehend."

The Princess wanted to observe the making of a game pie that she had noticed was a particular favorite of the Priest's. She would send a sudden command for it to be made, regardless of the day's other orders of work for Savour. If she were sleepless, she would send a messenger to force Savour to the kitchens from her bed. Savour would explain and demonstrate the procedures, and the Princess would somehow unravel the careful instructions between sessions.

"That wasn't what you said last time," she would correct Savour. "You seasoned it differently." "That isn't how it is prepared." She harangued Savour with a barrage of accusations and commandments.

Worse, the Princess insisted that it was her prerogative to instruct Savour in the proper techniques. She would seize the meat, hack it, malseason it, and then accuse Savour contemptuously of deliberately spoiling the perfection of her finished dish.

Savour scrupulously fished out the rings the Princess left in the pastry, so as not to be accused of theft. This was something Invisibles learned in their earliest training, to guard against the accusation of theft by those who determined to make them criminal.

Little is more poisonous to a craftsman who has struggled for mastery of a discipline than to be forced to yield to the deadly insults of masters who fuse arrogance, ignorance, and jealousy. Masters of this kind are often accompanied, too, by trains of weak followers, like the cattle egrets who ride on the backs of cattle, feeding on the insects that swarm around them.

Such people can in fact never be instructed; the asking of a question causes them intense suffering bringing them into the insulting presence of knowledge, over which they can have no lasting power. Love itself can be bought; only knowledge is always earned.

Those for whom ambition, power, and the naked adoration of wealth are substitutes for the hard-won work of a life, can learn nothing, not even at the feet of the gods themselves. For learning is wrought through a brief communion of god and human in pain and exaltation. The truth, even the smallest truth, survives those who die of it and those who die for it.

One night, several dark hours before the first light, Savour was ordered to the kitchen, again to make her game pie for the Princess. She stumbled across the courtyard groggily, beneath the full moon. She tiredly set out the flours, the mushrooms, the butter, and failed to hear the Princess enter the kitchen. She continued to set out the equipment, oblivious, until, with a shock, she heard a plate shatter.

She turned and saw the Princess, whose face was a mask of hatred. "You will greet me with the same joy I expect from any other servant," she said savagely. Savour remained expressionless, not awake enough to grasp the need to respond quickly. The Princess picked up the jagged half of plate, and violently threw it at Savour's face.

Savour did not turn with enough speed, and the sharp edge caught her left temple. Blood streamed onto the white marble of the counter. "You will remember from now on to smile in my presence," said the Princess. She dropped the other half of the plate on the floor. It shattered. The Princess turned her back and left the room. For the rest of her life, Savour carried a small scar, curved upward in the shape of a smile, on the left side of her face.

The Princess, who in all other ways was richly insensitive, possessed an insidious capacity to recognize what was prized by others, which she would then attempt to erode, compromise, or annex, unable to bear any inattention.

Even when her intuition was imprecise, she often managed to inflict a wound, like a bullet that ricochets. It was in this way that she was the means of separating Savour from her beloved companion, Candle.

The Priest had recently returned from an alliance-making expedition with a country famous for making superb tents from the fibers extracted from the leaves of a native tree. He had acquired a supply of these for the use of the Angelic armies.

The cuisine of this country also was renowned, for the subtlety with which it made use of all ingredients, rich or poor. The Priest described to his wife the dishes he had sampled. He had eaten vegetables steamed over seawater, soup made of rain and cream, and had been struck by the repertoire of distinctive braised dishes featuring cat, wild and domestic.

The Princess sent an order to Savour commanding a similar menu, whose centerpiece would be braised cat for one hundred guests. It was then that Salt gently advised her to send Candle away. It had to be done, quickly and secretly. The danger was too great that the Princess's eye might light on him, and inspire her to demand that he, too, be cooked.

Together, at the earliest opportunity, they put Candle in a basket, and took him to Salt's family in their Indigenous village. Candle was quiet and tranquil in the basket; as long as he could scent Savour, he was in a world he trusted. But when she left him there, and shut the door, he gave a high-pitched, anguished scream, like a child's. They told her he stood on his hind legs, and beat at the door with his paws, that he cried and screamed for her as if he were making a desperate attempt to become human in order to bring her back.

"It has to be done," Salt said, and actually took her hand to lead her away. "You will still be able to visit him now and then, and he will come to understand that you are not lost to him. Above all, he will be safe here."

Candle's heartbreaking cries were a dark miracle. They made Savour relive her long ago parting with Gate. Savour had never thought anyone would remember her, never expected to be numbered among the mourned.

It was the Priest who brought the agon of the Princess and Savour to a temporary end. He had made fruitful use of his forced marriage to change his relationship to the Princess's father.

The old King of the Angels was now his dependent in judgment and in influence. The King had made no objection when the Priest, ever preoccupied with the threat of the Indigenes to the New Kingdom, introduced severe new restrictions on the Indigenous population. They had long been prohibited from traveling to border areas. There was a persistent danger that they might form alliances with the neighboring Saints.

The Saints were a nation who had every reason to fear the Angelic ambitions for their own territory—or an Angelic attempt to drive the Indigenous out, forcing them permanently onto Saintlands. The Saints scrutinized intently any change in the Angelic treatment of the Indigenous in order to predict what the Angels intended for them. The borders between the two countries had already been the sites of brief, but violent skirmishes.

Now even travel between villages was to be severely controlled. The Priest was accustomed to the absolute obedience he commanded during the Angelic liturgies—the dance steps accomplished in unison, the precisely clasped multitudes of upraised hands, the dramatic prostrations among the congregants that gave the impression of row after row of wheat falling to the scythe.

The more he commanded the New Kingdom's political life, the more he was convinced that a similar submission must be required of the Indigenes, if Paradise were to be achieved. It had come to him that even determining the movement of the Indigenes would not accomplish this; their livelihoods themselves must be altered and subordinated to Angelic needs; the Angels held the power of death through their lavishly equipped army. But to conquer is not to rule. They would seize, too, the essential power of life; the power in food, in giving or withholding daily bread.

The Priest planned to accomplish this by requisitioning Indigenous reserves of food and Indigenous labor for the good of all; it would become the bread of Angels, stored in the silos of Paradise.

The Indigenes would then purchase food from the supply, according to their needs. In this way there would be both plenty, and unprecedented and permanent safety for all. The national stores would be filled, insured against future crises. And at last, every aspect of the Indigenes' lives would be ordained by the Angels of God.

Thinking about this plan gave him a kind of repose, a sign he always recognized as a good omen, an augur of success. He proposed to implement his program by a lengthy progress through the Indigenous territories, with a cohort of troops to enforce local cooperation. This would also give him the opportunity to inspect the current encampments at the borders with the Saints, and adapt them if necessary.

He did not propose, but informed the Princess that he intended to take Savour on his tour.

The Priest had become for the Princess the one being against whom she was powerless. "What good can she possibly do you in this project?" she asked, but with futile contempt.

"A great deal," he answered. "This is, in part, a military exercise. And Savour, in her way, is a strategist. She not only gives pleasure to the body with her work, but her work has the capacity to change the mind.

"The management of imagination is the chief necessity in taking men to war. It is also an important means of taking men to peace, and that is where Savour excels. My endeavor is to change the way the Indigenous people have lived for centuries on this land. You have no idea how useful she may be to me on this expedition."

So Savour set off with the Priest and his guard; she was charged with the task of managing the camp kitchens. Salt would remain to oversee the court kitchens, as he had before the Priest had purchased Savour.

Savour took on her tasks with joyous relief. The temporary freedom from the Princess's corrosive attacks on her was an utterly unexpected gift. The prospect of traveling in new landscapes, among unknown people, was a rare opportunity to add to the great library of her palate. The more richly she could taste, the more knowledge she would add to what she knew of the world she was inhabiting.

She was quietly proud, too, of the honor of being asked to accompany the Priest himself on the journey in which he began his magnificent task, the great work of his life, his part in restoring Paradise to earth. Savour, the only member of the company who was not an Angel, would witness the obliteration of hunger among the peoples of the New Kingdom, Angel and Indigene alike, the world as it had been in the days of Paradise.

She supervised the making of the eminently portable preserved foods that would see the Priest and his three-hundred-strong personal guard through a journey of several months, supplementing local supplies.

In addition to preserved meats, and parched sweet corn, she made hundreds of confections at the request of the Priest. He loved sweets, like all the Angels, but they were also an important element of the Angelic liturgy, symbols of the perfect fruit that had grown on the trees of Paradise, in all its eternal beauty and sweetness.

Savour packed box after box of many-colored sugar-jeweled fruit, crystallized eternal roses, and glistening buttery nut pastries buried in powdered sugar, to be eaten drowned with caramelized cream or syrups she would concoct wherever they camped.

Salt was stoic with regard to her absence—and painfully jealous—of her unexpected, if temporary, freedom. He made her promise to remember for him all the details of the regions forbidden to him. He begged her for seed samples from that unknown earth, which had once been Indigenous. The seeds, he knew, were the only way he would ever travel beyond the Angelic boundaries. If Savour succeeded in collecting them, he could still witness something unknown emerge into life.

They would travel first along the coastal route, gradually climbing into the mountains. The route was punctuated with deserted Indigenous villages, populated only by Angelic battalions. The Indigenes had been forbidden to live by the water, for fear they would rebel, reinforced by supplies and troops via the sea. They had gradually been resettled inland; the ripped-up fields and stumps of agate trees outside the walls of these villages gave them the air of tombs that had been robbed. The garrison village where they were to camp was like a stopped clock that contrasted with the cheers, commotion, and cries of "Life is Paradise" greeting the Priest's party.

Savour set to work with the battalion cook as her assistant. She sought to temper the melancholy atmosphere of this village through the sublimity of her cookery. She chose to make a dish of meat, nuts, quince, and rose wine, which at court was understood to represent yet another aspect of the union of ethereal Heaven and earth, life made paradise.

Here, though, the dish was a failure, received unenthusiastically, though perfectly executed. She was shocked to learn, for the first time, that perfection itself could fail—that the mediocre could be actively preferred to the excellent.

This was surely one of the flaws of Savour's work. Hers was always the restless, challenging food of philosophy, rarely the food of peaceful repose; she had not known the childhood dishes that gently renewed strength and prepared people for sweet sleep. She could build a cathedral, but not a house. These lonely Angels guarding the uprooted village did not want to be enchanted, but tranquilized. They wanted to imagine themselves living elsewhere. She could see and hear that they thought her work precious. It wounded her that she had not satisfied them.

She went for a walk on the beach at sunset, preoccupied by her failure. She wanted to feel the water. She entered the sea, standing ankle-deep in the waves, not one of which resembled another, one caressing her, one frisking at her ankles like a dog, one frankly trying to kill her. She tried to learn their lessons, the philosophy of the ocean.

"One wave is stone," she thought, "the next silk. One day my work does me honor, the next it disgraces me." She was so distracted by trying to absorb the teachings of the sea that she didn't hear the party of soldiers whose footsteps were muffled by the sand. She felt her head pulled back by her hair and saw a bright crescent of knife blade before she felt the metal touch her newly exposed throat.

"No one who is not of the Angels may walk on the shore," she heard one say harshly.

Savour's reaction to danger had always been a preternatural calm, as is often the case with those who are aware that though they have owned certain hours, they can never determine their fate.

She said with calibrated, purposive softness that she was the Priest Xe's cook, and had not known the shore was exclusively for Angels. Her calm calmed the soldiers. They herded her, as experienced sheep dogs marshal a stray, to the Priest's quarters.

The Priest himself emerged after a quarter of an hour, and confirmed her tale. The soldiers were awed at his appearance; they knelt before him.

The Priest put his hand on Savour's head. The face of power can be wolflike, savage, determined. In its other aspect it is radiant, rapt, beyond self-doubt or any other boundary. It subjugates not with violence, but with romance.

The Priest's ecstatic smile broke like sunrise, shedding overflowing grace.

"Savour is indeed my cook. Savour may go wherever she likes," he said. "She often forages for delicacies so that her work may refresh us—and she herself also needs a measure of refreshment from the smoke in which she works devotedly every day. I will write her a permit so that there will be no further interference with her." He silenced the soldiers utterly by himself escorting her on the path back to the shore.

Savour apologized to him for the disturbance. She summoned the self-discipline to apologize further for the inappropriately poetic food she had served to his soldiers.

"Don't concern yourself," said the Priest. "They won't remember it as long as tomorrow. It is a strange phenomenon, don't you agree, that despite the pleasure your work gives, it vanishes so quickly.

"I don't refer to the usual vulgar pleasantries about elegant food ending as no more than excrement, since those ignore the fact that its substance also becomes our flesh—our strength—our power to form a thought. And yet, we are not mesmerized by what keeps alive so much as by what may kill us. It seems the work of life disappears, while the work of death lasts forever.

"Yours is the work of making life possible—but for all your gift—for all the transforming beauty of your work—you are no more than a housekeeper on an epic scale. You are the world's wife, satisfying again and again the appetite you have just sated.

"You do not create fate. Your work is no more than an offering, a taste, sustaining life without changing it. And there lies the difference, perhaps, between a servant and a ruler. The servant will never know to what use her work is put, but the ruler knows what only God knows. He knows what will happen to his subjects tomorrow—even, it may be, the specific hour of their deaths."

A third of the art of being a woman is keeping quiet while men speak—and yet Savour would have said that we do remember pleasure—but that we remember it as we remember our lives before speech. We remember pleasure without words, in the way we live. What Savour cooked made each day remembered—and a day gone unremembered is a day unlived, lost as surely to the living as their days are to the dead.

Savour would have said if she dared, that though she did not create fates, she became at moments the conduit for the two things in creation as powerful as fate: memory and miracle.

She said nothing, though, except that she was needed again in the kitchens. Though it was still daylight, a half-moon had risen in the sky, ivory as a freshly cut apple.

They traveled a few days more on the coast; then they turned upward and inland toward the villages where the Indigenes lived. The countryside was noted for its velvety, fertile soil, where most of the grain that supplied the New Kingdom was grown. The region had been thickly forested as well, but the Angels had begun to thin out the surrounding forests; they hated the agate tree and all it symbolized for the Indigenes. Nor did they want the Indigenes to make use of the forests for secret conferences or surprise attacks.

The first villages on their route thus had a bullied look. With their neat fields, and houses well built in the folk style, they had the air of battered wives clinging to their dignity, as the Priest's party approached through avenues of tree stumps like broken teeth.

Messengers throughout the region had previously announced the impending visit of the Priest's entourage, so the village headman and a group of dignitaries were waiting to receive the Priest with the traditional black rose conserves and black rose sherbets in silver cups.

While they conferred, soldiers fanned out around the periphery of the village, and stationed themselves in parties of two at the door of each family compound. Savour was dispatched to set up her mobile kitchen, and ordered to concoct a meal impressive enough to honor the local authorities from the requisitioned stores. The village leaders made florid toasts of welcome to the Angels, which were returned by the Priest and officers of high rank.

Flushed with plenty and with wine, the village officials were dumbfounded at the end of the formalities by the announcement of the new law. They were ordered to deliver not only communal, but all private stores to the Angels.

Surplus food would now be managed for the benefit of the entire population, the Priest explained. "The Indigenes will share in the prosperity of the entire Kingdom. You will give in order to receive. We will at last be equals."

He raised his arms and spread them out in the universal embrace of Angelic prayer: "In the Paradise of our scriptures, it is promised that every good man who gives abundantly will be filled with good things. We will write our scriptures on the fields of the New Kingdom for you blessed ones to read. The ears of wheat are your keys to Paradise."

Collecting the stored grain from the village houses took two days; supplies were transported to the local mill, and put under guard. The village headman was ordered to recruit local guards to ensure that grain was not taken unlawfully from the fields. The harvest, too, would be for the common good.

The Priest's party held identical meetings at each community where they stopped, advancing from village to village over the next six days. The guards and the house searches made Savour uneasy, but she herself had often been peremptory with her staff in the effort to accomplish a task she understood better than they did. The Priest had steadfastly protected her from the dangers of the court; now he was trying at last to change the way the Indigenes were treated, too. Patience was the greatest skill those in the power of others must master.

On the seventh day, they crossed the river Song on the way to a village in the northern uplands, where they were attacked by a badly equipped band of young men. One soldier's arm was broken, but the rebels were quickly subdued. All fifteen were taken alive—one was no more than a boy—and hustled into a hastily erected tent for questioning.

Savour was touched by the sight of the brave, misguided children, and was profoundly relieved when a messenger arrived to request several trays of pastries from the extravagant supply the Priest had ordered at the outset of the journey. It was a sign of the Priest's fatherly forgiveness of these foolish and rebellious sons.

She selected some of her richest confections and syrups to seal the sweetness of reconciliation. These young men, once they understood the visionary generosity of the Priest, would surely become instruments of the coming peace between the Indigenes and the Angels. The grain collections at this village took place without further incident.

They were attacked again, though, as they approached a village even farther north; this time, the rebels were men, and one of them was lightly wounded. Again, the Angels subdued the remainder of the fighters. These were questioned, and the Reconciliation pastries sent for. The Priest was indefatigable in his refusal of revenge.

The Angelic party proceeded to the third northern village with much greater vigilance. There, the village elders greeted them hospitably, but told them the village had no grain to contribute. Their stored grain had been stolen by a band of marauding Indigenes, who had heard rumors of the collections taking place, and had determined to make a collection of their own. The Angels settled in this village for an uneasy number of days, despite the fact that it was missing supplies of grain. The Indigenous villagers were already suffering from hunger.

Nevertheless, the Priest parleyed with the village leaders, and pastries were sent for. News of Savour's well-stocked mobile kitchen traveled rapidly through the village streets. Dozens of children, cannily sent by their mothers, who knew they would be harder to resist, came in waves, advancing shyly, but silently. They came progressively closer, like ducklings in a pond when they catch sight of someone with bread. Savour began to give them food. She had no doubt that the Priest would approve; she imagined his face as it looked when he led public prayers, glowing and benevolent, blessing her efforts.

She had been trained to use the finest materials extravagantly; now she struggled to find ways to make each portion increase itself. She had plain bread baked, without the additions of sunflower or pumpkin seeds that made it delectable. She reserved the pulses she had previously used to enrich rice dishes. She nourished them with supplies that had once been mere garnishes.

The children's successful forays, rewarded with small packages of rice, sunflower seeds, potatoes, emboldened the women. They came discreetly, and singly, but they came. One woman with desperate, bitter eyes came two days in a row. Savour ladled out two cups of black beans, and a cup of nuts to pound for butter. The call to assemble sounded; the woman tried to scuttle off, but Savour knew how strict the assembly rules were enforced. She shepherded the woman toward the square, conscientiously setting a rapid pace. Still, they straggled;

the Indigenous woman she had been provisioning was too weak to keep pace.

Fifteen young men, their hands bound, stood between armed guards in the village square. Each had confessed to grain theft, and been condemned to death. She recognized some faces; these were the fifteen who had carried out the first attack.

Savour trembled; she, at whose hands so many animals had been sacrificed, had never before been in the presence of human beings about to be killed.

These were creatures whose lives spanned more and less than seasons, whose lives ended in a different way than animal lives, replaced identically by the next generation. The children of animals mastered exactly what the dead had once known; how to fly, hunt, breed. No one would ever know what these young men might learn or live, or fail to learn, if they were killed this morning. She was astonished to see them exposed there, in the village square.

"But they ate the pastries, the sweets of Reconciliation," Savour protested to the Indigenous woman who slouched beside her. The woman looked at her with contempt.

"Yes, they did. Trays and trays of them. What is it you think they do with these jeweled sweetmeats? If they want confessions from grain thieves, true or false, they feed these delights to their prisoners. As in a fairy tale, as many cakes as you could dream of. Until you are killed with honey, because they don't give you water. Some die of thirst, others confess—even when they are not guilty—just to get water in their throats. We have heard what has happened to the others who enjoyed the Priest's hospitality."

Savour suppressed a wail; she was a newborn again, torn into a world she had never imagined, where all her work, all that was excellent, might be put to evil use. Her stores were crammed with these painstakingly made, exquisite sweets, in the quantities the Priest had specifically ordered. She leaned on the Indigenous woman, suddenly weaker than her exhausted companion.

The cry went up for clemency for the young Indigenes, a clemency that depended on the Priest. According to the ritual, an altar was brought from his quarters.

He knelt there, at the feet of God, in rapt prayer. The words of his prayer were lit candles, by the light of them he would read the Divine Will. His face glowed almost golden, as he held his hands to his heart. He rocked back and forth on his knees. And then he rose, his face beatific. "I speak the word that God wills," he said. "Death."

The guards roughly removed the boys; one cried out, hoarse with outrage and despair, "Don't let me die thirsty. Give me water!"

After supper that night, the Priest called to Savour to bring him a plate of pastries. He dispensed with knife and fork, to feel the butter and honey on his fingers, and enjoy the added depth of flavor his flesh gave to the confections. His face was the face of a rapt child, tasting the sweet world on his tongue. Savour saw the miracle of innocence restored that the act of eating renews; even the most vicious criminal tastes his cake with wonder and pleasure, as if for a moment, he falls asleep peacefully at its breast.

Savour, however, had lost her innocence. She was now free of the Priest as she had never been, and in danger from him as never before, which is the effect of revealed truth.

She took risks she understood now, freely and subtly stealing from the stores, doing her utmost to hold life in as many bodies as she could. She noted the topography of the region acutely, the details of the soldiers' outposts, the depths of the rivers they crossed, with a wild animal's desperate perception. She was still and cautious, because now she was running for her life—and not only for her life. She was sharing her very body with other people now, with hundreds of people, this virgin who had never shared her body with even one.

She had seen courtly guests relish the food served at her table, but she had never seen the look of absolute fulfillment on the faces of the hungry when they had at last eaten enough. Her providence became a passion; for the first time, she felt physically, distinctly alive. She called on Heaven to rain bread upon the hungry; she prayed that the milk of Heaven would stream from her virgin breasts, so that her own body might become food.

What she was doing became rapidly known among the Indigenes, a secret they faithfully guarded. They, in their turn, with superhuman self-discipline, began to give her portions of their unique seeds, seeds they might have eaten for their own sustenance. But these were the seeds they wanted to outlive them, seeds that would carry their world into new life.

If samples of seeds were discovered in the possession of the Indigenes, the Angelic guards would toss them into the rivers; but if Savour were found with the precious seeds, the Priest might even honor her for her forethought.

The Priest had spoken with exalted sincerity on his return circuit through the New Kingdom, to village elders, diplomats, and regional governors' about the Angels' love of peace. Already, the countryside was severely short of food, but he reassured their leaders that there was ample grain in the national stores to be purchased.

As always, the price for food was labor—beyond that, when the scheme took root, there would be perfect protection from famine, for which these temporary stinging privations were the unpleasant, but temporary, price.

Even in villages that had been subdued violently, he evoked the just peace that he himself was charged to forge among them. He spoke of his pain at having been forced to meet violence with violence. Some among his audiences refused to meet his eyes, others tested a gingerly belief that the worst was over, that the innate fraternity of human beings had begun to prevail. Others saw the tenderness and familiarity with anguish in his profound and brilliant eyes, and knew he meant what he said.

Within a day of his return to the Angelic court, with the same look of gentle, mature, and knowledgeable pain, he informed his cabinet that war with a coalition of Saints and Indigenes was inevitable. He ordered the Angels to prepare for another war that was God's Will. He announced that he would offer a traditional Supplication Feast for victory in battle when the war councils were concluded.

For her part, as soon as she had put hidden what she brought back from her travels, Savour hurriedly sought out Salt. She had three urgent gifts to give him: the truth of all she had witnessed, her dire foreboding of his personal danger, and the three bags of seeds in her keeping that held the perishable knowledge and history of the Indigenes.

When she found him, he was in her place in the kitchens. He was calculating how long the kitchen's supplies of flour would last. The stores were ample, but he knew that cultivation was coming to a halt. She called to him. Salt turned around, walked to her, and embraced her, burying his head in her shoulder. She had a bizarre disorienting sense that she was remembering this embrace, instead of living it. "I know what is happening," he whispered into her shoulder.

He had already received the first and second of her gifts; the news had reached him, even behind the palace walls, of the Angels' works among the Indigenes.

When she tried to give him the third gift of the seeds, he shook his head, and pleaded that he was overburdened with work. He urgently needed her advice about the flour supplies. He would receive what she had brought after the kitchens were closed for the evening.

At the end of the day, when the moment had come, Salt said he had made a mistake in the provision books that needed correcting. He asked her to meet him in the cellars to look over the books, and she followed him, carrying the seeds.

He opened each pouch, and stared inside, as if the seeds were crystal transparencies, revealing some other world. Then he closed the pouches, kissed each one reverently, and handed them back to her. "They will be safer with you," he said. "Keep them and don't let me know where you have hidden them. You are a childless woman with hundreds of thousands of children in your hands."

"Have they taken the grain from your fields?" Savour asked him.

"Everything my family could not hide. There was a field with a fungus that they left."

"Will you have that grain brought to me?" she asked him.

"Only the desperate would find a use for it." He shrugged.

"The time may come. Besides, we can provision your family in exchange for it."

Salt agreed, and sat down on a barrel of molasses. "The time has come to teach you a kind of cooking that was not part of your apprenticeship," he said gravely.

She raised her eyebrows. "What is that?"

"The cooking of soldiers," he said. "The food of war. The art of roasting in clay pits so no smoke can be detected, the art of baking bread in shields, of fugitive meat, using spears as skewers."

"Where did you learn those skills?" she asked.

"I am a soldier," he said. "I have been training with the Saints since I was eleven years old."

A great stillness entered the room as if they had both plunged underwater. He had given his life into her hands as certainly as he had the precious seeds.

At periods when every hour is an uncertainty, lovers who may never have embraced in times of peace seek repose in each other. Salt and Savour were surrounded by treachery; the sense of trust they felt in each other was stronger than any romance. They needed to tell the truth as they needed water; they drew strength from the sense that when they were together they would neither harm each other nor be harmed. Their lovemaking was a form of telling the truth. They constructed a love, and sheltered in their mutual creation as if it were a house.

Savour had never before been with a man, and although the pleasure was never as precise as solitary lovemaking, holding Salt in her arms was a greater wonder—like holding a being that was simultaneously a child, an animal, and a god.

They did not have much time to be lovers; every day was more dangerous for Salt; Indigenes were being arrested on suspicion of collaborating with the Saints, and at any moment his time might come. Others had indeed slipped away and gone underground. Salt's years of trustworthy service in the employ of the Angels appeared to give him some immunity. But his impeccable reputation also gave him the opportunity to leave while it was possible.

He would not tell her the day, or anything precise about his plans; he wanted her ignorant if she were interrogated. He was so possessed by his passion to protect her that he failed to realize—even to imagine—that she was withholding valuable information she had gleaned from traveling with the Priest for the same reason.

Salt would not permit her even to guess which of the kitchen staff or courtiers sympathized with the Saints. "There is something, though, that directly affects you, that you must be told. The Saints are of course aware of our bond, in much more detail, I am sure, than anyone else here at court. The Angels spend their energies in controlling us, not in observing us; the lives of Invisibles belong to the masters, and as for us, all Indigenes are assumed to be both their enemies and their inferiors.

"The Saints are even more keenly aware of how uniquely you are placed to destroy the Priest—which they believe—and they may be right—will make the Angels' war impossible to carry out. I know you will be asked to poison him. And I want to tell them your answer before the question is asked with force, or in any way that frightens you. Would you kill him?"

Salt asked her this in the direct way they talked to each other. It was a question about the properties of her nature, about what was possible to her. They had worked so often together in the storerooms; now his question was about what furnished Savour.

"My answer is yes." Savour gazed directly at him. "I would. I will never forget what I have seen him do. And so my answer is also no. I will not—because I know that killing him would destroy me with him.

"All I have trained for is to put creation into my hands. This craft has been something different for me than for you. It is my mother.

"It gave me life. It is my teacher. I have followed it from one day into the next. It has shaped a history for me, which most Ghosts must live without. It gave me a human life, a life I can give, but not take.

"Death is present always in what we do in this work—but as sacrifice, not killing. There are warriors. But I am not one. I cannot use my own human life to take a human life.

"If I dared, I would bite his jugular with my own teeth. But it is forbidden to those born under the sign of sacrificed Souraya, the stars of the Knife. If one of us killed him, even that could not stop him. It would add to his power; it would make others become him."

"You consider him human?" Salt asked.

"Yes. And to say so is more terrible than any blood anathema. Because to say so is to know what I am."

"Many people may be killed before he dies." Salt turned his hands over as if he were holding a thousand unseen lives in his palms.

"I can only tell you it is as if I am playing chess with a powerful opponent. He has already claimed the power of death. I cannot use it as ably as he can. He is a great killer. He will defeat me. I know it."

Salt bowed his head, seeing her dead. "Then this is a risk you must not take."

"I must act within my limits," she continued, half-whispering as she shredded cold roast meat. Even the Angels were eating frugally now.

"I am an Invisible. What I know how to do is to gauge an appetite and to disappear in satisfying it.

"I can fight him only by making something else come to life. It is all I know how to do. I must bring him into relationship with his own actions. His own actions must hunt him down. His own hunger must devour him.

"We have a Supplication Feast to cook in three weeks. You have made this kind of banquet for the court before I arrived. Since I myself have never experienced the making of this kind of feast, I will have the scope to conceive something original. I shall make a revelation—in my own way—without using torture.

"I shall set the truth on the table, even before the Priest. Though I think he will no longer be capable of recognizing it. Tell the Saints that I invite them to dinner."

It was not long after this conversation that their parting day came. Salt wordlessly began to make a compact bundle of clothes. When she saw him gather up the implements he had used to teach her the dishes of soldiers and fugitives—the leather bag to ferment yogurt and cheese on the run, the spear that darkness transformed into a roasting spit, for chunks of meat and vegetables, the shield in which bread was baked, she knew. "It's tonight?" she asked. He nodded.

She looked at him covertly, cherishing the beauty of his body—the reality of his slight paunch, and thick bull-like legs. The eyes brown with changing glints of green that moved in the iris like river currents. The great trunk and branches of spine and vertebrae. The unexpectedly fine hands, on one of which glinted the thin silver ring of the Indigene.

She could idealize nothing about his body—it was flesh instead, that could only be loved and mourned. She was unable to believe, as she was unable to believe in the Angels' one inadequate, murderous God, that this being, this person, could undergo the sacrament of death, the transubstantiation into dust.

"Give me a day, and then report me missing." They stood supernaturally still, like animals sensing the presence of a hunter. They looked at each other with an absolute gaze—the gaze of someone looking out on the unfathomable sea from the deck of a ship. The children Savour might have had—their children—died in her eyes, as she faced him.

A wild resentment surged in him. Love had not failed them. Life had. Why could he not be a god himself, go to war in some other form, fight in battles where defeat mattered only to men, and live an endless life with her in some other place at the same time?

Instead, the gods had granted them the gift of loss—the only means of rendering immortal the loves of the Dying Ones, as the gods call humans.

So Salt set out on his ever-narrowing path, and went stealthily into the darkness, while Savour drew up plans for the eleventh dinner in her repertoire, the Feast of the True and False.

Separately they woke together. From now on, they slept with each other and without each other, living with and without each other, embracing and vanishing at the same moment, enveloped in their mortal love.

She gave him two days, as long as she dared, before she informed the Priest of Salt's peculiar absence. She was careful to show herself unconcerned, but impeccably dutiful in relaying the information. "Perhaps some concern has held him back in his village. I'm sure he will make his way here to do his part in the making of the Supplication Feast."

The Priest's expression of pleasant concern did not alter. "I will send an envoy to his village to see if he needs assistance of any kind."

And he did so. Every morning now before dawn, outside the palace walls, a group of skeletally thin women gathered to wait for the court linen to be brought down. They vied with each other for the chance to clean that day's laundry, a task prized for the thin gruel left behind in the water in which the linen had been starched. They struggled to sustain themselves by drinking the milky residue of the courtly garments, and they brought with them fresh rumors of the condition of the countryside, the only news most of the palace personnel received at this period. Women moved through the country unchallenged for the most part. They were too weak to threaten the soldiers, and the court could not do without their domestic labor as long as they were capable of it.

Five days after Salt's disappearance these women were the source of reports that troops of marauding Angels had razed the rings of Indigenous villages within a fifty-mile radius of the city of Paradise. Salt's village would be among them if the tales were true.

Savour often had business with the farmers of those neighboring villages, and could find a convenient pretext for an afternoon away to discuss contracts or commission certain crops. She set out for Paradise, and hired a man to take her the rest of the way into the ring villages and fields to see for herself if the reports were true.

When she saw the smoke as they approached the first of the villages, Savour remembered herself as a child, as a huntress. This time, though, she hunted not in forest nor lake nor sea, but through clusters of ruined houses, and what had been cultivated fields and orchards.

The uprooted corpses of agate trees obstructed her path. There had been no mercy for things growing. She passed a village cemetery, and saw that the Angels had even killed the dead. Everywhere graves gaped open and the ground was littered with a terrible mosaic of bones. It was as if the Angels had feared the dead would rise and defend their people.

She searched for living beings, but found none.

In many houses, the Angels had not had been obliged to do the work of killing; the inhabitants had starved before the massacre, and their neighbors had been too weak to bury them; or worse, had eaten the remains. She saw bodies missing buttocks that had been cut off for steaks. There was a heart carved on a wall in one house with the message, "We died in March, but send our love. Mother and Father."

She saw families too emaciated even to serve as meat, their mouths open, feeding on nothing. It was useless to think of her cat, Candle. Someone must have eaten him months ago.

She made her way across the bridge over the narrow river to the compound of Salt's family. Bodies, the shapes of what had days before been his sisters and brothers, their husbands and wives, were strewn around the courtyard, like toys a monster had played with. Salt's family had not died slowly of starvation, but had been cut down. She saw his twin brother and sister, her child in her arms. The child's rigid mouth was fixed on its mother's nipple.

She gasped as a black-winged corpse ascended overhead into flight—the Angel of Death. But it fell to earth as quickly as it had soared upward. Two vultures were contesting the body of Salt's mother, one on each shoulder. It was their struggle to feed on her that had lifted her into flight. This, then, was the lost Paradise of the Angels, the paradise they had made of life.

Then, alone among the butchered bodies of the people she had eaten and drunk with, Savour died with them. One can die, as she did then, although her life did not come to its end.

Some gods came into her, and she began involuntarily to sing a funeral song. Words she had never spoken poured from her, as blood that cannot be staunched gushes from a mortal wound. The stanzas came, breaking one after another, wave after wave, and she was helpless to be silent, as a child inside a woman in labor is forced to be born. She sang:

"Unknown gods we drove away, we invoke you.
You who are not named, but are not nameless,
Pardon our arrogance. Return to us.
Let the myriad altars we destroyed surge up again,
Ocean of gods, and lave the world with generous prayer,
Restore, we beseech you, your manifold blessings.

Let no one be called infidel unless
He seeks to harm another.
Let the curse of idolater be reserved
Only for the self-righteous,
Whose tyrannous faith brings war,
And permits any cruelty
In the service of its self-deity.
Let the charge of blasphemy fall
Only on the self-anointed,

Ventriloquists of divinities.
Once again, let no god be abominated,
Declared a devil by another's partisans,
Let none be despised, but all honored.

Terminus, god of border markers, return from Rome,
Teach us again our limits. Mark off the finite from the infinite,
Let no man claim the deaths he causes are the will of God,
That the bodies at his feet are the butcheries of angels.
Show the women their own deaths in the tortures they inflict—
Their children will tremble at the sight of them,
And drown on their own mothers' milk.
Abattur, come with your scales from Persia;
We need your judgment.
Anat of Canaan, goddess of war, wear your ostrich feather crown;
You alone knew the purpose of war, not to destroy other creatures,
Each born as it is, already in its shroud—
But to fight death.
Pattini, Lady born of a heavenly mango, share with the starving
Your miraculous rice, protect us from epidemics,
Both those we endure, and those we devise.

O Ptah, who created us in Egypt on a potter's wheel,
Make us serviceable and lovely.
Nu-gua, who made us in China of yellow clay,
Do not shatter us.
Huracan, who made us in America of cornmeal,
You who live simultaneously in eternity and time,
Watch over us in Heaven,
Watch over us on earth,
Watch over us in Hell.
Quat, who made us on his island out of boredom,
Inspire us to give our stories better endings.
Imrat, who fashioned us in India of butter,
And in the richness of divinity made other gods,
Remind us that it is not our limitations that are sacred.

Lowalangi, great guardian from Indonesia,
You speak of us tenderly as your pigs,
And teach us we are incapable of worship,
Until we see ourselves a thousand ways.
Nanse, Our Lady of Sumeria, Queen of Divination,
Tell us the awful truth—that this world is a faithful record
And clear interpretation of our dreams.
Omeototl, glorious Aztec, born of your own thought,
Keep us unfinished ones ever-thinking,
Revealed always by what we have caused to exist.

Patrons and Givers of Gifts, we summon you.
Juturna of the springs and wells,
Quench our thirst.
Egres, who first gave turnips to the Finns,
If we scorn your gift,
We repudiate the world.
Dua, god of daily grooming,
Reviver of mankind,
Patron of the perfume and the sacred bath,
It is your vocation also to wake the dead,
Your therapy through which they remember
How to use their limbs. Remind us of the
Resurrections hidden in our days,
Celestial incarnate in quotidian.
Cao Guo-Jiu, patron of actors,
Of all that is both true and false,
Sustain us in belief,
Protect us with doubt.
Hintubuhet, Androgyne,
Maker of Marriage,
Butterfly of both sexes,
Bless those who seek devoted love.
Tenenit, refresh us with the golden beer
Brewed first in your sky-blue lapis vat.
Marungogere, maker of genitals,

Thank you.
Arhats, enlightened ones,
Lend us your heavenly eyes,
So we might glimpse other worlds,
Read other scriptures, so those who
Know nothing of the earth they inhabit
Will not dare again to speak to us of Heaven.
Return to us, Pantheon,
Abundant in divinity,
Without you, we cannot be human.

Winged Nari, from the Heaven of dead children,
We petition you: have mercy on us.
Ran of Scandinavia, goddess of the drowned,
Lift the breathless gently into your nets,
Pray for us.
Freya, weep for us your golden tears.
Mayan Ixtab, Goddess of Suicides,
Show those in torment your inhuman mercy;
With compassion beyond blessing,
Receive them in your Paradise.
Greek Eirene,
Whose liturgies were never stained with blood,
Grant us peace."

This song is still sung, among those who celebrate the feast of the Cauldron, during the first night when that constellation is visible in the sky.

Savour, reared Invisible, succeeded in making her way back to the court undetected; she knew it was important for her to take her place in the kitchens, and to know absolutely nothing she was not told.

She thought of Salt, standing before the tormented bodies of his kin; she made of her steady, expressionless work that night a cabin where no one could touch him. The evening meal was nothing out of the ordinary, but she dedicated it as a funeral sacrifice for the destroyed villages, and for Salt's family above all.

A few days later, the Priest himself came to the kitchens, in the informal way he used to enjoy. He asked if she had had any word from Salt, and when she shook her head, he told her he now feared the worst—that Salt had abandoned them to make common cause with the Saints and the Indigenous rabble that were their allies.

Savour served for a convincing expression. The Priest must look at her forehead, eyes, and mouth, and be certain that he still knew more about Savour than she did about herself.

She told him that she hoped it was not true that Salt had abandoned the work for which he had such a strong gift. She hoped he would not sacrifice his life in a cause unworthy of him. She said that she would make that her personal supplication to weave among the supplications of the great traditional antebellum banquet of the Angels.

So for those who could read it, she began to write the book of wheat and curd, and to articulate the scriptures of cinnamon, saffron, and green almond. It was the most difficult dinner she had ever devised. The Priest must not realize that it was the dinner of his betrayal. And Savour must not be paralyzed by her old debt to the Priest, who had shown her nothing but favor and kindness.

The Banquet of Supplication, Savour's Feast of True and False, was a dinner in which nothing presented at table was what it seemed. It was a dinner of artful deception.

Each of the courses represented a quadrant of the New Kingdom, and served as a votive offering for the unity of all the Angelic territories.

Fifty small green-throated doves were set in nests made of crisp sautéed noodles for the first course. They were a variety of bird that could be found only in the southwest. Savour's cooking had always been a natural history of the lands where she found herself. But the doves, molded of white and green cheese, designed to form a sauce melting in accord with the rhythm of their consumption, also were a code, as the emblem of peace, that the southwest contained no military camps she knew of, was thought to be secure, and left undefended.

With the next course, celebrating the rivers region of the north-west, she sent out a course of fish, whose bodies were enrobed in twenty delicate layers of pancake, with olives for eyes. Striated ribbons of pounded greens gave them the illusion of swimming through rippling water—and the attentive now knew how many boats patrolled the rivers.

Racks of succulent pork ribs made out of the crackling sheets of dried bean curd disclosed the number of garrisons in the east.

Savour kept her tour de force for the end; servers wheeled in a table with a portrait of the New Kingdom and its territories executed in sugar. There were reproductions of important buildings, and as close to a contour map as possible of all the territories, done in colored sculpted sugar, with the Three Wishes Peaks towering over the table, and chocolate waterfalls pouring from its pinnacles. The guests broke off bits of the Angelic empire and sweetened their mouths with the walls of the Angelic palace.

Thus the Indigenes and the Saints were able to gauge where below the Three Wishes Peaks they could unite their forces.

We were told later that the Saints had begun constructing their rope bridge over the dizzying abyss that separated the two countries by forming a human bridge over the sheer drop. The first materials for building the bridge were passed over a chain of men, blinkered like horses, linked arms to legs, swaying over the abyss. It seems impossible, but no one has yet contradicted the story. The Indigenous guerrilla groups then joined the fierce Alpine army of Saints.

But perhaps the God of Battle, terrifying because he knows no fixed allegiance, favored the Indigenes that day in some measure because of the ingenuity of Savour.

She supplied the Angelic armies with bread tainted with the flour from Salt's diseased acre. The Angels found themselves fighting shadows. There were many Angels who saw three wavering soldiers where there was only one, thanks to the hallucinatory flour. Others were wrapped in visions, and still others were overthrown by nausea alone. The Priest himself was taken prisoner when he was kneeling and shielding his eyes in prayer, unable to defend himself from the multitudes of Indigenous dead who had risen to fight alongside the living army.

He was brought back to the Angelic court, now under the control of the Saints and the Indigenous, and placed under arrest. The Princess, her father, and other significant Angels were placed under guard in their own quarters, awaiting trial. All access to them, even by their servants, was severely restricted. They would have no further need of a banquet cook.

A number of their workers, even their Invisibles, were offered their freedom, and the chance at new work on the other side of the mountain if they chose. Most took up the offer, and lived their lives as the free people they had never been.

It never occurred to the Priest, nor to the Princess, that Savour might have had any role in their defeat. She existed for them, like all Invisibles, only insofar as she served their needs. And while the Angelicals had grasped the role of privation and scarcity in ruling a subject population, they had never conceived that defeat might also come through satiation.

Death, ironically, came to the Priest through his famous fastidious appetite. Even if Savour herself was no longer permitted to cook for the Angelical courtiers, he still requested that the kitchen reproduce some of the fine dishes for which she had been famous. The elegant food gave him pleasure, and perhaps momentarily put the taste of power back in his mouth. His jailors satisfied their own caprices to indulge him.

This was doubly cruel, as the Priest had been used to indulgence by command, not caprice. The intermittent satisfaction of his appetites made even his pleasure a humiliation.

In the end, it was a favorite dish that killed him. He must have died very quickly after he picked up his knife and fork to cut into one of the game pies that he craved. One could imagine from the fang marks on his throat that the pit viper he released from its concealment under the pastry struck the nearest exposed flesh with furious speed.

No one accused Savour, as she was no longer responsible for his fare, though some said perhaps the Princess had actually succeeded in learning this dish from Savour, and had added her own touch. Others disagreed; the Princess had always used the labor of others to carry out her wishes; and besides, the disappearance of the Priest was a great convenience for the new rulers.

It was only a short time, perhaps a week after the Priest's death, that we saw Salt again. Savour had been kneading bread dough that morning. Her strong, certain hands shaped and caressed the chaotic, ragged mass as if she were forming a human body from clay.

She had set an array of foods on the table, each dish, down to the smallest detail, made from her own hands. She poured a garnet-colored wine into a carafe the shape of an hourglass. The offering was simple, but still a feast in those days when the country was just beginning to recover from the Angelic famine. There was a round of warm bread, salt she had harvested herself, fresh butter, agate butter, cheese, ripe apricots, and a plate of black rose jam, as if she were expecting someone. She did not seem surprised to see him hobbling across the courtyard.

He was pale, and skeletally thin, and his eyes glowed in contrast to his translucent skin like candles in a paper lantern. He walked with a painful, lurching gait, as if the only victory he was now capable of was to take another step.

She did not run to him, but stood in the doorway, still and utterly quiet, as one stands over the cradle of a sleeping child. Salt was equally grave and quiet; he walked toward her. He looked neither to the right nor the left, but only straight into her eyes, as if only their light were supporting him and keeping him from falling.

He greeted no one else, and did not even seem to see the Indigenous child from the ring villages that had survived the Angelic massacre, and was now Savour's apprentice.

Savour stepped across the threshold and took him in her arms, embracing him with infinite delicacy as hands cup a flame.

"Are you hungry—my . . . dear?" she asked him. Salt smiled. Never during their entire acquaintance had Savour spoken an endearment; the language of attachment was a presumption forbidden to Invisibles; it was pruned from their vocabulary. She had almost winced with the effort of the tender phrase.

"I'm as weak as a newborn," he said. "All the way here I dreamed of eating bread from your hands."

They went inside and sat down at the table she had prepared for him. He ate slowly and attentively, as if he were an explorer approaching the shore of a new country. Savour noticed that he kept his left hand cupped tenderly over a round dome of bread, as if it were a child's head, or a woman's breast, even as he ate with his right hand.

"There is more," she said to him, but he moved closer to her, and rested his head on her breast, in luxuriant peace, delivered of the need to keep vigil.

No one ever saw him again. The next day he was gone. When I asked Savour where the Indigenous man was who had eaten with her yesterday, she replied, "In Paradise."

"He left for the city?" I asked.

"No," she said. "In the true Paradise."

"He died?" I asked. "And you buried him alone?"

"No," she said. "He was dead when he came to me." She had prepared for him the Twelfth of her Twelve feasts: the Feast of the Living and the Dead.

"Those who have mastered the art of the Twelfth can call someone beloved back to life, like a smoldering ember. They can briefly clasp hands between earth and Heaven. At that moment, the living and the dead can exchange a gift. But not for long."

There were those who believed her and those who did not. I saw him—I thought. But I was a child, and she was the adult who made the world for me. Such adults have always a magical power to instill their beliefs in the children apprenticed to them.

But what I did see, without illusion, was the constellation that appeared in the heavens some fifteen years later, after Savour had departed at her own request, to cook for a governor across the border in the country of the Saints.

She gave me most of the magnificent tureens inscribed to her by the teachers of her youth, though she would not part with her knives and three leather pouches she kept as close to her as if they were three infants. They were seeds she intended to have planted across the border—the heritage of the Indigenes, she said, that would outlive their ruined land.

They say that the constellation of the Cauldron appeared when these seeds took root throughout the territory of the Saints, as if the seeds also took root in the form of stars. Whatever the truth of that, I know that the constellation exists, and can be seen by others in the night skies of summer.

The men who made the heavens for us to see have filled them with gods, warriors, heroes, and victors, swords, stallions, and crowns. They have even arranged our eyes, so that these beings are what we find in the patterns of the stars. We see what we believe the heavens show us.

We might just as well trace the outlines of other objects, other creatures. You will be told the constellation of the Cauldron does not exist—but they also declared Savour at her own birth to be Invisible.

Savour had been born under the constellation of the Knife, the star of those unrecognized on earth, whose life stories are told falsely. Her own constellation, the Cauldron, is the star that guides us to question the tales told us about the heavens themselves. There is more to see than we have been permitted; there are heavens unseen behind the heavens of our perceptions.

Savour was a slave, a woman, and a cook. She was not a hero. You must say that she failed.

She saved few lives, though her great yearning was to save all.

She was able to bring only one of her dead back to life, and then only for a few hours.

She did manage to preserve the roots, rices, and wheats of the Indigenes. When the wind inclines the blond stalks of grain on summer afternoons, parents tell their children that it is kneeling like a bridegroom before Lady Savour.

But she was no messiah. She did not feed the entire earth, or wipe the tears from the eyes of all the starving. The world is still a world of beggars, who dream of dishes that they will never taste. But Savour is in Heaven, hungering to feed them—and only in Heaven can dreams be eaten.

If by any chance she is not in Heaven, then you and I will never be. If there is no room among the stars for mortals—for slaves and beggars, and the ones who yearn to feed them, the ones whose passion to feed the world remains unrequited—then there is no hope for you or for me.

Savour pours and pours her stars of grain over the earth, and we lift up our hands to share in that glittering, imagined abundance that we have yet to taste. They say that some of those stars take root on earth when they fall. They are the seeds of what we call miracles. They become the food without which our hearts die. They are the source of Heaven's weightless fruit—justice, mercy, love. We are the only soil in which they grow. Through us they become bread in reality. Feast on these, precious souls, and rejoice.

THE PROVERBS OF SAVOUR

The entire world can be seen within a kitchen bowl.
There are no truly childless women; there are no truly childless men.
Is there treachery greater than that of the host whose guests do not survive his dinner?
The wise anticipate at every dinner table the guest who will alter their fates.
The way food tastes is the first language: the primal alphabet of life and death.
All gods exist for their believers.
To insist that God is one is an arrogant underestimation of the divine.
Even one God metamorphoses.
Today's God of mercy is tomorrow's God of genocide.
The proper reply to the divine "I Am" is "What?"
All the elements of the universe—fire, earth, air, and water—are assembled in a loaf of bread.
The good hunter always remembers that he himself is edible.
The great hunter is the one who knows how to keep an animal alive.
The gift of brilliance in cookery flows from those who have never tasted mother's milk.
The great cook is the one whose food tastes not only of nature, but of human nature. And of divine glory.
A people's cuisine is its imagination of the world.
What a people eats is what it lives by—its economy in the mouth, made edible.
Cookery is a morality.
The table is the bed where dozens take their pleasure together.
A superb dinner is both a description of this world, and a message from the gods, a taste of paradise.
A seed is the emblem of the world to come.
The habitual expression on a man's face shows what he tastes like to himself.
There are five vocations that must be forbidden to those who have a taste for killing: butcher, soldier, hunter, king, mother.

The soul of a child persisting out of season within an adult is the source of all the world's tyranny.

The good mother is the one who does not destroy as much life as she gave.

The structure of a face is founded on the language a person speaks.

What we taste is the vocabulary of our first language.

The strangest of all desires, stranger even than the love of killing, is the lust to be hated.

We can recognize truth in our encounters with what we cannot create.

One can range the wide world within a skillet.

THE BOOK OF RAIN

THE THIRD CONSTELLATION: THE PARADISE NEBULA

TO THE MEMORY OF SAMUEL PLIMSOLL

The principle involved here is that the centre of power is identical with the centre of truth.

—VÁCLAV HAVEL

Once someone has tilted your head back and poised it at the right angle, you can plainly see the constellations of the Knife and the Cauldron in the seasons when they are bright. The Paradise Nebula, though, is a constellation that disappears and reappears, as the generations orbit through the ages. If you live at the wrong moment, or on the wrong fragment of the earth, you will not see these stars of fortune. They change position; they change eras; and their outline is so distinctive, that the entire cluster of stars seems, paradoxically, an illusion.

First, a group of stars appears, in the shape of a bird with a woman's head, its body made of night, its head and wings of stars. It moves swiftly across the sky, wheels, and hovers. A trembling rose of stars appears in the sky. And then a stem, diamond by diamond, and then a bush covered with sparkling blooms—and finally, on the cluster's outer rims, an orchard rich with what resembles fruit. The shimmering bird plummets into this celestial garden, and disappears.

Those fruits and these roses are not like the ones known here on earth. A terrestrial rosebush or cherry tree is a phenomenon of archetypal beauty, beautiful in ensemble. There each bloom or fruit shares the form and pattern of the other. In Heaven's garden, though, each single flower and fruit has individual features, as unrepeatable as human faces.

It is as if they have reached some new level of creation, some superabundance of existence. For an hour after this garden has formed in Heaven in all the colors of the spectrum, its fruit falls, a rain of jewel-colored starry leaves, and petals, and brilliant fruits, as you might see in the glass of a kaleidoscope. And then they float softly upward, in new configurations, and create a paradise utterly unlike the one that fell. This continues for an hour, until there occurs a spectacular rain of blue and gold stars. Then the constellation disappears, as if washed away, except from the minds of those who have seen it; they, in their turn, put it into the minds of those who have not.

Those who have not seen it, out of luck in time and space, deny that it exists. I can assure you though, in all honesty, that I have seen it, both with my own eyes, and with the eyes of others. It happened that during my time on the Peninsula the Paradise Nebula was visible.

I was employed there in the household of the man who became the most famous of the Peninsula's thirteen governors. This was Governor General Jarre. I was an eyewitness to the dramatic events that are the backdrop of his legend, a story that now periodically vanishes and reappears, like the Paradise Nebula.

The people of the Peninsula had successfully revolted, generations before, against their king, who ruled by divine right. But though they were strong, they were only a faction, and although they had killed the old king, they could not prevail against their loyalist fellow subjects, who preferred their traditional government, and enthroned a fresh king to maintain it.

The Peninsulans were driven across the border to the land they now inhabit. There, the decrease in the area of land they could inhabit and defend was compensated for by two superb deepwater ports, which shaped the Peninsulans as a trading people, and increased the yearning for the tantalizing worlds that lay beyond their own. For while no man wants to die, no one wants to live in a land he cannot ever leave. The contours of their new land gave them rich forests, fine grazing lands, and, as is so often the case, a new religion.

I am a traveler, having never settled in one land. I have had many opportunities to observe the rich variety of forms through which men perceive the sacred. I remember the holy liturgy in a country inhabited by former slaves in which the worshippers were kidnapped by God, and as they ritually struggled, screamed, and writhed, were imbued both with the horror of abduction, and with a power far greater than the merchants who sold them and the masters who held them in captivity could ever have possessed.

In another land, I participated in the cycle of festivities of a people who were possessed by a single god, a divinity who bitterly resented and persecuted all the gods who preceded him in this people's reverence. I saw bloody celebrations at which many of these helpless people, entangled by all the gods competing for their share of worship, were killed during the theomachies.

In yet another country, where by custom each woman was the property of up to five husbands, the devout were, oddly, mostly women. In their temples, God floated above them in starry domes, as if He were the first being they glimpsed upon waking. There, the face of God was that of the most tender, gentle husband imaginable, His arms outstretched in an embrace.

Do not mistake me, I am a believer absolute, but there is something undeniably singular in the ways God is revealed to men. The God of the Peninsulans, too, had his own characteristics and peculiarities of worship.

The Peninsulans were a group, who in their former country, formed almost a caste, of businessmen, craftsmen, tradesmen, but also at the lower reaches, peasants, peddlers, and thieves. They were never admitted into the aristocracy, either through their efforts, or through carefully wrought marriages. God, though, at the moment of his choosing, revealed himself to them as a king, infinitely more powerful than his earthly symbol, and with a much more exclusive court in the form of his church.

It was the monarch God who chose knights, the knights of perfect faith, whose royal souls were ennobled for all eternity. For the Peninsulans, there could be no cliques or factions, for their titles were granted by the King of Kings.

They proved they were truly of his elect by submitting to the body of Holy Peers a kind of spiritual patent, outlining not family ancestry, but spiritual ancestry, a description of the moment of election, and an account of all the examples and proofs of God's conversation and the favor that had followed. They too in their turn acquired the right to judge the authenticity of the marks of God's royalty.

Their King was so much greater than the mortal sovereign that they came to despise the earthly king, his presumption to grant privileges, and all his potentates.

They abandoned, too, the special consideration given to women at the old court, where birth could make a destiny. They realized that it was God who granted estates, God Omnipotent who instituted rank, stature that could never be challenged or altered, made before ancestry, before the creation of humanity itself, utterly outside of time. They came to scorn monarchy and all its trappings with an almost reflexive contempt. The most venerable monarchy was no more than arriviste in their conception.

Governor Jarre had all the attributes of one who had received God's crown. He had been given wealth with which to honor God, in the form of property, a son, and two daughters to devote to God's service, and in himself, those peculiarly magnetic facial features, a golden air of merited success, that made him look like a vision God had had of mankind.

He was a man so perfect in his faith, so at one with God's plan for the world, that at the famous border battle of Saldava, he smiled in unearthly exaltation during combat. His face, they said, was both grave and radiant when he had the first reports of the enemy casualties. Even when he received the news of the heavy losses of his own troops, he said with an exultant air, "Hallowed be thy name! Maker of War and of

Peace! The living do praise Him and also the dead! There will be souls in Heaven today!"

After arrangements were made for the prisoners, and the ceremony of surrender had taken place, Jarre gave instructions for the burial of the dead. He himself walked the battlefield to pay his respects. I was with him as he walked reflectively among the corpses, many of whom might have been his own sons. It was moving to see his face as he gravely and compassionately absorbed the sense of these men's fates. His expression could only be described as fatherly. "Many souls," he said, "have this day been delivered from their fear of death." He was a man who knew nothing of despair.

He was well rewarded for his victory at Saldava. He was given a site on a bluff where he built a stone house nearly in Heaven, and lived as if he had always lived there. It was surrounded by terraced vineyards, and he bred there the renowned race horses of the Peninsulans, the Peninsulan Smaraldians.

His service was also recognized with the gift of a marble villa on the seashore, with a perfect view of the summer boat races known as the Angel Flights, when the graceful Peninsulan schooners race against specially trained birds.

The end of those races is memorable for the sight of the fifty schooners returning to harbor at dusk, while overhead, the birds, laced together with the thinnest gold and silver chains, fly in the formation of a three-branched candelabra. They rise toward Heaven, returning the light to God that He granted the world. It is a marvelous celebration of man's perpetual task to yoke nature in glory to the spirit of God.

Little delighted Jarre more than those races; during the season, he would host parties, pouring wine from his own vineyards for his guests, gesturing from the great marble veranda with a poignant intensity of attention, as if he were in some kind of race himself. He and his dear friend and former comrade-in-arms, Admiral Annan, watched the contests together, leaning out over the water, their elbows on the balustrade, rapt as schoolboys drinking in the prowess of the men they hoped to become.

The women of the Peninsulans in those days were as obedient as it is possible to make women be. I do not know if it is still so, since I have not lived among that people for many years.

The Peninsulans held that the world had been inhabited only by men and creatures of the natural world until one man was seduced by a serpent and metamorphosed in his ecstasy into a woman. Hence their physical inferiority, an emblem of their inability to govern themselves—and the shape of their sex, bifurcate as a serpent's tongue, emblem of their duplicity.

They could achieve salvation only through the men who governed them, through the holy influence of their lost masculinity. For the sake of their salvation, they must suffer as God willed; it was forbidden even to alleviate their pain in childbirth. In any case, that God had ordained these terrible childbirths that killed so many of them, as well as so many of the babies struggling to be born, was proof of how far beyond God's kingdom they were.

Harsh justice was administered to women who defied God's decree with satanic opiates. The people of the Peninsula still talked in hushed tones of the case of Lark Inchin, a woman who was discovered to have brewed syrups against pain in labor, cunningly leaving bundles of mixed herbs for the concoction in a vineyard so she could not identify the women who used these drugs. She was sentenced to death, by a means specific to punishment of this crime.

The usual death penalties on the Peninsula were beheading for men, as a sign that they had betrayed God's gift to them of reason. Women were forced to leap from a cliff so that dying itself became a submission to the commands of men, and thus restored them to the obedience they had flouted. Lark Inchin, though, and other criminals of her ilk, was saddled and bridled, and ridden to the port, where she was hung from the leather bridle she wore.

The more talented among women had preserved in themselves a splinter of their original manhood. Even those, though, were empty vessels. The matchless Peninsulan doctors and scientists had determined that men were like the Smaraldian stallions they had studied. Males contained in their seed the invisible bodies and souls of the children the females received of them. Hence the description at races of colts as "by" the father, "out of" the mother. Only the childishly irrational attempted to contradict them, more out of a jealousy of the stature of the learned scholars than from any real intellectual dissent.

I am an avid student of anthropology, and have been fortunate to pursue my interests in many countries. I observed a curiosity on the Peninsula, similar to a phenomenon I have seen in other societies where women are fully governed by men.

It is this: that the most desirable women come to look like some creature or plant or even local craft that is highly prized, as if they are a kind of supreme incarnation of the national economy. Thus, among the Vanians, whose lands retain much of their primeval forest, and who make their houses and ships of that wood, the women look like trees, astoundingly tall, with thick leafy hair, and the balance that makes them famous dancers. Among the Roques, those great herders and cheese makers, nothing is more sought after than a woman with a dairy beauty, with creamy skin and lush breasts. The ceramicists of arid Buntu markedly prefer women with small waists and enormous hips, exactly like water jars.

This happens naturally, it seems, as the ruling men choose women who by accident evoke what they value, and after several generations, a pool of these women is bred for these qualities and marries intricately with other men in the aristocratic circles.

As for the Peninsulans, their standard of beauty for women was equine. The beauties among them looked like the fine Smaraldian racehorses, with long curving jaws, shining hair, and huge long-lashed dark eyes.

Jarre's wife had the Smaraldian looks, though she was not of a distinguished family. She had never lived in the fishing villages by the docks, but carried the honking accent of some grandmother who had.

In repose, her face was beautiful. Her carriage was perfect, even under the weight of the crown all Peninsulan wives wore to symbolize that they were princesses of God's court. But her nasal snarl and coarse vowels when she was speaking shaped her face into a sneer so that even when uttering endearments, she appeared to curse. Still, it was often the case that a woman with that physiognomy would find herself stabled, as it were, with her betters.

In any case, Jarre was impervious to her speech. All women's speech was a kind of instinctual lyric, as unrelated to reason as birdsong. If his wife cawed, her speech was simply a rougher version, an enhancement of the sweeter music of his daughters. Their son, already a junior minister, and still unmarried, lived in an adjacent seaside villa, when he was not abroad on mission.

They had twin daughters still at home, whose names were Dolphin and Rain. Like all Peninsulan girl children, they were given names drawn from the natural world, fruits, flowers, elements of landscape, as living prayers for grace and fertility, prophesies of their future embedded in their names.

And like all Peninsulan girl children, they were trained in the domestic arts, in dancing, music, and poetry—all that would make them both serviceable and delightful to men. The girls were approaching the momentous age of fifteen, the age at which a girl's future could first be decided. The Peninsulans adhered to a set of strict and highly ritualized customs in households with daughters.

They lived in a country with rich but restricted land and resources. Most of its revenues necessarily came from trade. However, there was precious little property to go around, and if death had not compelled periodic redistributions of properties, the country would surely have known great tensions, perhaps even civil wars. The cannier governors worked to conceal from the people that they lived on a deck of cards. The same cards were shuffled again and again—great change could come only from outside the Peninsula.

This economic situation made marriage portions a substantial share of a family's holdings. Therefore, what had originated as custom had become law: only one daughter of an oligarchy household, to be chosen by her father, could marry, to a husband also chosen by her father. One bloom would be plucked from the bouquet and laid in a husband's hand. This would be the daughter who, in her father's estimation, would secure the most advantageous marriage for the family.

Her sisters, if there were any, would be marked for a different destiny. These would be sent to the Houses of the Immortals, so-called because their occupants were removed from time. There they became perpetual brides.

The perpetual brides became, in effect, the property of the state, no longer members of their families. They were sent to a network of houses chosen for them, administered by respectable, often widowed, matrons. There, they entertained the men, local or foreign, who wished to purchase their services.

In a country where there was a constant flow of trade, and therefore of short-term visitors, it made eminent sense to secure the revenues of Houses of the Immortals for the state treasury. With this income, many of the finest public buildings of the Peninsula were built, many hungry families fed, and children educated. In addition, the brides polished the intricate silver of their former families, delivered to them weekly, and laundered their fine linens and laces. Through them, the state was cleansed.

The children of the perpetual brides, too, were of service to the state, often reared to take up a role among the Immortals, as only in this way could boys be furnished for the Houses. Or they were traded for goods, sent to other countries to serve the many uses to which children can be put.

Some of the Peninsulan mothers suffered for their daughters under the state system, but it had been so long in place that the suffering was anticipated, prepared for, accepted as inevitable. And the mothers lived in a strange emotional suspension; they could neither remember truly, nor truly forget, that they were wives and mothers at the expense of their lost sisters.

Every now and then, girls disappeared, rumored to have taken flight on a ship, or crossed the border into the old country, but most of the women were terrified of the world outside their sheltered lives, where, it was hinted, all women were held to be Immortals.

Many of the Peninsulan households were racked with tension and intrigue throughout their daughters' teenage years. Sometimes, a father made the decision early, so the other girls were spared the suspense over their futures, despite the bitterness that entered the household. But the bitterness was given by God, and must be blessed.

Often, though, there were secret family alliances, rumors spread, exhibitions of love for fathers that were as violent as duels, occasionally murders. This was the inevitable result of the double natures of females, the lovers of snakes.

None of this, though, was true in the domain of General Jarre, who was as famously impartial and impervious to influence in his household as he was on the field of battle. He had showed no hint of any preference. In fact, he often sat listening to music, the twins at his feet, his right hand smoothing the bright hair of one, his left hand of the other. It was a living sculpture of lordly tenderness.

Dolphin and Rain remained inseparable and loving sisters, each equally subject to the inescapable will of God and to the men who execute God's will, who for their own reasons, sometimes bring the wicked ones ashore and refuse the prayers of the drowning good.

No one can fathom an inexplicably happy fate. No one has ever understood what makes God hate one and love another. In General Jarre's case, as perhaps with God, it was the most subtle, unconscious, hairline infraction of his will that was decisive. The choice was made without deliberation, as on a stroll in the forest, a step will break a twig in half by chance.

Degrees of beauty were often the decisive factor between sisters, but Dolphin and Rain were equally gifted physically. Each danced like a seagull wheeling on currents of air. They were skilled in cookery and gardening, as befit those born under the sign of the Cauldron, or Savour the Provident, as it is known among polytheists.

Their manners were as disciplined as fired porcelain, and held as they were tested in their first participations in adult rituals. They wore their brocades to their first weddings, and sang with the correct, poignantly sensuous mixture of joy and restraint, their pendants representing the gold-harnessed birds of the Angel Flights rising and falling with their breath.

In mourning, by contrast, the Peninsulan women were supposed to give way to orgiastic sorrow, screaming, sobbing, raising their arms, falling to the floor as if Death himself were making love to them. It was a way of releasing the deceased for whatever awaited him in the afterlife. Mourning eased the weight of the icy dome of death, fragmenting it; its shards entered the mourning women, making the dead one able to proceed, to Heaven or to Hell. Groups of women were called on to provide this service at every funeral.

Dolphin and Rain, at fifteen, were eligible for the first time to join the seasoned women mourners. They were both apprehensive about performing the songs and dances of death in public for the first time, and awed by their responsibility to clear the path to the afterlife for someone who might otherwise be lost in death.

"What if we are the avenue to Hell? If we are the bridge to damnation?" Rain anguished when they were called to their first funeral. Dolphin lowered her eyes, and imperceptibly shook her head. The fear of Hell was ever present to the Peninsulans, most especially for women, who had ruined creation. The consciousness of their crime was a knife in the girls' hearts, each day. The idea that they could inadvertently be conduits for torment after death as well as in life was terrible for them.

Both acquitted themselves reasonably well at the grave. Dolphin tore her dress with admirable violence, though she was timid in striking her breast; Rain, while she sang a solo lament piercingly, remained subdued in her demeanor, dry-eyed and composed. Both girls were corrected, though leniently, and given exercises in mourning to rehearse at home.

Three months after their debut, they were summoned to an important funeral. The great chancellor Nunn, architect of Peninsulan education, and therefore of the continuity of the state, descendant of the first colonists, had died, rich in years. The Peninsulans did not conduct state funerals; it was for God to bestow honors. Nevertheless, the funeral would be attended by distinguished company, including General Jarre.

Women, save the ritual mourners, whose wild grief expressed the feelings not permitted to men, did not attend funerals. Even so, they often knew fragments of the funeral songs the ritual mourner societies so carefully rehearsed. Once a man's public stature was assured, the anecdotes of his life were sifted over the years by the ritual mourners, and his funeral opera composed even as he lived the prime of his life.

Once Nunn's family and friends had been seated, the songs and dances of death began. A cluster of women began a slow, weaving dance around the catafalque, as if they formed a collective womb, enfolding the dead man's body. One woman shuddered with a wail like wind on a rainy night, and the others took up her lament.

The poignant solos began, singing the stories of Nunn's life; Rain, who had an eloquent voice, sang a portrait of Nunn breaking his famous

Smaraldian to the saddle, a virtuoso aria in which she sang both rider and mare. Then came the great choruses, an outpouring of lament by all in Nunn's life that would mourn him. From his bed to his wineglass to his oar, all that would be bereft of Nunn cried out for him through the women's voices.

It was at this point that the mourning women, almost in a state of hypnosis, began to rend their garments, and shudder with sobs, shattering the music. They began to fall, writhing as they lay on the ground.

Dolphin fell so forcefully that she cut herself; a ribbon of blood appeared on her cheek. Rain, though, was inspired to continue her clear pure lament, and neither sobbed nor dropped to the earth. She raised her arms as if reaching to God, and sent her notes upward like captive birds to freedom. When she finished, she stood absolutely still, her arms at her side. It was a spontaneous and scandalous departure from tradition.

As the notables left the graveside, the harbormaster, feared and respected for his power over both trade and security, greeted General Jarre. They exchanged some remembrances of Nunn privately, before other mourners approached to share in the conversation. The harbormaster turned away, but gave Jarre a keen look. "Our sorrow today did not reach perfection. I do not leave him in peace."

Jarre felt an unfamiliar cramp, a pang; he, whose carriage was always martial, twisted sharply to free himself from it, his first sensation of shame. His unnatural twitch infuriated him further; he was insulted by the imposition of a feeling he did not command. He forbade it.

Annan, closer to him than any being in the world, put his hand lightly on Jarre's shoulder. "She is inexperienced. Yes, her tears should have flowed, she should have been prostrate, but with time she will master this art." Jarre looked at him with the same keen look as the harbormaster's, as if he were passing the identical gaze in relay. "Her tears will flow. She will be prostrate. She will master this art." He spoke as if he had closed the three doors Annan had left ajar.

When the girls had bathed and left their torn mourning costumes for the poor, they were called to the great salon that opened onto the marble seaside balcony from which they watched the Angel Flights. It was warm enough for the tall windows and doors to be open to the fresh sea breezes. Jarre and their mother were waiting for them, seated side by side. I stood behind his chair, as did the attendant on the lady.

Dolphin and Rain kissed their mother's hand, and genuflected before their father. They rose to their feet again; neither girl nor boy in the Peninsula was seated in the paternal presence without invitation. They continued to stand.

Jarre was still in his chair. He made no gesture. He spoke. His stillness gave his voice a disembodied power. "Dolphin," he said, "you have begun to master the craftsmanship of grief. You were admired. You may be seated."

"Rain." For a full minute, he was silent, denying her the privilege of his speech. "You were not admired. Why did you stand and sing instead of weeping with your face in the earth?"

"I don't know," she said.

"Did you think your gift of song was more important than doing the chancellor honor?"

"I don't know," she said, though her left leg began to shake convulsively. There were no answers to these questions. She peered through her father's words as if through the bars of a cell. If one had been reading these questions in an illustrated manuscript, one would see that the hooked question marks served as locks.

"Do you think you are too fine to mourn like a Peninsulan woman? Are you some sort of queen?" The accusation was a dark and double insult.

Arrogance of any kind was the primal dishonor of women, and was ruthlessly crushed when it appeared. And while the Peninsulans had conquered the old monarchy generations ago, they were still stung in some vital way by the memory of their contemptible stature in the kingdom, still tormented by a jealousy they could never admit of the people who excluded them.

"I don't know, I don't know," Rain could summon no other phrase. She was like a Smaraldian afraid of lightning, rearing and flailing in the stall, damaging herself against its walls in her desperation to be free of the terrible inexplicable fire.

Jarre himself wanted something from her that was obscure to him.

He wanted her to cry in desperation, fall to his feet, as she should have at the funeral. His desire, secret even to him, had transformed her clumsiness into defiance, in his eyes. Perhaps he was not wrong to detect a shade of defiance in her, a pride he had identified before she herself was aware of it.

As with God sometimes, he conceived at that moment an unanswerable hatred for one of his children. Though in the case of man, hatred seems to be born of desire, a way to compel satisfaction from something that persists as unattainable and causes unbearable pain. The cause must be different for the Creator of all, to whom nothing is unattainable, except the goodness of man.

"Then I erase you from the history that you scorn. You are Immortal, Rain. Your father gave your life, and takes it."

Even then, she did not fall to the ground.

Jarre called for the superintendent of the house. "I have made Rain Immortal. Remove her childhood from her room. Bring the toys and the masks." This was a heartrending ceremony marking a girl's entrance into Immortal life, her separation from her family and from her father's protection. I witnessed many such occasions during my time on the Peninsula.

We followed the superintendent to the young girl's room. There we took up gaily painted boxes full of her childhood toys: a box of dolls, a box of toy animals, a box of gilded balls and batons with which the girls played in rounds their charming toss and catch games, looking like muses playing casually with golden worlds.

The balls and batons, along with the girl's jewelry, would be given to Peninsulan philanthropies, an arrangement that greatly increased the scope of their works.

I took up the doll's house, as it was bulky and awkward to carry, fully furnished as it was with replicas of the villa's own pieces. All the girls of the Peninsula, even the less wealthy, were given these houses, toys that doubled as an education in the domestic arts, as they mastered the aesthetic and economic management of a household in miniature. Dolphin had an identical villa on a table in her own room.

We carried the boxes into the seaside salon where the family was waiting, Rain still standing, and Dolphin now standing beside her. Two servants emerged from the grand arched doorway opposite, carrying a small tent of finely worked golden mesh, which they threw over Dolphin. The material was so delicately woven that it was almost transparent; her features were clearly visible beneath it, even her tears. There, swathed in the precious meshes of safety, she was taken to stand in between her parents' chairs.

We then spread the floor with the thickly embroidered silk quilts we had taken from Rain's bed. And using scissors, knives, hammers, and our hands, we destroyed her toys one by one. We dismembered the dolls, and shredded the costumes for the girls' traditional dances.

The doll's house with its furniture was pulverized, roof crushed, windows broken, balconies dangling, looking exactly as real houses do in the aftermath of the earthquakes that were unfortunately familiar occurrences on the Peninsula.

The silk quilts were littered with arms and legs and heads with staring eyes, with mosaic fragments of gardens and ships from puzzles, with the heads of clay horses bridled in red leather. A little ballerina poised in an arabesque had kept her supporting leg, but lost the extended leg that defined the pose. Stars and a moon cracked like eggshell were scattered over the rubble, from the smashed nocturnal sky of a toy theater set.

An entire world lay in ruins on the cloth. It was an apocalypse, for toys are alive, toys are the children of children. They feel their first passions for the blocks, soldiers, animals, and dolls, exercise on them their first cruelties and repentances, deliberate maltreatment and tender reparation. To them, they say for the first time, "I hate you." And "forgive me." Here are the first crucifixions and resurrections, the first tragic intimations that they themselves might be toys.

Rain did not cry even at that scene, though when a brilliantly painted scarlet-and-lapis-colored bird plunged to the floor, losing both its wings, I saw her mouth shape an anguished "O" of compassion, as if she saw a living creature wounded. Some of the toys had stayed alive for her, even ones she clearly hadn't played with in some time. This bird was still apparently in flight in her, it was not a figure of the past, but had soared through it outside time into her soul. I saw her pocket the wingless body with its head still intact, bright-eyed, its mouth opened in song. Perhaps it was wrong of me, but I said nothing.

And when there was nothing left of her room's childhood to be destroyed, two black silk blindfolds were brought on a pillow and set before General Jarre. He stood, and bound one of them around Rain's eyes. I helped him to bind the other around his own. He pronounced the ritual formula of dismissal, "Your father sees nothing more of you." I led her away, blindfolded, to her room, now stripped of all her possessions.

She would not be sent away to the House of Immortals until her sister's marriage, though her life in her former family would never be the same. Her final glimpse of them would be at Dolphin's wedding.

Now serious suitors were free to come forward, knowing which of the Jarre daughters was the eligible bride. Hours of the general's time were taken up by conferences with the potentials. He studied scrupulously the account books and deeds they left with him, as well as examining the written statements outlining their religious lives that they submitted to confirm that they were among God's Crowned Ones.

The choice fell at last on a squat, fat man who had been a bachelor for perhaps longer than desirable, but who had his own fleet of ships, as well as a splendid villa on the sea, and farmland in the old monarchy to which he had managed to retain title, through impoverished aristocrats he'd made cooperative. The Peninsulans outwitted with a special relish the aristocrats who had been so condescending to them.

His extraordinarily moving and detailed account of the way in which God had made him part of the Holy Court decided the matter for General Jarre. He ordered the publication of the betrothal, set the wedding preparations in motion, and informed Dolphin of her impending marriage.

The vast copper cauldrons were set up for the wedding banquet, and the copper trays so large that it took eight men to carry them were readied to be set out in the great square for the poor, students, foreigners, and widows.

The ceremonial meals were prepared, as was the tradition, by pagan cooks, who were acknowledged to be the great masters of the kitchen, and were tolerated on the Peninsula for their unequaled skills. They operated taverns and inns throughout the Peninsula, always recognizable by the large painted signs outside with the image of the Cauldron constellation in glittering silver paint.

Their mother dressed the two girls for their weddings, for it was a wedding day for both daughters. Dolphin was dressed in white and her dowry gold, and Rain in red brocade. She gave them each a wedding blessing. "May you have many children," she said to Dolphin. "May you have none," she said to Rain.

She ushered Dolphin through the marriage door into the seaside hall, and handed her to her ape of a groom. She returned and led Rain to the opposite door, where in place of a groom, the governess of the House of Immortals stood waiting.

"Don't be downcast," the Lady Mother said. "Your sister obeys, and so do you. You are both alone. Dolphin has no idea what her future will be like, whereas you will never go hungry, and you know how you will live. The greatest blessing for a woman is a known fate. You are out of the wind."

After the vows, Dolphin was crowned, as a sign that she was now a Princess of the Elect. A magnificent banquet followed, and the last of the rites were performed.

Dolphin danced a slow, elegiac dance, her final dance, since birthgivers relinquished dancing. Rain danced a virtuosic dance, in which each movement was repeated at greater speed, until the steps ended in wild accelerations. It was the dance that signified her entry into the guild of the women who dance always.

They made wide circles around the room. Then they met in the middle to cross to the opposite doors from which they would exit, stepping forever from the path of the other.

The girls started toward the doors at their stately pace, but turned back, as if each had half the other's impulse. For a moment they held each other close, each one's head pressed to the other's shoulder. It was an unusual display, but they had been, as twins often are, deeply attached.

Blindfolded, Rain was taken by the governess along the sinuous roads that led away from the sea toward the mountains, where she was to be housed. She was not to know the route, or understand clearly where she was, a wise precaution of the system.

Unlike many countries, the Peninsulans did not permit the perpetual bride houses to be situated by the sea, but scattered them on the heights. Not only did this solve many of the common problems this service presented to neighboring communities, but it also served to regulate the crime sometimes associated with it, ensuring that all its revenues were strictly recorded and rendered to the state. So the state flourished through the repentance of women, and their tears were transformed into gold.

Visas were granted at the ports for men to visit the houses on the peaks; ingeniously, this served to identify precisely the men, foreign and local, who visited the Immortals. In this way, the Immortals were of further use to the state as a conduit for information about business and politics.

I, along with other agents, was dispatched each month to interview brides who had entertained men of interest to the state, and to make detailed reports of my findings for General Jarre and the other governors. With the use of the visas, particular men could even be directed to houses where brides had been instructed to listen with rapt attention to their stories. So garrulous were many of these men that one had the impression they visited the brides as much to talk as out of lust.

The House of the Immortals, for which Rain was destined, was surrounded by fields, cultivated gardens, and terraced vineyards, in which the aging brides worked during the days. They were charged with supplying themselves, and also the great households of the towns, with food.

"For those of us who have been taken out of time, labors never end," Madam explained to Rain impassively. "Though of course, we enjoy the repose decreed by God the King on the day of the Court of the Divine. A Crowned One ministers to us each week. And every resident of the house attends weekly Divine Court without fail." She was a handsome woman who wore the sober, elegant clothes of an impeccable matron. Her jade-green eyes were permanently narrowed, as if she were trying to see through a dust storm.

Over the arched doorway of the house was a carved and gilded Crown of the Elect, as was displayed on all the public buildings of the Peninsula. "Stand up straight," Madam said. "I saw that you are a fine dancer. Hold yourself like one." Madam was ever watchful and passionate about matters of deportment.

Inside was an arrangement of four houses, each separated from the other by an ample courtyard. They passed through the first house, from whose windows Rain could see men and women talking and laughing in an outdoor gallery. The noise was imperceptible in the second house, thanks to the arrangement of the courtyards.

In the center of the second courtyard, there was a party of men and elegant boys, for the men who preferred the children of the Immortals. Madam acknowledged the guests with practiced charm, and beckoned to a server to see that more wine and pastries were sent out. The guests raised their glasses to her, savoring her attention to their enjoyments.

The two women advanced to the third house, and again, there was an illusion of perfect separation; none of the laughter and chatter Rain had heard reached them.

In the center of the third courtyard was a raised stage for performance. "It is the house of dancers," Madam said. "This is where you will be lodged." A group of women, ranging from youth to elder, were sorting through trunks of costumes and arranging flowers for the evening's entertainments. She had not seen older women at the first house.

Madam divined what Rain had noticed. "This is the house with the greatest variety of women. The older women stay as teachers, as costumers, and the great ones as dancers, long after the women of the other houses are put into the kitchens and the fields. You are fortunate to have been chosen for this house.

"The clients are often superior as well. Some want simply to be thought of as polished connoisseurs of women. Some like the dancing women because to command their companionship afterward is like playing at marionettes. Some, though, love the classical dances, and will reward a girl for a well-made dance.

"Here, too, you will learn to sell them the finer wines, for the same reasons. And you will become expert. Those dark red wines change from one form into another. Money changes wine into shoes; the ruby in the throat becomes the red-heeled dance shoes in which you leap high enough to make the visitors buy more red wine."

They passed from the courtyard into a lavishly furnished great hall, the decor evoking the palaces of the old monarchy. From the window of the room Madam led her to, Rain could see another group of buildings set on a slope, surrounded by terraced vineyards and gardens.

"Those," Madam said, again divining her curiosity, "are the kitchens, the dining hall, and the houses where the brides bring up the children they have borne. Occasionally, if the father is known, he may choose to take the child and bring it up in his own country. But that is rare. The children belong to the house." She was careful to tell Rain very simply what she had to tell, as one tells a child of the murders and marriages in a fairy tale as they happen, never sure what the child might know of such matters.

The room Rain was given was fresh and pleasant, with a window opening onto the garden instead of the courtyard. Rain put away the small store of clothing she had brought. Most carefully, she made a secret nest of silk scarves, and hid the clay bird with broken wings that she had managed to conceal on the day of her Immortality. The broken toy was all she had to cling to. She smoothed the scarves and evened them, as concerned for the bird's comfort as if it were real.

She climbed the hill, as instructed, to take her meal. Along the path, there was a magnificent view down from the vineyards cut out of the mountain like angelic ladders, all the way to the sea. She could make out the customs house, and see the distant ships in the port.

She passed the house of children, caught in its cloud of music. From its various windows, she heard sobs and coos, screams of delight, soft voices singing lullabies, a brocade of all the traditional Peninsulan lullabies she had grown up with, and many that were unfamiliar, perhaps brought to the brides by strange visitors. She heard them, as if from the bottom of the sea, though she was high above it.

She thought, calmly, about finding an outcrop to make a fatal leap, but she had already been killed so much that day that she lacked the will to act. She could only absorb the day's death—she had been General Jarre's privileged daughter in the morning, but now, after the passage of hours, was some other kind of being. She was uncertain what she was now, except that it was the kind of being that was not a child. She was now the kind of being who had gained the first dreadful inkling of what an hour is and what it might contain.

Instead of dying, she found a terrace in the vineyards with a view down to that moment's glittering sunset sea. To the left of the vines there was a ruined stone pagan chapel, with the fragments over the door of the carved wheat sheaf and grapes that identified such buildings. Two untended rose bushes flanked the door on either side.

This place, for years to come, would provide the space in which she lived freely in the fragments of time that were hers alone. For what one experiences is not the whole of one's life. One can give birth to a child and bring it up, yet still fail to become its mother.

Here she thought about what had happened to her, and moved through it like the birds through the interstices of the stone chapel. She did there what we call living through what happened to her. She tasted this view of the sea every day, in its nuances and variations of mist, snow, star, storm, clouds, and currents of air—it was a place that was like a marriage to her.

Afraid to linger further, she returned to the path to climb to the dining hall.

There she was given dinner by herself in a room lined with couches on which one reclined to eat, in the old monarchy style. She was hungry and tired and so drank too much of the wine they gave her, though she would have fallen unconscious even without the overindulgence, thanks to the ample dose of sleeping drug mixed with the wine.

She was still drowsy when she woke in the dark without her clothes on, as one of the boys from the second courtyard put his hand over her mouth and raped her, as was the custom on a girl's first night as a perpetual bride.

After it was done, Madam, who had been working on her household accounts book outside the room, thanked the boy for his service with the traditional tip of a gold coin, and sent him away to his lodging. Then she went inside, carrying a blanket, and helped Rain, silent, lying doubled over on her side, to rise and walk back to her own quarters.

Efficiently, she put the girl to bed in the dark. Madam leaned over Rain, who was lying on her back as if paralyzed, her eyes open and blank. Rain had been brought to the place where there was nothing that could not be done to her. She would live in that place where every day was a new kind of dying.

"Is there anything else you need to help you sleep?" Madam asked. She was an expert apothecary; many of her charges needed and valued her skills.

Rain stared up at her. "You are damned, Madam," she said, hoarse with hate. "You are damned."

Madam smiled solicitously, and answered her in a soothing voice. "All women are. And so are you, little girl." She brought her face down to Rain's and kissed her maternally, consecratingly, on the forehead, and then full on the lips, kisses that were like the sealing stone of a tomb. "So now you know. Now you are a dedicated Immortal."

The violence of the boy had been only one dimension of rape—Madam, too, raped, but incorporeally. Madam murdered the last remnant of her hope of life, with her poisoned tenderness. Virginity in itself is nothing, unless its loss ends the power to love. Madam completed Rain's education, showing her that all the gestures of love can be ridiculed or perverted.

"You'll feel much more at home tomorrow," she said, and closed the door, leaving her in darkness. For the first time since childhood, that tearless girl at last wept as women are ordained to.

She had lived the rigorously disciplined life of women on the Peninsula, who lived as soldiers, soldiers who do not kill, but form the iron militia who endure life. But she had failed so far in the feminine discipline of sorrow.

Rape is a kind of physics, steadily obeying laws of action and reaction. The rapist suffers from his own violence. His only relief is to transmit it to the object he is determined to harm as well as have; when he has replaced love in her with terror, and the lust to kill, he is satisfied. He has then raped in self-defense.

Now, for the first time in her life, Rain felt desire; a passion to murder. She would murder Madam first, because she was to hand. And her death would be the doorway through which Rain could escape.

She imagined then shedding the blood of her sacred father, Jarre. She allowed herself to imagine tearing a piece of his dead flesh from his shoulder with her teeth, and then spitting it to the ground, stuff too contemptible even to eat.

The first blood-dark tide of hatred lapping at her feet was almost comforting in its warmth. She did not know how quickly it would rise or where it would carry her.

In the morning, Madam herself brought a breakfast tray, with luxurious fruits and breads too tempting to refuse. She saw to it that the brides were always well fed and well dressed.

"You must be feeling much better now, I think?" she said.

"I feel better," Rain said, echoing the answer implicit in Madam's question. She tested Madam's acuity, with the newfound feminine cunning that the Peninsulan men so abhorred.

Madam looked at her with genuine relief, pleased to receive her own answer to her own question. She was so accustomed to these necessary cruelties that she oversaw them as a doctor does surgery. She disliked being the object of lengthy resentment by the girls. It made her dislike them, and that interfered with her management of the house.

Rain did not meet her eyes. Madam found her modesty correct, even touching. Long years of mercantile experience had accustomed her to weighing the potential value of all the material of a girl, from the slimness of her wrists to the distinctive features of her temperament. Her own reactions to a girl guided her in choosing the clients whom she would best suit.

Shame was a precious delicacy whose flavor diminished over time. Madam quickly summoned an inner catalog of clients she imagined would pay generously for such a luxury. She thought of the money translated into repaired tiles, new kitchen copper, seed for winter wheat, and the endless installments of taxes she paid to the state.

Rain was, though, looking at Madam's throat, her eyes averted not in shame, but in rage. She wondered if her hands were strong enough to choke the governess. Her own throat burned and constricted with the feeling of the murder she was bringing to life. The murder would concentrate all that she had suffered, all that would be transformed, if she ceased to be a person and became fate itself. She was suffocating with her longing to kill; crucified on it.

Madam circulated the news that there was a new bride in the house, waiting to present Rain until she had stirred up the greatest excitement. It was a period she always enjoyed, this time when a newcomer was as completely in her own possession as a doll.

She even chose the new bride's clothes, trying different colors and styles to see the range of moods and fantasies the new body would yield. She made the brides walk up and down, lift their arms, turn, stand still, posing in effective light. She treated their bodies as she treated her compound: all were locked away from the world outside, but no locks were permitted on internal doors. Only Madam held the keys.

She cut the hair of the newly arrived Immortals, if she disapproved of their coiffures. If they resisted, having once been pampered with girlish freedoms, she menaced them with the scissors.

She applied their cosmetics herself, turning their heads right and left, tilting them up and down, threatening slaps if the girls were slow in absorbing and reflecting the features she designed for them, the magnified lips, exaggerated lashes, eyes ringed with black pearls when she wanted to emphasize a bride's expression of fear.

The obedience yielded in these sessions gave Madam a devotional sense of peace and security; she was doing sacred work, erasing the individual from the bride so that she might become Immortal.

(I have often reflected that the Peninsulans, like many other peoples, would do well to observe their nurseries more objectively. Their image of their children was so often a matter of belief, not of description—the classical evocation of the boy, like a god surrounded with the miniature fallen soldiers he had commanded and doomed, the girl helplessly tender as an apple blossom on a bough, compulsively rocking some sort of infant in any form of rag or wax. Yet the way of a girl with her dolls can be as fatal as the way of a boy with his army. I see these things clearly perhaps, because of my childlessness. Parents look into children as into mirrors, whereas all children remain opaque and mysterious to me.)

For the time being, Madam determined to withhold Rain—she would perform only as a dancer, until she had built a following, an audience among whom there would be wild competition to possess her. She did not want her in company with the other brides for the moment, either, frightened by rumors and quarrels. Rain was kept isolated. Madam thought the enforced solitude would sharpen her appetite for company when it would be useful.

She was sent to dance rehearsals in the morning and afternoon, supervised by a former principal dancer who had recently had a child, and was nursing it in the House of Immortal Children.

Rain's body was used as a blank canvas for the invention of new steps and new roles. She transformed her body into the world she was not permitted to live in. She was menageries, gemstones, architectures, oceans, landscapes—she danced them into the sequestered courtyard, she danced them into life.

If Rain could find an hour, she went to sit at the old pagan chapel overlooking the sea. She looked at the ships coming and going, and strained with all her imagination to leave on board one of them, but there she encountered, instead of freedom, the limits of dreams. Human imagination imports well, but exports with less success.

Madam permitted her these absences, recognizing an artist's needs. In the evenings, Rain sat alone in the gallery above the theater watching the performances, hidden by the carved wooden screens that enclosed the galleries. She almost panted under the weight of her hatred as she watched Madam at work, managing her domain. The sight of her was an unending torture, as if Madam was a malignant cancer inside Rain herself.

Rain's only relief was an odd ritual. At night, she would unwrap her wingless toy bird and stroke it, overcome with pity for this bit of broken clay. She felt her tenderness unfold inside her, like a pair of wings she might offer to the bird. To do this kept her human in some way.

Madam moved tirelessly back and forth during the evenings, inspecting the brides as they descended the staircases to the public salons, sharing a glass of wine with clients in one courtyard, attending some of the dances in the third courtyard, flanked always by men she selected to distinguish with her attention. She gave the selected ones conversation, jests, refreshments, the honor of good seats near the stage, as if she were offering hospitality, rather than calculating payment due to the house.

She was not given to praise of her girls and boys. "You were particularly graceless tonight," Rain overheard her say curtly and publicly to a bride who had danced a brilliant solo in a folk ballet about a hunted deer.

Madam turned her back on the dancer and walked away, but after a short time, as if Madam had conjured him, a robust man wearing large gold rings who had been sitting close to the stage approached the girl. He took off one of his rings, handed it to her with a gesture both placating and demanding, and led her away.

During the morning choreography next day, Rain and Azura, the choreographer, worked together on shaping steps based on the phases of the moon. (These later diffused themselves throughout the world as the five basic positions of what is known as ballet, in which the dancer emerges from invisibility through each phase until the culminating full moon of the fifth. Thus this soldierly society, with its harsh theological teachings about women, became known for its association with the most feminine of all styles of dance.)

Rain described Madam's display of contempt at the performance. Azura's reaction was surprising. Her posture changed. Her face, which glowed with the involuntary radiance of someone who has been dancing, became stern. She bent her neck, as if to a yoke, and looked as if she had lost a full head of her height. "Madam's judgments are always costly," she said.

Then she adjusted Rain's arms, and stood back to analyze how the pose would appear from a distance. Rain broke free from the pose, tormented by the image of Madam. "Let me dance," she said. "Let me dance tonight."

"No," Azura answered with authority. "The longer before you make your debut, the better off you are. Besides, you want to tell the truth. You want to tell what happened to you. But nothing will be worse for you than to find out onstage that the audience doesn't care. It doesn't matter to them. You are underwater to them. They can see you, but not hear you.

"I've learned—and you must realize—that nothing is more dangerous to you here than an audience you have shown something they don't want to imagine about themselves. It will enrage them. Everything for you depends on what you make them dream."

Rain suddenly thought of her sister, Dolphin, trapped too in the life that had been assigned to her. "You want to dance them to death," Azura said. "But that will only make them imagine killing."

Azura put her arm around Rain, the first gesture of affection that

Rain had known for months. She took the opportunity of the closeness to whisper to Rain to meet her at the pagan chapel in the afternoon. Then she quickly returned to drilling Rain, making her practice the boring repetitive movements of the feet, like sharpening knives, that would enable her steps to gleam with precision onstage.

Azura's own work over these weeks had guided Rain into several of the different worlds that coexisted alongside each other, even here.

Azura was a prostitute, but her dancing was sacred. She was teaching Rain that the worlds were permeable. She showed Rain how to enter dancing into an inexplicable heaven where no one could follow her without her consent. Rain approached the chapel with studied nonchalance, but she was filled with hope that Azura, who had mastered a kind of half-freedom, would disclose a way to escape altogether.

She heard a sequence of clear, piping rhythmic sounds, like birdsong. At the entrance to the chapel, in the full sunlight, she saw a baby. The child glowed like a planet on a blue and silver quilt, rolling in the folds as if she were swimming, singing the infant songs that exist before speech.

Azura, seated in the shadows, was watching her daughter play. She could see that Rain looked at the baby with the face of spontaneous love, which has always the intensity of reunion. Rain searched deep into the child's eyes as if she recognized her, as if she wanted to evoke a memory in this child who couldn't yet speak, or as if she wanted to restore some memory of her own.

"Is it safe for you to bring her here?" Rain asked, kneeling by the child, delicately touching her head as if she were a cup of water to drink from. She had thought there was nothing but violence left in her, but her hand on the child's head, to her wonder, was infinitely gentle.

Love was possible, even here. She had a strange feeling, as if she had lived in some other world than the Peninsula. It was as if she were immersed in another larger self, surrounding her like a body of water.

The child seemed to have something to tell her. It had no words but prattle; still it had the gift of making her feel what it needed her to know.

Yet Rain grasped something like complete sentences, made of flesh. She understood with the speed of breath that there was a vast difference between a being like herself that had ceased growing, and a being like this one, whose size changed infinitely every minute, and in every direction, including its own perceptions. That rapid metamorphosis in space was lost to adults like herself, but became a capacity to metamorphose in time, from woman to child to aged invalid, from life to death and back again.

She looked at the child with marveling curiosity, and then at Azura questioningly.

The child sang and played with its own body, handling its nose and feet like toys. Azura did not interfere with its games, but stayed near, as a kind of bridge for the child to cross toward her or away from her. Together, mother and child were like the first letter of some unknown alphabet, a bridge-shaped curve with a movable round punctuation mark, never in the same position. They were the first pair of this kind that Rain had ever seen.

Azura had meant her to see this. No matter what happened to her, beings existed, and would exist, who had yet to be destroyed. There was some threshold she herself might cross. She could see that, enter, and find out if their fates meant anything to her.

Every day on the Peninsula was shaped to frame life as it had been ordained. Here, locked in the House of the Immortals, within the canonical certainty of the Immortals' dedication, Rain had discovered the unknown. She had discovered questions within a world made only of commands.

"I want her to see the sea. I want to teach her to imagine leaving."

"Is that cruel?" Rain asked. "Since she will be a bride and die here?"

"Perhaps she won't," Azura said, and then wrapped her arms around the baby as if she were building her a castle of flesh.

"Do you know of any children who were permitted to leave here?"

"Sometimes a way can be found. Everyone tells one story that is almost certain." She leaned forward, and whispered, "They say Madam had a daughter, and that she managed to send her away. I believe it. It would have been very difficult for a child of hers to survive among the others in the House of Immortal Children. And even so, how could she have brought a child up here, in this fate?"

"She had a child?" Rain repeated, incredulous.

"The great governess and exemplary immortal bride. If I could find a way to prove it, the proof could force her to help my child leave the same way."

She didn't need to ask Rain to search on the child's behalf. The thought of harming Madam was immediately as strong as starvation. She felt a strange new physical coherence, of eye, muscle, smell, implacable will, as if she were a stalking lioness.

The strange sense of overlapping selves disappeared. She was as single as a weapon is, a knife, an ax, a pike, a battering ram. There is nothing more individual, more alone, more single in nature and purpose, than a weapon. They are instruments that cannot be paired; they cannot express more than one thought.

The dance Rain performed on the night she debuted on the Immortal stage is a legend of the courtesan repertoire, though now known largely through drawings and rarely performed.

The ballet was a technically complex pas de deux whose subject was a man and a glass of wine. Rain was the glass of wine; through her, the man was enchanted, charmed, and delivered to a radiant, transcendent vision of God. Finally, staggering, intoxicated to the point of drunkenness, he willfully shatters the glass and wastes the wine that has given him such pleasure and revelation.

Rain wore an ingenious costume consisting of a net of crystals over a red silk tunic. Her pirouettes modeled all the facets of cut crystal caught in light. Her partner sipped from the cup of her rounded arms. Her partner's virtuoso steps on the very edge of balance during his drunken scene were admired and imitated long afterward.

Few forgot the moment when the flickering crystals scattered over the floor, and Rain seemed to flow into oblivion, in agonizingly slow arabesques, until she disappeared, bleeding a ribbon of red silk. The audience applauded relentlessly, until they succeeded in compelling the dancers to repeat the final scene. The stage was pelted with dark red roses.

Rain could be hidden away no longer; after their debuts as soloists, the dancers became recognizable, and were expected to join the guests after the performances. The dancers stimulated high payments among the guests excited by their brilliant work. Freshly bathed, they walked among the guests like fires freed from the confining hearth that had been the stage.

Rain emerged, and went to join Azura, feeling the bond of dancer and maker of dance, as well as the protection of her presence. Spontaneously, appreciatively, they clasped hands. Madam approached, flanked by clients. "You are not here to congratulate each other," she said audibly, and roughly pushed their hands apart. "If there is anything to praise, God will praise it. Tonight, there was nothing to praise."

Azura's face fell. She knew that Madam's insults were one form of calculated prelude to a sale.

They were designed to leave a bride so bruised and humiliated that she would willingly accept a kind gesture from any of the guests. And they were a signal to the guests who had paid the fee to claim their brides for the night.

Azura was led away: her work was not over for this night. She saw that Madam brought Rain toward a short gray-haired man who reached out to touch her bare arm.

It was the harbormaster whose criticism of Rain at her long-ago funeral dance had stung Jarre into the almost competitive burst of fury that had brought her here.

"Her dancing has greatly improved since I last saw her in public," he said, daringly alluding to her existence prior to Immortality. "I congratulate you, Madam. I will drink my wine from this cup."

So Rain began her descent into Hell.

Human beings have wondrous capacities: they are the only creatures who can transform metaphor into reality. Unlike simpler animals, they feed not only on flesh, but also on dreams that they make flesh.

They do not even need to die in order to cease to live. They need no underworld to construct a hell. It is a strange kind of immortality.

Rain was conducted by Madam as a ghost is led by a god, to an underworld in which she ceased to exist except as the shifting shadow of a client's desires. If a client wanted a daughter, she must be the girl. If the client wanted a dog, she must be the bitch. If a client wanted death, she must be even less than the corpse. She was to be the grave.

For years to come, she spent her days thinking of the night that waited for her, when nothing could be refused, any more than a dying man can refuse to stop breathing. If her own father had come as a client to the House of the Immortals, Madam would have provided her for him at his request.

At times, she would see Admiral Annan, her father's boyhood friend, in the audience at her performances. He was known to be a connoisseur of the dance; she thought that was perhaps why he had not attempted to possess her. Her art gave her the power to enter his thoughts, perhaps even to become part of what he could see.

He would look at her with a strange gravity, but never speak to her, as if he were seeing a monument or a painting. In any case, it was against the Rule of the House for past history or identity to be acknowledged in any way by those who had been removed from time, and by their clients.

The admiral always left the courtyard after the dance with the same bride, a dark-haired and silent girl to whom he had apparently bought exclusive rights, as only the very wealthy can afford. She lived in her own quarters, to which they retreated when he visited.

Annan was so powerful and a Crowned One of such limitless wealth that he even took this girl with him from time to time as part of his entourage when he traveled to other parts of the Peninsula. She was the envy of all the brides for this patronage, which made her even more withdrawn.

Sometimes, among the tributes of flowers, jewelry, and delicacies she received after a performance, all signed by aspirants, and carefully reviewed by Madam, ever a ruthless abacus, Rain found bouquets she imagined Annan had sent.

They were elegant arrangements of coastal flowers, such as beach roses, that she had grown up with, always with a simple card enclosed that read "In Gratitude." Much more than the elaborate arrangements she received from greenhouses, they evoked for her the world outside the house, and in the most subtle floral code, the past.

Annan never offered for her, but a number of young men who had been acquainted with her as a daughter in the household of General Jarre bought her out of curiosity.

A portly bearded man bought her after an evening of folk dances, drawn from the dances every girl from the Peninsula was taught as a child. She realized that she had been purchased by her sister's pious husband. He did not acknowledge her, but made her kneel and serve God. He bought her at intervals over the course of a year, then he inexplicably disappeared.

He left her a sea-colored sapphire ring that she recognized as having belonged to Dolphin. Madam was scrupulous in delivering it—she never stole jewelry belonging to the Brides—though she divulged no information, if she had any, about why the ring was no longer on her sister's hand.

She was trained to speak only when she had divined what a client wanted to hear her say. For extra fees, the clients could make requests called prayers for particular needs or desires to be satisfied. They asked that Madam deliver Rain dressed in particular costumes, her face magnified through certain cosmetics, her skin whitened, or darkened, or rouged to the desired color. Once someone requested that she be painted gold, to represent a woman from another world in a popular fairy tale. Madam experimented with the shades of gilt on Rain herself, until she was satisfied that its radiance was sufficiently dazzling in candlelight.

Rain listened impassively as they spoke to her, and about her. She was schooled to understand that she was contingent, the client ultimate. The client had the power to tell her not only what she might say, but to declare what she was thinking, and force her to assent to the thoughts he created. She must never contradict. If she had other impulses or motives, she was to purify herself of them. Any well-brought-up girl of the Peninsula could manage that aspect of life in the house.

Sometimes clients wanted her as she appeared onstage; what excited them was to be with her in theater, not in reality. Fresh costumes were kept to answer prayers like these. She would be brought to them, bathed and newly attired in the duplicate costume, to give the illusion that she was the role they had seen her play.

Prayers were received from some who wanted her to be more beautiful than she was; others insisted that she be made more ugly. She was to be younger than they were—or older than they were. An aristocratic lady from the Old Monarchy to be debased, a peasant in local costume to be elevated, a mother, a battle talisman, they created her in their image.

The one thing that was never asked of her or of any other bride was the kiss on the lips, symbolic of shared love or of ultimate deceit. No man of the Peninsula would debase himself in this way, but a variety of superstitions was connected with the notion, fears of transformation, of losing the precious certainty of election, or even the power God poured into his Warriors.

They shed blood over her: the more absent and silent she was, the more rivals battled over the meaning of her gestures. Was a pause before she launched a whiplash series of steps significant? If one client felt she had singled him out with some look or hinted toward him with her hands, another felt slighted.

Something like a war developed between two factions of spectators who clashed fanatically over their opposite interpretations of a role she danced. This was a ballet in which she played the only female role, a young girl, who falls in love with a boy and runs away with him.

The third act is famous for its finale, a demanding, athletic trio in which the girl is pursued and killed by her father and brother. Rain took a last, abandoned, breathtaking leap directly into the audience, where the dancer playing her brother caught her in the air, and carried her back onto the stage to her death.

The controversy began after the performance over whether her character was innocent or had deserved to be murdered. A great deal of wine had already been served during the dance: the fighting escalated until an eighteen-year-old boy (who naturally identified with the young lover) from a well-known merchant's family was killed with a knife.

Rain saw the surge of fists and kicks, and heard the punished jagged breath of men giving and receiving blows as she came out to take her bows. And she thought she saw the knife come down, the swift decision that could never be changed; the boy was taken from the house elsewhere, so she did not see him die.

As a consequence, knives were prohibited on the premises, but this was impossible to enforce. The faction who contended that the girl's death in the ballet was justified considered that they had proved their point. Rain had, after all, inadvertently provoked the death of a boy simply by dancing a role written for her. The destructive power of women made even their innocence dangerous. They were fires that for safety's sake should burn only in the hearth.

Rain, during these years, was kept alive by love, hate, and work. It is a strange feature of the soul that each of these elements of human experience can heighten the other. Her dancing was where love and hate met—sometimes, her feet whipped at the ground as if she would tear the earth to pieces, at other times, she lay on the stage with her hands pressed to it as if to a beloved face. Love and hate struggled in her, or married in some necessity, in the way the human heart is bathed in blood.

Her hatred was for the men who bought her, but perhaps above all for Madam, who delivered her and the other girls to them, like the negligible little birds she served for expensive suppers with wine, birds that were eaten, head, delicate bones, and all. She learned to control her reactions to Madam's public insults, but even harder to endure was another technique of Madam's, the public feigning of love, the other sure trigger for a sale.

Madam would call certain brides to her, and seat them at her feet, stroking their hair as if they were lapdogs. Her displays of affection were above all exhibitions of the girls' submissiveness—they could not refuse her caresses or her false intimacies, a promise communicated to the clients. Her touch made Rain remember from childhood the scarred hands of a cook marked by burning sugar she was caramelizing.

Rain's loathing for Madam became irresistible, ardent, an assent to a dizzying world of cruelty without end. She suffered the most terrible, the most polluting of all human lusts—which is not, as commonly supposed, sexual desire, but the desire to kill.

And it was evident that Madam reciprocated her hatred; she hated all the girls she furnished, with an implacable, parental hatred. She hated them whether rebellious or obedient, hated their degradation, hated the way their very existence caused sin they could never be free of, as bodies can never be free of gravity, not even when they die, not even when they decompose. She hated women as they deserved, because they could not rescue her.

There are many worlds, though, within the same small space, and within the same soul.

Rain's hours with Azura and her baby daughter, Ocean, existed in the days, along with the nights passed in humiliation and violence. In their company, she was refreshed as if she had found her way to some hidden paradise, where love could never be exhausted, as unending as the death she knew at night was unending.

She died at night, and was born again each day, shocked by the reality of all she could still feel. Feeling love, that borrowed joy in these lives, made it possible for her to suffer here, unlike many of the others, frozen in the postures of seduction in which their captors had trained them.

Sitting on the soft grasses overlooking the sea, she timidly played with the child, hardly daring to touch it. She had been touched always against her will, and was afraid her touch would magically transmit her violation to the child.

When the laughing toddler threw herself in her arms spontaneously, Rain felt she was someone who had never been cauterized by hatred; again, she had a sense that she had another nature.

She discovered another, utterly unsuspected power, her ecstatic power not to kill. The swarm in the hive of her heart made a wild honey of its savagery.

She held the child in her arms, as if its whole passage through time was in her embrace. Her arms seemed to possess an infinite power, as if there were a thousand of them, muscled with her passion to do no harm. She seemed still, but was not; she was rain returning to Heaven, a celestial ship swift enough to change the order of the world, and hold Ocean as its cargo.

Ocean reinvented dance every time she moved; her prattle was like the poetry of another world that had yet to be translated. She was proof that the world was still being created. A life has signal images, they say, that return at the hour of death. Among Rain's would surely be a summer afternoon exchanging wild strawberries from a basket with a laughing child, fruits given by the little girl with a variety of solemn priestly concern, or riotous laughter followed by a somersault, or with a kiss.

When Rain fed her a strawberry in turn, she threw her head back as if she were floating in a world made of summer fruit; she tasted the fruit so completely that she became it. Then she ran back and forth between Rain and her mother, with strawberries in her hands, spilling over with the glory and generosity of her joy.

Mother and child were some other kind of human pair than she had known. And yet they did not languish in the dreamy mutual swoon of tenderness shown in paintings.

Instead, they cast changing lights and shadows on each other, each seeking some kind of delicate balance that touched Rain profoundly—what she witnessed, she thought, was a perpetual seeking of something greater than justice, an exchange of strengths and weaknesses beyond equality. They were not just in a natural relation to each other but, it seemed to her, in an ethical relation.

She did not just pass time with them, she believed in them. Azura and Ocean had formed this world of grace and trust beyond what Azura had undergone—beyond what Rain herself had undergone.

Paradoxically, it was this experience of human love that drove Rain ever closer to murder. She and Azura forgot, and the child had never suspected, the range of what could be done to them without their consent.

Early morning was the time of day that brought a kind of peace to the house. Tables were set in the courtyard if the weather was fine, for the sated men who had stayed the night to savor the final fillip of their pleasures, to complete the cycle of hungers fed.

They were served a country breakfast by the brides who had passed the age of active service, and were now primarily housekeepers and gardeners who had planted and harvested the corn and fruit for the house. If a guest wanted to be served by the bride with whom he had passed the night, and could pay the additional fee, she attended him.

Azura was often in demand for this service, as she had been a bride for long enough to have acquired a core of regular clients. There was no more envied position in the house; regular clients meant stability, regular and orderly payment, jewels to put aside for taxes, and, the greatest luxury of all, predictable nights, nights in which no unexpected facet of a client's mind would be revealed, and no unexpected danger would be faced. It meant that Azura was unlikely to be one of the women screaming for the guards at night, having been transformed into something hateful, a nightmare image that only the client could see.

Azura served well, even expertly, anticipating the logic of each man's appetite before her clients recognized their own preferences. A slice of cheese, a bowl of steaming milk and honey, a plate of house-smoked ham, a fruit liqueur if that was required by the indulgence of the previous night—she furnished them without her clients' ever sensing the want of them. Having a child had made her divination of others' needs, one of the supreme virtues of Peninsulan women, almost flawless.

At last, having ensured all payments were delivered and recorded, she made her way through the courtyards and turned through the vineyards to catch a glimpse of the ocean on her way to her own Ocean in the House of Immortal Children. She caught Rain's eye in the second courtyard, where she was teaching a class of six-year-olds folk dances; dancing was an important art for both the Immortal girls and boys to master, not least because the children's recitals influenced what they might become when they were of age. What was recreation now might become destiny later.

Rain returned her gaze flushed with helpless enjoyment of the movement and of the children's high spirits. They looked at each other with an almost guilty shared pleasure: they had sometimes spoken of the burden the Immortal children bore, their sometimes frantic efforts to charm, to divert, to invent the only happiness the house knew. The six-year-olds spun and leapt like toys frantically trying to come to life. Azura stroked the hair of a particularly earnest boy, and promised the class that cakes would be waiting to reward them in the afternoon at the House of Immortal Children.

Not more than an hour later, it seemed, Rain heard the pounding of the guards' boots, as a messenger tore through the courtyard to Madam, who was working in the First Circle.

A group of six guards followed him, carrying something in a sack.

It was Azura. She had killed herself. The Crowned Ones had requisitioned her little girl, Ocean, and Madam had taken the child during the night to deliver her.

Madam informed the Immortals of Azura's death at an assembly called before the hour when the clients were admitted.

Madam spoke contemptuously of Azura; she was guilty of the rankest blasphemy. Her body would be thrown from the Cliff of the Condemned, like a criminal. Living criminals were executed there, but in cases such as these, symbolic executions of lifeless criminals were held.

"God commands us to be exemplary in the lives He has chosen for us. Let those of you who challenge Him, as Azura did, see how He destroys the arrogant."

This warning, and the feverish tone in which Madam delivered it, looking into the eyes of Azura's friends in the company, gave rise to the rumor that Azura had not really killed herself, but had been killed in the act of trying to murder Madam.

"Not only was Azura's act sacrilege," Madam continued, "but it was born of selfishness. Her little daughter, born of who knows what father, is now a child among God's Elect, given to a Crowned family who chose this child for their own.

"That sure and perfect salvation of her child is what Azura died rebelling against. But God has chosen differently. We are helpless to defy Him. When I take a child, I serve you as God does, as God elects. The deaths of men belong to Him, and the children of women. Be grateful to Him."

She then called the names of those who would be assigned to entertain Azura's clients that evening. The Immortals dispersed, heads bowed, hiding what was in their eyes. In Rain's eyes was a vision of Madam, her skull crushed with a rock. The blood-smeared rock would be the anvil of perfect justice, where the wronged are restored to righteousness without remorse. It is there that knowledge passes into perfection, where questions end only with one answer, the divine command "So Be It."

"I will kill her—for you, Azura," she vowed. "She will die for you, Ocean." She felt a great invincibility, a holy prophetic certainty growing in her, overwhelming her despair. She could not restore Azura and

Ocean, but she would rebuild the world on the foundation of Madam's bones. She would sacrifice her own life in an ecstasy of sacred violence.

That night, alone in her room, she took her childhood toy, the brightly colored wingless bird, from its hiding place, and pressed her lips to it for luck. She was like it; she was already broken; all that was left for her was to shatter into glittering dust, and rise incandescent. She was uplifted, purified by hatred; she sought justice.

Vengeance, I have observed, is the first step on the path of hatred; vengeance is always messianic—and its goal, to restore through blood and sacrifice, lost innocence. The vengeful want to re-create the world as it was, fragment by fragment, out of life they shatter. The blood of murder is the blood of resurrection. Many on the path of hatred are destroyed here, at the outset.

Rain was greatly relieved for the time being to be spared contact with Madam, even through a seasonal assignment she usually loathed. Being detached from her deadly rapture would help her plan to kill coldly.

It was her turn to lead the annual troupe of Fiançailles dancers from her house. The dancers were commissioned to illustrate to the newly engaged girls of the capital the secrets of the marriage bed, from which they had so far been carefully guarded.

A festive band of the Ones Who Dance Always went from house to house, in splendid costumes, glittering with the jewelry they had earned, dazzling with their mastery of the profane arts, of song, poetry, and dance; education ended for the girls of the Peninsula when they married, when only knowledge that would be of use to or please their husbands should occupy them, so the savor of knowledge took on a sensual and forbidden air for them.

It was a demanding period not just because of the giggling, frightened, eager girls, but because the dancers of Madam's house were often returning to their childhood homes, not as daughters or sisters, but as perpetual brides.

The Fiançailles also often created conflicts between the perpetual brides and the wives, when husbands' other lives were revealed through the pieces of missing jewelry now sparkling on the dancers' wrists, hair, and necks. It had happened from time to time that brides died during the Fiançailles, poisoned by the traditional pastries, or met with some accident on the way to their quarters and were stripped of their jewelry by bands of thieves.

But there were also moments of keen poignance, the glimpses of childhood neighborhoods and former families for some, the luxury of an entire month without clients, the opportunity to display their exquisite mastery of the forbidden arts, and for Rain, breathing and hearing her beloved sea. She did not think she could have survived being walled inside the house without the view of the sea from the Pagan Chapel.

People lined the streets to see them as they paraded through the streets each night, singing songs of love, in diaphanous costumes as for the marriage bed, their faces and bodies painted with gold, covered with their collections of jewels.

Each dancer was crowned with lit candles set in a golden three-branched candelabra referring to the Angel Flights; a smaller candelabra was attached to left and right hand by a bracelet. On the fifth count of every song, they pirouetted with extraordinary precision, molten planets in orbit, surrounded by the changing foliage of shadows the candles cast.

When they arrived at the house that had commissioned them, they surrounded the waiting young wife-to-be at the door and ushered her inside. They paraded past the hostess and the cluster of matrons supervising the children too young to be left alone, indulging themselves in the lacy betrothal pastries and rose-colored wines, and reminiscing about their own Fiançailles. The dancers and the season's fiancées moved into a reception room in which a stage had been improvised.

There, the girls, blushing, gorging themselves on pastries, were seated in a circle around the stage. Songs and dances instructed them in the postures, caresses, and rhythms of marriage, the wall-climbing vine, the rising sun, the sweeping torrent, the leaping doe, the coral diver, the stalking tigress, the thousand waves, the moonlit cloud, the serpent-charmer, and the rest of the anthology, illustrated by the dancers, singly and in pairs.

Afterward, the girls rejoined the matrons, and the dancers filed past them, catching the eyes of former sisters, mothers, cousins, into the streets for the final nocturne. They rested in their quarters or walked by the sea under light guard until it was time for the next evening's entertainment.

It was toward the end of the month that Rain saw her sister among the matrons after performing at a seaside villa in which the stage was set up on a lavishly decorated and canopied dock, the fiancées ferried out in gondolas. The entertainment was made more dramatic by a sudden tempest.

As the dancers made their way back through the reception hall crowded with matrons holding drowsy babies or performing sleep rituals for toddlers, Rain suddenly had the odd sensation that the sapphire stone on her finger had expanded, as if she were not wearing the gem, but the blue night itself; the feeling connected her to the gaze projecting it.

She followed the angle of the invisible attention, and saw her sister in the act of realizing that she had seen her own sapphire ring, her husband's bridal gift, on the finger of a dancer. Dolphin recognized the ring before she recognized Rain. The ring seemed to hover over them; they met inside the sapphire.

Dolphin was holding a little girl who suddenly screamed like a butchered lamb. She held the child closer, to soothe its fear at the sight of the burning, otherworldly dancers. But the child screamed more heartrendingly, and fought her. She struggled in Dolphin's arms, trying to reach the dancers, and began to cry out "Rain! Rain!" The child was Ocean, Azura's daughter.

At that instant, these sisters understood their story simultaneously, as if they were angles trapped in their positions within a parallelogram of sapphire light. One sister held the child of the perpetual bride who had killed herself; the other held the ring of her sister's husband who had tried to father a blood child on her to take for her barren sister. Now Rain could not return the ring, any more than Dolphin could return the child, who wailed with a despair more hopeless and primordial than either sister had yet known, for her life.

The sisters looked at each other. Their own suffering had for a moment miraculously ceased; as they exchanged gazes, each became the other. Rain lived her sister's imprisonment as wife within an orthodoxy of marriage she must always fail, Dolphin knew herself the sacrificed bride who absorbed the violence of desires, and defended the world from destruction. Together with the unprotected child, they were a trinity, each alive as a self, each alive as the other, entrapped in infinite compassion and freed through infinite compassion.

Revelation came to them as revelations do, briefly, and in the form of disbelief.

They understood, yet without knowing, that there are no separate lives; each life and individual character exists in relation to every other life, dead, living, yet to live. They were like crystals, rotating within a lattice that extended in all directions.

The presence of Azura refracted through them, and through her the gleaming meshes of other geometries, other thousands of unknown bonds. Spontaneously, furtively, they clasped hands, feeling the symmetry and relationship of hand and hand, flesh and bone. It was the last time they saw each other.

Returning to the house after a month in the capital felt not only painful for the brides, after the excitement and quasi-freedom of the Fiançailles, but also unnatural; returning to nights of clients and governance by Madam after a month of physical integrity was to be forced back into some perverse infancy.

Madam had already drawn up new schedules for the returning dancers. "You won't like it," she said to Rain, "but I've assigned Azura's regular clients to you. They will spend at the same level for someone in the same style. I will have her clothes delivered to you. You will wear her dresses when entertaining her clients."

Rain had nearly forgotten Madam's sustained enjoyment of force-feeding misery like disgusting food, watching the face of someone struggling to choke it down. She was of the genus that finds human suffering desirable.

Madam had the added relish of orchestrating a subtle and certain double failure: Rain would disappoint Azura's circle by not being Azura, while she would be constantly grieved by remembering her friend through the clients. She wondered if Madam, cunning in small cruelties, was capable of savoring any other pleasures than this.

Madam was remarkable for her steady hostility to any semblance of human happiness. Her contempt seemed to add to her power—she could administer misery in calibrated doses, with predictable results. She needed to know nothing particular about any person under her roof in order to produce a conflict between wish and obedience.

To concern herself with the well-being of her charges would mean cultivating personal knowledge, making mistakes. The study of humanity too often ignores how much people hate personal failure; they receive it like a whiplash. Madam was infallible in the provision of misery; she had perfected it.

Rain was reminded of the stories she'd heard from trading clients about a country where the feet of highborn women were rendered porcelain ornaments by binding. This crippled them, but also contained them, and made their fates more bearable for being known; what would happen if they could walk? If the way they lived came from both inside and outside them, what might happen then?

Dressed as Azura that night, she waited to undertake a client who might be furious that she was not her dead friend. When the door opened, a young man entered. She had seen him irregularly, but often with Azura; he was the son of a prominent ship owner, and was often traveling. The jewels he had brought Azura, now the property of the state, came from many countries, the fruits of the many voyages he had already undertaken.

Rain stood up, displaying the courtesy due to clients, and waited in impeccable silence, with lowered eyes, for his orders. She was by this time a well-known dancer, with a fame that drew visitors from the Old Monarchy into the Peninsula to see her perform in her Immortal cloister. Now it was all the more important for her to exhibit the gestures of obeisance; nothing awakened more brutality in the men of the Peninsula than the pretensions of women.

She kept her eyes hidden, though long practice in staring out into an audience and pretending not to see them enabled her to look at the client unobserved. He was staring at Azura's dress, and not at Rain at all. Then she saw something she had never seen in her life, or even heard of. The young client sank into a chair, put his face into his hands, and wept. Rain stood correctly motionless, waiting to be told how to respond.

"I loved her," he said, when he was at last able to speak. "I thought the little girl might be mine."

They talked all night. Only their voices touched, colliding occasionally in questions and answers.

Since they could never marry, Enarch told her, he had planned to steal Azura and the child from the house, and settle them on one of the islands off the coast of the Old Monarchy. The rescue was to have been carried out two days from now. Azura and the little girl were to have been spirited out in a trunk placed among the luggage of the dark-haired bride who always traveled with Admiral Annan.

Rain tried to console him. "You would have taken an impossible risk. She would surely have been discovered."

"No. They had agreed to it, Annan and his daughter. She had persuaded him to help us."

"Whose daughter?"

"Admiral Annan's. The dark-haired girl he pays for permanently is his daughter. He never wanted her to end her life here. He does the only thing he can, and pays for her as if she were his lover. No one has ever touched her."

He began to sob again. "It's too late. Too late even for the little girl. There will never be justice." He tore a pillow apart with his bare hands, substituting it for the table he wanted to overturn and splinter. "I despise this world—which will be ruled forever by those I despise."

Then Rain spoke perhaps the first honest words she had spoken to a man in the house. She said, "It's not too late for the others. For the children of this house. And for the Immortal children in the other houses.

"Yes, I believe there will be no justice that we don't create. There will be no salvation unless we save each other. The question for us who suffer is not why we suffer, but what suffering we inflict?

"Who would we kill?

"Can we be just to someone trying to kill us?

"Can we save someone who is killing us?

"Whose suffering do we choose?

"Whose suffering do we ignore?

"Is there anguish that we need?

"Whose pain do we accept?

"Can we be just to someone who is trying to kill us?

"Can we save the innocent—and the guilty?

"How?"

Out of her questions, their conspiracy was born.

They planned first to make a census count of the children in all the Houses of Immortal Children, since neither knew how many there were, or how to plan the scope of the rescue. They could not hope to liberate all the women as well; children by their nature were easier to smuggle, but who would accompany them, and what would the mothers left behind be risking?

An intricate pattern of knowing and not knowing might determine who would die and who would live, according to which details each could give at the interrogations that would surely follow the rescue. And the rescue would have to be successful, because the act of failure is itself already a full and detailed confession.

Over the months, they made a count of the number of children in each house. Enarch would find several pages inside his map books, covered with small idle sketches of wingless birds in the landscapes where the houses were positioned. They had only to count the number of birds in each landscape to have a rough count of the children in each house, barring the new ones who were being born, and the others who passed into the service of the house each season, and were much more closely guarded.

Admiral Annan's daughter, Grail, with her freedom to travel with her father, provided this and much other useful information. Enarch was wealthy enough to be able to pay for costly nights of planning with Grail, despite the exclusive arrangement Madam had made with her father. And Admiral Annan, the connoisseur of Peninsulan dance, succumbed to a passion for Rain, and bought nights with her as well as his dark-haired girl. Such betrayals were always possible for a price; the house was expensive to manage, and the treasury of the Peninsula was steadily refilled with the revenues earned by the Immortals.

Madam managed these transactions discreetly. Her finesse in betrayal blinded her. It never occurred to her she might herself be betrayed. When it happened, as it turned out, she was both betrayed and betrayer.

On a spring evening, seeing to the service of wine to the guests in the first courtyard, she suddenly put her hand to her forehead, dropped her glass, and fell forward so abruptly that no one had the presence of mind to catch her before her head struck the ground. The body needs no partner to be unfaithful; Madam had had a stroke.

She was carried to her rooms, where she lay unconscious, cared for by shifts of her Immortal brides. Among them was Rain, who volunteered for the hours just before dawn. God had at last given her the chance to kill, that human desire that precedes sexual lust and often outlives it.

Rain stared at Madam, now defenseless in her bed, her mouth open, her breath rasping like a saw in wood. Remembered scenes of Madam slapping, insulting, seizing children, and distributing them like rations of wheat, Madam criticizing an evening's flower arrangements while girls screamed in rooms behind closed doors poured through her mind like a hemorrhage.

The life of the house had been conducted according to Madam's creed, her luxurious array of cruelties, her dream of God. Now Rain would be Madam's God brought to life.

All the lives Madam had harmed would, in a fatal ecstasy, be transformed into a sacrament of death. Rain's only desire was to eradicate this being of pure and absolute evil, and send her to the hell she had made for others; her desire erased the reality of the children, the work of the rescue, the escape from this house into life. She was far beyond the principle of the general amnesty that is given to the sick and wounded.

Rain had entered eternity; she had found the timeless perfect justice, the godly power, and the absolute innocence that all murderers possess. For it is the nature of that dark miracle that at the moment of murder, no killer feels a trace of guilt. Murderers give death to those who do not deserve to live.

She cut Madam's throat with her eyes. It would be a fitting death, a silence exchanged for all the screams she had muffled, the rapes that she had assisted as a poisonous midwife. God permits.

She opened a drawer, searching for a pair of scissors, or a knife. She found a fine knife with an image of the Angel Flights damascened on its blade, and gripped it tightly in her hand. Then, to her shock, she heard a child's voice in the room, and quickly, protectively, slid the weapon back inside the drawer, out of sight, but ready. She could never bear to see a terrified child in the presence of violence.

The little girl said, in her crystalline child's soprano, "I have some strawberries. Would you like me to give you some?"

Rain peered through the shadows. The child must be too shy to come into the room without permission. She needed to accept the gift, and with gentle authority send the girl home to her mother, far from what was about to happen here.

She went to the door, already somehow less tall, assuming the instinctive stoop of an adult about to miniaturize herself for a child. The hall was empty.

"You can feel how warm they are from the hot sun. I picked them for you," the child chattered.

The little girl had slipped inside. Rain turned again, peering into the corners of the room. But there was only one other person inside. The little girl speaking was speaking from Madam. Her eyes were open, but clear and soft, as Rain had never seen them. Madam had become another self, somewhere else. She said with melting, uncalculated sweetness, "I want you to have some of the strawberries too, Mama."

Later, Madam sang nursery rhymes, and begged for Rain to hold her hand. She spoke confidingly of her life at home—her passion for the family vanilla cake, how she hid her fear of her father.

Until dawn broke, Rain was both the killer with her hand on the knife of justice, and the resurrected mother of the lost, adorable, chattering girl child who had been Madam, and was alive again in her. She struggled to kill, and she struggled not to kill. If she stabbed Madam to the heart with the knife she held, she would also be killing a lost child.

Rain left when the next watcher bride arrived, and walked through the cloisters toward the Pagan Chapel, as the clients breakfasted. She was exhausted, but alive in a new way, with a strange new sense of power, the power of refusing, as she had never been able to refuse a client.

She had passed the night in the company of death, for murderous hatred brings a distinct physical sensation of being killed; of burning, of drowning, of being suffocated. Her lust to kill Madam had not left her—but she could not harm the child wandering lost inside the monster.

She had not killed Madam, though she had been given the perfect opportunity, even though Madam was entirely guilty of all she had done. Rain tried to understand why she had not done it.

She had not been afraid. She had wanted to give death. "But," she thought, "murder is, in the end, impossible. It can never achieve our aim. Human actions can never be so precise. The murder, it seems, is never of just one person.

"I could not kill one without risking taking the lives of others I don't know, from her past, from now, or from years to come. So then, we always kill the innocent with the guilty. She was a child tonight, intact in her childhood. Even our evil cannot ever eradicate all traces of our innocence. And there, too, I would have killed the innocent with the guilty. We cannot separate them.

"She may have a daughter, somewhere, missing her, imagining her, without knowing what she is. The nature of murder, like love, is that it spills over unpredictably into other lives; and if the death ricochets through so many bodies, the murderer herself might eventually die of it. Every murder is a genocide."

She spoke of it during the evening hours purchased by Admiral Annan, who had fully expected her to kill Madam, and had felt helpless to stop it. He was both relieved and made curious by her description.

"Then did you spare her out of love?" he asked.

"No, out of hate. And out of futility. I understood that if I murdered her, she would not live, but she would not die either. I would have rendered her immortal. God is an ironist. For those we kill enter us, and inhabit us like children we can never deliver. They never leave us; the murdered take our lives.

"I spent the hours with her in temptation. My hands ached with killing strength. I was torn through and in and beneath hatred as if it were a landscape surrounding me. It was like being struck by lightning. I saw strange things, rocks convulsing, dark clouds that were contorted human faces. They spat rain contemptuously. They shouted obscenities. The clouds screamed for me to kill them, and disappeared when I raised the knife. They mocked my powerlessness.

"This is what else I saw. I saw last night that we cannot escape hating, or being hated. These bodies expose us to it, as they expose us to love. But hatred can either strike us dead, like lightning, or illuminate us. It shocks us into seeing what is hidden in the landscape.

"Hatred can be confined to reason, but kept from the heart. You look at me skeptically, but we must hate with wisdom.

"We must not pretend we don't hate.

"I will hate Madam wisely, for what she has done. My hatred is a record of it all. There exists a true hatred as well as a true love. I am not sure, but I think without knowledge of hatred, our love will be an illusion?"

She studied a map he handed her of routes that led through the mountains down into the capital. She looked up at him and said, "It is clear how to mourn someone beloved: the questions that are not answered are how to mourn someone you did not love: how to mourn someone you hated."

The four conspirators debated intensely, while Madam was bedridden, how to initiate the rescue. Enarch had many contacts in the Old Monarchy, where the beliefs and practices of the Peninsulan colony were largely condemned. Raiding parties might save the most children and even women, and at the same time, divert suspicion from the Peninsulan collaborators. But were they risking igniting a war that would cost the lives of many more than sixty children? They discussed whether a fire, judiciously set, would be too hard to control.

Still, enough chaos and general evacuation could cover the rapid, coordinated disappearance of the children down the mountain roads, and onto Annan's ship, waiting in the port. They would identify the ship by its carved wooden figurehead of a wingless bird. Every alternative taught them a truth about the nature of risk: that every rescue plan carried with it the possibility of a failure that might cause more harm than the original situation.

"We can only hope to deliver the children from our own house,"

Rain concluded, and told them both separately. "The more ambitious plan is likely to risk more and save fewer. We have to hope that we inspire the others, that they will find their own ways."

When both Grail and Enarch protested, separately, Rain gave them both the same reply, in her characteristic manner of speaking, which advanced through questions that washed over one another like waves. "I have learned that I am no Messiah. I was born under the sign of Savour the Provident, who planted seeds so each of us might feed the other.

"We stand to fail all if we try to save many; it is dangerous enough for us all to try to do what is to hand. And we need to consider what will happen to these children once they are rescued, when their lives are beyond ours. That is something we should think about in our salvation fever. What good can come of salvation followed by abandonment? Salvation itself can be a form of sin, a drunken ecstasy, a lust for reverence. We are always admonished to fear God, but we would be wiser to fear ourselves."

Now, when Enarch spent nights in conference with her, he left with a jewel from her now substantial collection—each jewel would be an income for a child, whose mother had consented to the rescue. Jewel by jewel, they purchased a life to be returned to a child.

Rain acquired even more valuable gems through the spectacular success of her new ballet, in which she played two roles, one of athletic virtuosity, the other of flowing contemplative grace. No dancer ever again performed both roles, though naturally, the spectacular role of the first half was the more coveted.

The curtain opened, it seemed, on nothing. Then the wavering light that appeared unevenly onstage revealed the elements of a landscape, a miniature world of small hills, no higher than a child's knee, rivers on which boats glided, overlooked by houses and gardens studded with fruit trees and flowers. Finally, the light dawned slowly in the foreground and revealed, on her back, her arms and legs rippling like silver thread, Rain, a spider larger than the world.

She launched herself into the air with a backflip, and danced over the world, supporting herself in arabesque on the small trees, playing with the shadow she cast on the tiny rivers, balancing on point next to a house smaller than her foot. As she reached the opposite corner of the stage, she began a series of pirouettes, spinning diagonals punctuated by leaps, suggesting the form of the letter "X," as if she were trying to write an alphabet. When the sequence was finished, she glided backward.

The audience was silent for a moment; then it applauded loudly. She had danced a glittering, silver web over one half of the stage.

With a great leap, she flung herself into the center, and began what some thought the most memorable part of the dance, a pas de deux with her web.

She slid and darted and trembled in the silver orb, sometimes embedded in it, sometimes with limbs arcing independent of the web, while her hands caressed the silk. She used the web as a fresco, and moved inside and outside it, as we secretly wish the figures in paintings could do. But only God could inspire the painted shepherdess on canvas to lift her crook, and walk over the hill.

Rain, in this dance, found the great secret of theater art—the audience must see the performer revealed as only the eye of God can see her, the painting come alive, known intimately as God would know the unfolding of a life.

She revolved in the air, dancing with herself, and came to rest in the center of what she had spun, tenderly laying her cheek against her own web, in an ecstasy of self-love.

Then she tossed a shining filament upward; it drew her up to the ceiling, where she hovered, then floated down, her arms held overhead like a coronet, spinning five precise counts to the right, five to the left, crowning the air itself. She stood still when she descended, and held her position while the lights extinguished her. When they came back up, the audience roared its appreciation. One man stood up and tossed an emerald necklace into the web, where it caught and sparkled like a handful of stars. Others, delighted with the effect, hurled more jewelry into the web, until it shivered, studded with precious stones.

When the music began in the second act, a child emerged from the miniature village, and began a playful dance based on children's skipping games. Rain noiselessly descended from the web, and began to shadow all the child's movements, skipping when she skipped, mimicking her delicate chain of steps from behind her. Rain dangled a shining ribbon over the girl's right shoulder; the fascinated child seized the ribbon; then over her left shoulder, a second ribbon undulated. She took that in her hand, too, and Rain began to move her arms up and down, as if she were a marionette.

Rain amused herself by inventing the steps the child was now forced to dance, unaware that she was being partnered. Then Rain forced her to pirouette with increasingly dizzying speed, until she was tangled in the silver threads, and dragged up by them into Rain's arms, trapped in her embrace, to the music of a lullaby.

Then followed, to the sounds of horns, and traditional huntsman's chorales, one of the robust set pieces for male dancers that were often part of Rain's ballets. There was a comic trio of dogs, played by boys from the children's classes, and a vigorous flight and chase ballet, which subtly contrasted the masculine style of hunting, and the feminine style, as exemplified by the spider. For men hunt by pretending to be the brothers of the prey they seek, and women hunt by impersonating the mothers of their prey.

In a second act finale that equaled the first in daring, one of the hunter's arrows inadvertently passed scathingly close to Rain, casually destroying the foundation of her web. The freed child leapt into the wings, while the spider, with a series of steps that alternated falling and rising, caught a silver rope from the fragments of the web, and rose to the rafters clinging to it, doubled over.

There was some controversy over the third act, as some felt it conventional, and not the equal of the first two. The curtain opened on a new set, easily recognized as the landscape of the first act, with river, hills, gardens, and houses, the country of the miniature world now full scale. There a pair of lovers, Rain as the woman, performed a series of dances in a formal garden, using its statues and benches as partners, as well as each other. The dances were almost a conversation, teasing, intimate, tender. At the end of the act, the woman and man leave the stage, then return, having forgotten her wrap on a bench. The man lifts the garment and delicately drapes her in it. Her shawl is the cobweb, studded with jewels, which trails behind her as they leave the stage, arm in arm.

I listened to the criticisms of the third act, its lack of drama, its poverty of ambition. I did not agree. Admiral Annan passionately defended it. He argued that this act had been nothing less than Rain's introduction of love into the brutal milieu of the surroundings. I had no strong view of that, but I did notice something quietly and unmistakably radical. From the miniature landscape of the first acts to the restored full scale of the last, Rain had altered the proportions of the world.

With the jewels that had been showered on her with this dance, the four conspirators could now purchase the entire island where Enarch had planned to take his dead lover and her child, and settle the rescued innocents there. Annan's daughter Grail would sail with them, along with the five mothers escorting them. Annan would bear the disgrace of her disobedience with convincing indignation. Rain must remain in the house, so that only two of the conspirators would be exposed. He would then transfer his protection to Rain. At least if they could find no way to free her, he could offer her a privileged life within her prison, as he had done with Grail.

In the end, they settled on a natural disaster to draw the guards from the Gate of Immortals and as many people of the house as possible away from the children's quarters. They set a date for a fire in the vineyards, to be lit, as she said with a tired smile, by Rain. She was sure that the endeavor was hopeless, but she readied herself to carry it out, and light the flame. She kept her despair to herself, so as not to infect the others, and suspected them of doing the same.

Even in this house of rape, though, there were miracles. She had seen love; she had seen hate.

And by a miracle she had consented to protect someone she despised; in doing so, her loathing was transformed, not into love, but into an honorable and enlightened hatred, a hatred confined to reason, its hot light showing her clearly the features of what she hated, without possessing her own heart. Without hope, she was still able to remember that she was surrounded by more than she could see; she was like a figure in an icon, unable to see beyond the frame.

Beyond the frame, the earth shook.

In the afternoon, Rain was practicing dances set to traditional love songs, which had a special intensity on the Peninsula, as the combined practices of forced marriage and love slavery ensured that all loves were unrequited. Men and women who would never know the fulfillment of their desires had an insatiable appetite to hear songs about the invincibility of true love.

Rain soared up, turned in the air, and as she dropped and touched the floor with both heels, the earth trembled, as if her leap had shaken it to the core. She thought the leap had made her dizzy, that she had imagined the tremor.

She took a deep breath and practiced the leap again. This time there was a rattling sound, and the walls of the practice room took on a slow, strange elasticity, as if they were about to change places with each other.

She heard screams, and ran outside into the courtyard, where the tiles of the pavement had cracked, and the walls of the galleries were shivering. There was another series of slow, deep convulsions, but the buildings surrounding the dancers' courtyard held. The men and women who had poured into the courtyard wept and sank to the pavement in shock.

Rain and two dancers who were mothers raced through the arches, and up the hill past the Pagan Chapel to the House of Immortal Children. Grail was already there, urging the children and mothers into the small field where they played. She touched tear-stained faces as she counted. One wing of the house had been so damaged that it looked as if it might crumble through a careless footstep. They gingerly guided older and carried younger children through the ruined section, until the sixty were accounted for.

"The children are terrified," Rain said to Grail. "Nothing will soothe them if they sleep near buildings that could fall down and crush them." Grail understood.

"Yes," she said. Her eyes searched Rain's for certainty as she described her guess at Rain's improvised plan. "Until we know which buildings are secure, they will be safe only if they sleep outside the walls. Madam is in no condition to make the decision, but the acting governess will understand we cannot take risks with the children."

Rain nodded. "If the guards agree, under these extraordinary circumstances, we will bring them bottles of wine—as much as they can drink—and entertain them."

They repeated their dialogue for each of the five mothers who would escort the children, who began to organize them into the small clusters, the units they had planned when rehearsing the escape. The repetition was designed to teach the four what to quote if they were asked. If all went well, they would be outside the walls at sunset, and the guards would be blind drunk by dark.

They were to wait in the garden by the Pagan Chapel until Grail and Rain came to conduct them outside the walls. If permission was refused, the children were to wail and scream at the gates until no one could stand it, and the guards gave in. Many of the children were genuinely afraid, and others relished the chance at playacting tantrums. When they reached the port, they would be transformed into a group of shelterless refugees, fleeing the ruins of their houses. They would disperse in four groups around the capital, and wait for Grail to bring word from Admiral Annan that the ship was ready to board.

There were two things the Immortal brides protected in their house: their jewelry, which was their only safety, and the children who lived there, the only innocence in the house. Rain and Grail met little resistance to their plan; it was even given the flourishes of a pleasure outing, with pitched tents and picnic food.

They sent out bottles of wine to the guards, and climbed to the Pagan Chapel quickly, eager to get the children beyond the gates as naturally and quietly as possible.

Rain moved down the vineyards to the lowest terrace to see if she could get any sense of how much the port had been damaged. It was then she saw it. It was the black wall of love-killing water that nothing on the face of the earth could stop.

The shapeless sea became a fortress, stronger than any stone battlement, and hurled itself at the land. As the water poured over the sea walls, she saw one of the port's great docks set free; a portion of it slammed into a cargo boat moored nearby. The sea devoured a customs house, and lapped up the buildings on the shore like a beast with a thousand black tongues. Then she heard it, too, an orchestral roar of waters, the percussion of buildings cracking and collapsing, the choir of human screams, the symphony of death.

If she had killed Madam in her vulnerability as she had intended, she would have felt one with this destruction. If she had carried out the murder, she would have become of the nature of this wave, which damned all in its path.

She walked gravely and purposefully back to the waiting women and children. She described what she had seen to Grail. The tragedy might in the end work in their favor.

Grail was above all to gather the children just outside the gates and wait for her. She would watch from the terrace until she saw the waters recede; then they would make their way down the mountain and profit from the chaos of the town to get the children on board Enarch's ship. It was only then the two looked at each other, and realized that the wave might have taken both Enarch and his ship.

Rain returned to her perch among the vineyards. She put her hands in her pockets for warmth, and remembered that she had slipped her wingless clay bird in one for luck. She joined her heart for many hours with the ones in the water, wondering if her sister and the little girl, her brother, her former parents, were rising and falling in the floods. For a day and a night, she watched, she herself a wingless bird, unable to carry herself or anyone else to safety, until the waters receded.

She found another kind of flood in the courtyard, and outside the gates, a human flood of refugees who had fled their houses in the lower villages for higher ground. The guards had gone in the opposite direction, once they heard from the first dazed arrivals what had happened. They had families in the lower villages, and were frantic to find them. Already there were exhausted survivors camped in the courtyards, and outside the gates, and streams of people moving up and down the paths.

Hidden within the horror was a God-sent opportunity for the children of the house—they wasted no time. They set out in small, seemingly unrelated groups to descend to the port. Grail, a baby in her arms, was to lead the group to Admiral Annan's villa, where they would shelter. Rain, with a baby in her arms, brought up the rear. No one noticed anything questionable about a group of homeless refugees moving toward the capital for shelter, hoping to be reunited with their lost husbands and fathers.

For the first hour of descent, there was an eerie trace of holiday feeling within the little group. The children felt an exuberant thrill at being outside the walls for the first time, distracted by new landscapes, and the strangeness of the day's events.

As they approached the lower villages, though, their progress was hampered with fallen trees and thick mud. The river was high and running fast, and pieces of houses were streaming through the waters to the sea. Rain saw a head roll over and over in the waters, its gold earrings flashing in the sun when it turned faceup. Central streets were strewn with beds, forks, lamps, and other domestic paraphernalia. There were patches of brilliantly colored mud, from carpets whose dyes had soaked into the earth. The disaster had stripped houses of their facades, turning them into theater sets, households of the dead.

Occasionally, disembodied voices would call out from above them—people high in trees, either still afraid to come down, or waiting for help, having climbed too high to descend unassisted. But many others were roaming the streets and the outskirts, searching for neighbors, or possessions, or scavenging, oblivious to little bands of orphans and women on their way to the capital for relief. The women and children followed the route nearest the river, cautiously avoiding notice as best they could.

Rain heard a wild series of screams as they approached a thick stand of trees downstream. A man was lying on the bank, with one foot still in the river, while his new widow slapped him, screaming with each slap. An elderly couple stood over them, protectively embracing two children, so that their faces were turned from the inert man and the woman striking him.

Rain was possessed by a bizarre impulse. It was as if she had seen a picture of a group of mourners, and then her own figure had been sketched into the scene with swift, irresistible, ecstatic strokes. She, who had never kissed a man, ran to this one, and lay down on him, pressing her lips to his, passionately healing him.

She poured her breath into him, as someone blows on the embers in a hearth to restart a fire. She who had never given birth gave life. The breath she had not taken from Madam had been saved for this man.

She breathed into him with a transfigured violence; the force of the murder she had not committed added itself to creation, so strong and changed that it healed instead of killed. As if a dive could be reversed, the man soared upward from the depths back to the surface of the earth.

A person again, he turned on his side, his body curled like a baby's, and vomited feebly, until the air tasted sweet to him again.

A knot of people had gathered around Rain and the now-living dead man. The man's widow lifted the baby Rain had been carrying back into her arms, and touched her lips to Rain's. They would not let her go until she kissed each one who had witnessed her immortal kiss. And the healing kiss was taken through them up and down the mountains, and along the shores, and others who had died that day lived, they say. There is a legend that the breath Rain gave this man still brings life to people who have never heard of that flood. I do not know whether this is true.

I do know that Rain and her charges reached the capital, and rejoined the other Immortal children, waiting in the grounds behind Admiral Annan's villa on the bluffs. There Grail gently gave her the news that her sister and brother, with all their households, had been killed; the little girl—who might have been Enarch's daughter—the child awarded to Dolphin to live among the Elect had instead been delivered to her death.

Both Rain's parents had survived, though General Jarre was gravely injured. The port had sustained severe damage; the only way to reach or leave shore was by dinghy. No one knew whether Enarch's ship with the figurehead of the wingless bird had been crushed along with many other ships driven into each other, or against wharves and bridges.

The women waited with the children, refugees whom the wealthy and magnanimous Annan family sheltered at their own expense behind their locked gates. On the second afternoon, Rain heard the key turning in the lock. She and Grail exchanged a look and got to their feet. The somber, drawn face they saw was Enarch's, followed by Admiral Annan's.

He had been far out at sea on the rescue ship when what was to become the killing wave passed unnoticed deep beneath the *Wingless Bird;* they felt no more than a strong swell. As is so often the case in human life, they sailed serenely, ignorant of the suffering of others, unaware of the devastation that had reached the port before them.

Enarch was still in a state of disbelief; the capital he had sailed away from was barely recognizable.

Enarch took Grail and the first group of children to the dinghy; if they were challenged, they would say they were making use of the ship for housing these orphans until permanent shelter could be found. He and Annan would alternate escorting the children in small clusters until all were aboard. Then the brides would join them, with as much speed as they could manage discreetly. He dared not delay the sailing. All must be aboard ship by two o'clock.

Enarch led them with watchful, animal attention, as if he were a lioness transporting cub after cub to safety from a marauding predator. Group after group departed, until at last all sixty were aboard.

Then it was the turn of the five brides who were to make their way to the port, and board the waiting dinghy. Rain would leave with them, and take her own path back to the house, claiming that she had been separated from Grail and the children in the midst of the chaos.

The bluffs were crowded with makeshift camps of refugees. Rain guided the other women down along the paths she had known as a girl, until they reached a magnificent stone staircase, damaged, but still intact, flanked by houses on either side, descending some three hundred feet to the port. Men and boys were collecting stones that had fallen during the earthquake, while others had already begun repairs of their houses. Two men at work on reinforcing a house that was listing to the left side looked up reflexively at the women as they passed.

One elbowed the other. "Isn't that the dancer from the Fiançailles?" he asked. He had been one of Rain's guards during the betrothal month.

His companion looked at them, and nodded bitterly. It was bad luck to see an Immortal outside the walls of the houses, except during the Fiançailles. No wonder the killing wave had come.

The two hurried down the steps, pushing past the women to block them. They called out to the other men to help them pen the escaping Immortals; from below them and above them, a tide of men and boys, curious at first, and then enraged, engulfed the women.

The *Wingless Bird* sailed without them.

. . .

The morning of Rain's execution was golden; the tulip trees that had just snowed their blossoms made the world feminine with their perfume. On the five preceding mornings of the last week of her life, she had been forced to witness the death leaps of the five Immortal women who had conspired with her.

Each morning she had been taken to the Cliff of the Condemned to witness an execution, so that her own labor uphill when her day came would be quintupled; she must stagger beneath that knowledge, as if she were carrying the five bodies whose lives she had destroyed.

The night before, the traditional funeral garb was delivered to her cell. The condemned women of the Pensinsula wore a version of a bridal gown to their deaths, a black brocade dress embroidered with axes, ropes, and knives, and a coal-black veil. They carried a bouquet of red roses tied with black silk ribbon as they ascended the cliff to join a different kind of groom at a different kind of marriage altar, overlooking a sheer drop.

Rain had refused to spend her final hours in the company of a prince, as the priests of the Peninsula were called, so a guard delivered the paraphernalia silently, and left her alone. The bouquet was exquisite, lavish with perfect blooms. It seemed to her that there were more than a hundred.

She held it to her cheek; the petals felt like the velvet skin of children's faces. She counted the flowers, for the pleasure of touching them. There were exactly sixty, the number of Immortal children she had shepherded to safety. She caught a glimpse of white deep inside one central rose's heart. It was a scrap of paper, folded into a tiny, perfect square. She delicately dislodged it, unfolded it, and read its message: "In gratitude."

The ceremony began an hour later than usual, because of the difficulties the climb now presented to General Jarre, who had yet to master walking on even ground with his wooden leg. Madam, too, no longer had the strength for the ascent. In order to spare them further humiliation on this wrenching morning, we arranged to have all the high-ranking government officials carried up in mountain chairs. Jarre, Judge Pekrin and his son, Admiral Annan, Madam, and the triumvirate of administrators who had made the government function while Jarre recovered from his emotional and physical injuries, were in the front rank, along with myself. All wore the insignia of the Angel Flight, the team of birds pulling the three-branched candelabra.

When we arrived at the height, we were startled to see the cliff covered with bouquets of red roses, as if they were growing from the rocks. The faces of the spectators grew pinched; the peaks of flowers were a sure indication of some underground popular support for what Rain had done.

There would be an awkward interruption if we delayed the ceremony to clear them, as we could not even see how far they extended in either direction. Even that small success would be too much to grant to Rain. Jarre angrily ordered me to light the torches in the monumental golden candelabra soldered to the rocks, the signal for the procession to begin.

Rain ascended the hill, flanked by guards in black uniforms, their faces entirely covered with golden mesh, in which the design of the Angel Flight birds harnessed to their candelabra was outlined. This mask prevented executed and executioner from gazing into each other's eyes and being affected by the glance. It ensured that the anonymity of the guards was protected, and that the execution was correctly self-performed and voluntary.

Rain's black veil, twenty feet of it, flowed behind her in the breeze, as if she were being followed by a flock of black birds. When she arrived at the summit, she was made to kneel in front of the officials. A condemned woman had no right to speak, as her eternal fate ordained by God had been revealed, and nothing could mitigate her punishment.

"Woman, damned by God," Judge Pekrin read out, "obey your Creator. You are condemned to die." Rain got to her feet unhelped, looked each one of the officials, including her former father, Jarre, deliberately in the face. "You have condemned me to die," she said, and, characteristically, made her last words a question. "But will I?"

She walked to the edge of the cliff. Her face was drawn and her eyes wide, though her dancer's movements were as disciplined as ever. She could now count the very breaths that were left to her. The guards followed her, and took up positions, three on either side, drawing their weapons, kicking masses of red roses over the edge in order to stand close enough to the condemned. If she did not leap obediently, she would be pushed, an ultimate disgrace.

She took a deep breath and made a full dançer's leap, as if she, wingless bird, were flying into a partner's waiting arms. For a moment, it seemed, she hovered suspended in the sky, a sail without a ship. Then she fell like a black rose thrown from a balcony. And we no longer knew anything she knew, no longer knew anything about her.

Jarre never took his eyes off his former daughter. His expression showed the impassive, visionary pride of a man of faith, beatified by doing what is right, as God commands. His eyes glowed as in firelight, bright in his resolute face like semiprecious stones embedded in rock, and his soul was embedded in God.

Jarre felt a cold ecstasy after Rain's execution, the joy so central to his character in doing God's will, the mastery of passion perfected by ethics. There was an impersonal sense of resolution in this justice, as when a mathematical problem is solved correctly. The judges and executioners who stopped heartbeats and stifled breathing according to the law were doing what God did, though man's law made violence comprehensible. The law ensured that no one innocent ever died.

What had to be done was done. She had been an enemy of the state. To execute her was to assent to the world God had made. The indefinable satisfaction he had taken so long ago in making her an Immortal had been God's prophetic spirit working in him. And to tell the truth, to kill a daughter asked less of a man than to kill a son.

Jarre had done justice. But God had not. This great courtier of God was tormented by bewilderment and the rage that God had taken from him all He had given, as if Jarre had fallen from grace. God had snubbed him as if he were a steward who had been dismissed, although he had not departed from God's commands by one jot. Jarre's unquestioning service to the state had sustained him through Rain's trial and execution. But the very clarity of his actions made him even more dissatisfied with the illegibility of God's.

Once again, he began to sit in the rubble of his villa at night, staring out to sea on the half of the balcony that was left. His wife, once mother of three, now mother of none, picked her way nightly through the broken marble columns with his dinner. The gold-flecked fragments of wall mosaic were mixed with the sand deposited by the wave. They lay on the ground like shells, as if the house were still underwater, a sea of broken eyes and mouths, disintegrated dances torn from the scenes that had once decorated the walls.

Jarre ate silently, staring out to sea, as if he were waiting for someone to call. Some of his old friends did stop in to mourn with him and comfort him. They made him impatient, forcing him to attend to their needs when his own were absolute. It was as if the tortured were obliged to provide refreshment for the torturer. In any case, the guest he had invited was God, and God had not accepted.

Judge Pekrin, who had presided at Rain's trial, called from below. He had brought with him his son. "Bring a plate and some wine for Pekrin," Jarre said to his wife. "And guide him through the debris so that he doesn't bruise himself."

Jarre's wife fetched Pekrin a chair and sent me off to find him something to eat and drink; he sat down by Jarre, and put his hand on Jarre's shoulder. They were silent for a long time. Pekrin was picking his way through words like rubble, but could not find the means to build a thought. Finally he said, "I can say nothing better to you than this: all of the Peninsula is in mourning. We have all suffered under this terrible wave."

Jarre answered, "We have all suffered. But I have been ruined not only on earth, but beyond, in Heaven. I have nothing more to bequeath, and no one to bequeath it to.

"Every moment of my life has been God's. You cannot deny it. I rode the crest of God's will like a wave, my will lost in the sea of His magnificence. Why should I be crushed by this one wave? Answer that, Pekrin. We are all mourning, but I have lost everything."

Pekrin was conscious of his friend's agony. "God is our King. We cannot see the world and our lives in all details as He does. Your loss may be a mark of distinction, may be a sign of some divine honor you can't yet see."

Jarre shook his head with a convulsive movement of disgust. "I would call that kind if it didn't make me want even more than I do to end my life. Is God honoring me in company with the dead fishermen of the coast, and their barefoot children and their reeking wives? Does a tiger honor a stag when his fangs rip out its throat? God is a predator—whom I still worship, and whom I hate. Whom I adore, and will never trust again."

His wife said soothingly, "It is not right to question God." Jarre gave her a treacherous look, and she shrank. "A blasphemy indeed for you, but God gave reason to men, to speak to Him and know His will. Why did he give me a son and take him away? And my daughter dying at her birthday celebration, while an orchestra played. Where is my right leg? Yet the whores survived. Yet the whores survived. Why? If I can't question God with these questions, then He should not have created me. Or he should have made me a woman."

Admiral Annan, who had entered the villa, and found his own way to the balcony, stood in the shadows listening, before anyone realized he was there. Jarre's wife stood up to bring more food and wine, but he shook his head and thanked her. "I'm not hungry," he said, clearly strongly affected by Jarre's words.

Pekrin's son, a junior advocate at the stage of a young man's career when his view of the world is shaped by the joyous rightness of his place in it, spoke a shade tactlessly. "God never chastises without a holy purpose, to rescue us from doing wrong. He is like a prosecutor, relentlessly searching for the truth of our actions. I see this wave as an instance of God's terrible, majestic grace. It was an act of Almighty mercy, which we cannot grasp, since the scale of divine mercy is so different from our own.

"It was a disaster, it is true, but for our sake, and for our protection. Without it, we might never have known about the traitorous intentions of your daughter Rain. It is a bitter thanksgiving, but we should praise God in all humility. He has struck us down to renew our country and ourselves in His grace."

Jarre was pale with fury. "Rain was no longer my daughter the day I made her Immortal. As to her treachery, we do not need God's revelation that there is no honor among prostitutes. We did not need a tidal wave to remind us that we should keep a closer watch on the houses of the perpetual brides. Why was it necessary for the sake of our national revival for me to lose my only son? My health? My fortune?

"We agree that God is of such unutterable power that He can make a wave tall enough to destroy our city, a wave that killed everyone in its path.

"I witness this power. I assent to it. I am a soldier. We kill all in our path when it is necessary.

"Why, then, isn't God less like us? Why can't He make a wave that kills the guilty but spares the innocent? Why can't he make a wave that elects, as He does among men? He has that power, too, all power—the Maker of sharks and doves. You insult him if you think otherwise. You should pray for forgiveness."

Annan broke in gently, to spare the boy, and make peace between them. "Whether we love God or rail against Him, we cannot fathom Him, any more than we could the tidal wave He sent against us. Even as we talk tonight, we cannot establish whether we have witnessed creation or destruction. Perhaps we cannot even see how many tidal waves we endure. Perhaps there are tidal waves that are not made of water. Age is also a tidal wave."

He turned to the boy. "I remember what you are living now—my perfect aim, my endless breath, the certainty of my balance. Now I waver when I walk, I am breathless, and my bones are dissolving inside my body. I am not underwater, but I am drowning. I had no more warning of it than we did of the tidal wave. My body is being swept away from me while I am speaking to you. Isn't that a miracle?

"There may be still other tidal waves, tidal waves of ecstasy, in which we are changed as in death, but not killed. The only knowledge I have of God I have found in the unexpected and the unforeseen. We can never guess how or when He will appear. Even if we could, we might not recognize Him. Or ourselves. He makes us weep. But I sometimes wonder whether we ourselves, each one of us, are the tears shed by God."

Jarre had fallen silent. His wife saw though that his angry face was wet with tears; she made a sign to the guests to depart without ceremony. I stepped from the shadows behind her chair, and lit them out through the remains of the villa.

Men are such creatures that even if the sky fell and the apocalypse were total, the pitiful remnant left would crawl from the shards of the world, search for timber, and lay the foundations of their new houses. As birds must nest in the spring, men are helpless against this instinct. The coast stirred with the work of rebuilding, but Jarre had no heart to join it.

The loss of his children and his prosperity overwhelmed him, but the loss of his leg also incapacitated him bitterly. He resented his loss of mobility, of being forced to hobble and mince as if he were wearing a skirt. Until that moment, everything that had happened to Jarre, it seemed to him, could be reversed or changed to his advantage if he wanted. The tidal wave and all its consequences were Jarre's first experience of the unalterable. The idea of the permanent in relationship to himself came very late to him.

No one could guess how long he might persist in this state; three of his staff deputized for him, making gubernatorial decisions as they would never before have dared.

It was equally unthinkable that anyone would call for Jarre's resignation; the awe in which he was still held, and pity for his suffering, kept him in his seat. So his deputies presented their acts and policies as his, and scrupulously reported to him on the authority they had exercised in his name, to which he seemed indifferent.

There was also at that time a welling up of strange phenomena, offshoots of the upheaval undergone by the Peninsula, which they did not report. Bizarre graffiti had been appearing scratched on dusty tiles, on the inner walls of houses undergoing reconstruction, on the smooth surfaces of rocks, mounded by the wave or by workmen.

They were mostly images of birds: birds without wings in flight, birds without wings flying with arrows in their breasts, birds in flight whose wings had been replaced in some fanciful way. I remember two in particular: one showed a bird with flaming torches substituted for the wings, and the other, even more bizarrely, a bird whose outstretched wings were trees, utterly reversing the conventional relationship of bird to tree.

As soon as they were effaced, similar images appeared—one of the quotidian annoyances most galling to public officials. Other images and then slogans cropped up, in other quarters. Empty wineglasses were suspended over certain streets, hung from ribbons printed with the legend, "We are parched."

This was a legend that appeared again in rather handsome leaflets one would find blowing about the streets. These were painted with what looked like a full moon. One half of the moon was a barren desert, while the half above was painted a magnificent garden blooming under a mist of spring rain. The streets proliferated with images of roses, their petals sparkling with crystalline drops, over slogans like "Let us flower" or "We flower."

The three deputies took little note of the images at the beginning. They seemed to appear at random times and places, and were regarded as a nuisance rather than a threat. More than anything, they seemed to be stifled outcries by the poor or newly impoverished, pleas for swift relief from the civic authorities. They avoided discussing much more significant matters with Jarre; to bring up these folkloric laments of the poor would be to record the whimpering of the puppies abandoned in the outskirts.

Even when the images began to appear more steadily, suggesting more hands cooperating, no one paid much attention.

The Paradise Nebula, that constellation of disappearing and reappearing stars, unseen for generations, had appeared in the night skies. Along the coast, people sat on the shore and along the cliffs, and watched the breathtaking theater of stars. Some wept when the stars disappeared, and gasped as they took shape again, emerging out of the darkness in new forms. Many took the constellation as a divine consolation, a sign of a heavenly covenant with the drowned. It was likely that this rare celestial apparition was stimulating the production of the images and messages in the capital; the roses, birds, and wineglasses expressing some poignant wish for contact with the dead.

Within months, though, governors of other districts were reporting sightings of similar slogans and pictures in their own territories. The pictures multiplied, but the makers remained invisible. At that point, the deputies decided the matter warranted more exploration, that our eyes should do more than appreciate the art bestowed on us.

I had been reluctant to leave General Jarre's side—he needed me to lean on while he learned to manage his artificial leg, and occasionally, when he was exhausted, I would even carry him up and down, enduring his harsh reproofs and commands. I understood that he needed me to feel the whip; I was to carry him like a battle horse, not like a nurse.

Now, though, there were discussions about returning to my regular circuits among the Houses of the Immortals. They had been neglected during the period after the tidal wave, when the port traffic was so disrupted. What seemed a wise idea became more urgent after an incident involving General Jarre's still uninhabitable villa.

One morning, we woke to discover its walls nearly covered with images of wingless birds, its intact ceilings, floors, and doorways flecked with drops of silver paint that looked like falling rain. When the four Supreme Judges left their separate residences that day for court, they were drenched with torrents of water mixed with silver paper pouring from buckets ingeniously poised over their doors. They took their seats in court that day with stray flecks of silver glinting in their hair and on their shoulders, a furtive silver like the eyes of animals peering out from underbrush.

The artists seemed to have passed from cryptic complaint to childish prank, but no one advanced a convincing theory about their purpose. Jarre remained indifferent. "To deface my house," he told me, "is to add a bruise to a corpse." Nevertheless, the triumvirate of deputies sent a number of us back into the field without informing him.

I went with young Pekrin to my old district, the villages and the two substantial towns on the cliffs above the port, where Madam still nominally presided over the most exclusive House of Immortals in the vicinity.

Her brides had always been drawn from the most influential families. It was natural to wonder if her house, which had been one of the centers of the Immortal rebellion, harbored any leftover dissidents or sympathizers. An informer we had relied on in the past told us he had heard rumors of buried treasure, but had nothing more concrete to offer us.

We thought at first the rumors must refer to the looting that had inevitably occurred in the wake of the tidal wave; these particular troublemakers, though, seemed to have a political purpose. Their graffiti was exhorting others to thievery; they must be storing their takings to rebuild their shattered movement.

I found Madam herself in even worse condition than General Jarre. Though she had suffered nothing so devastating as his losses, she seemed to me unhinged, perhaps by the tidal wave, perhaps because of the disgrace Rain's execution had brought to her and her impeccably managed house. She kept to her bedroom, no longer able to involve herself in the day-to-day administration of the house. She was said to have grown grotesquely fat.

I was told she now often failed to recognize the faces of those she had worked with for years, so I was prepared for her to be confused, when the new governess discreetly left us alone in her room. However, I saw in her eyes that she recognized me at once. She knew exactly who I was. She screamed when she saw me as if I were someone who had come to kill her. "She's dead! She's dead!" Then she screamed again, "She's alive! She's alive!"

"Who is alive and who is dead?" I said in the most hypnotic tones I could muster to soothe her before she created a panic or made anyone think I was hurting her. "Both of them! Rain," she answered. "She doesn't die! Azura doesn't die! But my daughter dies. My child is dead." She began to weep and writhe under her covers.

"These are absurd fantasies," I said to her, creating a tone of voice as an actor does, this time of reassuring paternal ridicule and teasing warmth. I said gently, "You are suffering for a dream daughter. You have never been a mother. And you were standing near me when we saw Rain executed. She leapt from the Cliff of the Condemned, and died. You dream about her, and in your nervous state, take the dreams for reality."

"I see her," Madam said.

"I'm sure you do see her," I said, "but she is not alive. No human being could have survived that fall."

Madam grew silent, and calmer. "Now let me tell you what I have been asked to do here," I said, glad to turn the conversation to something concrete, instead of hallucinations.

After I explained, I had Madam send for the acting governess, a self-possessed, wiry woman, who had previously been responsible for the vineyards, and was said even at her age to be able to prune and crucify the tough arms of the vines into the shapes of intense beseeching that made them yield the finest grapes. Her work was recognizable; her vines looked like ascetics in postures of prayer. She looked like a gnarled vine herself, and had capably taken on the task of the daily administration of the entire compound.

The house, like all the residences of the Immortals, was quieter than before the wave. Many men had died, many had less money to spend, and the traffic of ships in and out of port had still not attained its previous levels. The courtyards were full of refugees whose houses had been destroyed along the coast, and in the lower villages.

Among the refugees were a number who had inherited the kiss of Rain, and survived because of it, or so they believed; they seemed to have no view of her conspiracy. They were only grateful for the miracle that had happened to them. They watched intently at night as the dance troupe continued to perform the repertory of dances she had created, veined with Rain's experience of cruelty and grace, as if they were trying to understand whose breath they now held in their lungs, from whom they had been reborn.

The brides had retreated into the children's quarters, now silent, after Rain, Grail, and whoever else had helped them had dispersed the children to whatever fates awaited them outside the gates, across the borders, on other shores. Not one of them was recovered, to my knowledge. A generation of Immortal children had been lost.

Their mothers protested that they had known nothing of Rain's vainglorious plan to rescue the children, and spoke bitterly of having been cheated of the fruits of their labor, the one joy of life as an Immortal bride, and the one hope of security among the aging. But that, of course, could not have been as true as they uniformly insisted. Not one child remained with its mother. There must have been some kind of pact.

Three kinds of beings can never be suppressed in human life: the informer, always hidden in the crowd to ensure that no secret goes unknown; the torturer, always ready to practice his unique physical intimacies on behalf of his beliefs; and the seeker after love, whose vulnerability often renders the first two superfluous. It was among the third group that we were able to recruit the unwitting dreamer whose sweet hopes cradled the knowledge we were seeking.

Sheaf was the youngest of the child-bearers among the Immortal brides. Her son had been eight months old—and her first child—when Rain had led the groups of children over the mountain passes, and down to the ships waiting to take them off the Peninsula to other lands.

I sent young Pekrin toward her whenever there was an opportunity. She was quite pretty, and it was also clear that Pekrin's ambition to serve the state would keep his attraction to her purposeful and in proportion. He was like the lord of a great inheritance, hunting a bird. The bird thought its nest was its refuge, but the nest was situated on the lord's own property, bounded by limits the bird could not recognize.

It did not take long for Sheaf to confide in him. She told him she had been promised by Rain that the selfless action of sending the boy from the Peninsula would deliver him from a youth enslaved to the clients, and a maturity as a jailor both of his own mother, and of the next generation. The brides swore to Rain that if she succeeded in freeing their children, they would do everything in their power not to bear children into the life of the houses.

So Sheaf had agreed to send the boy to freedom with the other children, but instead of exaltation, she now felt aimless longing. She had made her sacrifice of the child, but not of herself. She had failed at becoming selfless.

In reality, in herself, she wanted the boy back no matter what would have happened to him. His life was her life. She wanted love more than what is called the good; she wanted the flesh of the child fragrant in her arms, and the music of his prattling more than any other future. She mourned him inconsolably. She wanted young Pekrin to make her another one. I gave him permission.

And yet Sheaf hesitated, though Pekrin had been given a rare privilege, and granted enough money to make her exclusively his. She asked him to allow her to wait forty days, apparently to make some sort of personal feminine expiation, to the lost child. Pekrin, with admirable cunning, and utterly without my advice, agreed.

But he was careful to insist that only hours filled with her company and conversation could ease his deprivation during this period.

He treated this interval as a courtship; an irresistible seduction for a bride, accustomed to being given for the asking.

"I want to know everything about your life here," he told her. "Where you walk, where you pray, where you think, wherever you are your most true self."

To be treasured like this was to reenact in some fashion her experience with her child, but this time without sacrifice. Now she herself was the child, but cocooned securely, shielded from loss or painful choice. Pekrin relentlessly gave her what she needed, mixing like a chemist the elements of human love, with its strange proportions of ever false and ever true.

She even received him in her private quarters, though this had by previous custom been forbidden. No client was ever permitted to enter the sections where the children were housed. But now, Sheaf thought, it cannot matter. There are no more children.

She did not understand, nor did Pekrin, that there are always children where women are, that there are always children where men are. And the more invisible the children are, the more haunting their presence.

Adults carry the child they once were inside them into death itself. The unseen, undying child who accompanies them is like a candle whose light they cannot see by, but which cannot be extinguished. The first self they were before they believed in death is what they understand of immortality. For this reason, no man has ever truly known whether he is mortal or not, even though each understands that death comes to all.

So Sheaf, against all her training, trusted like a child, much as she had trusted Rain, and young Pekrin, against all his rigorous training, played like one.

He followed and hid and opened the doors of rooms when no one was there. He threaded his way from the attics to the underground storerooms, but it was always as if someone had just closed the door and left the room he was on the verge of entering.

He found nothing unexpected—the most personal possessions in this house were the toys and furniture of the missing children, collections that functioned unsurprisingly as shrines. The brides guarded them jealously, refusing to share their children's possessions with the refugee families.

Sometimes whispering, otherworldly music could be heard, at no fixed hours of day or night—the women apparently still sang lullabies to the lost children. He couldn't make out the words. He listened as he walked among the other courtyards, but the only music he heard from them was song or ballet, in rehearsal for performance. The music from the House of Immortal Children had a more personal and primitive quality—by some acoustical trick, it seemed to be coming from beyond the building itself.

Pekrin formed another strategy. He would disappear for a few days, to let any habits that had been suppressed while he was there reappear. He would return at an unpredictable day and late hour, and walk the compound like a thief to see if the darkness had anything to reveal.

The courtyards were quiet, melancholy, debased with cooking utensils, laundry, and makeshift shelters. Luxury required an assumption of stability, the abundance of being granted more than one's own life, unlike these survivors who had been left with nothing more.

He still had nothing to report, other than Sheaf's confession to him—the testimony of one bride implicating the others in the escape of the children. The others could just as easily reverse her story.

Frustrated, he turned to me at last for advice. "You are looking outside," I said, "when you should be looking inside. If you want to find where the secret is, look inside. In this way, you will become a part of the secret you don't know. And you will find the truth, because once you are a part of the secret you will not be able to hide from yourself."

Pekrin began to hide himself: he hid in the shadows of the Pagan Chapel, in wardrobes, in random rooms. This was something he did not like. The tension of a person in hiding has a primal desperation, whether that person is the hunted or the hunter. He realized, though, that before, he had been looking only for what he expected. No one will ever make a discovery if he is not afraid of what it is he might find.

Pekrin found what he was not looking for in a long sealed-off underground passage that linked a cluster of dusty storerooms.

Its walls were lined with stone compartments carved with now faint names and clusters of grapes. He looked inside a compartment.

He was standing inside a vast cupboard of bones. He recognized that he was inside an ancient pagan catacomb, of a type not unknown near the coast.

He opened the door of a storeroom. Its walls were covered with frescoes of small miniature portraits, the famous pagan "faces of the blessed." It had clearly been a pagan chapel, as had the second storeroom, though it also contained beds, chests, and trunks packed with old clothes and theatrical costumes. Three trunks were stacked in the center of the room. Suspended above them on a thin silk cord was a painted clay bird without wings.

He went close to it. There was nothing out of the ordinary. It was a common child's toy, although a child would have thrown away a bird once broken, not hung it from the center of a room. Pekrin began to look for an alcove within the scattered furniture to serve as a hiding place.

It was dull to wait, after the initial sense of triumph in coming across the icon of the rebels. He wondered if it had simply been abandoned here, if they had felt watched and moved elsewhere. He fell asleep. He was unsure whether it was still day or night, when he heard a hushed choral chant, and footsteps in the corridor. He saw them as they entered, eight of the brides, the first carrying a crystal pitcher of water, the others holding single candles. Some men and women who he was sure must be refugees were present, too.

The celebrant set the water in the center of the trunks, which, he now saw, served as an altar. The others ringed the pitcher with their candles, so that the images of the flames wavered in the trembling water. The wingless bird swayed overhead.

"We are parched," the first woman began the ceremony. The others sang the phrase, in soft repetitions, like lapping water. "We are parched, we are parched. We thirst." Then a mesmerizing chant began, one word pronounced by each singer: "Rain. Soften. Our. Souls. Rain. Make. Our. Salt. Tears. Spring. Sweet. Rain. Make. Stone. Ground. Flower. Wash. Death. From. Us. Falling. Rain. From. Heaven. Rain."

He recognized some of the strange, distant strains of music he had overheard, he realized now, from underground, the rhythms transforming each word into a single, delicate drop of rain. They sang the chant perpetually and softly, during the brief liturgy that followed.

The woman presiding, with a priestly gesture, lifted a candle from the table and held it high with both hands.

"Beloved. You, the betrayed, and raped, hunted and tortured, silenced and murdered, you seekers of revenge, pilgrims in Hell, may the Storm refresh your souls.

"Know now what she knew: Our souls wander barefoot in the magmas of hatred as well as the gardens of love. She was seared. Our palms burn too with the blood we would spill. We walk with her through the crucible of hatred, and come to know, as she did, that we are neither perpetually wronged, nor delivered by wrong to perpetual righteousness.

"Rain, wingless bird, your fall renews the world. Help us to see by our darkness as well as by our light. Make the suffering we inflict as clear to us as the pain we endure. Let our hatreds not destroy us, or those we hate, but illuminate us, with them, like this flame." She set the candle down. The full light on her face allowed him to see her features in detail. The priest was the former vineyard mistress, now the acting governess.

Two brides brought twelve glasses from a battered cupboard against the wall. The priest held the crystal pitcher high above the flames of the candles. The other women and men circled with the glasses in their hands, and paused before her as she poured water for each.

When all had received the water, the priest raised her own glass and said: "May those who hate know the kiss of grace, lucid and perfect as water; may those who love know the kiss of grace, lucid and perfect as water."

After they drank their glasses, rinsed them, and removed them to the cupboard, they circled the makeshift altar again. One woman pulled a dark red rose from her dress, and laid it on the table. The priest sprinkled it with water drops that jeweled it in the candlelight.

"Rain and fire shape the flower. O wound become the offered rose."

Then they left the room quietly, but no longer furtively, touching each other affectionately, with a hand on a cheek or a caress on a shoulder. Their expressions were serene and glowing, as if they believed themselves in Heaven.

Most of the people's faces were obscured by the shadows, but Pekrin saw the priest clearly and unmistakably. He waited until he could hear neither murmur nor footstep. Then he stepped from the cavern the furniture had made for him, and moved toward the trunk that had been the altar. He reached up and ripped the wingless clay bird from its silk cord. He had their toy, and now he would compel these catacomb women and men to confess to him whatever it was they were playing at.

I did not make it my affair, though Pekrin correctly informed me of his discovery. He could scarcely conceal his wish for his first authority, his first success. His discipline in offering me a share of the victory he longed to claim uncompromised was a measure of his self-mastery and his iron patriotism. It was the boy's first real opportunity to distinguish himself among his generation in the service of his country, and to prove himself to his father.

I offered only one piece of guidance—that he must at all costs uncover the truth about this ring of women, but I stressed that it was as important to learn the identities of any men involved with them.

Pekrin let two days and the morning after pass without action, allowing the house to go about its business unsuspectingly. I took the opportunity to assemble for him, dispersed into the lower-lying towns, a small group of soldiers to have at hand if needed. The roads were still difficult, with washed-out sections, and stretches strewn with debris, so the extra time to bring the men up was welcome.

On the afternoon of the third day, Pekrin asked Madam to arrange an appointment with the acting governess. He watched her as she walked with her air of crisp purpose across the courtyard.

A concealed person watching someone he expects coming toward him is like a world the other is entering unawares. Pekrin watching and waiting in the shadows in his little anteroom felt he had a fatal knowledge of this woman, as if he were in the act of creating her. He was standing as she entered, and able to see in detail how her face distorted with the surprise of seeing him instead of Madam. She recomposed her features quickly and rather brutally, like an artist dissatisfied with a sketch.

Then he stepped aside, to administer the second surprise. She saw the wingless bird he had taken after her ceremony hanging from a silk cord above the table, swaying slowly in the circles of its impossible flight.

Pekrin found her demeanor at that moment fascinating. Her gaze had the splintered look of a person a split second from death, as if the soul were glass breaking into a thousand fragments. Then she closed her eyes and, bizarrely, smiled, as if she had just heard the voice of someone she loved.

"Sit down," Pekrin said. "I see you recognize this toy."

"It would serve nothing to pretend that I don't. The question is how do you recognize it?"

"I saw you praying to it three nights ago. You and eleven other women."

"I assure you, we were not praying to the clay bird."

"You hung it above a simulated altar, and performed some sort of ritual. You seem to address it. We have also been following for some time the appearance of images like this one in the port."

"Of those I have no knowledge."

"I doubt that very much. But first, I want to know what the toy means to you. You say you don't pray to it. But you—and others, whether you know them or you don't—apparently accord this bird some reverence. Do you think it has some magical power?"

"Absolutely not. That would be unthinkable for us. We are not practitioners of magic. It is a symbol for us, a memory, a relic, an inspiration, a reminder of what God asks of us."

"And what does God ask of you?"

"To fly without wings. To do what seems impossible. To cling to our loves through the rapids of our hates. To know that God charges us with the task of making these miracles. They exist between person and person, as flame goes from candle to candle. To know that all we can know of right or wrong is through the way our acts are revealed in the lives of other people. There is no other way to see God. It is not given to us."

"These are not the beliefs of the Peninsula."

"They are indeed. She was born here, after all."

"She? Who are you talking about?"

"Rain."

"The traitor, the plotter against the Peninsula, is the source of these beliefs? The abductor of children?"

"No. God is. Rain was no traitor. She was God."

Pekrin realized from his sharp intake of air that he had been holding his breath as if he were underwater. The sacrilege was so appalling that he felt a kind of exhausted pity for her. He would have to see this woman executed, even though she was mad. It would bring him all the honor of killing a rabid dog.

He gave her another chance. He poured her a glass of water.

"Drink this," he ordered her. "Compose yourself. Now think carefully of what you really mean to say. You cannot mean that Rain was God our only Sovereign."

"No, I did not mean that Rain was God our only Sovereign."

He was relieved. He might after all guide this babbling lunatic back to safety. Women never understood the grandeurs of doctrine; they were natural conduits of ceremony and ritual. Their skills were best used in repetition; in rocking the cradle, not in studying the science of reproduction.

"Then why did you call her God?"

"Because God is not a sovereign. God refuses power. God came to us incarnate in Rain to experience hate and love."

"God is all-powerful."

"Love is impossible without the relinquishing of power."

"God is all-loving."

"God made us incapable of experiencing love without experiencing hate, as the chisel shapes the jewel. God suffered both as we do. She submitted herself to our blindness, our uncertainty, our precarious humanity."

"So you think God appeared as a mortal girl, sequestered and used by men in whatever way they desired, and then executed?"

"That, Lord Pekrin, is exactly what I think."

"And she did nothing to defend herself, your God? Used not one of her infinite powers in her own behalf? Gave no command to her followers?"

"God does not command. God asks. We do not overcome evil through orders, but through questions. Rain said, 'We do not overcome evil through "you shall not," but through "why do you?"'

"It has always been for us to protect God—and we fail. God asks for us to protect, to shelter, to feed, to embrace Her as if She were mortal. As if She were a child. Rain said, 'A child has no power, but a child is not weak.'

"She asks us to contemplate each mortal person as if they were infinite. As if they were dying. As if they were divine.

"We cannot see God. We cannot speak in God's behalf. We cannot do God's will. God is invisible. We can know God only through our own acts and their consequences. Like all of us, you are blinded by your own face when you look at God. And you don't see mine. But your soul is reflected in my face, as mine is in yours. Rain said, 'We are metaphors describing God, each life. And how we treat each other is how we treat God.'

"Commands are human, Lord Pekrin. The Divine has no need of them. The act of cherishing is divine, and demands something greater and more difficult than obedience. Rain said, 'Tell the truth about what is inflicted on you. And tell the truth about what you inflict.'

"Rain said, 'You cannot imagine the degree to which God shuns power. You cannot imagine the degree to which God is not a warrior, or a king. You who rule women because they are the life to come on earth, you who claim to rule even over the life to come in Heaven.'"

Pekrin could not tolerate another word from the woman. "I am sorry for you, then. I will tell you your story. I know better than your God how your story ends. You are going to die for this She-God who cannot save you."

"You know my fate because it is you who make it. But my fate is now transfused into your life. Rain said, 'A belief in one's own righteousness is a form of superstition.' And I am sure that your God will, in His turn, demand a death of you."

Soon after, the time of the purges began. As always, when interrogations are determined to find evidence of guilt, many innocents are swept up along with the criminals. Some are condemned through coerced confessions, others through an accidental personal antipathy they provoke in the interrogator, others through motives that have nothing to do with the accusations.

Families, as always, settled scores and punished, expressed favoritisms, took revenge, made alliances through denunciations, just as they did through the marriages they arranged. One girl of a fine coastal family was executed for Rain worship after being accused by an uncle, who had been in fact himself drawn to the sect. His feelings of guilt over his own wavering made him more suspicious of true believers, as he later admitted. His strength in the face of temptation earned him exoneration.

General Jarre, invigorated, pored over maps and studied the transcripts of confessions. He helped establish the special tribunals necessary to examine the accused and render verdicts. The prisons were overburdened with suspects, and it was a subtle business establishing who was a genuine worshipper, or simply a curious observer.

Jarre's former malaise disappeared, as he comprehended the glory of what God had planned for him. He was a pure gold chess piece in the Champion's hand. He was instrumental in ferreting out cells of Rain worshippers, though he was never successful in learning the fate of the abducted innocents. They had simply, miraculously, disappeared.

The Rain worshippers' cunning and invention in improvising chapels was challenging for God's courtiers. They needed so little for their sacraments—a glass of water, a candle, a rose, a broken bird—that they were frustratingly mobile.

Throughout the Peninsula, in basements, in clearings and coves, abandoned buildings and caves, they were hunted down. Hundreds were executed, women and men, although children, permeable to all adult influence, were taken to camps to be purified and rededicated to the faith of their fathers. Toy birds were banned, and figures of angels, and all images of creatures with wings.

The heightened tension made for many night raids on innocent celebrations. Entire villages along the coast lay in ruins, or were difficult to reach, so zealous captains instead showed their efficiency by harassing respectable gatherings, it must be said, sometimes surrendering rather than capturing, sitting down to carouse with the hosts in the absence of culprits.

Port guards patrolled the waterfront, though only for display, as the area was generally off-limits for women. They, too, took to sitting down to the bottles of wine offered on their random and routine inspections of the ships in port. That was how six guards on the verge of getting pleasantly drunk heard a soft whispering chant, like rainfall, that seemed to come from belowdecks on a relief ship laden with rice and dried vegetables for the refugees of the wave.

They looked at each other and then at their hosts, conviviality replaced by tension. They called for the captain of the ship to authorize an inspection below, but he was not on board. The highest-ranking officer available was quickly located and ordered to lead them below. As they neared the hold, they made out distinct but incomprehensible words, in the way that rain itself seems to whisper a subtle, once-known language.

"Rain. Soften. Our. Souls. Rain. Make. Our. Salt. Tears. Spring. Sweet. Rain. Make. Stone. Ground. Flower. Wash. Death. From. Us. Falling. Rain. From. Heaven. Rain."

Two guards kicked the door open. Candles burned in the center of the room. A wingless clay bird was suspended from a piece of mooring line, swaying rhythmically. Eight men moved in a circle underneath it, holding up glasses for the clear water Admiral Annan poured for them from a crystal pitcher sparkling in the light of the flames. The port guards were so accustomed to showing deference to the legendary seaman that for a moment they stood frozen.

The worshippers and the guards simply looked at each other, hesitant like fathers and sons reunited after a long separation. But instead of rushing into each other's arms, the guards seized the worshippers, and to the awe of the onlookers who recognized Admiral Annan, marched them through the streets to prison.

One might have thought Annan's heresy would be a deathblow to his old friend and comrade-in-arms, Jarre, who had already suffered so much. But Jarre met the news with a mixture of contempt and exaltation.

The disgrace of his friend, paradoxically, restored his shattered faith. He was now confirmed beyond doubt in his knightly service to the Sovereign King of the Universe. He was forever God's liegeman.

All that had happened to him had seemed like wanton punishment, but had in fact been revelation.

The one sentimental concession Jarre made was to allow Annan to be condemned for heresy, not as a traitor who had abducted children consecrated to the service of the state. He took no part in Annan's trial, but paid a final visit a few days before Annan was to be executed. The great bond that had existed between them was severed, but Jarre was fascinated by his friend's fall, as people are by fatal accidents. He was gripped by the need to understand what had eclipsed the great sun of his former friend's mind and soul.

Jarre's stature was such—and even more so now—that he could arrange to meet Annan outside his cell, in perfect privacy. For the sake of Annan's human dignity, he wanted to ensure that no eavesdropper had the opportunity to broadcast Annan's ravings.

Annan was brought in by a guard; he still had his air of vigorous health, solid as a thick-trunked tree, which made his imminent death seem even more unnatural.

Annan sat down quietly opposite Jarre. "I did not imagine you would want to see me," he said.

"I am haunted by questions only you can answer. I want to know if you really are one of these who believe that my dead daughter is a deity. Or was this a ploy for rallying support for the political ambitions you must have harbored for years? To be candid, I want to understand if you are mad or sane."

"And I will be candid with you. I believe. Not absolutely, in the way you do, the way I used to. We are not creatures made for the absolute, our breath is too wavering, our perception too flawed, our doubts too necessary. But I saw God in Rain. She is alive in everyone. Even you."

"What sort of God is it who has no power, who makes no miracles? I know you are going to talk about the kiss she gave that brought the dead man back to life. I have never witnessed such a kiss, but in any case, this deity saved only one life."

"You cannot know how many other miracles one sole miracle begets. She was not a savior. She did not confer salvation. She said we were to be the saviors. She said we know God only through each other. That God is not in us, but between us. That we deliver God to each other, like a flame passed from cupped hand to cupped hand. We bring God to life in each other. And in any case, she did perform other miracles."

"What other miracles?"

"She led sixty children to freedom under hopeless circumstances. Therefore she gave life without being a mother. That is a miracle.

"She was stronger than you are, though your word is law. She was stronger than I am. That is a miracle. When you saw her, you saw a being who had descended into Hell and struggled there. She returned not as most do, a gladiator, but a dancer.

"She did not kill, in the face of the most excruciating temptation. She refused to bring into the world the cruel God her tempters wanted to beget with her. That was a miracle.

"And there was yet another miracle. She made me into a human being."

Jarre stared at him, incredulous.

"After a lifetime as a champion of God, a Prince of God's Court, you are capable of believing that a woman could be God incarnate? That God would deign to enter into a woman? Into a being polluted with sin and blood, the slave of men and even children, too weak even to defend herself? You know God's teaching as well as I do. Man has a soul, woman has a nature.

"You sicken me. God is omnipotent, the creator of the world. No one can measure His power."

"You say that God has created Heaven and earth," Admiral Annan replied, looking at his boyhood friend steadily. "And yet He is unable to imagine a woman in any way different from your own conception of her. He has apparently never been able to create a good woman.

"You say God is omnipotent. And yet He might incarnate in a man, but is incapable of incarnating in a woman without desecrating Himself, without being destroyed. So then, out of all creation, in your belief, only woman is more powerful than God. Which of us, do you think, is the heretic?"

Jarre stood up without a word, turned his back on the man who had been his friend, and left the room.

Annan was beheaded two days later, in the presence of Jarre, according to the law of the Peninsula.

Despite the purges, the devotion to Rain was not completely crushed on the Peninsula, and remains very much alive to this day. But Jarre's pursuit of the heretic cult gave him a new sense of mission; he was reborn as the hero of God he had been at the battle of Saldava.

And to his wonderment, he once again knew the joys of domestic life. He built another villa with a sea view, this time on a bluff, using much of the material from the one that had been destroyed. He divorced the wife of his youth, and married a girl of good family, with fine Smaraldian features.

Within the year, she had given him twin boys, and by the time my own work on the Peninsula was drawing to a close, she had borne a girl, a third child to replace the three who had been killed. All that he had lost was restored to him.

Shortly afterward, to our mutual regret, I left his employ. I had been offered a post in a much larger country, and despite my affection for Jarre, I wanted to make use of my skills to serve on a larger scale. But I left having fulfilled what I had set out to accomplish.

I had been entrusted—inspired—honored—by God—with the task of selecting an impeccably good man for a jointly administered experiment, a test of faith in the face of unmerited suffering. And in Jarre, I was certain that I had chosen perfectly. Here was a man ruthless only in the love of God, a man whose every action was taken in a spirit of angelic necessity.

I recognized in Jarre a man who understood the pure symmetrical division of good and evil, right and wrong, male and female, animal and human, adult and child, rich and poor, earth and ocean, darkness and light, sacred and profane.

He lived by the precise and invariable principles through which God created the world. His life was an expression of everything he had learned of the Lord of All. The supreme clarity of his mind made it like a quotation from a poem of God's. It was heartrending to see him suffer so unjustly, though I knew he would ultimately prevail.

I was scrupulously conscious of my responsibility in this mission. For I have always considered myself a friend of God, and a lover of mankind, whatever you may have been told. Despite this, I have known nothing but abuse, generation after generation. I have borne it patiently, though I think no one, even Jarre, has suffered as I have. Nor have I ever been thanked for all I have given to the world.

It is a gross insult to say I am an enemy of God. On the contrary, I hold God in the greatest esteem and even affection, even though I do not love God with the devotion I hold for human beings. Why would I? God created them; but they created me, for which I adore them, though my creators' doings are often as opaque to me as God's are to them. God's will comes to me through them.

I am no rebel, no troublemaker. When I fail people, it is out of sheer incomprehension—but I always do, to the best of my ability, exactly as they tell me.

Mistakes, though, are always possible, as always between languages, as they attempt to translate the words of God to them, and I to translate their words to me and to execute their will. The work I had to do on the Peninsula rendered me frantic at times.

Of course, you want to know if Rain was God. Might it be that God is actually human? How can I know? I have never seen God; I simply follow God's instructions as clearly as possible when I receive them from my creators. And that can be a difficult task, unless someone knows right from wrong as infallibly as the blessed General Jarre, and the other elected ones. For it is perfectly lucid, what is right and what is wrong. It is for this knowledge that I am welcomed among the good, and am sometimes called the Bringer of Light.

Otherwise I can find myself in a vortex of contradictions, as on the Peninsula, where some deserve to suffer, yet do not, and others are blameless, yet tormented.

There it can seem the innocent are guilty, and the guilty good. There rape, torture, murders are crimes, yet at seasons perfectly justified by God's law.

There love struggles into birth through some strange intermittent partnership of hatred, and Heaven exists in Hell, and Hell in Paradise, and an imprisoned sacred prostitute, damned by her own father, might have been an incarnation of God.

At such times, I can only renew my vow of devotion to my creators, and marvel with gratitude at my existence, created not by the One, but by the Many. I was made to serve the humans who brought me to life.

Through their protection and their generous love, I survive throughout the generations. In my eyes, they will always remain sublime, a radiant, unapproachable, and magnificent mystery. I kiss the hems of their garments. All praise to my creators! I adore them! I adore them! I adore them! No matter how I strive, I will never be worthy of them; I will never be their equal.

THE PROVERBS OF RAIN

One sees in God only what one worships.
All souls burn: some give light.
Hatred can be as true as love.
Perfect hatred leads to enlightenment, not conflagration.
The wisdom of hatred must be earned with neither rejoicing nor violence.
Much can be learned from hatred: nothing from revenge.
When hatred leads to murder, it is as terrible as goodness without mercy.
When they say, "I hate you," do not protest. Rather, ask—"Tell me the story of your life."
Hatred, examined, leads to freedom from hatred.
We do not need to love those we loathe, but to treat them ethically, and to understand our loathing.
Misogyny is often justified, but can never be sacred.
Each human being must be fundamental to God; therefore misogyny, as theology, is heresy.
Women, it has been said, are inferior, amoral, animal, satanic. In which case being born is either insulting, or meaningless.
Believe only when you grasp the consequences of your belief.
He who would be a king of ashes must keep his kingdom in flames.
Those who know nothing of this world are great scholars of the next one.
Hatred, correctly disciplined, torments only the one who hates.
Dogs are taught by commandment; human beings learn through questions.
To hate without violence begins the work of love.
Your hatred is corrupt if the children of those you hate suffer it.

Like a grape, hatred must be crushed, but not obliterated. Crushed, then tasted, tasted and then known, until it is transformed into wine.
Nothing good can come of innocence.
She who has not hated will never love.
She who has never hated will never know how to forgive.
Men call the hatred they do not recognize "honor."
There is no being who feels himself more innocent than the murderer as he kills.
There was only one innocent in the Garden: the serpent.
The death of one woman is the death of countless men.
The death of one woman is the death of countless women.
The death of one woman is the death of countless children.
Violence begun in reason will end in madness.
Murder cannot kill; it splits a being into a thousand ghosts.
Inside the rib cage of his victim, the murderer is locked.
Death may end the life of the victim, but murder is eternal in the killer.
In the marketplace of souls, one may sell a soul, but not purchase one.
Praise Divine Death who protects even those who torture from infinite cruelty.
Hatred reveals to us that even demons suffer.
No one has yet measured the force of the Divine Will to refuse power.
Men and women will not become human until they refuse to be God.
Hatred is the pit in the olive: the fruit cannot form without its stone.
Hatred joined to violence is like love without thought.
We need fire to cook, and hatred to motivate justice; the key to both arts is the management of flame.
And God said: Unless you know every word of every language, living or lost, forming, or unspoken, you know no more of me than the child whose whole idea of the world is formed from the only two words she knows: "Mother, Father."
And God said: Speak all the words in all the tongues of all the world, but there is one word forever forbidden to human beings: "infidel."

IV

THE BOOK OF SHEBA

THE LOVERS' CLUSTER: THE FOURTH CONSTELLATION

TO THE MEMORY OF IDA B. WELLS

This constellation has never been hidden. Yet such is the irony and wonder of the human relation to Heaven, that the vision of certain stars, celestial geometries, and orbits has often been limited to what human beings are determined not to, or are willing to, see.

You will remember how long it was believed that the sun circled the earth in an ecstasy of hierarchical reverence, and that this belief was enforced by law, through the means of torture, or even penalty of death. No cancer has tormented or killed as many men as knowledge decreed or its shadow, knowledge denied existence. The one ends in damnation, the other in despair.

Both bar the rare revelations we are granted of truth, an apparition as graceful, fleeting, and difficult to embrace as a nymph glimpsed just beyond a waterfall. For science is a matter not just of intellect, but also of desire, for worlds that we would wish, while lovers cling to each other with their yearning rapturous minds.

Few enough speak of the Lovers' Cluster, yet it is the glory of the heavens. It is a constellation of many unknown features, still being studied, since after the fall of the Shebans the people were obliged to refer to it as the Warriors, and their astronomers ordered to illustrate it as an image of hand-to-hand combat.

See, if you choose, countless symmetrical terraces bejeweled with stars, glittering in a hundred shades, amethyst, jade, sapphire, ruby, topaz, aquamarine, amber, pearl, pink, emerald, in perpetual motion, as if the stones of a mosaic were constantly rearranging themselves.

These surround a central region in which a magnificent double star, opalescent and variable, a celestial couple absorbing and returning the colors of the cluster, revolves like a pair of lovers in each other's arms. The changing translucent colors of the Lovers, now transparent and shimmering, now fiery and blinding, make their embrace a composition of infinite variation.

We know that the double stars of this cluster are so powerful that at its center, where they embrace, is a region of permanent light. It is said that the jewels that lovers universally give to each other as presents are crystallized fragments of the stars of this constellation, scattered on earth by the Lovers, the All-Givers whose love is so abundant that it overflows in generosity and in knowledge as well as beauty.

In the country where Sheba was born, jewels were not a form of money, but of knowledge. Jewels told stories and described in their forms and colors the most excellent qualities possible to humankind. There jewels were to educate, first as toys, through which children transcended greed, then as ornament, through which young people transcended lust, and finally as art, through which older people looked through a thousand eyes of different colors than their own, and transcended the limits of their narrow ways of seeing the world.

Jewels were considered a kind of incorruptible speech, words for divine qualities that had suffered through trials and succeeded in keeping their meanings until they were always true. A word of truth, the Sheban saying went, is a jewel set in the heart's amulet; they also had many folktales in which the words of love were metamorphosed into jewels flowing from the lips of those who loved, their meaning so intense that the words themselves became palpable.

Words were important to the Shebans, and were likewise considered jewels; their ceremonial rulers, a king and queen, were always a pair of singers, the two considered the greatest practitioners of their generation of the Sheban epics. It was unusual for a king and queen to be married to each other; rather, it was expected that the queen not be married to the king, as the Shebans, unlike their neighbors, had a horror of dynastic marriage, and did all they could to discourage it.

Thus, there were no conventional Sheban features or complexions, as the Shebans never organized themselves in tribes, and habitually married foreigners. In this way, too, by limiting clan alliances, the people of Sheba were not decimated by the bloody tribal feuds that ravaged families just beyond their borders. They were masters of the art of not having children, who could be conceived only by mutual consent. This was a source of sharp controversy and official disapproval by many of their neighbors, though privately, they were openly envied, and it was speculated that perhaps fewer Sheban children were unhappy to be born.

However, Sheba's parents, unconventionally, were partners in bed and bread as well as in song. The Queen's flesh, betraying her Ellushan forebears, was black as the darkest night. When she wore her diamond necklace whose gems were set in the form of the constellation, the Lovers, it seemed those stars themselves had emerged from the tender night of her breast.

Her husband's skin was a rich copper, a sunset color, and his belts and chest plates were set with turquoise, the same distinctive blue as his eyes. Their children, Sheba and her older brother, Quiran, recombined the qualities of both: their dark skins were opaline, black glowing ruby in firelight, and changing notes of autumnal ambers, golds, and grenadines.

Every generation, families seemed to change skin colors; the Shebans considered complexion seasonal. This was consistent with their view of the Divine: they believed all gods were God, and that God was at times many, like a chorus, and at times, one, like a soloist.

Their house was filled with the traditional volumes of songs and poems, on whose black pages words and notes were illuminated in raised gold shapes, so that the tellers could perform them by their own light. During the Tellings, Sheba's parents wore the magnificent, justly celebrated garments of the Sheban songmakers, tunics of velvet and satin, brocaded with lines of poems and song stanzas from that evening's recitation, the phrases punctuated with jewels.

No one knew when the country's epics had first been compiled and sung, but they were unique, in that the principal heroes of the epics were not only or primarily men, but also women. Unconventionally, the heroines and heroes of the Sheban epics sought not glory, but fruitful and illuminating love. The Sheban singers emphasized, generation after generation, that humankind studied, knew, and understood far more of war than it did of love.

In undertaking that subject, the cycles of the Sheban songs were far more tragic than the martial epics of their neighbors, as love is more rare than glory, more unpredictable than battle, and exposes all who love to the greatest dangers imaginable.

Those wounded by the sword die once of their wounds, but the wounds of love recur, replicating themselves through both male and female in each generation, destroying those who never knew or understood the source of their destruction. The wounds of love kill not only warriors, but women, and most terribly of all, children.

Many more have died of attempting love than victory, and countless numbers hate love more than war. Honor has often been the dear prize awarded to the killers of lovers. The epics of war have always and still outnumber the epics of love. For those who love deeply and greatly gain a clairvoyant, excruciating awareness of the fear and suffering of the world along with their joy, which few warriors could endure. Who is not more truly afraid of a love story than of a tale of war?

Nevertheless, the poetry of war has always been treated with a dignity and accorded a prestige denied the poetry of love. But the Shebans persisted in singing of love in all its aspects. There was the tragedy of Nenufar, a girl who could not love human beings, and of her successive unrequited loves for a swan, a face on a coin, a stone wall, and finally for a diamond necklace that strangled her.

There was the lengthy cycle of the exploits of the warrior Bano, who boasted to God he had no fear of death, and was undefeated in his marvelous adventures until the twelfth book, when his muscles trembled and failed in the task of cherishing as he held his beloved Orania, dying not from wounds on the battlefield, but in their bedroom, in his arms.

There were tales like that of Mana, an epic of maternal love, in which a mother embarks on a quest to rescue her captive daughter, a great role for a virtuoso coloratura, with its spectacular complex arias celebrating the timeless sacrificial love of mothers, each more dramatic than the next, only surpassed by the denouement, in which Mana fails to recognize the unaccompanied voice of the escaped daughter whom she herself had had imprisoned. This was one of the most splendid among the many works that explored what grand public rhetoric serves to conceal, and how often false love is nearly indistinguishable from true.

The Shebans had also evolved an entirely new genre of romance, in which the happy endings of their neighbor's conventional comedies served as the beginnings of the story's action. They thought any story a failure if it came to an end.

Finally, there was the sublime, unending cycle of Eno and Aiyesha. Every year the reigning queen and king composed a new book of the inexhaustible story of this couple, charged with the perhaps impossible task of creating love in a loveless world.

The great epics and songs were sung to the accompaniment of a unique stringed instrument of Sheban invention, the oar, originating, as you might guess, from the oars of that seafaring people. The basic chord setting the rhythm of the recitations evokes an oar moving through the water, the rowing beat driving and percussive, contrasting with the music of the water, lapping, or viscous, or leaping in white-capped waves, expressed by the combinations of the strings.

It was the custom for the oars to be crafted by pairs of adolescent girls and boys, as this was considered the only means of successfully fashioning an instrument that combined the anatomical qualities of female and male. The oars were ornamented with figures of red, gold, and mother of pearl drawn from the images of the epics, and the bodies of the instruments made of highly polished wood. The Sheban oars could be played horizontally, like guitars, or upright, like cellos, producing different tones.

Sheba, the saying went, was surrounded by the sea, and by song. City inhabitants lived in buildings that formed the walls of quadrangles ornamented with scenes from the epics worked in mosaic. In the shared central courtyards of the quadrangles were pools lined with colored tiles inscribed with quotations from the songs.

The courtyards were bordered with both real trees and flowering bushes and invented trees, vines, and bushes of gold, coral, and other precious materials, hung with fruit and flowers in various stages of ripeness and bloom, made intricately of jewels. At dusk, when the fragrance of the natural blooms was subdued, the immortal trees gave off their own fragrances, by means of ingenious mixtures of the famous local aromatics, perfuming the quadrangle throughout the night. It was through these fragrances that the Shebans told time. Each of the eight hours of the day corresponded to a fragrance on the incense clock, so that they woke to the hour of Bread, and lived the sequence of their days through the hour of the Ocean, to the bedtime hour of the Rose.

The eight hours of sleep at night were mutable, designed for each individual's preference, so that one might dream through the hours of Almond or Bonfire, another to the Hour of Lavender or Lemon or Cut Grass.

In this way, the Shebans admitted the mysterious elasticity of time; the hours of the schoolchild whose clock infused the fragrances of gingerbread and ink were dreamed differently than the hours of a young man who dreamed of sleeping blissfully with the eight girls whose perfumes fixed the hours of his incense clock. This was what any Sheban traveling in other countries would speak of nostalgically, the incense that woke them at dawn, and the exquisite scents that rose at night from their gardens of dreams.

Anyone who was drawn to a particular jewel on the branch of a dream tree could pick it like a grape or a rose, and wear or contemplate it until another jewel beckoned, speaking a message in its inaudible, but real language.

There, children, Sheba and Quiran among them, fed and tended the rare water silkworms who lived in the pools, which spun the extraordinarily strong and flexible threads that furnished the strings of the oars. The use of the water silk was responsible for the inimitable melodies accompanying the songs, each instrument capable of producing eighty-four thousand notes, not only the full known range of the musical scales of earth, but also of the marine scales.

A Sheban orchestra was organized so that players on the right-hand side played the music of a character's actions, and on the left, thanks to these additional scales, the music of a character's unspoken feelings.

These song cycles were the basis of their children's education. As soon as the children were weaned from their mothers, it is said, they began to suckle instead from the breasts of poems and songs, words and music flowing into them. Thus, the children began life with learning to assume many forms. This, the Sheban sages said, was the difference between humans and animals, which were confined throughout their lives to one form only. Animals never imagine themselves people, though people are constantly impersonating animals.

The Shebans considered the goal of education to be the most difficult of all arts to master—the art that could never be perfected—of loving wisely. An important function of their arts was the education in desire.

They were roundly mocked for this in most of the world outside their borders, where any degree of wisdom mixed with love was held to kill passion and pleasure.

The Bana, to the north, denied the existence of love altogether, and coupled only for procreation.

The Ellusha, to the west, lived for pleasure and could never get enough.

The Philosophers, to the south, lived for wisdom, which they considered incompatible with love. They thought it better to renounce pleasure altogether, and could never get any.

And the Zealots, to the east, believed that love was simply an aspect of war, another means of acquiring territory.

The Shebans taught, to the contrary, that wisdom would reveal new passion and invent new pleasure in love, and that the art, science, quotidian life, and even the inventions of a civilization with this aspiration would be of a different order. They endured the contempt of their neighbors (who, despite their condescension, made up large numbers of the rapt spectators of the Tellings) not always with grace, but impassively. Instead of being mutilated or kidnapped at their initiations, Sheban children were trained to craft and sustain their roles while exposed to taunts, heckling, and coarse insults from an audience.

This was a culture of performers; the courage to risk humiliation was the work of every day, and greatly valued among them. The initiation, though, introduced the children to more than the troubles faced in an evening's performance, but showed them a beginner's glimpse of the dark eternal perversity they must always face without despair.

It was the players' work to draw the entire audience into a mutual embrace, as lovers must hold not only each other in their arms, but the hostile, unrequited world.

The Shebans were not ignorant of the epics of their neighbors. Many of the Tellers could recite long passages of those works, and all knew at least the stories they told, as Sheban troupes traveled widely.

Theatrical companies were an important Sheban export, not only in the neighboring regions, but also in the entire extent of the world known to the Shebans. Troupes were commissioned by courts, universities, festival organizations, theaters, and great houses, for periods ranging from one month to three years.

Each month, orders were placed through the various embassies for groups of particular songs or performances of specific epics. These orders could involve delicate negotiations and adjustments, since songs were not simply texts and notes. The players and musicians themselves were the songs and epics, and to order a title was to order the troupes trained to embody it.

Sheba's uncle, Kito, who was responsible for the oversight of all foreign embassies, could recite long passages of any number of the great foreign epics. Sheba and Quiran spent some of the enchanted afternoons of their childhood in his grand suite inside one of the buildings lying in the park that housed the complex of theaters that were the very heart of the country. The children's visits were a poignant, unacknowledged gift on the part of their parents, since Kito was a widower and had no children of his own.

Their indulgent uncle permitted the children, when they were very small, to play with the tokens each resident ambassador presented to the kingdom of Sheba during his tenure. The custom was for each mission to present its hosts with a jewel identifying its country.

The Philosophers, for example, gave a brooch of a golden book inscribed with a passage from one of their honored thinkers. When their representative arrived, she detached the second page of the brooch during a ceremonial reception, and gave it to Kito to display during her stay. She wore the first page of the golden book as a kind of passport. The Ellushans gave a crystal plate, heaped with fruit shaped from precious stones; their ambassador wore a pendant of the fruit, while Kito displayed the plate. The Zealots gave a silver target, inscribed with the device "True Aim," and their ambassador was recognizable as he wore the Zealot spoke, a circle of five golden arrows, symbolizing that they were invincible in all directions. In this subtle way, not without a certain discreet charm, the Sheban governors kept track of the comings and goings of visitors in their land.

Kito also gathered and compiled information about each country's economy, geography, and language, and was celebrated for his map-making skills. He was a prodigy, able to give detailed and accurate details of the topography of countries he had never visited. And no one knew the terrain of Sheba in such detail, as if he himself had created it before it was set down on earth. The children pored over the maps, and listened rapt to his store of stories about the other worlds beyond them.

"Knowledge," he would say impressively, glancing at them with his keen eyes the color of blue flame, "is as important as love."

Quiran hesitatingly drew a relevant-seeming paradox that the children of his year had recently been set to study. "We cannot . . . we cannot . . . ," he stumbled, "love without knowledge. We have no knowledge without love."

"Very true." Kito nodded. "But above all"—he smiled—"no one can love without eating."

He offered the children a plate of the marvelous Ellushan creams, the golden cloud of cream buried inside the centers of caramelized roses, and proposed to recite an episode from a Zealot epic. He went into a private storeroom just off his public suite, and returned with a Zealot instrument, a kind of hand-held harp. The music was ritualistic, repetitive, and compelling, as if to convey with each phrase that nothing else could have been said, with each event that nothing else could have happened.

The tale was a love story in the Zealot style, of a great hero who landed on the shores where a beautiful queen ruled. The hero and the queen conceived an uncontrollable passion for each other, and had a son. Then the hero abandoned the queen in the middle of the night, without saying good-bye, overwhelmed by the revelation of his divine destiny. The gods had chosen him to sail to an unknown country, and battle its inhabitants in order to found a great city.

Kito sang it impressively. The song changed his face, as the songs one sings form the underlying architecture of each face. The song turned his face from a man's into a monument's, like the armored statues he had described seeing in the Zealot capitals to which he had traveled. As he parted from his love, he sang of his destiny as a battle from which he must not run away. Kito was so moved that he actually stood, carried out of himself, and enacted the final passage in which the hero ascends the path the gods have chosen for him.

The children were quiet, as much because they had seen Kito's familiar features change into a marble mask, as because of the story. Kito himself was impressed by the silence of the two usually boisterous children. He escorted them to the door, let them each take two more creams from the plate, and kissed each one on the cheek. "Give my love to your mother," he said, and went back to his work.

In fact, despite the power of the music, the story seemed false, and for nearly a year, became a feature of the brother and sister's secret satirical repertoire. Sheba, being smaller, took the part of the hero for comic effect. She stood on a barrel, as if it were a statue's plinth, and wore a makeshift helmet like a mocking cherub. "A hero must embrace divinely destined life," she sang, her jaw set, and her piercing eyes searching the horizon in the fearless quest for her immortality, "and sails toward fame at night from his ungodly wife."

"And stinking child . . . and stinking child," Quiran added a chorus, his eyebrows raised with compassionate but condescending regret, one reluctant hand on his imaginary massive chest, the other raised in a gesture of inexorable and self-aggrandizing farewell.

They outdid each other in assuming the facial expressions demanded by the rhymes and rhythms of Zealot epic. They competed in molding their eyes into the gaze of a hero chosen to look into the face of the world, but not into human eyes. They imitated the cast of lips formed only for the sublime kiss of fate. They would collapse in laughter, unable to be statues long enough for destiny to take them in hand.

Their parents were amused when they stumbled on the children in midperformance, and delighted at their precocity. Brother and sister had already instinctively grasped that styles of acting could be codes declaring, even prescribing, ideals of how to feel and how to live.

It was proof of their talent that they had caught the way the heroic Zealot style abdicated personhood. All the hero's actions must be radiant, surrounded by a nimbus of glory; even his cruelties were superb, belonging ultimately, as did his powers, to the God that ordained them.

The parents smiled at each other in unconfessed relief. Sheban artists of their stature secretly dreaded the prospect of having untalented children, and lived under years of considerable strain of concealing their fear, or worse, their disappointment. The children's comic performance freed them of this anxiety. "But," said Sheba's father, with a slow-dawning smile, "there is something new to be afraid of."

"What do you mean?" his wife asked.

"That they are so talented they will see the flaws in our own styles," he said. "We are trained as epic singers; but we may find ourselves in satire at last." They collapsed in laughter.

At the age of ten, Sheban children were taken to the crafts workshops where, for the first time, the force, precision, strategy, and struggle with which jewels were formed was revealed to them. Sheba never forgot the shock of this introduction, long after she had left the kingdom.

The children, even though warned by their elders, were overcome with fear when they witnessed the master jewelers demonstrating the explosive angled blows with which rocks were split so that the gems inside them emerged with the capacity to refract maximum light.

The rocks were struck with an executioner's force and keen placement; a number of children invariably burst into tears at this moment. Sheba shivered, and thought of the terrible moment in the epic of Gil when an elephant stamps on the hero's skull and crushes it.

But when a stone breaks beautifully, it finishes in an existence of ever-changing light, not in death. The children were taught in the workshops, without realizing it, the first terrifying lesson of love—that no heart is truly capable of love until it has been broken. And it was their first true experience of the core of Sheban teaching; these people held that love educates through metaphor, and imitated its methods as best they could.

"If they break beautifully—perfectly—they can then receive their facets," explained the chief geometress, who demonstrated the cutting, "exactly like souls receiving experiences. When a stone breaks badly, we call it destiny. But when a stone breaks beautifully, we call it living."

She held up a ruby, which shed glowing flecks of light, like drops from God's wineglass. "It seems motionless, doesn't it?"

She handed the gem to Sheba. "But turn this one in your hand. It is your hand that moves it, but it also leads and guides your hand. Can you feel it exploring light in all its motions? Now let your mind play in the light like a dolphin in water. Remember the pictures that come to you, and eventually you can learn to read them as a fortune-teller does."

Sheba passed the gem to the boy next to her. The geometress handed her a destined stone for contrast. Its color and the light that it refracted was muddier, warped, imprisoned. "The brilliant gems are the ones that break beautifully. It is as if they give themselves to the chisel. When your turn comes, do not be afraid to let your heart break." Sheba heard these words with foreboding. She was secretly determined that this would never happen to her.

In the evening, before the current rehearsal—for their seasons were marked not only by nature, but also by rehearsals and performances associated with the changing year—Sheba approached her father and asked him to explain.

He put down the music he was carrying, and was quiet for a moment. "I remember the Breakings vividly, and the geometress who explained it to me when I was your age," he said.

"What she meant," he continued, "is that love is not like death. There is nothing inevitable about it. Death is inevitable. In the realm of love, anything can happen, or not happen. All die: but many never love. It is a path of perpetual surprise, in the way the jewels you saw give and receive changing light, speak new languages."

It was the practice of Sheban adults to speak freely and candidly to their children about death as well as about love, in the simple style they believed imitated the speech of angels.

Their Philosopher neighbors called death "apotheosis," which, Sheba's mother had often remarked, made it seem rather superior to life, and something one could hardly wait to achieve. Their other neighbors, the Zealots, had their own euphemism; they called death "passing," as if it were a form of excretion.

The Shebans admitted that they were always failing in their own practice; still, those who were squeamish about the reality of death could hardly teach their children about love.

Sheba's mother had entered the room with Quiran, and added, "It is in the song of Oriana: 'We die by destiny, but we love by choice.' You know that song."

Her father said, "Even when we don't recognize that we have chosen. Love is the only invitation we receive that we can always refuse. No one—not even the deities—can compel love."

Sheba had stopped listening; her brother was bouncing a golden ball she found irresistible. She dove for it, like a gull for a shellfish, and he began to pummel her. Their mother rose impatiently to separate them. "When are you going to struggle for what is yours, not what is his?" It was the first thing anyone had said to her that day that Sheba confidently understood.

This was the only day of her childhood that Sheba had hated. She did not want her heart broken, or anything to happen to her resembling that pulverizing and chiseling.

She wanted things to stay as they were in her good life, safe with her adored brother; she wanted to savor the secret greatest bliss of children, the perfect security of parents who loved each other well. She wanted the incense of the immortal trees to draw her dreams toward them when she slept, and wake from her nightmares to find all as it was. She wanted to run away when she was afraid, and then be called back and comforted. She wanted to learn the great songs and love them, but not to be an important singer, always preoccupied, and always anxious, preparing for the next performance. She was, in the local assessment, a merry soul, interested only in comic roles. She wanted to do what she wanted. Which was to dive.

She was almost an underwater creature; when she plunged into the blue and green world below her, she felt paradoxically as if here at last she could truly breathe, her body in love with the sea, in the way some of the songs described that feeling. The ocean was her first love. But Sheba was a creature drawn to cyclical action; she adored tracing fluid circles underwater, as if she were a paintbrush; she loved diving partly for the sake of returning to the surface. She was only devoted to things that ended well.

After the Day of the Breaking, Sheba followed her brother into the conservatory for performance classes. From age ten to age fourteen, the children were schooled in Metamorphosis. The first year, the students could not play anything human, or use any known language; they played animals, rivers, rain, meats cooking in pots.

The second year, they could play only adults and elderly people, and express themselves only in song, which was like a great storehouse of all articulated human experience, which they could enter to try out what they had not yet felt.

In the third year, they polished their speech, and played only children, to examine the nature of what they were beginning not to be.

And in the fourth year, the girls could play only boys and the boys could play only girls, since to comprehend and interpret the qualities of the other sex was essential training for the performance of tragedy, while no comic role could be played successfully without that skill. It was an attribute of all the great Sheban Tellers, both a source of envy and a scandalous outrage to the theaters of other nations, whose players were not schooled in those techniques. It was in the fourth year, too, that the students also mastered the crafting of the oars.

At the age of fifteen, Sheba began the classes in the rhetoric of love that were reputed to be the most challenging of all. A private tutor was assigned to supervise small groups of students. It was rumored that after you had mastered the history and rhetoric of love, you were initiated into a great secret.

The years of schooling culminated in a distinctive farewell ceremony. Those who were leaving the academy were given three costumes, a wardrobe for the first three roles they would play in public.

Often the initiates disliked the costumes they were given, but there was no explanation and no appeal; no one ever knew how and why they were assigned these particular roles.

After receiving and displaying the costumes, each tutor kissed the graduating apprentice on the lips. Then the tutor leaned toward the apprentice and whispered something in his ear. The audience read many meanings into the expressions on the faces of the tutors as they delivered their inaudible messages, but no one was able to decipher the words of these silky whisperings, any more than one could interpret falling snow. The apprentice was sworn to reveal only indirectly the message given, in compliance with the performer's code, and that code was honored through all the course of Sheban life.

No Sheban, for instance, ever uttered the words "I love you." They considered this phrase extraordinarily primitive, expressing so little that it could mean anything or nothing. This lazy, amorphous cliché was putty in the mouths of liars, the viscous verbal syrup the abuser poured on the child, the formulaic words prostitutes were paid to say to clients. The proof of this was that no memorable song made use of this phrase; rather, lover and beloved described some element of the world precisely to convey their experience, or sang of each other.

Sheba's tutor was the most venerable and beloved of all the teachers of the theater arts—Noctis the Bridge, who, like all the sages of theater, had earned a personal title honoring a distinctive quality of her expression.

Noctis the Bridge had been queen four times in her life, though she was now frail, in too much pain to perform, and sometimes could not stand to demonstrate a gesture or gait. This, however, forced her students to experiment to find her meaning, rather than to reproduce her performances.

She taught in a large hall, which was lined with white plaster casts of the faces of generations of Tellers, molded on their features at different epochs of their lives. She was distinguished for her use of casts of the same Teller playing a famous role, but at different ages.

She opened her tutorials seated in an armchair set on a rehearsal stage. At times, she would close her eyes, which were a distinctive gray-green, like certain leaves, and tighten her lips with angry concentration before answering a question or giving a criticism. "When I am in dialogue with pain," she explained to them, "I wait to answer until I am sure that I am really the one speaking, to you, not a ventriloquist's puppet."

But on the days when she had little pain, she relished her freedom, and reveled in her physical reprieve. She held their young faces between her hands as if she were picking fruit, and showed them in close work, how to set their expressions, using the language of their own features. She even enfolded her apprentices in her arms, if necessary, to demonstrate a stance or evoke a possible response.

When Noctis was delighted with a successful moment, or fresh reading, or had brought them to applause with a passage from one of her own great roles, she broke into a smile that dazzled on her face like the sun on water, currents of radiance mobilizing every feature, shifting from eyes to mouth to cheeks.

Noctis guided them in the subtle art of communicating the pain, grief, or violence of a death without torturing the spectators.

"The epic singer is unique in this," she taught them. "She herself enters the song. The singer then becomes part of the story. He must never use the audience as an occasion for his own sadism. She will destroy the role if she indulges herself in the punishment of the audience. The suffering, cruelty, and love in the story enter him, and become the gates through which she enters the song." Madame Noctis, in the Sheban style, freely alternated the pronouns of gender.

Sheba heard this with an impatience that concealed her panic. The last thing she wanted was to be trapped in a song too grand, operatic, and out of scale for her, with no exit. In truth, she thought, she was lazy. She wanted as little suffering as possible. No more than the slight chill of the sea that became voluptuous once she was used to it, the bitterness of almonds that became desirable and delicious.

She had no ambitions to be ascetic, but dreamed instead of a life expressed in laughter and largesse, a magnificent giving of gifts, as if she were the head of a household of inexhaustible generosity. "Can we enter the song through laughter instead, Madame Noctis?" she asked.

"Yes, certainly, it can be done. But I warn you, it will not be an easier path; rather the reverse. Don't fall into the error of so many, like the Zealots, or the Philosophers, who think comedy is trivial, light, negligible. Their comedies are superficial because they don't know how to write any others. They write inferior love stories because of what they believe love is. The Zealots look at love as a form of war. They are a martial people for whom a kiss is a soap bubble unless it draws blood. And for the Philosophers, love is only fatal, a wedding of skeletons."

Her quicksilver face rapidly took on the stock expressions in the style of a Zealot, then a Philosopher actor. "Remember that tragedy tells the story of the inevitable, actions that make us prisoners, that could happen in no other way, conclusions that cannot be changed. Whereas comedy tells the story of the impossible, the divine, the unimaginable, what could never happen. The tragic hero drowns, the comic heroine walks on water. Which story do you think is harder to tell?" Noctis laughed. It was a laugh of a kind that Sheba had never seen before, her head thrown back, her throat as exposed as a bird's, as if she were about to take ecstatic flight.

Noctis showed them how to fight and strike each other onstage without doing harm. She trained them in the art of touching each other passionately without hurting each other—"one of the great arts of lovers as well as actors." Much later, she exposed them to the far more advanced and difficult craft of expressing ardent joy without stirring anger, jealousy, or despair in the audience.

"No one doubts the reality of death," she told them. "But the truth of love is always in question, and many—perhaps you yourselves—do not believe in its existence. Many may never come to one conclusion. But you can examine this physically, through stagecraft, much more usefully than through any words of mine."

She called on Sheba, and on an acrobatic boy already known for the poise and clarity of his movements. Far had a strength, balance, and grace that made his actions legible to the spectators in the highest, farthest tiers of the theater. He was the only apprentice of their year who had already played in the Arena, taking the athletic and taxing role of the risen corpse in the cycle *Comedies of Spring.* Sheba was daunted by his reputation, and blushed to find herself next to him on the practice stage.

"You are a couple," said Noctis. "You are angry with each other. Perhaps you are frustrated. Perhaps you are jealous. It doesn't matter. You are both angry. Build the quarrel in your bodies. Show it in your shoulders and hands. You can either sing or speak, whichever feels natural. Then you, Far, strike her, and you, Sheba, fall to the floor. Then stand up and strike back. Far will fall. Watch him carefully; I have not taught any student who falls with more art than Far."

No one thought Sheba the laughter-loving water nymph could be capable of such a rending scene, but the apprentices had to play whatever role they were assigned.

The couple began to improvise the ugly, menacing rhythm of a pair quarreling. A quarrel between three, or six, is an incident of more diffused power more open to dissent or mediation from one of the company, but a quarrel between two can only escalate farther and farther until their bond is broken, and one prevails. The only chance of ending a battle of two is through the work of both together in partnership. Battles between two opponents are the fights that most often end in death, equaled in violence only by a rampaging mob.

Far and Sheba began by alternating their speeches, first in low threatening tones, then with insults and unfair mimicry, each taking a facial expression of the other and distorting it into ugliness. Far flung down a series of phrases as if he were planting a field; Sheba wildly uprooted every word.

They stirred a primordial childish fear in their audience, each of whom had a child's terrified memory of being powerless to stop a similar adult fight at least once. The scene evolved until the pair no longer spoke words, but only made sounds, their hatred so great that it overpowered speech, and it no longer mattered if either spoke the truth. Even their movements were frightening, though the spectators knew perfectly well that a stage fight is more like a dance than a duel.

Sheba thwarted Far's effort to turn his back on her. Far, provoked beyond measure in his liberty to move, raised his arm, and let it fall toward her, inexorably as a cut tree, which gave Sheba time to prepare her own fall; she beautifully conveyed that the blow was a defeat for Far as well as a victory. Then Sheba paused ominously, leapt up, and, with the shocking precision of a viper, struck Far three times in the chest, so that he fell and lay facedown.

The students broke into applause, a rare tribute to a scene particularly well played. Sheba helped Far get to his feet, and they sat down side by side on the edge of the stage, their legs dangling, while they waited for Noctis's comments.

She did not come forward, but said, "I want you to do one more thing before I say a word. Stay just where you are, but turn toward each other, and kiss each other, believably—tenderly, like lovers."

The pair followed her instructions, and the tentative kiss with which they began became more and more convincing, and showed no signs of concluding, until Madame Noctis said, "Excellent," a shade drily. Then she made her way to the stage, sent Far and Sheba into the audience with the others, and addressed a question to the whole group: "Now what have you seen?"

One after another of the students spoke about the tempered violence of the fight scene, the stabbing rhythms with which the actors had composed their invective, the clarity and finality of the gestures with which they struck each other.

Noctis held up her hand. "You all speak, as I thought you would, only of the impact of the fight scene. Yet they played a second scene. No one has mentioned their embrace. Why?" The students were silent, recognizing now that Noctis had something particular she wanted them to know. They saw she was now directing them into a scene with her; this was the way she taught. Not one of them wanted to risk the humiliation of answering wildly off her mark.

"You can find the answer in your own descriptions: 'finality,' you said, 'clarity.' Violence simplifies everything; a blow has a clear beginning, purpose, and a decisive end. The action defines sharply: Who is the stronger? Though remember, it may turn out to be the victim, tempting the other into anger, luring the aggressor toward disintegration.

"Violence is strenuous, but simpler to play. And with its stark lights and shadows, it simplifies the response of the audience, as it did yours.

"Which is why it is the basis of theater in all martial societies: gladiator fights, dramas as occasions for the display of new and ingenious weapons, or wrestling holds, sports that excite through risk to the players. The audience reacts viscerally, for or against.

"The ones who enjoy and need the violent spectacles are often soldiers, reliving battles without threat to their lives, temporarily absolved from the memories of their own kills by watching combats in which they do not participate. The ones who are distressed and recoil feel an instant reassurance, granted an escape from being either the pursued or the killer. To cheer for the hero is to share his virtue.

"But who is stronger or weaker in a kiss? Instantly, we are in a more mysterious realm, moved out of time by an action that can never be completed, this exchange of life's breath that aims to begin again as soon as it ends. It is easier to enact a slap than an ocean, and easier to describe, too. Through a kiss, the actors leave the stage, and travel somewhere we can't imagine.

"We also saw, as Far and Sheba took each other in their arms, a closed circle. The audience does not share in the kiss; it belongs to the lovers, it excludes them. And to what effect? It reveals something private to each witness, about himself, some secret of his own heart, something she may never have guessed. An audience can be molded into collective response with a violent scene; but there is no collective response to a love scene.

"A quick exercise now: you in the front row, remember their kiss, and quickly imagine a reaction to it."

"Envy," said the girl in the aisle seat. "Hope." "Longing." "Fear." "Wonder." "Despair." "Nostalgia." "Wanting what I can't have," a boy said with a furtive glance at Sheba. "Wanting what I can't have," the boy next to him said, with a similar furtive glance at Far.

"And if there were an arena, with every seat filled," Noctis said, "imagine the infinite, unpredictable variety. Now I give you one more thing to notice before we finish today. This will be equally useful to the ones who become Tellers, and the ones who don't.

"Sheba and Far have no quarrel: and yet, they quickly created a conflict. They were able to end it just as quickly, because they were playing . . . inside reality and outside of it at the same time. That is what our education aims for—to make us the slave of neither reality nor dream. For what we insist is reality may be as unreal as any hallucination.

"Sheba and Far are not lovers. And yet, their kiss was as intense as if they were. You should go home filled with awe at the power of these gestures to turn us to their purposes—and make use of this occasion to remember how easily you may be deceived in both war and love. Good afternoon."

Noctis had been more acute than even she knew in teaching that a kiss revealed the secrets of a heart. The kiss that Far and Sheba gave each other had not really ended; it had only paused. Each discovered, separately, but simultaneously, that they wanted it to begin again.

That night, in their different neighborhoods, each remembered in extraordinary detail the features of the other's mouth and arms, as if Sheba's kiss had formed and created Far, and Far's kiss had formed and created Sheba. It was as if they had discovered some new form of indelible personhood in this act. And each deliberately remembered it again and again, hoping to dream it when they fell asleep.

They began to tamper subtly with their days, remaking hours so that they would yield occasions to meet and talk. Like all first lovers, they looked at each other as mirrors, enraptured not only with each other, but also as truly with their own charmed glimpses of themselves. Far was enchanted by Sheba's sparkling, sweet temperament, like an island with a perfect sunrise every day. "You were created to laugh," he told her, charmed by noticing that her face, even in repose, showed the delicate contours of a smile.

"And you were created to be a great Teller. Even the sound of rain falling sounds to you like an audience chattering about a performance during intermission." Not long afterward, they followed their first kiss where it led them.

Sheba shyly commissioned a new nocturnal incense mixture for her clock. The scent-makers teased her gently; for generations, this had been a sure signal of first love. Now she slept all night enveloped in the essence of burned sugar, to be reminded of the scent of Far's body.

During the final year of the Metamorphosis, a presentation costume chest was crafted for each graduating apprentice by the masters of stagecraft, who were responsible for the physical aspects of every production, set and costume designers and makers. A council of these makers was present throughout the schooling of a class of apprentices, and it was this council who designed the wardrobe chests for each student. Not one was alike; for many Shebans, the chests were the most precious possessions of their lifetimes, and their first performance was always formally dedicated to these craftsmen.

On the day of the initiation, the Sages of the Tellings waited onstage as their students were called up for the presentation of their coffers.

Far was called forward to receive his costumes; he acknowledged the Sages, and then approached his own tutor, Noctis the Bridge. He knelt before her, and kissed her hand. Two craftsmen brought his chest from the wings onto the stage; they could not suppress their smiles of delight, for these occasions were as joyous as they were solemn.

Far's chest was of rare blue wood, stained in many shades. The top was decorated with a carved bridge, alluding to his tutor, dividing a blue sky and blue sea, on which mother of pearl glistened like the sun on water.

Inside were his three costumes, each one the garment of an epic character. He turned pale at this greatest honor and obligation. When Noctis stood to whisper his initiation words to him, his expression grew grave, and he put his hand on his heart.

Then it was Sheba's turn; she ascended the stage of the Arena. She made her way to Noctis, and swooped to the floor in front of her, curtseying like a wheeling bird. Her coffer was brought out; she nearly cried out with pleasure at its beauty.

Its top was of transparent crystal, with the four phases of the moon in mother of pearl in each corner, the crescent moon a witty reference to her ever-present smile. The brass clasp was in the shape of a bridge.

It was lucky that she had been so delighted with the chest, because she was less pleased with the costumes.

One was for a minor character in a comedy, an old woman who plays the ribald nurse of the heroine.

The second was much more pleasing, since the costume was for the same comedy, but this time it was the dress of the heroine herself.

And the third was a sour disappointment. It was a famous costume worn by her mother playing the lost prince Horizon in a tragic epic that Sheba did not like, since it had no clear resolution. The audience never agreed when the curtain fell about what had really happened, while it was a great challenge for the player, who did not know either.

It was a beautiful costume, of dark red silk brocaded with gold and scarlet pomegranates, but Sheba did not want to play a role of her mother's, and she had no grand ambition to act in tragedies, even though the lost prince was a starring part. She turned to Noctis for her initiation words; the only response the audience could read on her face was incomprehension.

For some, this would begin the long journey into the great characters of their epics, a path of selflessness difficult for a culture of performers who were eager to be magnets to the audience's eyes. Finding the voices and gestures, learning the lines, living the life of these men and women who lived in them and in whom they lived, learning to be someone else, was recognized as a form of religious pilgrimage by the Shebans.

Springtime opened the season of the Tellings, which always began in the great central Arena, with a performance of the first book of Eno and Aiyesha, and closed in early autumn with a performance of the most recent, written, produced, and played by the current King and Queen. It was also the opening of the season of weddings, celebrated after performances; many foreign spectators who were indifferent to the dramas bought tickets for the sake of the magnificent spectacle of the marriages.

The bridal processions set out from the Arena, each departing from one of its twelve exits, a great wheel of brides and grooms and attendants whose trembling jewels made them look like a human galaxy. It was considered auspicious to be married during the Tellings, the new couples joining their lives framed by the ancient stories of love; thus the world began again.

Elegant celebrations were held in the courtyards of the honored artists' houses that surrounded the Arena. Not only were the festivities open to all, so that guests strolled from house to house, but the host and hostess of each reception were by custom strangers to the brides and grooms, another good omen, since to celebrate the love of strangers was a foundation of Sheban hospitality.

There are sometimes years that seem to crown the lives of people with so much joy and fulfillment that they have the effect that sorrow sometimes does; the only way so much joy can be borne is to dedicate it to other people, make a gift of it to those waiting for joy, or deprived of it, pour it out so that it does not overwhelm the heart.

For Sheba and Far, this spring was the crest of such a year. They were now experienced enough players to take on substantial roles. Sheba had one of the light comic roles she adored, as the principal boy in a famous coming-of-age comedy, playing an adolescent in love with his elder brother's fiancée. Her brother Quiran, to complete her delight, would play the title role.

Far had been chosen for a role in the second book of Eno and Aiyesha, surely a first step on the path to be chosen as a king of Sheba. And they were to take their own place in the spring wedding processions and to be married.

Even Sheba, with her untroubled childhood, had never known anything like this abundance inside her matched with the abundance outside her. The lengthening days were the image of a love extending into the unknown future, the swallows celestial comedians, the new flowers in all their colors were the kisses from some divine being who could not stop making love to the world.

The man-made season, as they called the performances, began well, too, opening as always with the shorter works, alternating with concerts, building toward the majestic epics that began at the summer solstice, and culminated in the autumn.

Each work marked a particular turn in the year, and its words and music seemed to have a particular taste, anticipated like the foods that ripened and were savored successively in each season. Sheba's work was finished in the first month of the festival; Far's would begin at the end of summer, when they were already wife and husband.

Noctis was present for Sheba's fourth and tenth performances. Sheba had an impulse to beg her not to come, or at least to come for only one performance. All Noctis's students dreaded the special tension of her presence, and the matter-of-fact rigor of the criticisms that she delivered in the dressing rooms while the stage cosmetics were lathered away. She was a critic of acute taste and no personal malice, which made her judgments the more formidable, as authoritative as if they were posted on a wall in sheets of calligraphy.

"Oh, my dear," said Noctis, "let us keep our stage frights in perspective. Why should you be afraid of my being in the audience? Comedy is sacred to God, and it is God we play to. And God is patient, having waited thousands of disappointing years for us to master the happy ending. There is no genre we play so amateurishly.

"Not only will I be at the fourth and tenth performances, but at the seventh, too, I think. I will be of more use to you that way." She mischievously smiled a statue's inexorable smile, a mime she was famous for.

Few of Noctis's students ever equaled her in her ability to translate herself into a statue, a falcon, a chalice, a cypress tree. It was for that gift of moving between beings as if between languages that they called her Noctis the Bridge.

Sheba had not only received Noctis's criticisms, but also passed through them, changed, like a jewel refracting the light from a new angle. She understood even better now how Noctis the Bridge had earned her title. She had found playing in the Arena more satisfying than she had imagined, but now she was delighted that her part in this season's Tellings was done.

She had a refreshing period in which she avoided the Arena altogether. She listened to the passages Far was preparing, marveling at the stately beauty of his voice, even though his work was just beginning, and his delivery uncertain. When he sang the great section describing the preparation of Eno's bridal chamber, he built the room with his voice, filling the air with insubstantial wood, marble, and sheets of beaten gold that surrounded Sheba, but could not be touched. His singing turned her thoughts to their life to come; it was now her time to marry.

They had chosen a section of one of the Tellers' courtyards to house them, and Sheba gave herself the joy of furnishing the rooms as if she were furnishing their future life. The windows were still of clear glass; at the end of the season, they could claim their first colored glass window, worked with their images in their first official roles.

The fruitwood costume chests inlaid with abalone shells were fortune-tellers, the silk carpets woven with the scenes of epics were omens, the chimes hung with the golden letters of the Sheban alphabet were invocations chanted by the wind.

She could hardly wait to live there, with Far; and then sometime with the children she imagined with the nervous shyness of a hostess anticipating important guests. Impatient to know how the house felt at night, she arranged a makeshift bed so she could sleep there the night of the summer solstice, a night when dreams were said to reveal the future to the solitary sleeper, and even more marvelously, to allow the dream to know something of the dreamer.

And so that year, her dreams fulfilled both promises. Far had walked with her to the house, carrying the heavy embroidered coverlet they had been given as a wedding gift. Sheba brought her incense clock in its jeweled case, with its nighttime fragrances of burned sugar already mixed and set in position to kindle when it was dark.

He tried to tempt her and charm his way into the house, for the sheer pleasure of the love-play. Sheba allowed herself the subtle pleasure of temptation to which they both knew she would not yield. There is no greater freedom than to be tempted by a trusted lover, which offers all the charms of seduction, with none of the danger of betrayal.

Sheba drew away from him, denying him voluptuously. "You know it is the solstice. I have to sleep alone tonight, my love, and so do you, or the true dreams will be mixed with things that will never happen, and we won't know which is which."

"I want to dream of you, and I want you to dream about me, every night, forever."

"I already do, and you know that I do. But tonight, I want us both to dream of our children. They will show themselves to us only if we are apart tonight. And if we succeed in coaxing them to come into our dreams, they will be able to see us, too. When they are born, they will be born in trust; they won't wail when they come into the light, able to recognize the mother and father waiting for them.

"You know they say that each minute they are with us tonight, means a year without tears in their lives—if we dream of each other in a true dream."

Far smiled at her intensity. For him, their future children were faceless, but he could imagine the feeling of trust a child could have for someone who was already imagining them outliving her. It was a good sign. He could trust her with his own children. She would not be one of those mothers who hate their children for outgrowing their childhoods, who struggle to stay young by feeding on their children. "Then dream a true dream. I will, too. I hope I see children who look like you. Good night, love."

"In a month, we will be living here together. Dream of love," she said, the traditional Sheban good-night wish. They smiled twin smiles, and kissed lingeringly.

Sheba went inside, closing the door, but opening the windows to draw in the perfumed breezes of the courtyard. She walked through the rooms, slowly, in communion with the house. It had already undertaken the task of houses, which is not only to shelter the inhabitants, but to make them see things from ever fresh perspectives, to change the ways they move, and speak.

Tonight, the house offered her the golden letters of the alphabet sculpted by the last of the sunset, the breezes lifting them into words that formed momentarily, and then vanished.

When it was dark, she laid out her bedding in the half-furnished room, lit her incense clock, and prayed that she would dream true. She tried too hard at first to fall asleep, and stayed awake for a frustrating hour, defeated. At last, without realizing it, she found among the doorways that opened to new thoughts, or fears, tomorrow's tasks, or memories, the one that led to sleep, and entered it.

In her dream, she was walking at night in a mountainous landscape she didn't recognize. A child appeared and gestured to her. It was dark-skinned, like her, and seemed to be a boy, but she could not see his face. She excitedly moved closer, and called to him. "Let me hold you, love. Let me hold you, so when you are born you can recognize the first face you will see in the world." He began to play catch-me with her, like a real boy, looking over his shoulder from the shadows to make sure she was following. She began to run, but he picked up speed whenever she drew near.

She had nearly caught up with him, stumbling over the rocky path, when he swerved sharply to the left. She looked down, and tripped fortuitously, just before she ran off the ledge where he had led her, into a sheer fathomless drop off the edge. She fell, not into space, but to her knees, the pebbles she dislodged in her fall spraying into the chasm.

"Be careful," he called to her. Now he descended at breakneck speed, to the base of the mountain and led her running, across a beach of shining black sand. "Follow me," he called, "or you won't find me." He raced across a dock, and in the way an experienced cavalier mounts a horse, leapt into a waiting boat, unmoored the vessel, and waved to her to hurry. "Get in, get in," he called from the boat, "they're coming for us."

She followed him breathlessly, looking over her shoulder behind her. She plunged into the water to swim to the waiting boat. She dove underwater so as not to be obstructed in her course by the strong winds suddenly stirring up. And as she pushed deeper into the water, she saw five black sharks with golden fins, rising to force her into the center of their circle. She swam upward again, but they were faster. She hurled herself onto the beach, but these sharks followed her even onto dry land, and surrounded her, rearing upward, forming a stockade around her. Their teeth gleamed red in their mouths, lit by the five fiery suns that burned overhead, reddening the coarse, clotted black sand she lay on. The boat carrying her child was far out to sea already, sailing out of the world.

She tried to scream, but could not make the piercing sound emerge from her dreamer's throat. With two more panting efforts, she managed a guttural moan; projecting the sound out of the dream and into the world began to wake her. She half-opened her eyes, then closed them again, blinded by the red suns she could still see. "Get up," someone said, and shook her shoulder.

She opened her eyes, now fully awake. Five red torches burned above her. The dream had moved from one world to another, and reassembled itself around her bed. One of the deepest archetypal fears of women had come to life. She lay in her bedroom surrounded by five strange soldiers. They wore black uniforms, and on their left shoulders, the golden spoke of the five Zealot arrows flickered in the torchlight. "Get up and get dressed," the first soldier repeated. "Are there others of you here?"

She was afraid that saying no would render her even more defenseless, but in fact, so would saying yes. Either way her risk was pure and absolute. She was lost in this knot of soldiers as in a forest. And there must be more of them. She could not escape them through a discoverable lie. She took the truth as a compass, a useless defense, but a possible pathfinder: "I am the only one here."

"Your name?"

"Sheba."

Another soldier handed him a sheaf of papers, and he leafed through it, as precise with the sheets as a card player. "Get dressed quickly, please. We are a nation of soldiers. We are used to women dressing and undressing without ceremony. Our women are soldiers like us and are trained out of false modesty. We drill them naked as children to prevent it."

Perhaps the women were trained to ignore the assessing stares of the men, but the men had not been trained not to examine the women in insulting detail. They watched her as if they were mapping her; two of them indulged in cartoonish facial expressions, grading her body, without provoking any response from their superior officer.

"If you are Princess Sheba," he stopped at the page he was holding, "then you are the daughter of the King and Queen, sister of Prince Quiran, and the niece of the Foreign Minister, Kito. Correct?"

"Yes, I am," she said, "except we have no princesses or princes. Our Kings and Queens are chosen every year at the festival of the Tellings. There is no dynasty, only a changing crown, and the honor of having worn it. I have answered your questions. May I ask one of my own?"

"We are permitted to answer certain questions."

"Why have your soldiers come here? Your embassy represents you here, not your army."

"Our embassy is also our army, Princess. Our ambassadors are soldiers. Our teachers are soldiers. Our artists are soldiers. Our children are soldiers. Our dead are soldiers. But we are here in force because there has been a change in government. We are here to protect you. We are here to ensure that the transition that is now taking place occurs without any violence that could affect our people or yours. Come with us now. We are going to take you to safety."

She cast an involuntary look around the rooms as they passed through them, looking with momentarily unguarded yearning at the costume chest that held the costumes for the first three roles she had been assigned, when Noctis the Bridge had held her two hands and whispered the initiation secret in her ear.

"Don't be concerned. This will all be sent after you once we have escorted you to shelter. We are soldiers. We are not thieves. We ask that you follow us now, and refrain from speaking until we have taken you to your assigned shelter."

They led her out into the courtyard, where hundreds of silent women and children under Zealot escort were being led to unknown destinations. Older boys were efficiently separated from their mothers, and led elsewhere. There were no men visible except for the soldiers. The soldiers were, despite the officer's claim, stripping the jeweled trees of the courtyard of their gems by the handful.

"I thought you said you were not thieves," Sheba said to the officer.

"We will not requisition personal property. But these jewels, which you treat as some sort of mystical charm, are nothing more than money to us. The soldiers have permission by law to collect them. They must serve to pay the expenses of coming to your defense. I ask you again not to speak until we have reached your shelter."

Sheba was, in fact, led back to the Tellers' compound nearest the Arena. There, in the courtyard, were her mother, along with Noctis the Bridge, and most of the famous women Tellers and Sages of the epics. She could see among them some of the singers still in costume who had been playing that night.

She recognized two of the greats, Nira the Heron, and Rasanna the Sea, superb in their costumes and the heavy makeup that made their faces gleam like planets, visible to the farthest tiers of the Arena, and even, according to Sheban folklore, to the angels in the heavens who watched their performances, and applauded by throwing handfuls of stars when they were pleased.

The soldiers apparently knew exactly which woman was Sheba's mother. They took her directly to the corner of the courtyard, past a knot of children whose mothers were singing a question-and-answer song with them to keep them calm.

The Queen was sitting on the edge of a silkworm pool. Sheba was delivered to her mother, who stood up and fell toward her daughter with a passive force, as if she were driven by a strong wind. Sheba caught her as a child catches a falling leaf. She was shivering in the mild summer night. A sharp cry echoed powerfully through the courtyard, which like all Sheban architecture featured sensitive acoustics. A woman had gone into labor; she walked haltingly from the courtyard supported by her companions, under armed guard.

"A bit excessive, such a squadron for a woman giving birth. Do they think the baby will be born fully armed?" At their feet, Noctis the Bridge, obviously in pain, lay on cushions brought from one of the houses. Several soldiers had consented to bring the pillows out to her when a delegation of the women approached them.

Sheba knelt by her side; ever liberal with affection, especially for her apprentices, Noctis touched her cheek. "I would have prevented them if I had known the request had been made. They transform us into suppliants, so that every request fulfilled becomes an exhibition of magnanimity. It is a classic posture of false love, to steal in private, and then to bestow in public. Any child of our kingdom recognizes it. You remember the song of the Philanthropist in the Notios cycle?"

"I know it by heart," Sheba said, with the absurd reflex of a student eager to please her teacher, even though they were now confined together out of doors under the vigilant eyes of black-uniformed soldiers. She leaned forward as if to adjust a pillow, and whispered, "Where are the men?"

"Held in the Arena, with soldiers posted now at every entrance and exit. Your father and Far are there, I saw them both," Noctis answered. "It began during tonight's Telling. Your mother and I were sitting together in the audience for the performance. I had my notebook on my lap, as always, and was writing the comments to be delivered to my performers in the morning. Halfway through the second act, two thirds of the audience stood up and stormed the stage. The rest stayed calmly in their seats, thinking this was an experimental choreography. I knew it could not be, but what could I do against this universal disbelief? What could I do?

"Then, abruptly, the lights were extinguished and we were in thick darkness; from the top tier of the Arena descending to the ground, the entire Arena was ringed with countless golden triangles, in precise formation. It was like being trapped in a kind of musical staff, with only one note, repeated again and again.

"When the lights were restored, we saw that the triangles were the golden tips of the arrows of Zealot soldiers, each flourished aloft in one hand, ready to be fitted to the bow. The stage had been cleared.

"Your uncle Kito, who speaks their language perfectly, was escorted to the stage flanked by two Zealot commanders. They spoke, one after another, and he translated their speeches. He was fluent, but evidently speaking under strain. They obviously had told him what he might say.

"'The Kingdom of Sheba is in the grip of a rebellion,' he said. 'Our allies have come to our assistance. I beg you to cooperate with them until we have arrived at a better understanding of what is happening. Go with them as they direct. I ask this of you in concern and love. I love you all. I wish for nothing but your safety and prosperity. Good night.' And then we were brought here."

Sheba heard a rare rasp in Noctis's carefully tended voice, and stood up to find her a pitcher of water. In a few steps, she found herself confronted by the officer who had supervised her waking.

She asked for water, and he went himself to fetch a pitcher, presenting it to her with exaggerated gallantry.

"Permission for water," Noctis said bitterly, "permission for water in our own courtyard." Nevertheless, she was parched, and she drank. They could just hear noises coming from the direction of the Arena. There was a kind of collective gasp, as of dazzled admiration, and then burst after burst of applause.

A young soldier hurried into the courtyard, and approached the commander. The boy was clearly awed by his contact with someone of such high rank, and his face was contorted with the effort to deliver his message concisely. His mouth moved with a snapping motion, and his hands jerked spasmodically, though he kept them at his sides. The commander nodded meditatively, and, in contrast to the boy's agitation, moved slowly, almost langorously, to the center of the courtyard and addressed them.

"We find ourselves in a surprising and suspenseful situation this evening. However, in one instance, we have been given an unexpected gift. We also find ourselves in the company of great artists. It is an opportunity we would be foolish to waste. We ask you to oblige us by singing for the company, to share with us some of the Sheban music that we so admire. We know it is your wedding season. It would be a sublime favor if you would perform for us some of the renowned Sheban wedding songs. Come forward, please, into the center of the courtyard, and do us the honor of performing for us those songs of celebration."

He turned to the young soldier, and spoke quietly to him. The boy began to make the rounds of the courtyard, handing seated women to their feet, and gesturing for them to follow him. Several of the women followed resignedly, and began to position themselves in their choral groups. Groups of soldiers followed his lead, herding the women into the central plaza.

The commander gestured pointedly toward Sheba and her mother; the boy hurried off to fetch them. He took the Queen's arm; she cast a helpless glance at Sheba, who was talking with Noctis, and gestured to them to follow. Sheba half obediently, half protectively stood up to go with her mother.

Noctis, though, stubbornly stayed seated, leaning against the silkworm pool, her back supported by cushions. The boy leaned down to offer her his hand, but she stared ahead, ignoring him. Another faint burst of applause sounded from the Arena.

Above the staccato of the overheard applause, the Queen sang a line of a wedding night serenade, "So male stars and female end their exile," another woman took up the next line, "begin the crossing of their brilliant mile," and a third wove her voice into the song, "accept the union that completes their trial . . ."

"Please join the singers," the boy said to Noctis.

"My child," she said, calmly, since this was a considered estimation of the boy's capacities, and any insult incidental to the judgment, "I have spent a long life as an apprentice, and then, a guardian, of art. It has mattered too much to me to offer it to you under coercion. It would be as if I gave you permission to rape my daughter. I will not join the singers. I do not admire them for singing, though I do not blame them."

The serenade continued, with the sopranos in unison: "And fuse and form in wedding life to life," now answered by the altos, "that human constellation, man and wife."

The boy's mouth tightened. He was being tested and humiliated in public by an old woman. He looked furtively toward the commander, and realized that he was observing the contest. "You must join the singers," he said. It was no longer a request, but a threat.

"There is only one command artists obey: that we obey no commands. If we did, we would forfeit the power over power that is the strength of art. I must preserve myself for the great role I still hope for."

The boy was sick with rage as only a young man can be whose first authority is challenged. He dragged Noctis to her feet, hoping he might casually break her rotten old arm. "Your great role is to sing with the other women in this courtyard. That is your great future," he said, and began pulling the balking old woman toward the singers.

She said one more simple word to him: "No." He dropped her arm, then swiftly and savagely kicked her three times, like a horse he had lost patience with. She fell to the floor, and lay still, her head and neck angled like a snapped branch dangling from a tree. The singers gasped and fell silent in mid-phrase.

A group of soldiers quickly clustered themselves around the old woman and carried her away. The Zealots were famous for the quality and daring of their doctors, having wounded so many.

"Sing, sing," the commander urged. "She will be cared for."

The Queen gave the pitch, and the women began to sing again, from fear surely, but also to take refuge in the architecture of their accomplished voices, and to sing their men to safety inside it. They sang the song of the marriage chamber, their voices playing among the verses like candles illuminating the corners of a room.

Noctis the Bridge was the only woman who died the night of the Zealot invasion. Her body was taken to the Arena, and placed on the platform erected there with the bodies of all the Sheban males over the age of ten who had been in the capital that night.

The wedding songs of the Sheban women had muffled the sounds of killing, as had the great camouflaging unison bursts of clapping that were the specialty of the Zealot women's battalions, arranged in percussive patterns choreographed for such occasions.

The young Zealot soldier who had trampled Noctis in the furor of his first mission was himself executed in disgrace. He had shown himself unworthy of the military code. A soldier must never kill from an impulse of personal rage, which could taint the action with ambiguity, but in the collective certainty of justice, beyond any repentance.

The Zealots spared the younger boys of Sheba, who were almost always malleable enough to be remolded as soldiers, and released them to their mothers. The ranks of the great male Tellers were decimated, though a number escaped from the provinces, and went into hiding. It was rumored that an eminent former King, Caspar, who lived in retirement in the countryside, had not been captured.

As was the Zealot custom, the bodies lay in state for two days, two being a sacred number for the Zealots. And now the famous squadrons of women soldiers appeared in public, for they were the patrols of honor: guardians of the dead, census takers, information gatherers, and the superintendents of prisons. Their service was to function as restorers of order after combat.

Zealots were brought up on the principle that every element of the world was dual in nature, and that every word and act that did not incarnate a dual purpose was wasted. At the Zealot coming of age ceremony, the boys and girls pledged as soldiers with their hands on a sheaf of gold-tipped arrows, and spoke the army oath, "False for truth's sake: architect of what I break: I do and I do not."

The two days of lying in state under the patrols of honor exemplified the principle. They not only served as homage to the sacrificed, but also ensured that anyone who was feigning would be discovered; at the sign of a flickering eyelid, a breath, the sound of a groan, the soldier women would quickly administer the coup de grâce.

Sheba's betrothed, her father, and her brother were among the kingdom's dead. The Sheban women, under the direction of the soldiers, dug the collective grave of their husbands, their sons, their brothers, and their fathers.

On the third day, the women mourners gathered in the Arena for the funeral procession. The commander took the stage and addressed them.

Kito stood beside him, hands slack at his side, a stunned expression on his face, as if he were not quite sure he could trust the sensations of being alive. The order had already been disseminated that he would lead the new government of Sheba.

The commander lifted his hands in benediction. "I come before you today not only as a soldier, but as a priest—a priest who has presided over a great, a noble, and painful sacrifice.

"For the men of Sheba have not been murdered; they have been sacrificed. They lived for peace; and they died for peace. If your neighbors to the north had shared our love of peace, there would have been no need to annex this territory, on which they had designs. They left us no choice.

"For in the cause of peace, the life of the individual may be consumed, like a small flame in a great fire, in the name of the greater good. We pledge to work with you, to restore what you have lost tenfold; for as our oath says, we are the architects of what we break, and we shall return to you a new kingdom, a new Sheba.

"Much has been asked of you, as we have asked much of ourselves. But what will be accomplished will be the work of peace, and, you will realize, the work of love, that value so central to your culture.

"Now we ask of you one more sacrifice. We ask that you do not indulge yourselves in weeping as we return the sacrificed to the earth. We do not cry when we eat bread in the morning, we do not shed tears while we sleep, for eating and sleeping are necessary to us. We do not mourn the necessary. To weep during this ritual would be an insult to the sacrificed, and an insult to us."

The women stood while the shrouded bodies were lifted by the patrols of honor. Kito took the Queen by the arm, and led her to the head of the procession. She leaned against him heavily, and he touched her hair in a gesture of comfort so tentative that it was almost invisible. The commander solicitously offered his arm to Sheba.

The train of women walked to the burial field slowly and soundlessly, as if they were the ghosts of their men, their faces contorted and their lips twisted with the effort to repress their tears.

Contingents of foreigners who had been culled from the audience at the last Tellings and were hastily returning to their own countries halted when they saw the mourners, and stood in respectful silence.

When they arrived at the burial grounds, the silence remained profound. The bodies of the men had already been shrouded, and dropped into the crater the Sheban women had dug. All along its rim, the Zealot women's patrol of honor stood at attention, ever watchful for signs of life.

Kito escorted the Queen forward and stepped behind her, retreating so that she could sing the first funeral call. She did not lift her head, her eyes fixed on the ground. Her lips trembled; it was clear that she did not dare words, let alone attempt the music.

A series of cracked, inarticulate stammering noises emerged from her throat, terrible caricatures of words, as if her tongue had been cut in half. It was a dark, unprecedented disgrace for the chief epic artist of her country; several women gasped, gripped by a sickening awareness that the Queen was being used, an exhibition of the death of Telling.

She had been forbidden to mourn the deaths of her husband, son, friends, and colleagues. Without mourning she could not sing the truth, could not produce the words of funeral, or the correct pitches of the songs, any more than she could order a child to say "I love you" to her and have the declaration mean anything. Without explicitly forbidding what words might be sung or said, the Zealots had succeeded in making the funeral songs false.

Sheba could not bear her mother's wounded babbling. She withdrew her arm from the commander's proprietary support, and walked with forced, deliberate serenity to the Queen's side, to assume the leadership of the funeral ceremony. She held up her right hand, in the traditional gesture of the leader who would signal for the response of the chorus.

"As is our custom," she bowed to the commander to acknowledge him.

Then she threw back her head and laughed, in delicate trills. She directed the women to answer, and they laughed, a perfectly coordinated mass of trilling laughter. She repeated the trills, and her mother took them up, joining the chorus.

Then Sheba changed the tempo, and the laughter became clipped and staccato, as if their laughter was mocking the sound of marching boots. The chorus drilled out its laughter in response. Sheba's leading laugh took a new tone; she howled, and the women howled chorally, as if supernatural jackals were howling in mirth in some predatory heaven.

Then Sheba led them in peal after peal of violent laughter, forcing a faster and faster rhythm, like the convulsive ringing of bells. She laughed until the tears ran down her face, and the women followed her, their bodies rocking and their faces contorted with laughter. At her signal, the women formed a closed circle, their arms around each other, eyes streaming, shoulders racked with wild laughter, until at a sign from Sheba, they abruptly fell silent.

"We don't expect you to be familiar with all of our customs," Sheba said to the commander, when the funeral chorus had ended. The commander looked for a long time at Sheba, with speculative, severe, and admiring eyes.

"Then I must set myself to learn them," he said.

The women were still again, after their possessed laughter; several of the women's faces were fixed in smiles, as they wiped the tears of laughter from their brilliant eyes.

On the return from the burial, the commander did not take Sheba's arm, but dropped behind a pace. Kito put his arm protectively around the Queen, and held her close. Sheba walked alone.

She saw nothing, heard nothing, except Far's voice, wrapping her like a cloud in one of his ritual phrases of love: "You were born to laugh." He had told her the truth, but she had understood only a half-truth. She had been presumptuous; it seemed she had been born to laugh—but not, as she had thought, to be happy.

She was back in the quarters of her childhood; the room was intact, but the childhood was shattered. The personal belongings that had been in the lodging where she and Far had planned to live had been retrieved and delivered here in her absence.

She opened her costume chest and took out her incense clock. She emptied the incense from the hours that measured the night, the hours fragrant with the burned sugar that reminded her of him. Then she knelt before Far's costume chest, opened it, buried her head in it as if it were his grave, and cried as violently as if she were being eviscerated.

Within the first week, the Zealot caretakers had provided the Shebans with a constitution, outlining the people's rights and responsibilities as a Zealot protectorate. This document became the source of the weekly decrees issued and statutes established during the next two years, as Sheban life was remade in the Zealot image.

The Zealots proclaimed that they would sustain the theater school, and the central place of drama in the life of the Shebans, so much so that they would allot a portion of their own budget to commissioning new epics and lyric plays. Thus, war became a subject as prestigious in epics as love.

Noctis the Bridge had always taught that the study of love included the study of war, although the opposite was not true, but the Zealots were more intensely concerned with the kingdom's future than its past. The school would no longer train its students to perform only Sheban works, but would be open to candidates from all territories protected by the Zealots. Thus, a body of Zealots would be qualified to teach the Sheban techniques fitted to Zealot stories.

The greatest change in the life of the kingdom was the incorporation of all able-bodied Shebans, women and men, into the Zealot army. The Sheban peoples had never sustained a standing army; they had considered the stage their territory and their country; Sheba itself was ultimately the stage a Sheban mounted to perform, the excellence of the Sheban epic craft was the only defense possible for a country that altered from night to night, with each Telling.

Now only active performers would be exempt from Zealot military service, which was carefully designed not only for dominating Zealot neighbors, but also for the purpose of dominating the Zealots themselves.

The Zealot army was at the heart of its government and education; its centrality spared the Zealots the dissent and rebellions that were such a danger to other aggressive nations.

Parents, teachers, leaders, doctors, priests, were all soldiers. The walls of Zealot nurseries were covered with images of the children's parents, holding their weapons. A Zealot child could never separate herself from the army, any more than he could separate his life from his body. Zealot children were taught to stand in respect in the presence of any soldier; a child who refused, with the most innocent obstinacy, was put under observation; troublemakers were identified from the earliest age.

The army functioned even more insidiously as a perfect system to ensure, without struggle, the submission of that other potentially rebellious group, the Zealot women. The forced incorporation of women as soldiers ensured their permanent subordination.

Since few could equal the men in combat, they could never rise in the structure of command. And there could be no dissent, since they were always under the orders of men of higher rank, and to disobey was treason to the collective. As never before, Zealot women could be used as their men saw fit. Their two highest ranks were as Soldier Breeders, and Justifiers, the spokeswomen whose serious, pretty faces, cleanly braided hair, and training in heroic rhetoric ennobled each action of the Zealot army.

For Sheba personally, the greatest change was the alteration in her mother, still known as the Queen of Sheba, but now the bitter, narrow-eyed wife of Uncle Kito, who had married her protectively. She no longer performed, except to sing strange lullabies to her new baby son, in which all the refrains about night and sleep and rocking cradles took on a foreboding air. Epic was lost to her now, even in the truncated form approved by the Zealots; she had lost the power to believe their cyclical patterns, or in the quests for love the epics described. She could sing only of premonition.

In the kingdom as it was under the Zealots, there was no more privacy. All rooms and lodgings were now lived in as barracks, subject to inspections at all hours. No subordinate woman, man, or child could refuse a visit, and all Shebans were considered subordinate, and perhaps would be for generations to come.

All locks were removed from the doors of anyone below the rank of officer; old trees were cut down in gardens and forests, even lilac and rose bushes were lopped to a height that could not provide cover for an assassin. Only those of high rank could sit under tall trees, behind high walls, roaming through orchards discreetly guarded by the patrols of women, in the Protector's gardens.

Now the commander roamed through the kingdom at night, entering random darkened houses whose sleeping inhabitants, abruptly roused, leapt from their beds to offer him a glass of wine and a plate of nuts and sweets, in terrified parody of their former spontaneous hospitality. He also began to make unpredictable but regular nocturnal visits to Sheba's quarters, often finding her lying in bed, learning the lines for the new Zealot roles she was to play.

"I want to ensure personally that you are resting well, and have everything you need," he would say, and sit down on her bed, dismissing his guards.

Sometimes he entered the room after she was asleep, seated himself on the edge of the bed, and rhythmically stroked her shoulder until she awoke. She would have liked to be able to receive him formally, dressed, sitting in a chair, or standing, but his solid, armed body on her bed made an obstacle between her and the freedom of any other posture. In order to reach a chair, she would have to dislodge him, and even if that could be managed, he would see her undressed. As if he intuited her discomfort, his visits became later and later, so that he would almost always discover her asleep, as if he wanted to enter her dreams.

These visits seemed to unleash something necessary to him; he would stroke some part of her body absently, as if it were a body of water through which he was rowing, and tell her stories of his battles, and of his childhood.

He told her about his first two wives, or "conquests" in their language; they had lost their lives in police actions. He spoke about his third wife, with an expression of great pride; she was an extremely pretty girl who was training as a Justifier, one of the teams of women soldiers who met with civilians, explained the actions and customs of the Zealots to them, and clarified Zealot law.

As he spoke the stroking never stopped; once or twice when he was describing his first childhood Triggering, he gripped her shoulder violently. The Triggering was the beginning of military training for Zealot children.

At the age of three, each child was called into his parents' bedroom. There he was shown a picture of a woman or man who he was told was hunting him in order to kill him; and so the children learned their survival was in their own hands.

They were instructed in techniques of camouflage and outdoor survival, and how to escape traps and master the deadly weapons they would need to eliminate the killers.

Throughout their childhoods, trained adult soldiers dressed like the stalkers' pictures would suddenly cross their paths or loom behind them as they went to school. They were haunted by these specters, never realizing that the stalkers were carefully trained to terrorize them, but never to inflict physical harm.

The commander's Triggering, he told her, began with the apparition of the killer at his bedroom window; he now knew it was a soldier impersonator, but his career had begun that night, with rolling under the bed at lightning speed, and holding his breath, while he heard the killer's footsteps in the room.

He laughed now at his childish ineptitude; of course the impersonator had known exactly where he was hiding, but he could still taste his own blood in his mouth, where he had bitten his lip to force himself to keep his breathing quiet and to lie still.

Sheba never spoke during these visits, nor was she questioned or invited to speak; the commandant stroked her hair, her shoulder, at times the edge of her breast, during his monologue. Or he would take her hand, as if it were his own, and pat his knee with it, or his thigh, moving it close to his sex, but only rarely touching it.

"I want you to think of me as a father," he told her one night, "to take the place of the father you have lost. I want to make up for that loss. I will be the father who never leaves you."

Those words made Sheba fear him with an absolute, uncontrollable fear; she realized that he believed this; he believed as certainly in all that he felt, as a crowd believes a skillful orator. He had no doubt that he was showing her paternal affection. In that belief, he could absently kill her someday, and believe it was a fatherly act. His was a somnambulist's soul.

"Yours is a culture incapable of defending itself," he said meditatively. "Yet I have learned much about the charms and grandeur of love here. It seems it is after all a force as irresistible as death. I am grateful to your uncle Kito for bringing me here."

"My uncle Kito?" It was the first question, and also the last, that Sheba would ever ask of the commander.

"It was the maps your uncle sold to us from his remarkable collection that enabled us to secure the city and the outlying districts so quickly. He is a true man of Sheba; he gave everything for love. It was his only chance to possess your mother.

"He has taught me that a lover may be more like a warrior than I had ever understood. Your mother means more to him than life; like the great generals I have known, he would stop at nothing." He patted her, patted and stroked her, lost in the contemplation of her uncle's love.

At last he stood up to leave, with a look of tender regret. "I would not have been capable of such feeling. It is not part of our culture. All our relations are tinged with strategy, with gaining or losing advantage through alliance. Your uncle had no strategy; your mother is all he gained. And she is all he wanted. I had heard of such things, but until now, I did not believe in them. It is remarkable."

He fell silent for a moment, staring at nothing as intently as if it were a painting. "I will leave you to your own company. Dream of love, as you say here."

It was that night she had her first dream of Noctis the Bridge. She saw her great teacher seated in her old armchair on the practice stage, her lips moving soundlessly. The sight of her longed-for face flooded Sheba with delight, a momentary return to the life before the Zealots had come. Within her dream, she felt an unbearable craving to see Far, and hoped that she could somehow call him into the dream. Noctis smiled at her with her old knowing affection, then said admonishingly: "Are you practicing every day?"

"Almost," Sheba said. Noctis smiled as she used to do when she heard the truth confessed, with the expression of someone hearing a pleasing musical tone.

"But I don't spend a day without thinking of you," Sheba told her. "Nothing here is the same. This is not the place where you and I lived. They are assigning me roles I am not suited to play."

"Yes, like so many, you now find yourself body and soul in the wrong story. One sees so often rich people who are poor, and poor people who are rich, beauties who are ugly, and plain people who are really exquisite. History is full of provinces forced into alien nations. It is a terrible business for a comic actor like you to be trapped inside a tragedy. That is why you must leave this place. It is time for you to find a way to return to your own story, now, before it is too late."

"And my mother?"

"Your mother's heart broke badly, and lost its brilliance. Her story is no longer your story. You cannot live if you will not leave her. I warn you, I am telling the truth."

"How can I escape this? They will never let me cross the border."

"You will leave three times. You will leave as an old woman, as a boy, and as a girl who is not you, but is very like you. Play these roles that belong to you well, and they will take you where you have to go. You were born under the Paradise Nebula, a constellation that vanishes and reappears. Its natives were born to reveal the truth of what is thought not to exist.

"Open your costume chest. The path across the border begins inside it."

"If this is true, what about you?" Sheba asked Noctis, longing for her to say she would come back. "How can you return to your own story? You counsel me to play my own roles, but you were killed because you refused to play yours."

"I have returned to my own story, my dear, and the great role—the greatest of my roles—that was waiting for me. After all, if you notice, I am a dead woman producing a perfect illusion of a living one, thanks to a lifetime of observation. And that, I say without modesty, is a role only masters are given to play.

"I do not know whether you or I will share a dream again. I can only tell you to leave here at the first opportunity. I wish you courage. I wish you luck. Dream of love."

In the days that followed, an elderly woman, still vigorous despite her habit of sighing and clutching whatever part of her body suddenly gave her pain, offered her domestic services to several inns in the foreign quarter.

The foreign quarter was teeming with tradesmen from the various Zealot colonies, eager to find a foothold in the newest addition. None of the innkeepers had work for her, though one knew of five Philosophers living in a rented house while they studied Sheban thought and customs. These five might be glad of a personal servant, especially a woman of her age, who would pose no temptation to the men.

The Philosophers were ascetics whose lives were given over to thought and prayer; they were forbidden to have relations with women outside marriage, and to avoid marriage itself, if they were strong enough. In their youth, they studied in the Academy under their greatest thinkers, and they spent their young manhood wandering from country to country, learning as much as they could of the ephemeral world in order to grasp the eternal one. Paradoxically, the more their principles detached them from the temporal world, the more their education emphasized knowledge of the physical world; they had produced many important works of physics and a substantial number of respected naturalists.

The five young Philosophers knew a great deal about the seven heavens above earth, the mathematics of music, and all the beautiful hierarchies that ordered the cosmos, but they knew nothing of such mundane realities as how fevers were treated and food made edible. This knowledge they were encouraged to avoid, so as not to dilute the purity of their contemplation, and so as to cultivate indifference to physical comforts, and to the fate of the temporary body. They were glad to have the old woman bear the brunt of this sordid aspect of life on their behalf.

For several months, Sheba spent sporadic hours housekeeping for them, and perfecting her impersonation of an old woman.

The Philosophers were not demanding employers; they were all gaunt, eating only food sufficient for the mind to function. Sheba compelled herself to respect their sense of virtue, though she mischievously permitted herself to make their grains and vegetables temptingly palatable.

She enjoyed watching the tallest and most skeletal of them learn to taste food. The others ate absently and continued reading at the table. But this one tasted the unfamiliar food slowly, a questioning look in his blue eyes. She liked his willingness to think about everything, even this aspect of life he had been trained to dismiss. This one occasionally showed her his notebooks, and recorded her answers to his questions about Sheban life.

Sheba usually became old near the marketplace, where she bought their modest supplies of food. The double life was natural to her; it was how all Sheban people lived now.

She worked as she walked from the market on perfecting her elderly gait, suitable for the old woman she now was, rapid, but unbalanced, negotiating the invisible mountainous terrain on which all old people walked.

This morning, there were strange sounds coming from the Philosophers' house, which was usually quiet except for pages turning, and the lapping sounds of brushes against paper. She found the tall Philosopher hunched over the table where he usually worked, his arms limp as if he had fallen, his shoulders racked with his gasping sobs.

She leaned down to him, touched his shoulder with infinite gentleness, and made a soft sound that was not quite a word. He lifted his tear-marked face and spontaneously laid his head against her breast, nestling in her arms as a normal grief-stricken man of Sheba would, though he had probably not been this close to a woman since childhood.

A messenger had brought news an hour ago that his beloved and brilliant five-year-old brother, for whom he had replaced their dead father, had been killed by a snake's bite. The boy had leaned down to pick up a clutch of tiny eggs he'd found; the mother snake attacked him before he had time to close his hand around the charming miniatures.

The Philosopher was too distraught to make arrangements to travel to the funeral. Sheba promised she would act for him, and offered to go with him.

That evening, she made a bundle of her costumes and stage cosmetics, along with the few jewels she had been able to keep, and dismantled her Sheban oar, concealing it among the clothes. Her father used to say that song was a more certain living than farming, since it was unaffected by drought, storm, or season. Now she would put his maxim to the test.

She went to her mother's rooms to say good night, hoping that she might somehow find a way to speak the truth to her. But her mother looked up from the eerie lullabies she was singing to Kito's unwanted son, and stared at Sheba with the opaque general loathing she felt now for the world itself. She was finished with further truths.

Sheba said a good-night her mother ignored as if she had been a stranger, absorbed in her incessant songs. Sheba never saw her again. A year after she had crossed the border into Ellusha, a report circulated that the woman who had been Queen of Sheba had killed that child, and then herself.

Sheba and the Philosopher crossed the border without incident; the Zealots were not particularly concerned with the comings and goings of the elderly, and elderly women were the most negligible of all, having exhausted their animal and military value.

Traveling had its odd narcotic effect in which strangers talk as they have never talked with intimates, telling unrepeatable truths. At least the Philosopher did, during the three days' journey to the Ellushan capital; Sheba kept her own counsel, but asked him question after question, not only out of caution. She began to realize as he answered her that he needed the questions; the only way for a Philosopher to heal his grief was to think.

He spoke of his dead brother, and of the supreme pleasure he had taken in giving him his first lessons, in botany, music, and physics; "as if I saw a soul being born in the house of flesh," he said.

He described some of those lessons to Sheba; and as surely as if she had a special optical instrument, she saw him through the child's eyes. Perhaps a fragment of the boy entered into her own soul.

The Philosopher showed her worlds that had always existed all around her, that she could never have discovered without him. The undifferentiated flights of birds overhead became real and specific, as he showed her the different rhythms of the wing beats, the sublime collaboration of bone, wing, and current of air. It was a rare gift he gave her with this knowledge—a piece of the world he loved, as real as a key or a lamp.

He sketched the ascent and descent of a gliding sea bird, showing her how the wings themselves changed shape each time the bird rowed in the air. The Philosopher made her imagine what it would feel like if her body changed its very shape each time she took a step.

He gave the old woman the sketch to keep; an access to the freedom and mobility that had once been hers.

Sheba prized the tactful generosity hidden in the gift of the sketch; whenever she brought it out to look at afterward, she felt the rush of wings. That soaring and swiftness later entered her voice as she sang the epics, hovering, floating, and gliding fleetly and delicately from note to note.

They dismounted to walk through fields of sunflowers that were taller than Sheba. For Sheba, entering the forest of green and gold flowers was a world of surreal beauty.

The Philosopher, though, had a different view: "You do not see flowers if you see them only as fragile and beautiful. These flowers are male and female fused, as most of them are. You are at the center here of the sheer force of breeding. We breathe it. We eat it. The whole world exists to seduce us." With this knowledge, he gave her something he feared.

At night, as they camped under the stars, he asked her to sing passages from the epics, and she did, as old people do, revealing the anatomy of the passages, but failing the notes and quavering poignantly on certain phrases. He questioned her about Sheban teachings on love, and compared them to the Philosophers' ideas on the subject.

"We think of human love itself as a hopeless quest," he explained to her. "Though we are not among those who are taught to avoid love on the grounds that women are flawed men."

"I should hope not," Sheba said. "Because by that logic, men can only be perfect women."

"I don't understand," he said, "how your people have so much faith in the illusion of human love. How can you believe so much in an impulse that fails more often than it endures?"

"We don't have faith in it. We don't believe in it. Remember, we are trained from childhood to spend our lives on stages, making imaginary people exist. We create it."

He gestured toward the sky. "In all the history of humanity, not one pair of lovers has ever been united in Heaven. Only the perpetual hunters and their hunted, warriors, and rapists glitter there, separated lovers, the unfaithful shamed through light, women turned into animals through the shame of seduction."

"Not true," she said. "Have you never seen the Lovers' Cluster? It is faint at this season, but you can make it out." She led him away from the fire, searching for an advantageous perspective from which to view the constellation. "There, look up," she said, and showed him the lovers in their shimmering embrace at the heart of the constellation. "Can you see them?"

"Yes, I think so. Though they could be wrestlers or combatants."

"I suppose they could be, if that is what you have in your eye."

Sheba concealed the sadness she felt when they reached the city; she knew that she would accompany him no further. As the Zealots had no use for an old woman, the Philosophers had no use for a young one. In pleasure-loving Ellusha, she could make her living singing and play-acting, though she had heard from her Ellushan mother that they did not always appreciate listening to songs more complex than the ones belonging to the national repertoire.

Just before dawn, Sheba dressed and tied her small parcel to her back. The Philosopher was sleeping soundly in the room above. She quietly closed the door behind her, and taking deep breaths of the fresh dawn air, set out to see if she could find her way back into her own story in Ellusha.

By late afternoon, it was clear that she had vanished. The Philosopher questioned the proprietor of the house where they had rented rooms, but neither he nor anyone in the quarter had seen an old woman on the street early that morning, though someone thought he had seen a fifteen-year-old boy he didn't recognize, carrying a pack.

The Philosopher could discover nothing more, and could wait no longer to return to the road. He traveled on alone, carrying not only the weight of his brother's death, which increased as he neared home, but a galling sense of failure: there had been something profoundly important he had not understood, and that was a sharp torment to Philosophers.

It was not hard at all for Sheba to find work tavern-singing; the

Ellushans loved their wine and their entertainments, though they were not the kind of audience she had been used to; they listened sometimes, but sometimes hummed and sang with her, as if this charming fresh-voiced boy was simply an echo of all their collected voices.

Only one man truly listened intently, and he began to appear with a regularity that worried her. He might be a lover of boys, in which case she could only disappoint him; or he might be a Zealot scout, a bounty hunter lying in wait for escaped Shebans.

She joined him apprehensively when he sent her an invitation to take a glass of wine with him at his table.

"Thank you for meeting me," he said. He had an oddly distinguished face, for someone who spent time and money watching simple tavern singers.

"I have been admiring your singing since I discovered you, as you may have noticed." He leaned toward her intently. "But I can perhaps find you work that would suit you better than tavern-singing."

She froze defensively, setting her wineglass down. She could not afford to be courted by this man, and she could not afford to tell him the truth. "The voice is good," he said. "But I want to make a man of you."

She stood up to leave the table, crafting an expression of polite regret. He pulled her firmly back into her seat. "Oh, not that way, my girl," he said. "Your mother's work as a boy was much better than yours when she wore this costume, playing the Prince Horizon, the year I was made King of Sheba."

"Are you Caspar?" she whispered. She thought now that she could see a resemblance to the plaster casts of Caspar in his exemplary roles that Noctis the Bridge had used when she taught.

"Yes," the man replied, "I am. I escaped the butchers by playing a side of beef, and I have brought many more fine carcasses across since then.

"The Zealots can't tell an actor from a steer. They think a prison is the same thing as a country, and that a theater is a place to make war. They are confident that they can kill our epics along with our land."

He doubled over, laughing angrily. "Poor brutes. We have made the only heroes who can die but never be killed, the women and the men of the Tellings. In the end, we will put the Zealots into our songs, and they will be no more than coarse adjectives.

"For the moment, I am the only living King of Sheba. But there are enough of us to make a troupe. And if you join us, I can make you a Queen as great as your mother was, Queen Sheba."

So Sheba joined the troupe of King Caspar, training by day, and playing by night, sometimes in houses, sometimes in parks—the performances were never held in the same locale, to protect the troupe from Zealot retaliation.

Caspar did not allow her to play women's roles: "You don't understand enough about boys' and men's roles to play the girls well," he said, "but it will come with time."

The troupe rapidly gained a following; it was a novelty at first to hear the stumbling rebirth of the true Tellings of Sheba, but the superficial Ellushans actually developed a taste for the epics; favorite passages were hummed in the marketplace, and even the tavern singers attempted versions.

The Sheban refugees began to give lessons in building the oars, and playing them. It became fashionable for Ellushan children to be trained in the Sheban arts. The songs were quoted, the songs were sung, and scenes from the Tellings were played again. The songs moved across borders faster than flame; the formidable troops of the Zealots were outmaneuvered by not only men, but women—the heroines and heroes of the Tellings, who were bringing the world of Sheba back to life.

So young Sheba remained a boy, and it was in one of her masculine roles that the Philosopher first saw her play on his return to Ellusha, a place that continued to haunt him. He had been given permission to make a study of Ellusha, though he also admitted to himself that he longed to learn something simpler; he wanted to understand what had happened to him there.

The Philosopher had heard a rumor of a Telling to take place on a ship in the Ellushan harbor; he made his way to the port, where he was unwittingly, rapidly, and expertly tested by a small network of passersby, before he was approved and allowed to pay to be rowed from the quay to the ship. He took a seat on the deck, and as dusk fell, the performers took their places to enact the seventh book of the Horizon.

The Philosopher was absorbed and intrigued by the unique tones the Sheban instruments produced, but it was Sheba's recitation, costumed as Horizon, in the prince's red velvet tunic, and the turban clasped by a pomegranate-shaped and -colored jewel, that shocked him. He fell into a rapt concentration beyond even thought, as he had never before experienced.

To be carried beyond thought frightened him. He found himself entering an entirely new world, as he had done the night the old Sheban woman showed him a constellation he had never seen.

The Philosopher dutifully took notes, recorded interviews, and learned the language of Ellusha during the days, but at night, he no longer studied.

Instead, he made passionate efforts to find out where the Tellings were being presented, and if the marvelous boy was playing in that night's performance. Like many inexperienced spectators of theater, he confused the performer with her roles. Soon he began to seek her out after performances, to try to talk with her, or at least to hear her talk.

When she caught sight of him, Sheba recognized him at once. He was waiting for her to emerge from a wine cellar where that night's performance had been held. He sent a bottle of wine to the players' table with his compliments for the boy who had recited Horizon. She thanked him as she was leaving, and he invited her to take another glass with him so courteously and with such disciplined eagerness that she could not refuse.

Besides, she was overjoyed at the utterly unexpected appearance of the man who had unwittingly saved her life without realizing it. It was as if she had found a talisman she had lost.

He now appeared regularly at her Telling evenings, and as regularly waited to spend an hour with her afterward, or two if he could get two. Now the days when they did not see each other lacked savor. Soon the days when they did not see each other lacked purpose. It was when the days that they did not see each other began to seem to gamble with the nature of reality that each of them became privately terrified.

Sheba knew that it was a matter of luck that he followed only the Tellings in which she played a boy; on other nights, he would have had the chance to see her play the old woman who had been his servant in the capital of Sheba. And there would be no end to that confusion.

As to the Philosopher, the growing danger that life and thought could be affected absolutely by the mere presence of another person was exactly what he had been warned against, a snare and a risk to immortal life. He was at least lucky that they were of the same sex. The Philosophers were expected to mentor and educate boys in a fraternal and paternal fashion, to conduct new generations across the boundaries of time into immortality, as his own great teacher had led him.

Sheba still loved to swim, and whenever she had the opportunity, she would make her way to a secluded cove overlooked by a pavilion, all that remained of what had been a magnificent palace destroyed by fire. The water of the cove had the wonderful property of being at times smooth as a lagoon, at others, passionate as a miniature sea. On this warm afternoon, the Philosopher was reading in the pavilion, which he had also privately discovered; loving bird flight as he did, he cherished the rich variety of water fowl drawn to the cove.

He looked up from his book; his adored actor was kneeling by the water's edge, letting the water ripple over his hand. Apparently, the temperature pleased, because the boy stood up and kicked off his boots. The Philosopher watched, indulging himself in the sweet pleasure of watching a beloved unaware, glimpsing the extra dimension of someone engaged for the moment in nothing but living his own life.

The boy unwound his turban; a flood of dark hair cascaded to his waist. He swiveled, and slipped out of his tunic, his breasts shining in the golden sun just beginning to set. She dove into the water.

"Oh, God," the Philosopher said. "You're a girl." His book fell from his lap as he raced to the edge of the lagoon, and plunged in, still in his clothes. He swam to the girl. The pools of her long hair swirled around him, like the inks of a calligrapher erasing his first picture. In an ecstasy of horror and exaltation, he took her in his arms and embraced her.

In the pavilion, they made love for the first time, with the moving courage and extreme vulnerability of all lovers willing to stand before each other naked. And their lovemaking cannot be described. No one yet has succeeded in describing lovemaking, except through the most oblique and fleeting glimpses: for making love returns us to a state of being that exists before memory, and makes us miraculously present at our own conception. And the act of love is itself description, as each lover describes with body and soul the other's body and soul.

As they lay entwined in the pavilion afterward, the Philosopher caught sight of the constellation of the Lovers' Cluster, and pointed it out to her. He told her how an old Sheban woman had first taught him to see it, relating the story of their journey and her inexplicable disappearance. Sheba, in her elderly quavering voice, sang him the same song she had sung by firelight that night.

"Oh, God," the Philosopher said. "You were a boy. Are you also your grandmother?"

"Of course," said Sheba. "That too. And a boy and a beech tree and a dolphin. At times a devil. A man, too, and a baby. Even now and then, a goddess and a god. Like all Shebans. And like you, if you knew it."

"Then we Philosophers have made grave errors in our thinking. We are taught to renounce the company and love of women. And yet, if women are as you say, it is not women who are false; it is our own laws that are false. We have based them on a premature idea of what a woman is, instead of exploring them as beings whose dimensions we have still to discover."

"As is a man," she said.

In the two years that followed, the Philosopher discovered a truth he had never been taught: that love and learning could never be separated, and that the sages of love were far fewer than the sages of philosophy. His education began gingerly; he learned not to be afraid or embarrassed to inquire and speak as candidly, courageously, and searchingly of love as he did about the nature of good, evil, or power.

At times during these years, he was tormented by love, as he had been schooled; at other times, his thoughts were as ecstatic as his body; he made love with his mind, he learned with his body.

Love educated Sheba, too; she learned that an epic was not only a poem, but that a person, the living of a human life, could also be epic. She saw this in the way the Philosopher loved her and, at the same time, struggled with his love for her. She saw it in the way the world was greater for her when she could see some of what he perceived. They never knew the same stories. The earth she saw was different from his; the Heaven he saw was different from hers. Yet at times, she could live on his earth, and he in her Heaven.

There was no better time, they discovered, to tell stories than after lovemaking, in the darkness and quiet lit only by the glow of their bodies' bliss, the perfumes drifting from Sheba's incense clock telling the hours. It was then they amused themselves by comparing the stories they had been told, of the origins of fire and jewels, the creation of the world. One night, inspired by a rainstorm, he told her a story of a flood that destroyed the world, except for a family who survived on a wooden ark.

When he finished, Sheba said, "I have heard of that story. But the version we tell is quite different. The characters do not have quite the same names. But we also call it 'How the World Was Saved.' Do you want to hear it? Or I could tell you 'How Love Was First Invented.' "

"I am on fire to hear how something so dangerous was invented."

"We would be in even greater danger if it had not."

"But it always requires suffering."

"I would say almost always," she said, and put a finger to his lips.

"Almost always," he said, with a Philosopher's reluctant smile of concession at the end of a debate.

"But if the world wasn't saved, love could not have been invented. So let me begin where I should," she said, and sat up, pulling a silk shawl over her shoulders.

"Only a traveler who had had the good fortune to range the earth as widely as a migrant bird could have seen vineyards as beautiful as No's. The vines were set in terraces cut out of chalky cliffs high above a glittering blue sea. The terraces descended to the sea with the thrilling symmetry of a perfectly played musical scale. No and his wife labored in these vineyards, and they grew rich on the dark purple wine, the color of an empress's carpet, that they sold in barrels."

"What was No's wife's name?" the Philosopher asked, reaching for a pear and a piece of blue cheese.

"Now you have asked a profound question, a true Philosopher's question. Her name was Malista."

Sheba took a sip of water, and continued. "The couple prospered not only in the abundance and excellence of their grapes, but in their own fertility. Malista brought three sons to the light of earth's sun, and each of these married well in his turn. No added the substantial dowries of the wives to his own holdings, and built an imposing walled compound to house the family and, he hoped, all its future generations. It was built on the highest point of the surrounding countryside, and from it, No could look down the sweep of the terraced vineyards all the way to the brilliant sea. He had built his estate in the exact spot his God had found for him, as he had been told in a dream.

"In all his good fortune, No did not neglect the God he worshipped. He sacrificed to his God in perfect accordance with the prescribed ritual, and poured out the correct inch of wine from every cup to give God his taste of the vintage. He was vigilant over his family, seeing to it that they worked hard and did not wander far from the compound except for commercial or religious necessity, so that they would not fall into temptation.

"He was not entirely free of faults; he was rather too fond of his own wine, and periodically drank himself into oblivion. As is sometimes the case with upright men, he was bitter and insulting when in his cups, and given to violent cursing, as if drunkenness unleashed all the pent-up resentments and hidden angers he carefully controlled.

"Then he would harass his sons, accusing them of laziness and ineptitude, and mock their tenderness for their young wives as if he were jealous of them. And he would call Malista to him, and beat her, the mother who had reared such inferior sons, with rather more force than the light correction with which a man is entitled to chastise his wife, sometimes even leaving visible marks, though that was expressly forbidden.

"On those occasions, Malista would weep and refuse to speak to him, and would run through the vineyards to the shore when her husband finally collapsed in a stupor. These occasions brought her to despair. She longed to please No and was as conscientious a wife as she knew how to be, rising before dawn, and working tirelessly in house and vineyard, always awake long after the household was asleep. She searched her conduct for faults severe enough to warrant punishment, and could find none.

"So she ran to the shore and desperately leapt into the sea, and let the salt water heal her cuts and bruises, while she struggled with the thought of swimming out as far as she could see, to death or some other miracle.

"Instead, she would make her way into town, exactly as No forbade. It was a place of godless cheats and dissipated rabble, he said, and to be avoided as much as possible. He knew all their tricks; he traded with them, after all. The townsmen wrangled ruthlessly to evade a fair price for the wine, and once agreed to, it was the devil to get them to pay on time. And perhaps worst of all, they often cut his beautiful pure nectar with water, or blended it with other wines, and resold it under other names, contaminating the work of No's hands, the fruits of the labor he dedicated to his God.

"The first time Malista walked through the town, the people she encountered fell into an uneasy silence. A cut on her cheek that she thought had closed had begun to bleed again. She walked through the central marketplace, and was calmed by the sight of the heaped-up breads and cheeses; the clarity of the actions of buying and selling seemed stable and comfortable after No's incoherent attack.

"She would have liked to stop and buy a piece of fruit, or a bunch of garlic, for the sake of enjoying the predictable exchange that would accompany the transaction. But unlike normal merchants, no one called to her to show off his wares, or chanted a rhyme praising the perfume of his fruit. Instead, the sight of her seemed to stop conversation.

"A sudden gush from the wound dropped on the bodice of her dress, staining her chest with a setting sun of blood. She put her hand to her cheek, and saw that it was as red as if she had butchered an animal. Embarrassed, she hurried away from the center of the town, and walked toward the secluded orchards beyond.

"Several groups of children were seated in circles under apple trees, reading in turn, or answering questions their teachers put to them. The sight of them made her remember her own children's school years. Young children, even when tutored privately, like hers, always had their lessons under apple trees in fine weather. For some reason—no one remembered why—these trees were associated with knowledge, and said to stimulate the appetite for learning and its fruits.

"She saw a gaunt, gray-haired man lean over, place his hand on a boy's shoulder, and whisper something in the child's ear. The boy frowned, as if trying to absorb a complex lesson, then stood up and raced past Malista. She could not have touched him even if she had tried; he was as swift and wheeling as a swallow. No one spoke to her. She was ashamed; they must think she was a witch or a wandering madwoman, and sent the boy for help. She thought she must now hurry back along the shore, and climb toward home. What would happen if they detained her here?

"She turned back on her path, and began to retrace her steps toward the town, walking with the new pulsing energy of fear. She saw an unmistakably pregnant woman and a child coming toward her on the path, and gave way for them to pass, making herself as inconspicuous as possible.

"The boy was the same one who had run past her as if he were her prey. He looked at her, looked at the pregnant woman, and without speaking to either of them, seemed to take wing toward the orchards where the groups of children were clustered.

"The pregnant woman spoke: 'Will you let me clean the cut and give you something to eat?' She neither smiled nor reached out her hand. Her tone was so simple and lacking in seduction that Malista knew she was being offered only those things. And in that security, she recognized that those two things were just what she wished for.

"That meeting began Malista's acquaintance—her first—with anyone outside her family and clan. The pregnant woman, who was a doctor, serving that town and two others nearby, was surprised to learn who Malista was.

"She had never seen any of the women of the vineyard clan, though she knew exactly who No was by sight, and had drunk his wine, and heard years of stories about this uncompromising tradesman, who never drank a glass with the merchants, unlike the other traders, who sold their barrels through a haze of toasting, impossible boasts, and raucous, slurred drinking songs.

"After that day, Malista would escape No's spontaneous and unpredictable furies by slipping away from his palace on the rooftop of the world to town as she had that day. No never questioned her about these absences; his silence was a form of contrition for his rages.

"In this way, Malista came to know the doctor, whose name was Ember, her fleet little son, and her husband, who led a silk workshop. Over the next months, she came to know many of the townspeople, the teachers she had seen on the first day, the baker who invariably cheated her when she bought his confections to give as gifts, the town drunk, who could never afford No's wines. As soon as he understood who the stranger woman was, he stubbornly harassed Malista, begging to be treated by the great vintner's wife.

"To escape him, she began to periodically leave a sum with the wine merchants for his entertainment. Now, when he caught sight of her, he would raise a glass and toast her with an elegant gesture, like a prince in disguise under his tattered clothes.

"Malista bore the beatings now with true resignation; she had discovered another world, a world that had also discovered her. From visit to visit, the place and the people who lived there became more real.

"She would never forget the moment when Ember put her new daughter into Malista's arms, born three weeks ago, after her most recent visit. She relived the extraordinary sensation of holding a sleeping baby, the feeling of superhuman, protective strength in the face of its fragile and absolute being, the surge of oceanic, inexhaustible tenderness.

"She kept the image of this child in her mind during No's outbursts, knowing she could make an occasion to see her again. Every time she returned to the town, the child had a new feature or expression or gesture, like a book whose story was so true that it was capable of turning its own pages.

"Malista was doubly grateful for this unexpected grace, as her husband was becoming more and more irascible and distracted. He was sleeping fitfully, woken by fearful dreams; he went through the days with the red-rimmed eyes of someone tortured by sleeplessness, and called earlier for his wine, in order to substitute unconsciousness for sleep. Instead of drinking the wine reclining in his courtyard in the fresh early evening, he took his cup outside, and stood overlooking the sea, or walked, sipping and gesticulating as if he were in conversation with someone. He grew thin, as if a giant were feeding on him.

"Several times, Malista brought him out a plate of hot food, but each time, he waved her away, and ordered her back inside. 'I have no appetite,' she quoted him, reporting to his sons and daughters-in-law at the table.

"She tried a fourth time. That evening, he struck the plate from between her hands, and then slapped her across the face. 'God is talking to me,' he said. 'I am talking to God.' He turned away from her, and she saw him put his right hand on his heart, in a pledge-making gesture. She retreated and saw the household safely into sleep.

"She was shaken awake by No himself in the dark of the night. 'Beat the drum, and assemble the household,' he told her. 'I have seen what God has shown me. God's will be done.' She dressed and hurried into the courtyard, lit the torches, and took down the large drum whose sound was the signal for all living in the complex to gather. No one straggled; they came, frightened out of sleep, and sat at his feet.

"No spoke, his face transfigured, his words burning. 'I have seen God this night. It was not for the first time. But tonight, God made a promise. He promises to destroy the world.'

"'"I hate my creation," He said. "I have come to hate mankind, except for you, No. You alone, and the family you govern, are worthy in my eyes. I will kill these others, who have become nothing more than parasites. But I will not kill you, No, or any of yours, if you do as I command."'

"'"From you, I will make a new earth. The floods will rise even over the peak where your house stands, and all will drown, except for you, No."'

"'"You will build a great ark, and on it, you will store seeds of all the plants of the earth. You will house all the species of all the animals, insects, birds, and reptiles of the earth, a pair of each for breeding. And above them all, I have chosen you. You alone will be the seed of new humanity. You are my vintage. But if you deviate from my command, I will pour you out. You will surely die. You have no time to lose. The waters are already rising.'"

"As soon as it was light enough to see, the men set out to choose and cut timber for the ark. The women began the work of examining the breeding stock to select the finest specimens. They picked the finest pair of swans from the silvery pool No had had dug, and the cow who gave the richest cream, the bull with the noblest physique. They took cuttings from the oldest vines, and from the newest.

"No's little grandsons fought over whose puppies, kittens, and baby lambs would have the honor of frolicking over the new earth. And the ones who had hesitated in their hearts that night looked down and saw with awe that the waters were indeed already rising.

"Malista directed the labor of the women, with the impeccable energy and attention to detail she had always contributed to the household. She worked even more scrupulously, because she had a secret to keep at all costs.

"She had begun to have her own visions; she realized with a profound sense of sin that there was no terror for her greater than this salvation. She dreamed, those nights, of the remnant floating in precious safety, drawing draughts of pure air deep into their lungs, as they sailed on the waters of annihilation, taut beseeching arms fathoms below clutching dead children, anguished faces of the invisible dead the foundation of the burnished, purified new earth.

"Yet, God had given No a sign and a command. And as God commanded No, so it was her holy vocation to fulfill her husband. Every day of their marriage, she surrounded him with invisible services and protections, enslaving herself so she could free him for God. With every tray polished, every vine pruned, every loaf kneaded, she had avidly measured the extra hours of life on earth she had given him for life in God.

"Now the day began with the sound of hammers on wood, the carpentry of the ark, unfamiliar animals braying, cawing, farting, and growling—and the waters whispering the messages the winds gave them. The waters rose steadily, inexplicably, a foot a day. They had already laved Malista's beach at the foot of the mountain, except now the tide did not go out.

"She wondered what Ember and the people of the towns that lay at the base of the cliffs thought was happening. She should warn them, at least, to go to higher ground. But she hesitated. What good would that do them? They were not among the elect. Perhaps her interference would prolong their terror to no end. And they would see an evasion in her eyes, the false expression of hope from kin at a deathbed. Someone would intuit and scream her forbidden question: What is God going to do with all this death?

"Still, their faces remained in acute detail in her mind, even as she watered the newly acquired peacocks, and watched her prized fig trees savaged by the vegetarian giraffes. She thought of Ember and the silk shawl embroidered with grapes that her quiet husband had given Malista as a gift. She thought of their son, Wing, always running so lightly and so fleetly that she fantasized he might be able to run weightlessly across the rising waters.

"She thought of the teachers and the cheating baker, who had too many children. She thought of the town drunk, who still tippled steadily, but with exquisite deliberation, almost philosophical pleasure, when he was given a ruby glass of No's vintage. These were the first people among whom she had dared not to keep her own counsel.

"Most of all, she thought of Ember's new baby, who had just begun to smile, and followed certain faces with the expression of rapt delight with which she would never have the chance to dazzle a lover. She did not know what she would tell them, but she could not let them vanish as if they had been imaginary. Even if she told them nothing, she would see them, and hold them helplessly, remembered, but unrescued, in her gaze.

"In the frenzy of preparations, she had far more than her usual opportunities to slip away unnoticed. But in her terrible knowledge that God had chosen only the Noan clan to outlive his deluge, she hesitated. She did not have the courage to warn them.

"She would go, she promised herself, when the waters themselves had delivered the secret. She would go when the threat was so unmistakable that they would already have understood there was no hope. She would announce neither their condemnation nor offer false hope. She would only go to say good-bye to the ones who had been her friends. And to the ones who had not been her friends. And to the ones she had never known at all.

"She waited, meaninglessly storing precious household items, carpets, jewels, copper trays with domes incised with images of vines, inside the cupboards concealed in the stone walls. None of this would survive. It was forbidden to bring on board anything that could not grow or breed, but she had been the custodian of these objects, and had prized them. She wrapped them and fastened them, and put them gently away, as if she were putting children to sleep. She felt an embarrassment at her triviality; these things were precious to her, but not to God.

"At last, when she judged that the town would soon be unreachable, when the great ark was nearly ready to be launched, she made her way on now muddy paths to the place that had once been her refuge.

"She found the place in a chaos of packing and of weeping, frightened children; they saw they had no choice now but to move to higher ground. The place they had lived would be swept away, but they imagined they would at least keep their lives.

"She made her way to Ember's house; Ember was struggling to pack as much food as possible compactly enough to carry, along with her medicines and her other healer's instruments. The men were absent, having climbed the cliffs to make a temporary encampment well above the waters, where they would take shelter.

"The women embraced spontaneously and silently. Malista looked and could not bear to look at the dismantled house, as if she had caught sight of someone naked. Ember saw her discomfort, and shrugged bitterly, trapped in a disorder not of her making.

"Ember took the baby from her cradle, and the three stepped outside to escape the ruin of the interior. Ember, exhausted, sat for a moment, and handed the baby to Malista while she rested.

"'You are lucky,' Ember said. Malista shivered involuntarily, and looked at her, startled. 'You will surely lose some vineyards, but no waters will reach you on your cliff. You can at least stay where you are. You can at least salvage your household. We will be ruined.'

"'We are leaving our household, too,' Malista blurted out, in a futile impulse to share her friend's hardship.

"'But why?' Ember stared. 'From where you live, there is no place else to go.'

"'There is one more place to go. My husband had a dream. He was given the idea to build a kind of floating house. So the dream was built. We will live inside it until the waters recede.'

"'We might have done that for ourselves. Now there is hardly time to try. Why didn't you tell us about his dream?'

"Malista could not answer. Her tears welled up and fell in heavy drops on the baby's face. Overwhelmed, she confessed the truth to her friend. She told her about the dream God sent No, about the ark and the seeds and animals. She told her about the end of the world. 'So you must tell them to climb, tell everyone to climb. Our buildings will be empty. Our grounds can hold many more. Eat from our garden. Take your meat from the animals we are leaving behind. Take refuge there. God may yet relent. I will pray for it.'

"She held the baby out for Ember to take. 'I don't dare stay longer. I will be missed. But no door will be closed to you. I will see to it that nothing is locked. Climb there. May God have mercy on you.'

"'Then I have a favor to ask of you.' Ember put her hand on Malista's forehead, and touched it in the traditional gesture of beseeching. 'Take the baby,' she said. 'Take the baby onto your ark.'

"Malista hung her head. She could not look at Ember's face.

"'Please. Let the baby live. Take her into your husband's dream. Save her. I know you can do no more, and I do not ask for more.'

"'How can I defy God? Or change my husband's dream?'

"'In the beginning, I could not believe him. Like a good wife, though, I did as I was told to do. I gave everything expert in my hands to his mad project. I hoped he would wake up from his dream of death. But he was right. This world is lost. You see how the waters are rising, just as he said they would. The rest must happen—will happen—as he saw.'

"'There are things he may not have seen. God sends thousands of dreams. For nine months, this child was in me like a dream, and now I hold that dream breathing in my arms. Look at the face of this child, who does not know death exists. She may have been in some corner of the dream unnoticed.'

"She put the child into Malista's arms, her head against Malista's heart. Malista involuntarily looked into the baby's sleeping face. Like a cloud, her malleable features softened and altered perpetually as she slept, responding to all the unmediated influences of the world passing over her and through her.

"She had an eerie sensation as she held this creature that was still shaped like a handful of apples, its face like a fruit articulate with feeling. It is not only ghosts that come from the unseen, but also the children who are its other messengers, creatures not of afterlife, but of the life before.

"Malista felt her heart matching the rhythm of the baby's heartbeat; it was as if she had been given a second heart outside her body. And in that second heart, there was a reservoir of courage, decision, and passion utterly beyond Malista's own meager resources, so abundant that it could coexist with the fear of what she was about to do. 'I will find her a place,' she said.

"The women exchanged glances. Malista had regained her fear of death, the fear denied to the elect of the ark. She had become once again Ember's equal. She turned and began to climb the path home, terrified, holding her courage in her arms.

"She reached the great lake where the divinely imagined ark was now moored; it was a great floating fortress, its deck railings ornamented with mounted shields, for defense against potential hordes that might try to swamp the vessel.

"Yet the decks themselves were the bearers of paradise, five stories of fruit trees, flowers, sown fields of grain, an outdoor garden that was a record of creation. When the seawaters rose high enough, as they soon would, the ark would be ready to be carried off from the surface wherever God willed it to go.

"They had begun to board the animals when she arrived; they were so preoccupied with the skittish, rearing horses, bleating lambs, and scratching cats that no one took notice of her at first. Malista made a makeshift hammock for the baby, and hid her in one of the builders' lean-tos on the shore, praying she would not wake and cry. She had no better plan than to simply carry the little girl on board and hide her until there was no turning back.

"Then she walked toward the ark, allowing herself to be discovered. She joined her daughters-in-law, folding and storing blankets and warm clothes for the voyage in chests that were carried aboard as soon as each was filled.

"The hours passed in silent, exhausting work, until No satisfied himself that every corner of the ark was filled. Then the pairs of little cousins were marched on board. No had ordained that the boarding should have a liturgical quality, to demonstrate their gratitude to God, and their consciousness that this was no ordinary voyage, but a journey from annihilation into life.

"Each child clutched the one toy permitted them. The littlest ones staggered under the weight of the personal store of grain each person was to carry. No had ordained strict rations for the voyagers, in order to preserve the supplies of food stock as long as possible.

"They were conducted into a special shelter, which had been engineered with special rope mechanisms to lash them all together if necessary. The delicate bearers of the human future must ride the deluge; their parents knew their own lives were forfeit to No and to God, if any of these unsuspecting miniature brides and grooms were swept overboard.

"An anthem was sung for them, and when it finished, a second began, the signal for their parents to board. Malista emerged from the lean-to, holding her friend's child in her arms. The baby was awake, but quiet, seemingly attentive to the music, its enormous eyes vigilant but trusting. The children of No and of Malista boarded, as formally coupled as they had been at their weddings.

"They positioned themselves on the deck, singing a hymn honoring Malista, the symbol of the ark, who had carried her sons into life. She came toward the great, wide gangplank, which she would ascend, followed by No, the last living creature who would board the vessel of salvation. No looked at her with an expression of solemn reverence as she approached, an expression that swiftly altered when she set her foot on the gangplank, and he glimpsed the child in her arms.

"'What is that?' he asked sharply, his eyes now as narrow and territorial as a venomous snake's.

"'This is my store of grain,' Malista answered. 'This is my sheaf of wheat.'

"'Where did you get it?' No's voice deepened, the thunderous voice that meant God was in possession of him. 'Put it on the ground,' he ordered her, 'and board the ark. All that God has chosen to be saved is aboard, except for you and me.'

"It was the voice that always terrified her. She held the child and closed her eyes, knowing that if she looked at him, her soul would faint into a twilight beyond will. Then he could take the child from her, and carry her on board.

"'I have made a promise,' she said, almost inaudibly. She clung to the child as a passenger overboard clings to a raft.

"'Then you are a fool,' he said. 'You have made a promise. Look up at this vessel; you see a promise—a promise God made. Do you think God will honor your promise, and break His own?'

"'Not really,' she said weakly. 'No.'

"'Then board, or stay here with the damned.'

"Malista stood still, speechless, unable to move forward or backward. No turned, and without a backward look, mounted the gangplank, and ordered it hauled up. It swung into place like the raised palm of a huge hand."

"All were now aboard the ark. It looked from where she was standing that her middle son had stayed on deck, his head in his hands. The water was beginning to reach Malista's feet. The power to move was restored to her, and she began hurriedly to retrace her path. The baby cooed and giggled, entertained by the gentle jolting motion produced by Malista's haste.

"She scrambled up a hill, and stopped to catch her breath in a grove of trees. From the depths of the shade, she could see the ark. It was now sealed, with neither entrance nor exit.

"She climbed steadily upward. When she reached the imposing group of buildings on the cliff, she took the child indoors, and brought down again her eldest son's cradle, which she had carefully packed away. She made a soft, warm bed for the child, and fed it.

"She cleared a path through a poignant chaos of dolls, toy soldiers, balls, and cloth monkeys, which lay where they had been dropped; the toys ultimately abandoned by her grandchildren. No had held them strictly to the rule that they could choose only one toy each.

"Then she set about opening all the cupboards she had locked, so that the refugees could easily find supplies. She went around the courtyard, opening all the doors and windows that had been shut. She noted with relief the many outbuildings that could house refugees. Many people could survive here for as long as God willed.

"There were already refugees on the peak, and more were climbing the terraces through the vineyards, and still more on the road. Malista asked them to see that the strongest camped on the grounds and high terraces, and to leave the inner courtyard and houses for those in greatest need of shelter.

"As night began to fall campfires were lit, and the procession of refugees climbed toward them. They were as calm as pilgrims on a holiday, and today, or tomorrow, was the holy feast of Saint Death himself. Some were even singing as they ascended, laden with food and blankets.

"She was relieved to hear the singing. She tensed in the wish that they might sustain this spirit. The fear that they would die struggling against each other to live at the other's expense was as real to her as the fear of death. Malista shut her eyes, unsure who to pray to, the God of the salvation of the ark, or the God of the destruction of the world.

"In a parody of her former lavish hospitality, she began to distribute rations of water to the arrivals, with the same gestures she had once brought out salt, bread, and wine. A refugee girl of about seven approached and asked if she could rock the baby in her cradle; she sat down, legs crossed, and swayed the child gravely back and forth, steady as a clock.

"When Ember and her family passed through the gates into the courtyard and caught sight of Malista there, she instantly grasped what had happened. She made her way to Malista, her son and husband following her.

"The women looked at each other wordlessly; Malista lifted the baby from the cradle and placed her in her mother's arms. Wing, the boy who had never even accepted a cake from her hands, threw his arms around Malista for a sharp sweet second, and then raced behind his mother, as if a bird had circled her.

"He whispered something to his father, who nodded, and then the boy disappeared outside. He wanted to climb a tree to watch the state of the flood; there was no reason to refuse, it was as safe a shelter as any, perhaps even safer. He was at the age when boy and animal were still woven inextricably together, and the energy of it gives the boy a touch of immortality. They leap off bridges and swim to the surface unhurt, run like falling rain downhill, and watch the unwary in majesty perched in trees they have climbed.

"She knew it was irrational, but Malista could not believe in death when she watched this boy race through the courtyard, wheeling through the throngs and clusters of campers like a swift plunging through crowds.

"It is the weakness of parents, she thought. We believe in our own deaths, but not in our children's. And in my case, it is true. This young boy who barely touches the ground will die, but my own grown sons will live, sheltered inside their wooden walls.

"Malista worked to settle the arrivals as comfortably as she could, moving from group to group, to see what needs she might supply. She felt unnatural without her daughters-in-law gracefully following her directions. Strangers clasped her hands as she wove through the circles of people sitting on the grounds. She touched their palms with hers apologetically, conscious, as they were not, that she might have lived.

"There were strange, explosive sounds outside—below them, trees were being uprooted, and houses torn from their foundations, a man who had witnessed the eradication of his village told them.

"Suddenly, there was a shout: 'The ark has sailed, the ark has sailed.'

"Wing had seen the sea rise to the level of the lake, and watched the great vessel, like a monstrous fish holding a world in its belly, inch forward into its element. It could only be hours now, Malista knew. Her hands were frighteningly cold, and, suddenly, she felt as exhausted as if she had already finished her death struggle. She wanted to be with Ember's family when it happened. She searched them out, and sat down with them in the firelight.

"A man who looked familiar made his way to their circle, and greeted Malista with an elegant inclination of his head. She recognized the townsman who had always been drunk, now quite sober. He asked her with great dignity if he might have the honor of breaching the barrels from No's cellars and offering the company a glass of wine, 'to drink to our health and to the health of our hostess,' he said.

"They exchanged gentle smiles, and a long, deep glance of shared fear and shared dignity. Malista handed him the keys that were in her pocket.

"Cup after cup of wine was sent from hand to hand, as if the wine were inexhaustible; carafes were carried out to the ones camped on the hillsides, where there was the smell of fresh bread, of meat and vegetables roasting, savory fragrances still stronger than the smell of the dampening earth.

"Malista moved the cradle rhythmically back and forth, and looked around at the firelit faces filling her rooms and courtyard, at the man who had been the town drunk, now serving others with discipline and grace, at Ember, who had wiped away the blood of her wounds the first day they had met. Her fate was interwoven with the fate of each one of these people, and theirs with hers, as mutual as if the fingers of their hands were enlaced. Within the meshes, both apparent and invisible, waited their death, but also a feeling of absolute communion, an incomprehensible freedom even from the death they were bound to die.

"She sipped her cup of her husband's wine; it was the amber-vermilion color of the early morning sky said to be the sailor's warning. With her other hand, she rocked the baby girl in her cradle, with a sound and motion that kept her dreaming as if she were floating in a skiff on soft summer waves.

"The baby suddenly opened her eyes, looked into Malista's, and held her gaze, with the exact look of knowledge that had deepened and brightened the eyes of all the adult company, as if their eyes were filled with tears not of weakness, but of illumination. Malista had never seen such a look of such clarity, of such equality, on the face of a child.

"She leaned forward, thinking the wine must be giving her this illusion. Then, there was no doubt: she heard a distant musical sound, as if the wind had moved the strings of some instrument, and an unearthly soprano voice, not a man's or a woman's.

"Malista instinctively looked up at the night sky; she saw a sky full of stars drifting in patterns she had never seen before. They gathered like musical notes, shimmering trebles and basses, starry notes flickering in staves that glittered like mica. 'This is the ark,' the baby in the cradle sang. Malista frowned at herself, her senses deceived by the wine during these, the final hours of her life. 'I am the ark,' the child sang its tune, without any variation. 'You are the ark.'

"Malista furtively looked up to see if anyone else close by had heard the child's music. She caught Ember's eyes; the woman returned her gaze and it seemed to Malista that they had exchanged eyes, that the tears in her eyes were the tears of Ember's sorrow, that Ember's eyes were now filled with Malista's tears. Yet the music seemed inaudible to her.

"'She is the ark,' the child sang. Ember, still deaf, it seemed, to the music, leaned forward and impulsively clasped Malista's hand. She wove Malista's fingers with hers, as if their joined hands made a basket. 'That is the ark,' the child sang.

"Malista stared from one end of the courtyard to the other. The center by the fountains and all the galleries were crowded with people, their frightened, resolute faces intermittently visible by firelight. Many held hands, or had their arms around each other. 'These are the ark.'

"Malista looked down again at the child's face, her eyes still holding Malista's. She felt a tide of love that curved her over the cradle, as if the crest of a wave had washed over her and carried her to shore; she unself-consciously lifted the child into her arms, and kissed her cheek with infinite tenderness. She rocked her back and forth, but it seemed to her that it was the child who cradled her, and drew her deeper and deeper into the embrace. 'This is the flood,' sang the child.

"Malista must have fallen asleep because she woke abruptly when she heard a hoarse cry at first light; she shifted suddenly in the shock of waking, and startled the baby sleeping in her arms, who began to wail. She heard the cry again, someone shouting incoherently with all the power of his lungs; she stood up, to prepare herself for whatever was to come next.

"She saw Wing circling through the groups seated at the far end of the courtyard, dipping toward one person and then another, his face red with shouting. Some people jumped up and began to race outside.

"Wing's father stood up and called to him, so that the boy could locate his family among the crowds. With an impossible leap, soaring through the air as if he could never fall, Wing threw himself into his father's arms. 'The waters are receding!' he shouted. 'The waters are receding.' They hurried to the bluff where the child had watched the night, and saw that it was true. The sea was withdrawing, with a superb slow formality, like a courtier in the presence of majesty."

The Philosopher reached for a cluster of grapes from the bowl beside the bed. He was always hungry after a story. "What happened to No?" he asked.

"Who knows?" she answered. "None of them saw him again. I imagine he stayed on the ark he was inspired to build as his wife stayed on the ark she built."

"Is it a true story?" the Philosopher asked, smiling involuntarily when the wine inside the grape flowed into his mouth.

"I don't know. Is the one you tell true? All I know is that I know different stories than you do."

"And all I know is that I don't want you to be lost in some story different from mine. My two years here are nearly finished. Will you let me travel home to ask my teacher for permission to marry you?"

"Are you sure?" she asked, knowing that marriage would mean that he could never be inducted into the Academy.

He kissed her hand; Sheba said her irrevocable "yes."

Now an elegiac period began for King Caspar's troupe, during these last months before Sheba's Philosopher returned from his own country to marry her and bring her to the house near the Academy he had gone to prepare for her. There were large audiences for her last performances, which ran very late, since the news of Queen Sheba's departure had spread. She was kept onstage by call after call for encores of favorite passages from the epics. People watched with minute attention, memorizing every intonation and gesture, straining to keep true pictures for themselves about how this last Queen of Sheban art chiseled her phrases like the gems the people of the kingdom had so loved.

The troupe itself was packing away costumes and props, and readying for its own journey onward.

Caspar's beloved plants, the link with his lost estate in Sheba, were carefully packed for transport. Caspar had become increasingly uncomfortable being situated so near the Sheban border; he had decided to take up an unexpected and opportune offer to accompany a grand court returning from a seasonal trade expedition on its celebratory journey home.

As the epic players used to do, Caspar and the players of his troupe would entertain the court as it crossed the mountains, and then to sea, to its country. If the players pleased King Melchior, there was a chance of establishing a permanent theater in his capital. His was a country of lengthy summers, which was always an advantage for actors, who were in steady demand as storytellers during the golden nights when the sun did not set.

Word came from a first rider that the Philosopher was two days away, then from a second rider that he was a day away, then from a third that he was waiting for Sheba at their familiar pavilion on the lagoon, where they had first declared their love.

The sun glittered on the water as it had the first day. Sheba saw him looking toward her, tall and elegant, slender as the columns on which the Philosophers loved to perch as they confronted all that existed in the cosmos.

She wound her arms around him, and held him close. He returned her embrace, but strangely, weightlessly. She drew away, and looked into his eyes with the question. Even his eyes were different; the color of water, they changed like water, but now they were opaque as stone.

"I see you already realize what I have realized."

"What have you realized?" she asked.

"That this is impossible. And always was."

"But why? It has been possible for nearly two years. No, it was greater than possible—it was true. What makes it impossible now?"

"Perhaps your skin, the color of your skin."

"You have always loved the color of my skin."

"I was reminded at home that we marry the fair. How would it be for you to be the only visible exception?"

"Look at the boat on the lagoon." He gazed in the direction she pointed out.

There was a fishing boat on the water, motionless in the blinding brilliance of the sun. In the great confluence of the torrent of light, the boat was black, as were the figures of the fishermen, and their darkness made every detail of their shapes as achingly precise as sculpture.

"It is inside this amount of radiance that they are revealed as dark," she said. "Besides, I don't believe any Philosopher would refuse love for the sake of the way the flesh catches light. No matter what color my skin is, in any case, one day it will disappear, as I will. What is the real reason for your change?"

"You are right, it has nothing to do with your skin, but something far deeper and more absolute. My teacher at the Academy, the teacher who is to me what Noctis the Bridge was to you, spoke to me with all the force of his wisdom.

"I am the son of his soul, and he spoke to me as a son. He reminded me that among us, great Philosophers do not marry. We are for what is immortal alone. We sacrifice the cosmos we would make sacred if we choose profane love instead of divine love. The body crumbles our great structures of thought into dust."

"And you are sure that it is our love for each other that is profane?"

"There is no doubt about it."

Then Sheba's heart broke utterly and cleanly as the gemstones she had seen as a schoolgirl. It broke with such force that it catapulted her beyond despair to some other vantage point in the world. From this perspective, she could see not only the Philosopher, but also watch herself looking up at him. She could see herself as if she were a director observing a player enact a life.

Her broken heart seemed to break her into many selves, like the facets of a gem, as the geometress had said it would. Feelings she did not recognize emerged, as if freed from some ancient prison, a strange sensation of selflessness, without effort or deprivation, as if she had died.

The new emptiness in her made her every thought and feeling resonant, like the acoustics of a grand concert hall. There seemed nothing left in her but the mysterious space of the future that lay before her, without him, the bearable, permanent sorrow of facing that life, and her astonished, passionate wish that whatever he loved would be full and true for him.

Her heart had broken, her life's wish unfulfilled, but she could still feel love. It was as if her unbroken heart had had a touch of stone, and served to contain more love than she knew was possible. Now it lay in fragments, swept outward by the feelings it had held back. They flowed freely beyond her, beyond her, beyond the Philosopher, surging into the world. No, she had not died; she had outlived herself.

She had loved the man in curiosity, detail, delight, and passion; her love was now this concentrated wish for him to live, with her or without her.

"I must hurry back to the troupe," she said, "and inform King Caspar that Queen Sheba is still a traveling player. May the life you choose bring you joy and all you truly prize."

They embraced in the new way, as if they were clouds colliding. Sheba was overcome with a wave of exhaustion, and she left quickly. The Philosopher watched her walk away, his smile radiant and fixed, a greeting to the new life he had won.

The annual journey toward Melchior's kingdom was particularly festive that year, and the itinerant court especially brilliant. King Melchior was a gourmand of knowledge, and of art, always willing to prolong a journey or make a detour to see something of value.

Every night King Caspar's troupe performed songs during dinner; after dinner, the troupe would set out the great terra-cotta urns containing the Sheban herbs from Caspar's lost garden. They were leafless bushes at this time of year, but their appearance was always the sign that the comedies or scenes from the epics of the Tellings were about to be performed.

If the landscape of a day's traveling was not particularly interesting, Melchior and selected guests would ride behind an elephant that carried a flat wooden platform mounted on its back, a portable theater, on which the actors played for them. Melchior delighted in saying that he was not only traveling home, but also straight into the epic tales he followed as he rode.

These royal homecomings were always furnished with a company of botanists, zoologists, and selected court painters who recorded every step of the journey, and every wonder encountered on the way with sketches and paintings. The sketches did a second service; some were sold at each halt to replenish their supplies of food.

It was through these sketches that the Philosopher was able to trace her footsteps as he followed Melchior's court; he recognized the images of Sheba dressed in the costumes in which she performed the lost Prince Horizon—the first stage role in which he had seen her. He had renounced her in order to become a great thinker; now he could think only of her. He set out to find her, in a desperate quest to recover the sacred love he had been taught to believe profane.

Now King Melchior had gotten word of a marvelous newborn child who was performing miracles quite beyond the miracles that all newborn children can perform. And consistent with his reputation, he could not resist changing the court's route to witness a reputed beauty or a wonder of the world. He had never regretted making a pilgrimage for such a purpose.

So Melchior turned his retinue north, and out of their way, toward the snowy country where he had heard the child could be visited. Some of the party grumbled, impatient to reach their own temperate shores instead of being dragged deeper into winter. The artists, botanists, and zoologists, though, were delighted at the prospect of sketchbooks filled with views never before seen, and recorded the journey with redoubled energy and delight.

The Philosopher followed the sketches they left behind at each stop, navigating by the images of Sheba as a sailor does by the stars. He turned north when they did, and traveled by night as well as day to overtake them.

When Melchior's party reached the icy pass that should lead them across where the miraculous child and his parents were lodged, they found it impassible. Melchior was extremely disappointed to have taken his court so far for nothing, but he was not willing to risk the lives of his followers, even for a miracle. He asked Caspar to use his trained, resonant voice to call out their greetings, and their regrets. Slowly and gingerly, the court made ready to retrace the arduous path by which they had come.

They could hear voices calling from high above them, and Melchior held up his hand to halt the retreat. They saw a couple above, a man and woman who were without coats, apparently oblivious to the cold that had Melchior's court shivering.

The woman was carrying a child, whose face glowed with a radiance that lit the darkness above them; she held up the child as if it were a living candle, and the ice and snow melted away from the path in smooth ribbons.

Melchior and his company ascended the alp, following the lightly dressed couple to a cavern in the mountainside.

All along the meadow, there were pilgrims, some camped by firelight, others moving toward the cavern where the child sat on his mother's lap. Inside the cavern, though it was bitter cold outside, people were warming themselves by the child as if he were a hearth fire. An old peasant couple, which had clearly never known comfort in winter for all of their lives, held their knotty hands near the infant's head, luxuriating in the warmth.

Melchior's group dismounted, and King Caspar signaled to the troupe to sing for the pleasure of the pilgrims. Noticing that all the pilgrims who were filing before the child carried some gift of a trinket, a cheese, a pear, Caspar trudged to the packhorse and broke off a branch of the herb native to his country.

Melchior caught sight among the theater properties of a gold paper crown, studded with sequins. He asked Caspar if he might take it; he was an experienced grandfather, and knew its glitter would please a child. Sheba followed the two kings, taking the incense clock that was the only thing suitable in her luggage. The court painters hurried behind, clutching their notebooks, brushes, easels, and crayons in hand.

The wonderful baby could already sit upright, barely supported by his mother's gentle hands; his face was indeed miraculously beautiful, because of the effect it had. No one could look at this child without his heart dissolving with tenderness, even people who didn't ordinarily care for children.

Melchior handed him the gold paper crown, which he turned over in his hands, as amused as the old king had known he would be. He touched the baby's cheek, and drew himself up to speak a word of congratulations to his father. Caspar put the branch of herbs into the baby's tiny fist, and joined Melchior at his father's side.

Queen Sheba knelt before the child, looking into his eyes with the peculiar intimate reciprocal delight some women share with babies. The baby fingered the incense clock she set before him; though she thought it was not her most precious gift. That was still the love the Philosopher had made her able to feel. It endured.

Her ebony face glowed under her golden turban, its changing tones, and the contours of her natural, poignantly involuntary smile, brought out by the light of the child. It is a moment captured by many of the court painters and their successors; perhaps the familiar image of this precise moment explains why so many confuse Queen Sheba with the young prince Balthazar, the son she later bore who resembled her so much.

The child's father touched the elbows of Melchior and Caspar, who had fallen into conversation. He gestured toward his wife, the child's mother, who held out an offering to Melchior; the gilt paper crown transformed to solid gold, its cheap sequins now precious gems.

In the baby's left hand, the dry branch of herbs was covered with silvery green leaves and blue flowers. His mother took the branch, and returned his gift to Caspar. Under the baby's right hand, clouds of incense from the clock suffused the cavern, as if he had touched it with an invisible flame. Balthazar, the child Sheba had conceived with the Philosopher, stirred faintly inside her.

It was then that the Philosopher emerged from the shadows. He came toward Sheba slowly, and she slowly rose and went to him. They embraced, the pale tall Philosopher, and the dark, small Queen Sheba, meeting like the tall and small hands of a clock, at midnight, or at noon, when the hour is fulfilled and perfect, on earth for a moment as it is in Heaven, in the constellation of the Lovers' Cluster.

Sheba took off her turban, and her long hair tumbled down to her waist; she lifted her face to kiss the Philosopher. They came to life through each other, each incarnate through the other's kiss.

Then all over the mountainside, pilgrims turned to one another's kisses. The old peasant held his wife's face in his hands and warmly kissed her; the baby's father kissed his mother's lips. Father kissed son, brother kissed brother, sister kissed sister, stranger embraced stranger, as if each were simultaneously, tenderly newborn to each other, or as if each had restored a treasure long lost to the other.

The baby smiled a luminous and unending smile, at the gift they had brought him, this dedication of the most beautiful of human gestures, the exchange of life's breath, the consent of soul to body, of earth to Heaven, in the form of a kiss. They brought their gift to the newborn of what he, and they, had been born for.

He raised both his hands in a gesture of blessing that was both a joyful and a reverent benediction of human love, always hard won—heroic—and divine.

It is a shame that the beautiful canvas that records this moment was stolen, and has yet to be recovered.

THE PROVERBS OF SHEBA

All marriages are arranged, except those in which the wife invents her husband, and the husband invents his wife.

We pretend love is inexplicable, because we fear its iron logic.

Those who love money will marry it.

The misogynist and misanthrope do not need the matchmaker's services.

Do we submit to God? Which partner dancing a pas de deux submits to the other?

Love is not submission. Love is improvisation.

God said: I have furnished you a world; now create it.

The master will always in the end desire to be dominated by his slave.

The desire to submit masquerades as the desire to dominate.

Torture is the weapon of the cosmically jealous: an attempt to destroy the capacity to love.

War is the master of the world; yet love outlives slaughter.

Thousands of years before we read and wrote; thousands more before we love.

More are deceived by the belief that they love than by the belief that they are loved.

Men have seized the privilege of naming the stars; but it was women who invented Heaven.

Heaven is not Heaven if Hell is Hell.

Weapons give men the illusion that they are not flesh.

In times of war, men's worth is measured by their bodies; in times of peace, by their souls.

Men have always feared the unarmed more than they fear armies.

What do men fear more than peace?

Wise love is possible, innocent love never.

The ascetic who starves herself for the love of the poor never asks how many of them must stand watch, exhausted, at her deathbed.

He who demands innocence in love is seeking something that he himself does not possess.

Only those ignorant of love believe it exists only to make children; in every true act of love, something is born.

We speak of Eros as an anarchic force, but his ungovernableness disguises his well-disciplined obedience to his mother.

Like Zeus, men pretend women are cows so that they can pretend to be gods.

Contempt for women is the expression of men's secret scorn for God.

The goddess of love is always described as the essence of desire; but her real power is far greater; she can feel with precision and think ecstatically.

The great art of love is to think and feel at the same time; love poem.

A good parent is one who refuses to be the fate of his child.

Those who seek to save themselves while the rest of the world is destroyed will never realize they themselves are drowned.

Love is the only way we can escape our fates.

Do not ask: Do you love me? Ask: Should you love me?

Love and Knowledge are aspects of each other: which is why lovemaking takes the form of a perpetual question perpetually answered.

Here is the most terrible secret: One way or another, love is always requited.

ACKNOWLEDGMENTS

I am deeply grateful for the privilege—and joy—of working with Erroll McDonald. I thank him for the brilliance, tact, freedom, and elegance of his reading, and for his enduring friendship.

I thank Lynn Nesbit profoundly for all she has done to sustain this book. Her wonderful letters always arrived at just the right moment, with just the right words of encouragement.

Mona Trad Dabaji's painting takes me every day into a world where beauty is an aspect of courage.

It is my loving obligation to thank Dan Rabinowitz, Ann Thomas, Prudence Crowther, Reem Abu Jaber, Sarah Kerr, Peter Devine, Nancy Devine, and Emily Flint, for everything.

I am one of many for whom Barbara Epstein is an irreplaceable loss and an undying presence. I thank her always.

This book came to life in three places: the Catalan coast, the Connecticut coast, and the Swiss canton of Vaud. In each, I have had the great good fortune, with my beloved, to catch a glimpse of heaven.

ALSO BY

PATRICIA STORACE

DINNER WITH PERSEPHONE

Travels in Greece

"I lived in Athens, at the intersection of a prostitute and a saint." So begins Patricia Storace's astonishing memoir of her year in Greece. Mixing affection with detachment, rapture with clarity, this American poet perfectly evokes a country delicately balanced between East and West. Whether she is interpreting Hellenic dream books, pop songs, and soap operas; describing breathtakingly beautiful beaches and archaic villages; or braving the crush at a saint's tomb; Storace, winner of the Whiting Award, rewards the reader with informed and sensual insights into Greece's soul. She sees how the country's pride in its past coexists with profound doubts about its place in the modern world. She discovers a world in which past and present engage in a passionate dialogue. Stylish, funny, and erudite, *Dinner with Persephone* is travel writing elevated to a fine art.

Travel/Memoir